Praise for Frank Peretti's Writing

"Peretti fans and readers of mainstream thrillers will snap this up
. . . expect *Monster* to be a major hit."

—*Library Journal*

"[*Monster*] is Peretti's best and most down-to-earth novel yet."

—*CBA Marketplace*

". . . Peretti is a bona fide publishing phenomenon."

—*BookPage*, regarding *The Visitation*

"In the world of Christian fiction, the hottest novels are those by
Frank Peretti."

—*Newsweek*, regarding *The Visitation*

"The king of the [faith-based fiction] genre is Frank Peretti."

—*Time* magazine, regarding *The Visitation*

"Potboiling adventure is combined with a distinctly conservative
theology."

—*The New York Times*, regarding *The Visitation*

"One of the biggest surprises in publishing . . ."

—*People* magazine, regarding *The Visitation*

"Not only is Peretti the country's top selling Christian fiction
author, but he has become, by any standard, one of current fiction's biggest stars."

—*Chicago Tribune*, regarding *The Visitation*

". . . Peretti's book set a suspenseful standard in spiritual warfare
story-telling that has rarely been matched by his contemporaries."

—*Amazon*, regarding *This Present Darkness*

FICTION

"... plenty of spine-chilling mayhem ..."

—Amazon, regarding *The Visitation*

"... the world's hottest writer of spiritual thrillers."

—www.bookbrowse.com

"What makes Mr. Peretti stand out among Christian writers is his focus on the craft. He is a master storyteller with a knack for realistic dialogue, scene-setting, and adept pacing that engages readers."

—Dallas Morning News

MONSTER

MONSTER

FRANK PERETTI

THOMAS NELSON
Since 1798

NASHVILLE   DALLAS   MEXICO CITY   RIO DE JANEIRO

Published in Nashville, Tennessee, by Thomas Nelson. Thomas Nelson is a trademark of Thomas Nelson, Inc.

Thomas Nelson, Inc. titles may be purchased in bulk for educational, business, fund-raising, or sales promotional use. For information, please e-mail SpecialMarkets@ThomasNelson.com.

Publisher's Note: This novel is a work of fiction. Names, characters, places, and incidents are either products of the author's imagination or used fictitiously. All characters are fictional, and any similarity to people living or dead is purely coincidental.

ISBN: 978-1-4016-8521-8 (repak)

Library of Congress Cataloging-in-Publication Data

Peretti, Frank E.
   Monster / Frank Peretti.
     p. cm.
   ISBN: 978-0-8499-1180-4 (hard cover)
   ISBN: 1-59554-152-9 (trade paper)
   ISBN: 1-5955-4032-6 (IE)
   1. Northwest, Pacific—Fiction. 2. Wilderness areas—Fiction. 3. Supernatural—Fiction. 4. Monsters—Fiction. 5. Hiking—Fiction. I. Title.
   PS3566.E691317M66 2005
   813'.54—dc22

                        2004030836

Printed in the United States of America

11 12 13 14 15 QG 6 5 4 3 2 1

To Barbara Jean, my true love,
and my best friend through it all.

ACKNOWLEDGMENTS

It's not so easy finding capable people who can get excited about somebody else's book when they have their own projects and commitments. These guys are special, and I thank them profusely for making this whole story such a pleasure to tell:

Jonathan Wells, postdoctoral biologist and senior fellow at the Discovery Institute, whose book, *Icons of Evolution*, first got my creative wheels turning, and who helped me clarify my main story idea over a pleasant lunch.

Dr. David DeWitt, director of the Center for Creation Studies at Liberty University, who, besides being a brilliant scientist and technical advisor, is quite an imaginative story crafter in his own right.

Dr. Paul Brillhart, my family physician, who loves to tell stories and went beyond the call of duty to provide me with medical details.

Nick Hogamier, a real, honest-to-goodness tracker, whose knowledge and fascinating stories became the model for the character Pete Henderson.

Thanks to all of you for making *Monster* such a great adventure!

Frank E. Peretti
April 2005

ONE

The Hunter, rifle in his hands, dug in a heel and came to a sudden halt on the game trail, motionless, nearly invisible in a thicket of serviceberry and crowded pines. He heard something.

The first rays of the sun flamed over the ridge to the east, knifing through the pine boughs and morning haze in translucent wedges, backlighting tiny galaxies of swirling bugs. Soon the warming air would float up the draw and the pines would whisper like distant surf, but in the lull between the cool of night and the warmth of day, the air was still, the sounds distinct. The Hunter heard his own pulse. The scraping of branches against his camouflage sleeves was crisp and brilliant, the snapping of twigs under his boots almost startling.

And the eerie howl was clear enough to reach him from miles away, audible under the sound of the jays and between the chatterings of a squirrel.

He waited, not breathing, until he heard it again: long, mournful, rising in pitch, and then holding that anguished note to the point of agony before trailing off.

The Hunter's brow crinkled under the bill of his cap. The howl was too deep and guttural for a wolf. A cougar never made a sound like that. A bear? Not to his knowledge. If it was his quarry, it was upset about something.

And far ahead of him.

He moved again, quickstepping, ducking branches, eyes darting about, dealing with the distance.

Before he had worked his way through the forest another mile, he saw a breach in the forest canopy and an open patch of daylight through the trees. He was coming to a clearing.

He slowed, cautious, found a hiding place behind a massive fallen fir, and peered ahead.

Just a few yards beyond him, the forest had been shorn open by a logging operation, a wide swath of open ground littered with forest debris and freshly sawn tree stumps. A dirt road cut through it all, a house-sized pile of limbs and slash awaited burning, and on the far side of the clearing, a hulking, yellow bulldozer sat cold and silent, its tracks caked with fresh earth. A huge pile of logs lay neatly stacked near the road, ready for the logging trucks.

He saw no movement, and the only sound was the quiet rumble of a battered pickup truck idling near the center of the clearing.

He waited, crouching, eyes level with the top of the fallen tree, scanning the clearing, searching for the human beings who had to be there. But no one appeared and the truck just kept idling.

His gaze flitted from the truck to the bulldozer, then to the huge pile of logs, and then to the truck again where something protruding from behind the truck's front wheels caught his eye.

He grabbed a compact pair of binoculars from a pocket and took a closer look.

The protrusion was a man's arm, motionless and streaked with red.

Looking about, the Hunter waited just a few more seconds and then, satisfied that no one else was there, he climbed over the log and stole into the clearing, stepping carefully from rock to stump to patch of grass, trying to avoid any soil that would register his footprints. The truck was parked in nothing but loose soil, freshly chewed by the bulldozer, but he would have to deal with that problem later. He was planning his moves as he went along.

He reached the truck, slowed with caution, and then eased around it, neck craning, in no mood for gruesome surprises.

What he found on the other side was no surprise, but it was gruesome, and definitely a complication. Cursing, he leaned against the truck's hood, warily scanned the tree line and the logging road, and started weighing his options.

The crumpled body on the ground was obviously one of the logging crew, most likely the foreman who'd lingered alone too long on the site the previous evening, judging from the stiff condition of his body. He lay on his belly in the dirt, his body crushed, dried blood streaked from his nose and mouth, his head twisted grotesquely on a broken neck. His hard hat lay top down several feet away, and the ground around the truck was littered with metal shreds of what used to be a lunch box and scattered, chewed-up plastic wrappings that used to hold a lunch.

I don't have time for this!

The Hunter quickly stifled his rage. He needed to calculate, foresee, plan.

His gaze shifted to the pile of logs. That might be an option. He could make it look like an accident that would explain the bent, torn, rag-doll condition of the dead man.

Were the keys in the bulldozer?

Leaving his rifle by the truck, the Hunter ran to the bull-dozer, clambered up on the big steel track, and stepped into the cab. He sank into the worn and torn driver's seat and searched the panel for the keys. Then he sniffed a chuckle of realization: Of course. This wasn't in town, where idle punks drifted about looking to steal anything not locked up or bolted down, and this machine was no car for joyriding. The key was in the ignition.

It had been a while since his college summers with the construction crew, but if this thing was anything like that track hoe he used to operate . . .

He clicked the key over to *Preheat*, waited, then turned the key to *Start*.

The dozer cranked to life with a puff of black smoke.

His mind was racing, still planning, as he put the mountainous machine into gear and got it moving. Reverse came easily enough. Forward was easier. With careful manipulation of the brakes and levers, he brought the dozer to the back of the log pile, then left it there, still running.

Hauling the dead man across the ground would be messy, but it was the only option. The Hunter grabbed the man's wrists—the right arm was intact, but the left arm had been snapped above the elbow and flexed like a rubber hose—and started pulling. He tugged and dragged the body over limbs, grass, rocks, and debris. The man's head dangled from a wrung neck and scraped on the ground. When the Hunter reached the front of the log pile, he let go of the arms. The stiffened body flopped into the dust.

Seated once again in the dozer, he edged the machine forward, reaching under the logs with the bucket. With a calculating, steady pull of the lever, he raised the bucket, lifting the logs, lifting, lifting, until . . .

The pile upset. The logs rolled and rumbled down, bouncing,

tumbling one over the other, drumming the ground, kicking up dust.

The dead man's body disappeared beneath a jackstraw pile of logs.

No time, no time! The Hunter eased the dozer back to its resting place, switched it off, and leaped to the ground. He ran back to the idling truck and pocketed every metal scrap, every torn plastic wrapper he could find. Then, slinging his rifle over his shoulder, he spotted and grabbed a broken-off evergreen bough and went to work, retracing his every step, brushing and erasing each footprint with rapid side-sweeps as he backed out of the clearing.

As expected, he heard the slowly rising sound of a vehicle coming up the logging road, climbing switchbacks, lurching through gears, rattling over potholes, and growling over gravel.

He crouched and headed for the trees, tossing away the branch. Just as he slipped into the forest, a truck pulled into the clearing on the other side. He stole through the crowded timber, planting every footstep silently in the soft, pine-needled ground. Truck doors slammed. Voices lifted, followed by cries of alarm. Those loggers were going to have quite a morning.

■ ■ ■

"So we stay on the Cave Lake Trail for 3.4 miles, and then we come to this fork where the Lost Creek Trail branches off to the right—Beck? Are you following this?"

Rebecca Shelton, twenty-eight, looked up from her compact, unhappy with her clumpy mascara but resigned to leaving it as it was. "W-which trail?"

Her husband, Reed, a six-foot hunk and very aware of it, was trying to be patient, she could tell. She'd seen that understanding but slightly testy expression many times over their six years of marriage. He pointed once again to the map he'd spread out on the hood of their Ford SUV, their route boldly marked with orange highlighter. "This one. Cave Lake. Then this one. Lost Creek."

"Mm. Got it."

She'd been trying to pay attention and even scare up a little enthusiasm all during their long drive, or as Reed called it, "Insertion into the Survival Zone." They'd had a nice picnic lunch—"Preexcursion Rations"—on a log, and even now—at "The Final Briefing" on the hood of their car—she was doing her best to match Reed's excitement, but it was hard to be interested in how many miles they would hike, the hours it would take to get there, the trail grades they would encounter, and their available physical energy. This whole adventure was never *their* idea in the first place, but *his*. He was so *into* this stuff. He'd picked out all the gear, the boots, the backpacks, the maps, the freeze-dried apricots and trail mix, everything. He let her choose which *color* of backpack she wanted—blue—but *he* chose which *kind*.

"If we average four miles an hour, we can be there in . . . three hours," he was saying. There he went again. Beck sighed, and Reed stole a sideways glance at her. "Uh, but considering the rough terrain and the two-thousand-foot climb, I've allowed for six hours, which will still get us there before dark. Got your canteen?"

"Chh-ch-check." Well, *check* was supposed to sound cool, but the word made her stutter flare up, especially now, when she was upset.

"Potable water only, remember. Treat any water you collect before you drink it."

"B-beaver fever."

"Exactly."

Beaver fever. According to Reed, beavers pooped and peed in the creeks, so they weren't supposed to drink the water or they'd catch whatever contagion the beavers were passing, something she wouldn't even try to pronounce.

"Beaver fever," she repeated, just for the satisfaction of saying it clearly. *B*'s didn't bother her much, especially when she was alone with Reed. *W*'s and *s*'s were the toughest, especially around people or when she was on edge. *R*'s and hard *c*'s made her nervous; that was why her name had shrunk to Beck—she didn't have to say an *R*, and once she got the *c* out, the task was over.

"Now, you're going to need a minimum of two or three quarts of water a day," Reed said, "and that's if you aren't exerting yourself, so don't push it too hard on the way up there. And pay attention to your urine output. You want at least a quart in a twenty-four hour period."

"R-r-reed!" She was incredulous.

"Hey, you're looking out for dehydration. If enough water's going out, then you know enough's going in."

"Sss-so are there any b-bathrooms up there?"

Reed smiled playfully. "Honey, what do you think your camp shovel's for?"

Oh, right. Those little collapsible shovels hanging on their packs. Wonderful.

"You did bring toilet paper, right?"

She couldn't help rolling her eyes. "Yes. I've got s-some in my pack and some in my pocket." It was the first thing she packed, and she brought extra. It was the last vestige of the decent, civilized, sensible life she was being ripped away from—besides a folding hairbrush and a small makeup bag.

"Ah, good. Leaves and grass can get a little itchy."

She'd worked up the perfect angry wife look over the years, and now she gave him a good dose of it.

But it didn't faze him. He laughed and gave her a playful rub on her shoulder. Her tension eased. "Don't worry, sweetheart. Once you get up in those mountains and start learning how to survive, you'll wonder why we never did this before."

"I'm w-w-wondering why we're doing it *now*."

Reed studied her face a moment. "Because it'll be good for us." She was about to counter, but he headed her off. "No, now, it's something we need to do. We need a week away from the grind, away from TV and cell phones and the little holes we've dug ourselves into."

"You and Cap maybe."

"Sing's coming too."

"It's a guy thing. You and Cap. Admit it."

"No, come on, *you* admit it. You need to stretch a little. Comfort can be a dangerous thing. You stick around home all the time where it's safe and nothing ever changes, and before you know it, you get set in your ways and you quit learning, you quit changing, you don't grow anymore." He gestured toward the mountains before them, vast, towering, fading from sharp green to soft blue in the immense distance, with snow still visible on the rocky crags. "This will keep you growing. There are things out there you've never seen, never felt, things you need to experience. It'll be worth the trouble." He gave her a knowing glance. "Sometimes even the *trouble's* worth the trouble."

"Are you talking down to me?"

Now he was openly miffed. "I'm talking about *all* of us."

"Right. All of us." She gazed at the mountains, then down at her hiking outfit—rugged boots with high socks, khaki shorts with pockets for just about everything, and on her back a very slick and efficient backpack with a million zippers, cinches, and Velcro flaps, a sleeping bag, and a tiny, rolled-up tent that really did unroll and become big enough for two people to sleep in. Reed had already seen to it that they'd taken three—not one or two—short, "shake-down hikes" to test all this stuff: the fit of the clothes, the weight of the packs, the effectiveness of the hiking shoes, how fast they could set up the tent, *everything*. "Well, I'm not home and I'm not c-comfortable, so I think you can b-be satisfied."

Reed looked pleased. "It's a good start."

She wanted to hit him.

He turned to the map again, and she tried to follow along. "So, all right. We take the Cave Lake Trail from here to the Lost Creek turnoff, then take that trail for another 8.6 miles, and we should have no trouble reaching the hunter's cabin before night-fall. It's right here, right on the creek. Randy Thompson'll be there waiting for us."

"With dinner?"

"If I know Randy, he'll show us how to build the fire our-selves, without matches, and how to cook our own dinner from what we can find in the woods."

"That'll take forever."

Reed cocked an eyebrow. "Randy can whip up a pine needle tea in under two minutes—and after this week, we'll be able to do the same thing."

Beck made a face. "Pine needle tea?"

Reed shrugged, undaunted, undimmed. "I understand it's not too bad. We might even like it."

"He's not going to make us eat b-bugs and worms, is he?"

Reed wouldn't give up that playful smile. "Mm, you might like those too."

She drew a breath to make a snide comment—

"We'd better get going." He folded up the map and tucked it away in one of his backpack's many zippered compartments, then hefted the pack to his shoulders and put his arms through the straps.

She followed his cue, and Reed held the pack aloft as she

wrestled and squirmed her way into the straps. The thing wasn't as heavy as it looked—and then again, maybe it was.

Reed led the way across the gravel parking lot to the trailhead. Beck followed, looking back once to be sure she hadn't left anything behind, besides her sanity. The SUV sat there all by itself, like a faithful dog sitting in the driveway watching his masters leave.

"You're gonna roast in that jacket," Reed observed.

Beck regarded her fringed buckskin jacket, a gift from her father—he was an outdoors nut too. She never wore it, but for this outing, it seemed appropriate. "S-so I want to be Daniel B-boone, all right?"

"You'll be carrying it."

"Just look out for yourself, Mr. Know-It-All."

Reed kept walking, a spring in his step despite the load on his back. He was so pleased Beck was sure he had a screw loose. "Yeah, this is just what we need."

What I *need, you mean!* Part of her could have, peradventure, at a better time, admitted he was right, but right now she wasn't in the mood to admit anything.

The moment came. Feeling like a Neil Armstrong, Beck followed her adventurous husband and took that One Small Step out of the parking lot and onto the trail. Other steps came after that, and she looked back twice before the deepening forest hid the familiar world from view.

Then, looking back no more, she pressed on, leaving one world for another.

■ ■ ■

Road 228 was "maintained" in the summer, which was Idaho's way of saying it would be filled back in if it washed out, and you could still drive it if you didn't mind the washboard rattle under your wheels, the blinding dust, the constant growl of the gravel, and the rude bumping of the rocks.

Dr. Michael Capella, a stocky, dark-haired college professor in his thirties, was driving 228 in a Toyota 4Runner, climbing, ever climbing into the mountains, his eyes intent on every curve, every bump, every rut as he maintained a speed just a notch short of dangerous. His wife, Sing, a lovely Coeur d'Alene Native American, sat next to him, her face clouded by a list of concerns, not the least of which was his driving.

"Incredible mountains," she said, admiring their beauty.

Cap nodded, gripping the wheel.

"Cap, there really is some great scenery out there."

"And your point is?"

"It's just a little after four. We'll make it to the resort with time to spare, so relax. Kick back a little. Isn't that what this trip's all about?"

He eased off the accelerator. Sing said nothing, but a faint smile traced her lips.

Cap allowed himself a quick look to the right, where the edge of the road dropped off sharply to the St. Marie's River below and a lone osprey circled above a fathomless, forested valley. He drew a breath and loosened his grip on the steering. "It's hard to let go of things."

She smiled. "You may as well. They aren't there anymore."

He pondered that a moment, but shook his head, still unable to grasp it. "No, *I'm* the one who's not there anymore. And I keep thinking I should be, because they *are*."

She chuckled. "You and that confidentiality agreement! It makes you talk in riddles—ever notice that?"

"Sorry. I know it must seem rude."

She touched his hand. "You don't have to say anything, and you don't have to prove anything, especially to me. I know the man I married."

He nodded a deep nod just to avoid the debate. They'd had this conversation before, and she'd been right, but he'd had trouble buying it. He still did. "Well, call it a sabbatical, then. Call it a break."

"It's a sabbatical. It's a break. And Reed had a good idea." Then she added, "I think."

Cap shifted his thoughts to the coming week. "Well, Reed says Randy Thompson's the best. He's a Native, by the way."

"Well, there *are* some of us still around."

"Randy's up there right now, getting the cabin ready, laying in supplies. He does these survival courses all the time, winter or summer, it doesn't matter. Reed says you can drop that guy anywhere in the world and he'd know what to do to stay alive."

Sing gave a barely audible sigh and looked out the window a moment. "So what do you do while you're living? Staying alive is nice, but you can't do that forever. It's *how* you live the life you have while you have it."

Cap smirked just a little. "I should stick that on the refrigerator."

"I'll write it down for you." She turned her body to face him and put her hand on his shoulder. "Cap, you did the right thing. I'm proud of you."

"At least the house is paid for." He forced a smile. "It's where we go from here that bothers me."

She smiled. He felt her acceptance, as he was. Without changing him. "We go into the mountains, we learn to survive, and we hear from God. That's enough for now."

He drove quietly for a moment, noticing mountain peaks and waterfalls for the first time, and then placed his hand on hers and gave it a squeeze.

Thirty miles of grinding, growling, gravel road later, they reached Abney, a once-booming mining town that had long since withered and now had trouble remembering why it was there.

"Well, it has ambience," said Cap as they eased down the main road past sagging storefronts, well-used vehicles, and mangy stray dogs.

"Rustic," Sing observed politely, kind to choose even that word. They drove by a forlorn clapboard tavern with one corner sinking into the ground, an auto garage with dismembered cars and trucks scattered about and a snow cat up on blocks, a combination hardware store and mining museum—noteworthy because this building actually had a new front porch—and a post office not much bigger than a phone booth. They had yet to see a human being.

"Can't wait to see the *resort*," Sing quipped.

"I hear it's the real thing, right out of the rich, historical heritage of Idaho."

They drove to the end of town—not far from the beginning—and found a large log cabin to which someone had added another story, to which someone added another wing and a dormer, to which someone added another bedroom, to which someone added four more bedrooms like a motel and then tied the whole thing together with one continuous wraparound porch that bumped up and down to line up with all the doors to all those additions. A sign strung on a chain over the driveway read, "Tall Pine Resort." On the rail fence was a weathered VACANCY sign with an empty nail for hanging a NO in case that should ever be the case. Judging from the scarcity of vehicles in the parking area, the Tall Pine was not seeing a booming business at the moment.

Cap pulled in next to two pickups rigged with high sides for hauling firewood and a station wagon with a sad old dog—he must have been the sire of all the others in town—staring at them through the back window.

"Hm," Cap mused. "Reed said this place is really hopping this time of year."

The lobby was a cubbyhole wedged between the café and the souvenir shop, with trophies of moose, deer, elk, and bear crowding the walls, and one huge chandelier made of antlers that hung over the front desk.

The white-haired, leathery proprietor broke into a silvery grin from behind the front desk. "So you must be the, uh, the Campanellas . . . ?"

"Capella. This is my wife, Sing."

Sing shook his hand. He had gnarled fingers that had hewn many a log and tanned many a deer hide.

"Sing," the old man said quizzically. "It's gotta be short for something."

"Sings in the Morning," she answered. "My parents like the old traditions." Not that she didn't; her and Cap's home boasted some of the finest Salish artwork, and she often wore her long black hair in traditional braids as she did today.

The silvery teeth showed again. "It suits you." He extended his hand to Cap.

Cap gripped it firmly. "I'm Michael, but my friends call me Cap."

"Arlen Peak, pleased to meet you. Now we're friends and I can call you Cap."

"Got that room?"

Peak slid a room registration card toward Cap to fill out. "One-oh-four, just right for you and the missus."

Cap started scribbling, a hint of a smile on his face, his first since they'd left Spokane.

"So . . ." Peak said, watching Cap scribble, "Randy says you're planning on a week up there."

"Yep. Our friends ought to be getting there right about now. We're going to hike up and join them tomorrow morning. We're a day late, but we'll catch up."

"Had to wait to get off work, I suppose."

"Sing did."

Sing shot him a loving but scolding glance, then she broke the silence with a question. "So what's this cabin like?"

Peak chuckled apologetically. "It's not the Hilton, but it's in good shape. We gave it a once-over a little while ago, me and some hunter friends. Put in a new floor, patched the roof, got it all up to snuff again. You understand it's just a shelter for hunters. It's got a few cots, some shelves, and some hooks for hanging things, but that's about it. Randy prefers it that way. Helps people get into the wilderness frame of mind."

"We're ready for it," said Cap, sliding the completed card back across the desk.

"Yeah, well, Randy headed up there this morning, so he's ready for you." Peak thought for a moment. "But you'll wanna be careful. Keep your eyes and ears open, and don't, uh, don't hang around if . . . you know, if you think better of it."

Cap and Sing looked at him, waiting for more.

Peak met their eyes. "Kind of late to be telling you, I know."

Cap sensed something in Arlen Peak, a warning they should heed. "Is there a problem?"

The old man's face became grim. "Well, Mr. Capella . . . Cap . . . we've never had any trouble around here. Randy knows that, and that's what he tells all his clients, but like I tried to tell him, something's not right. Wish he would've been here a few hours ago and seen that whole herd of elk come through, right in broad daylight, all going someplace in a hurry. That's not like them. It's too early in the year for them to be down this low."

"What are you saying?" Cap asked. Both he and Sing were motionless, their eyes on the old man.

He seemed hesitant to answer. "I've lived here a long time, Cap, right here in this lodge, and when you live in a place a long time, you get to know how things are supposed to happen." He leaned over the counter for a better view out the front windows. He pointed as he spoke. "I know when the elk are supposed to migrate to the lower ground, and I know what time each day the deer are going to cross that road to get to the river. I know when the bears are going to run out of forage and start coming down here to raid the apple trees. I know when things are all right." Then he looked at them again and added, "And I can tell when they aren't." He gave his hands a little toss up. "But you have to live here awhile to understand what I'm saying."

Cap drummed one finger on the counter. "Is there a *specific* danger we should be aware of?"

Peak thought it over, came to some kind of agreement with himself, and answered, "You may have noticed there aren't a lot of folks around. Not that I don't want their business, I surely do, but what I know, I tell 'em, 'cause I know what I know, and nobody's gonna tell me I don't." Then he nodded toward a yellowing poster tacked to the wall.

Cap thought he'd seen this picture before, a blurry blowup of a massive, apelike creature. It strode on two legs across a log-strewn riverbed. Suddenly his uneasiness melted away.

"*Bigfoot?*" Sing said. Cap could tell she was holding back a smile.

"Don't laugh."

"No, no, I'm not laughing."

Peak's eyes were intense as he listened to something only he could hear, an old memory playing in his mind. "I heard one howl once, maybe eight, nine years ago. It wasn't like anything I ever heard before. Chilled my blood."

Sing leaned forward, obviously intrigued by the old man's earnestness. "What did it sound like?" she said.

He wrinkled the bridge of his nose, listening some more.

"Something between the howl of a wolf and the roar of a lion. Real long, and echoing. Scary."

Cap wasn't doing much to control his smile. "But that was nine years ago?"

Peak locked eyes with Cap, not smiling at all. "That was the first one. But I was meaning to say, I've heard it again the last few nights. Sounds like more than one, and they're upset about something."

Cap had read such nonsense before on grocery-store tabloids. He leaned back and crossed his arms over his chest, allowing his eyes to wander toward the cluttered shelves behind the old man.

"Nine years without making a sound," Peak insisted, "and now they're making all this noise? Cap, they don't howl for nothing. Something's wrong."

Cap met his gaze again, indulgingly. "It could be a wolf. I understand they've been reintroduced up north."

The innkeeper raised his hands in a brief sign of surrender. "All right, believe what you want, but just do me one favor—be careful."

Cap nodded. "We'll be careful."

Sing was looking at a glass display cabinet immediately below the poster. Inside were yellowed news clippings, photos of footprints, and in the middle of it all, a plaster cast of a huge footprint. "Huh. Look at this."

Cap leaned against the counter, detached and happy to remain that way. "Guess you're quite the Bigfoot enthusiast."

"Not by choice," Peak answered.

"Ever seen one?"

"Nope. Ever seen a wolverine?"

Cap thought the question a little strange. "No."

"Very few people have, but it's out there, isn't it?"

While Sing perused the contents of the cabinet, Peak pointed at the plaster cast. "Got that from a Sasquatch researcher just a year ago. He found that footprint right around here, right up in these mountains."

"And you paid good money for it, I suppose," said Cap.

"Well, that's between him and me."

Sing leaned for a closer look at the cast.

Cap had to grill Peak a touch longer. "But how many people have lived in this county all their lives and never seen a thing?"

"These creatures are smart, and they don't *want* to be seen. Did you ever think of that?"

"That still doesn't mean—" Cap didn't like the look on Sing's face or what it told him she might be thinking. "I'd say someone did a real good job carving that out." Sing unfolded her glasses and put them on. She began tracing a line on the cast, eyeing it over her finger. "A *very* good job."

■ ■ ■

The hike was going well—physically. Beck always ran two miles before breakfast, so she was up to the arduous trek, and Reed, being a sheriff's deputy, prided himself on his physical condition. They maintained a brisk pace, Reed bounding along the trail, fully demonstrating the strength and efficiency of his muscles and cardiovascular system, and Beck keeping up just fine, not about to be one-upped. The day was getting warmer, and okay, Reed was right about her buckskin jacket: she'd shed it only a few minutes into the hike, and now it was draped on the frame of her backpack.

Uphill, uphill, uphill had been the rule of the day. They'd just climbed along a steep, forested slope, half a mile one way, then around a switchback and another half a mile the other way, then back again, the steep mountain drop-off on their right, then their left, then their right, and so it went.

It was when they finished that climb and descended a north-facing slope into old-growth forest that the hike turned from a physical competition to something almost . . . profound. This wasn't common, everyday forest with trees the size of telephone poles all close together and stickery bushes between them. No, this was something out of a Tolkien or Lewis fantasy, a wondrous, otherworldly place where the earth was soft and deep with moss and peat; where tiny white wildflowers twinkled in the green carpet, iridescent bugs with fairy wings flickered in the sunbeams, and every footstep was muffled in the pulverized red bark of a million trees that lived there before. Now, *this* caught Beck's fancy. She'd read about this place, even written her own whimsical stories about it when she was a girl. This was where hobbits and elves, fairies and princesses, knights and ogres had their adventures and intrigues, and where all nature of mischievous creatures lived among the snaking, claw-foot roots. This was where—

"You can eat cattails, did you know that?" Reed still had not run out of things he knew and just had to share. "You can eat the stalk; you can eat the pollen; you can even eat the roots. Of course, they grow in swamps and wetlands, and we're up a little high for that." He sounded like a forest ranger on a nature hike, and he was past getting on her nerves.

She held her peace and concentrated on the coarse, furrowed sides of the huge trees. How old must they be by now? How many centuries had they seen? How many—

"Hey, a slug. Did you know those are edible? 'Course, they're supposed to be better if you cook 'em, but you can eat them either way."

Enough. "R-reed. You c-can barbecue one and s-serve it with A1 Sauce and I will never eat it. Change the s-subject."

"How about grass? Remember that meadow back there? We

could have cooked up a kettle of grass stew, maybe even made some tea."

"If I recall c-correctly, we have p-pine needles for tea."

"*Now* you're learning. Hey, you know how to find north and south without a compass?"

"D-do you ever stop talking?"

"Beck, we're supposed to learn all this stuff."

"Reed, I am happy with my life, I really am! I have a novel to work on, two paintings, and a stack of research. I could be doing all of that right now and enjoying my life, but *nooo*, I have to be hoofing out in the middle of nowhere, listening to my back-to-earth husband talk about eating slugs."

"One of these days, Beck, you're gonna wish you knew this stuff."

She fully intended to learn it, but she wasn't about to tell him. She did sneak a look at the slug as she passed by. Ooookay. That settled that.

Reed held back, which gave her precious time to mellow and enjoy things—well, more than just enjoy. She already understood what Reed had been trying to tell her. There were sights out here she'd never seen, and there were feelings that could only be felt by being here: the solitude, the wonder. The unique song of the woods could only be heard in nature's kind of *quiet*. She wanted to capture it, but what camera was capable of conveying the depth of such an image? What words could evoke the emotion? God spoke through His creation, and the message went past the mind, straight to the heart. It was all so—

"Uh-oh." Reed stopped, and in her reverie Beck almost ran into him.

"What?"

"Is that the cabin?"

Ahead, the trail meandered downward into a quiet, tree-shaded ravine where an ancient fallen log formed a bridge across a creek. On the other side, the remains of a man-made structure huddled against the slope in what could have been—should have been—a quaint setting. Once it had been a crude but effective shelter built from hand-hewn logs and split shakes, perched on footings of river rock. Once it had a sheltered front porch, a front door, and a window on each side. Once it had been just as Randy Thompson's survival brochure had described it—"a wilderness retreat well worth the hike."

They kept an eye on it as they silently worked their way down the trail, the cabin peeking and hiding, peeking and hiding through the trees. With each new view came more woeful news: The porch roof had collapsed, its support posts snapped in two; just visible under the sagging porch roof, the front door hung crookedly from only one of the two strap hinges; on the shallow creek bank below, the remains of a cot lay ripped and crumpled, the frame splintered like matchsticks.

At the log bridge, the cabin was in plain sight. Reed rechecked the map and Randy Thompson's detailed instructions. "This is it. This is the cabin."

One window was shattered; the other was torn out, frame and all. Through the window, and on the porch, and on the ground around the cabin lay gutted food containers, shredded wrappers, crumpled cans, spilled flour.

"Someone's been here," said Reed. "Maybe a bear."

Beck called, "M-Mr. Thompson! Mr. Thompson!"

The only answer was the mournful sound of Lost Creek moving under the bridge.

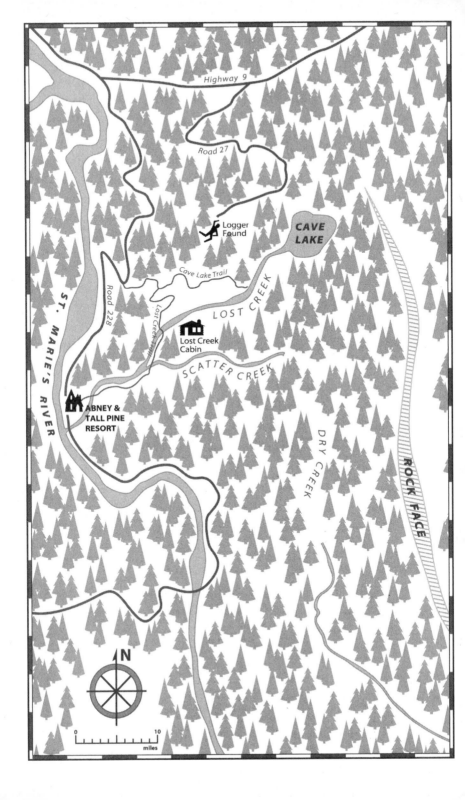

TWO

Reed didn't like not knowing. He started toward the cabin. "Guess we'd better check it out."

"I-I'm n-n-not going i-innnn there!" Beck protested, staying right where she was on the log bridge.

"Okay, fine." Reed slipped his backpack off. "Stay here and watch the stuff."

He grabbed his digital camera from a side pocket of his pack, snapped some wide shots from the bridge, and then went across to the other side.

The cop in him was coming out. He stepped carefully, not wanting to contaminate the site with his own disturbances, moving over the rocks, avoiding the softer areas that might reveal footprints. He snapped some more pictures of the litter, the cabin, the torn-out window, the collapsing front porch, the broken cot on the creek bank.

He ducked under the sagging roof, pushed the broken door out of the way, and took a look inside. The other cot was still here, but splintered like the one outside. Shelves along the back wall were smashed, and the shredded, depleted remnants of the food supplies spilled all over the floor, along with a rusty shovel, most likely the cabin's "toilet." A sack of pancake mix had been ruptured, dusting the floor and shelves with a translucent layer of white. At his feet lay an empty bread wrapper, a can of Spam torn open and licked clean, a crinkled and empty package of jerky, a canteen still full of water.

Beck called, "Is anybody in there?"

"Yeah. Me."

"Very funny!"

He ducked back outside.

Beck had ventured close enough to pick up and examine an empty can of beans, its torn edges jagged as if it had been bitten or clawed open.

"There's more of that inside," he told her. "Had to have been a bear. That's what happens when you leave food around. That's why you never leave food in your camp. You store it up high, out of reach, away from your campsite."

For once she was listening, with no comeback or protest—not with that torn can in her hand.

"But that makes me think somebody's been here recently," Reed said. "The food around here was all fresh stuff, like somebody just brought it."

Maybe he shouldn't have told her that. She sighed, threw up her hands and brought them down with a slap against her legs, twirled in place, scanned the forest all around. "Oh, that's just g-great! So w-where is he now?"

"Beck."

"Looks like your b-b-big vacation plan just went s-south—"

"*Beck!* Come on, now. We're adults. We're professional people. We work the problem!"

Good. That seemed to hit home. Beck breathed a moment, brushed a lock of her reddish-brown hair from her face, and asked him, "So w-what do we do?"

"We get a grip—"

"I've got a grip! What do we do?"

Well, this was his moment. He was the stud here, the man with the plan. He drew a breath to buy a little time. "We think things through. Now, we've only got an hour of daylight left. We'd better get our camp set up."

She cocked her head and looked at him with unbelieving eyes. "Y-y-you—"

"Yes. We're going to camp here. We don't have time to hike back down."

"S-s-s-so w-what if the b-bear comes-comes back?"

"We've got our shovels and there's a shovel in the cabin. We can bury all this garbage so he doesn't return, and then we'll camp somewhere else and hang our food up in a tree far away from where we're sleeping. No problem. That's the way campers do it all the time."

"S-s-s—" Beck sputtered and spit through her fumbling lips in frustration. "So w-where's Mr. Thompson—that's what I want to kn-n-n—"

"Beck, we're in the wilderness. The rules are different out here. If we don't keep ourselves alive, Mr. Thompson isn't going to matter one way or the other."

Beck finally sighed, "Ooo-kay."

He led, she followed, and they found a suitable spot farther up the creek, high, dry, and mostly level, encircled by hefty firs and pines. It provided a good view of the cabin below, but was hard to see from below—Beck liked that part. Reed got out a length of rope, and between the two of them, with some shin-nying and climbing, they were able to suspend their food containers on a clothesline between two trees a suitable distance from their camp. Other than the food, they didn't unpack much. Reed spread out a ground cloth, and they unrolled their sleeping bags on it.

In the ebbing light, Beck changed into jeans and a warmer shirt. Now the cool air moving down the ravine made her glad she'd brought that buckskin jacket. She gladly put it back on.

Their camp prepared, they sat on their sleeping bags in the deepening dark and munched on cold sandwiches.

"We'll stow our sandwich boxes and wrappers up in the Remote Storage Apparatus along with the other rations," Reed said.

Beck's sandwich was cold and soggy. "So much for hot pine needle tea."

"Maybe tomorrow." He snapped a few pictures of her.

She smiled, a shade of smirk on her lips despite the wad of sandwich still in her cheek. "So I wonder what happened to Mr. Thompson?"

"The bear wouldn't have raided the cabin if he'd been here. I'm guessing he went back down to Abney to bring up more supplies."

"Well, Mr. Survival wasn't too smart to leave all that food in the cabin in the first place, am I right?"

Reed nodded, conceding the point even as it puzzled him. "It sure didn't work out, did it?"

Beck swallowed her bite of sandwich before she spoke again. "Maybe he's planning on coming up with Sing and Cap in the morning."

"That's why we need to sit tight. Stick with the plan."

Beck chewed and thought it over. It did make sense. Sometime in the midmorning, Randy Thompson would come up the trail from Abney. Cap and Sing would be right there with him carrying in more supplies. Everything would fall together, and they would all make the best of it. She allowed herself to breathe a little easier. Reed seemed to have a handle on things. Maybe she'd trust him. Maybe.

She lay back on her sleeping bag, finishing up the last bite of her sandwich. The treetops converged around the circle of darkening sky. The first stars were visible. She had to admit, this part of it was pretty nice.

■ ■ ■

It couldn't have been more than a half hour since they crawled into their sleeping bags that Beck sat up, blinked, stared straight ahead, and saw nothing. She turned her head, felt her eyes moving in their sockets, blinked to be sure her eyes were open.

Where was she? The darkness was so total, so enveloping, that she had to tell herself she was in the woods, somewhere along Lost Creek, above a torn-up little cabin.

She couldn't see the cabin. She couldn't see the creek or the trail.

She groped for her flashlight and found it just inside her sleeping bag. *Come on, come on, where's that button?*

It clicked on and almost blinded her.

Okay. Squinting in the sudden light, she could see the trees encircling their camping spot. She could see a few bushes, ferns, roots, and rocks, stark in the flashlight beam with nothing but bottomless black behind them.

What happened to that wondrous place she'd seen by day, that enchanting forest where the elves and princesses and heroes had their adventures and intrigues and little bugs with fairy wings floated in the sunbeams?

Obviously, that was *then*, and this was *night*. Suddenly she felt lost. What were the rules *now*?

"What are you doing?" Reed's voice made her jump.

She settled, breathed, her hand over her heart. "Y-you—" She stopped without saying, *scared me*. "N-nothing. Just looking around."

"Go to sleep."

She clicked off the flashlight. Now the darkness was darker than before and she saw nothing but afterimages floating on her retinas.

Go to sleep, girl, she told herself. *This is night. It happens every day. No, every night. Every—what?—sixteen hours or so? No, more like eight hours that start after sixteen hours of daytime. Anyway, it only lasts so long.*

She lay back and closed her eyes.

Snap.

She froze, her eyes wide but unseeing. "Did you hear that?"

Reed didn't answer. She wanted to nudge him but didn't.

There it was again, only more of it: a twig snapping, a bush swishing. *Crack!* Definitely a stick on the ground breaking.

Now she did nudge him.

"What?"

"There's s-something out there."

Reed propped himself up on an elbow with a sigh of exasperation and listened for at least half a minute. All was silent. He turned as if to chide her, but then—*Snap!*

Reed's stomach wrenched inside him. *Brother, now she's got me worked up.* But he couldn't deny it. He heard it too: something was moving in the deep blackness beyond, somewhere down in the ravine.

A rustling. *Thump!* Something heavy and wooden tipped over.

It's wildlife, he told himself. "It's wildlife," he whispered. "You know, deer, elk, something like that."

"A b-b-bear?"

"Well, it could be the bear. Animals do a lot of foraging at night. There's nothing weird about it."

She insisted, "W-w-what if it's the b-bear?"

"He's after food, remember? If he goes anywhere, it'll be to the cabin to clean up whatever's left. He doesn't even know we're up here."

There was a breathless moment of silence.

"Oh, shoot," Reed whispered.

"What?"

"I forgot to hang up the sandwich containers. We still have them here."

"M-m-maybe he won't s-smell anything."

"Air moves downhill at night. We're upwind."

But then it was quiet, and stayed quiet.

Reed spoke first. "Guess it's over." He lay back down.

Beck sat up for another moment, then eased back and pulled the sleeping bag up to her chin. She lay on her back, then one side, then the other side.

Finally, she whispered, "Arrre y-you asleep?"

"No," he answered out loud.

"How you doing?"

"I'm okay."

"M-me too."

"You sound nervous."

"I'm not." Silence. "Well, aren't y-you?"

"Nope. Not me."

"You're not asleep."

He sighed and rustled around. "You woke me up."

He was getting to her again. "I'm r-reeeally not afraid. I can handle this just as w-well as you can."

Well, *he* wasn't afraid, no way. "Beck, you know what? The

only creatures out here afraid of the dark are us. All the other animals are out there stomping around in the dark like it's nothing, and here we are, scared to death—"

"Oh, *w-we're* scared to death?"

"I'm talking in *group* talk here. We're a team, we're—"

"Oh, w-we're a team? Well just-just tell me this: Which t-team has the advantage here? I mean, just *who* is on *whose* turf?"

"The animals don't mind. They're just doing what animals do—"

More noise. Something moving.

"I th-th-think it's near the c-cabin," Beck whispered.

"The cabin's *that* way."

"W-what way?"

"That way."

"I can't see where you're pointing."

"Well, just sit tight and—"

The sound was nothing like they had ever heard before, and it wasn't quiet. It was so clear, so loud, that even though Reed knew it was somewhere down in the ravine, it seemed as if it was *right there* next to them.

It was like a woman wailing in grief and anguish, weeping over the corpse of a loved one, her cry rising, wavering, holding, then falling off into a hissing sob, then . . . gone. Silence.

Snap! Crunch. Whatever it was, it was coming up the ravine.

The woman wept again, her voice quaking, the note rising to a nerve-rending peak and then trailing off.

Beck saw nothing with her eyes, but her imagination was providing the most horrible images of dismembered witches, transparent banshees, rotting corpses walking about seeking revenge—

Oh, stop it! she scolded herself.

Reed fumbled for his flashlight.

"D-d-don't-don't turn that on! She'll see where we are!"

Reed's voice was shaking. "Nothing's gonna sneak up on me—I mean, I just, I just wanna get a fix on it."

Then came a quieter whimper, as if through clenched teeth.

Reed found the button. Suddenly, shockingly, the beam of his flashlight cut through the darkness, reached as far as the immediate trees, then stretched itself into oblivion in the tangled forest, bringing back only dim images of leaves, dead branches, dancing shadows. Beck didn't look—she was afraid of what she might see.

"What if it really is somebody out there?" Reed whispered. "What if they're in trouble?"

"Th-th-then w-why don't they say s-so?"

Reed hollered, "Hello? Is anybody out there?"

No answer.

Beck thought, *Well, if* he's *going to holler* . . . "Hello? Ar-rrr-re you okay?"

Nothing.

They waited. They listened. Was that thing *hiding*?

"I don't think it w-was a woman," Beck whispered.

Now Reed was whispering. "It sounded like one."

"N-no, no it didn't."

"I think we made it go away."

A growl and a short snuff. It was low, quiet, from the other side of the ravine, somewhere high up the slope. Beck envisioned something big, with lots of teeth and a bad attitude as it crouched in the bushes, feeling intruded upon—

There it was again, more insistent this time, edged with anger. It was moving. The direction was hard to tell, but it could have been away from them, which was great, and so far, it was *out there* and not . . .

A chuckle sniffed out Reed's nose.

Beck thought that was quite out of place. "W-what are you laughing at?"

"It's a joke."

Somehow she wasn't ready to accept that.

"It's a joke," he insisted. "Cap and Randy Thompson are trying to scare us."

"W-what makes you so s-sure?"

"Well, it's obvious. Everybody knew we'd be coming up here one day before Cap and Sing, and then Thompson just happens to not show up, and then we start hearing stupid noises out in the woods. It's a big put-on."

Beck sat there, her frightened face indirectly lit by Reed's flashlight beam. She longed for him to be right.

He kept trying. "Don't you remember when we were going to United Christian and we went to that party for the young couples' group?"

"Sure."

"We all went for that hayride in the back of George Johnson's truck—"

"A-a-and the truck b-broke down, and a bear came out of the w-woods." Her nerves calmed. "And it was just what's-his-name—"

"Mr. Farmer wearing that bear rug." Reed snickered. "But you sure were scared."

"I was young! And so were *you!*"

They sat still and listened.

"S-so you think that's what it is?" Beck asked.

Reed hollered, "Okay, you can come out now! Very funny! Ha-ha!"

"Very funny, Cap!" Beck shouted. "Cap?"

No answer.

Then they heard, of all things, a strange, hissing kind of whistle, like a teapot at a boil, but bigger, louder, warbling a little. It sounded like it was far up the opposite bank of the ravine. It could have been moving . . .

Another whistle answered the first one. This one was much closer, on this side of the ravine, off to their right. Between the pounding of her heart, Beck heard something leaving heavy, munching footfalls on the dead needles and twigs.

"What if it isn't a joke?" she asked.

"Hey—"

"N-no, no, what if it *is* Cap and Mr. Thompson, but they're testing us, trying to demonstrate something, t-trying to show us w-what the mind can do in the dark, in the woods, late at night?"

Reed thought about that. "Like a simulation?"

"Y-yeah. To show us how e-e-easy it is to panic and d-do the wrong things."

Reed nodded. "I've done those before in the department's training sessions. Crime scenes and hostage situations . . ."

"Yeah."

"That could be it!"

"So . . . how do we handle this?"

"Well, if it's supposed to be a bear, then we should holler and make a bunch of noise and chase it away."

She looked at him; he looked at her. They got to their feet, shouting, hollering, shooing. "Yaaa! Go on! Get out of here!"

The woman outscreamed them in length, in volume, and definitely in terror effect, her cry searing up the ravine like black fire as she thrashed in the brush.

A wooden creak, a splintering snap, cloth tearing.

That broken cot in front of the cabin. She was that close.

A very loud, throaty growl shattered the air and rippled through the trees. Whatever had made that first whistle was bursting out in anger or fear or—whatever it was, it wasn't good. They heard footfalls moving quickly, pounding and thrashing up the bank.

The woman screamed in reply, splashing in the creek, then moving up the bank as if in pursuit.

Reed and Beck shied back in the dark. Beck clicked on her flashlight to match Reed's. They swept the perimeter. Trees. Brush. Bony, dead limbs. Blackness beyond.

"Th-th-th-three of them," Beck said, her voice broken with terror.

"*Think*," Reed said, to her *and* to himself. "Don't panic, just think."

Beck thought out loud, "B-big, hungry beasts, two t-t-tender, chewable people—"

"You're letting your imagination run away with you."

"It's *my* imagination!"

She exhaled, trying to steady herself.

It was quiet out there.

"I'm think-th-thinking something," she said.

"I'm listening."

"Cap and Sing w-wouldn't do this. They'd never b-betray our trust. George Johnson, yeah, but not Cap, and not Sing."

Reed mulled that over for a precious second. "You're right." In a moment, he came back with, "But if something out there was hunting us, it wouldn't be making all this noise. It would've sneaked up on us."

More listening. More silence. Then some rustling and movement up the bank. Whatever the creatures were, they were still there.

"I s-say we get out of here," she said.

Snap! Thud.

"Don't panic. If we panic, we're sunk." He tried to steady his voice as he quickly added, "If we stick with the plan, Mr. Thompson and Cap and Sing will know where to find us. If they get here tomorrow and we're not here—"

A howl up in the woods. Something—and it was no small coyote or wolf—was very upset.

"They might be going away. Don't panic," Reed pleaded.

"You're s-s-scared too; come on."

"I'm not scared."

"Come on, your voice is shaking!"

"I'm cold."

"W-w-well I'm wearing a jacket, s-so there!"

Reed started scrambling around the campsite.

"What are you doing now?"

"I'm getting rid of these sandwich containers."

"You, youuu can't hang those up in the trees now!"

"I'm gonna *throw* 'em, just get 'em away from us!"

"Yeah, and leave me here?"

"What's the matter, you scared?"

She didn't answer. He turned, his arms full, and left.

She stood there, alone in the dark, her flashlight shining into a black infinity. The quiet out there was not comforting. At least when those unknowns were making noise, she knew where they were.

Uh-oh, there was that growl again, somewhere up the bank across the ravine. Now it sounded alarmed. But no response from the wailing woman. Where was she?

A whistle! Long, loud, like escaping steam, warbling—and close.

Beck swept the woods that direction with her flashlight. Tree trunks. Dead limbs. A broken snag. Nothing beyond.

What on earth . . . ? Now she smelled something. She sniffed, first one direction, then another. It was terrible, like the worst body odor, like something rotten.

"R-r-reed? D-do youuu smell that?"

No answer.

"Reed?"

Something rustled behind her, and then came that whistle

again, this time low and hissing. She spun, her hands shaking, and shined her light up the hill, across a row of tree trunks, past a black chasm of nothing, over some more trunks—

Something glimmered in that black chasm. She returned to the darkness between the trees.

She knew what it was. Anytime Jonah, their dog, looked back at a flashlight beam, anytime a cat would look into their car's headlights, the eyes always reflected the light back like . . . like what she was seeing right now.

Two huge eyes, like silvery green headlights floating slowly in the dark. They blinked at her, then vanished as if blocked by a hand or arm. *Heavy footfalls, snapping, crunching!*

Beck plunged into the trees, looking for Reed. She may have been screaming; she only knew she was running, dodging tree trunks as they leaped from left and right into her light. "R-r-r-r—" His name just wouldn't form. She abandoned consonants and let any sound leap out that would.

"Here—"

This time a scream came out easily, without forethought or construction, mainly because she ran right into him.

"Whoa, whoa, easy!"

She screamed and stuttered and spit something about seeing the eyes and the smell and how close it was and how high off the ground those eyes were and the noise it made and how—

Screams! Savage screeches! Howls! The rage and thunder of demons, banshees, black minions of hell, roared, echoed, crackled down the hillside, reverberating off the trees, quaking and bouncing through the ravine, rippling up the creek. The beasts were close, so close, the thump of their footfalls like subwoofers in the ground.

Reed and Beck found the same tree in the quaking, sweeping beams of their flashlights, a tangled, half-dead cedar. Both had the same thought: *Climb! Climb and never come down, never ever*—

He got one hand under her foot to give her a boost. The first limb she grabbed wore a shirt and gave way the moment she touched it. A bloody, broken arm dropped out of the tree. She didn't scream this time. No sound would come. She only fell away, numbed by the sight, as she dropped for a slow-motion eternity before landing in a tangle of bushes.

A wide-eyed, crazed-faced man dropped into the beam of their lights. He was upside down, swinging, flopping, limp and purple with death, his legs snarled in the branches, his long braid dangling like a black viper below his head.

The man's head was barely attached.

They ran, through tree trunks that flashed and flickered across their light beams, over uneven, leg-grabbing tangles of growth, into endless night and darkness, oblivious, reckless, mad with fear.

Their backpacks were nearly an afterthought, but a shred of wisdom still remained, and they grabbed them up as they passed by. They didn't know where the trail was, only that it was below them in the ravine, so down they went, over the bank, grabbing roots, plants, tree trunks, anything to keep from tumbling headlong as they dropped down, gripping, heeling in, slipping, grabbing, dropping again.

The beasts, the demons, the spirits of the forest were still screaming as if in the throes of battle. Their voices were everywhere, so loud that Beck had to scream to be heard. She sputtered something about seeing the trail.

One more leap and they were on the path, running up the trail out of the ravine, hoping and praying it was the right one, the one that would get them out of this hellish place and down to Abney, a town they'd only heard about.

They ran as fast as they could see to run, adrenaline rushing, the trail, the trees, the turns quaking in their light beams. They climbed, cut around switchbacks, clambered over rocks, dodged around windfalls, getting distance, getting away, getting distance.

But another enemy was stalking them, overcoming them like a slow, creeping death: fatigue. The steep grade, the altitude, and their heavy packs pulled them down, stole their breath, consumed their muscles.

Beck was in the lead, groping up a steep, precarious portion of trail on all fours, gasping for breath, whimpering. She looked over her shoulder. Tears streaked her face. "W-w-where . . . ?"

"I don't know." Reed stopped, trying to stop panting long enough to hear if they'd outrun it.

There was a moment when they couldn't hear anything. But only a moment.

The woman was still out there. She wailed again and wouldn't stop screaming while another beast howled, its voice rumbling and fluttering from a deep, slimy throat.

"Behind us," Reed finally answered.

They kept going, inch by agonizing inch.

They made it up out of the ravine, and the trail finally began to head downward. They stumbled along, feet like lead, legs screaming in pain, lungs laboring for air.

Beck's legs collapsed. She went down and stayed there. The ground felt good. Not moving felt like life itself.

Reed crumpled just behind her, gasping, slick with sweat, wiping salty perspiration from his eyes.

They listened, eyes darting.

The screaming and wailing had stopped. Maybe it was over. Maybe they'd outrun the danger. Maybe the rest on the ground and a few precious molecules of oxygen were bringing the inkling of hope now rising in their hearts, the vague and dreamlike notion that they just might get out of this alive.

Reed pulled the map from his pocket and unfolded it, the crinkling, creased pages rattling loudly in the dark.

"Oh, quiet, quiet!" Beck pleaded.

"Got to see where we are, where we're going."

He shined his light on the map, turned it right side up, searched up and down the page for something familiar. "The trail's going . . . southeast, I guess."

"Sounds right."

Wump! Thump! The ground quivered.

"Oh, dear Lord, no!" Beck cried in a whisper.

Reed clicked off his light, then tapped Beck, who did the same. They stifled their breathing and heard it plainly: heavy footfalls and snapping twigs, something moving above them, moving fast, moving . . .

It stopped. Not a sound. They waited, longing for air but hardly breathing, probing the darkness with inadequate eyes.

"If we keep quiet," Reed whispered in Beck's ear, "maybe it'll give up and leave."

But Beck touched his nose and sniffed, a signal. Reed sniffed quietly. They'd both been running, panting, sweating like crazy, but nothing coming from them could match this stench. Beck pointed up the hill, and he understood. Night air moved down-hill. That thing was above them somewhere.

Then came the whistle, long and steady, with a little warble at the end. It was closer than they'd thought.

Sitting still wasn't going to work. They eased back onto the trail and started to run again, but their legs were feeble and tee-tering, their bodies exhausted, and they had no choice but to use their lights.

The whistle sounded again, keeping pace.

Faster, faster!

The footfalls and thrashing in the brush did not fade back but only came closer, louder, closing the distance. They were being hunted. That thing was running them down, keeping up with no problem, and *it* could see.

Beck heard the rush of a waterfall. Abruptly, the trail cut through a streambed, snaking through and over slick, sharp-edged rocks. Reed stopped, stumbling on the rocks, his legs wobbly. He bent as if searching for rocks to throw, a stick he might use as a club, *anything*.

Beck just wanted to get across, get on smooth trail again. The waterfall was loud, close, just to her right—

The rocks broke away under her foot. She tumbled side-ways, then fell headlong over the precipice, flipping end over end—

Her backpack absorbed some of the impact with the rocks, but she was still tumbling, her flashlight flipping in midair.

Her head hit. A blinding flash exploded in her brain.

Reed heard her go down, and he searched with his light.

"Beck!" There she was, flailed like a rag doll on the rocks about ten feet below the trail, her leg dangling in the flowing water, a streak of blood reaching down her face. He found a way down, a slow but sure course through brush, limbs, and saplings. "Beck!"

He grabbed the first limb and swung himself down, then another limb, then a fistful of brush. Lower, lower!

"Beck! Say something! Talk to me!"

There was a commotion across the stream. *Oh dear Lord, don't let it be—*

The beam caught the silvery-green glimmer of two retinas suspended within a massive black shadow that swallowed up his light. He screamed, half out of his own terror, half to cause terror. Would nothing chase this thing away?

The shadow moved so fast he lost it. He searched, waved his

light about. It caught one fleeting image of his wife's body swept up like a toy, arms limp, long brown hair flying.

The shadow enfolded her like a blanket. There were heavy, bass-note footfalls up the bank, and then . . .

Nothing.

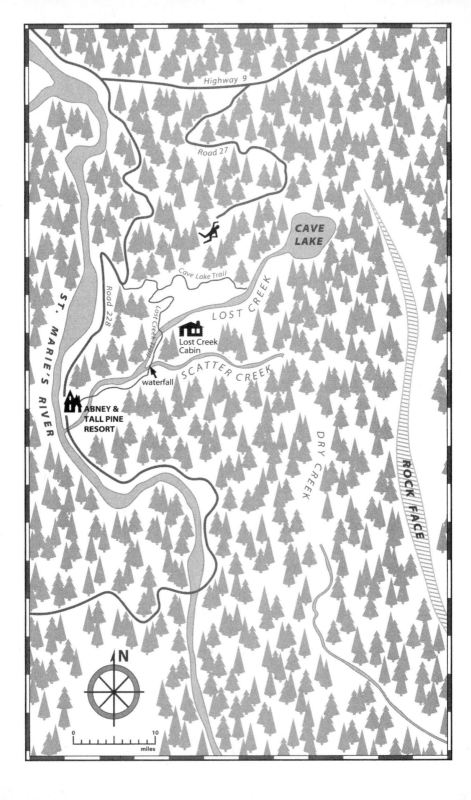

THREE

Reed dashed across the stream, frantic, shining his light in every direction but seeing only thick, tangled forest. The stream and waterfall made so much noise he couldn't hear anything else. He got out of there, clambering up the other side, only guessing which way that thing went.

"Beck!" he called.

No answer.

But she wasn't dead. No. He would not allow himself to think that. She was alive and breathing, and any moment she was going to hear his call and answer. If she screamed for help, he would hear her.

Think, he told himself. *Don't panic. You can't see much at all, but can you hear anything? Can you smell anything?*

There! He heard limbs snapping farther up the slope. He raced along the trail, probing with his flashlight. A broken tree limb! Then another! He slipped out of his pack and dove into the trees, probing, climbing, looking for signs, listening, then calling.

From deep in his mind came a warning: *You have no gun. No weapon. You need to find something—*

Another rustling sound grabbed his attention and spurred him upward. He found a game trail where the ground was disturbed by hoofprints of elk and deer. Among these prints he found a deep, half-round impression, perhaps a heel print. With new strength he climbed, and then traversed the slope, then zigzagged as he lost, then found, then lost the game trail. With the trail gone, he followed sounds, any sound.

"Beck!" The forest swallowed his voice.

He hurried, he struggled, he climbed, he doubled back, he climbed again, then descended, then climbed, until fear and desperation gave way to exhaustion and he began to realize that he was like a mite in a carpet. As loud as he might call, this wilderness stretched farther than his voice could reach. The light from his flashlight had dimmed to a dull orange glow, but the mountains had darkness to spare, plenty to swallow up any light.

The seconds had stacked up and become minutes; the minutes had stretched into hours. Steps had become yards, and yards had become miles, but the forest had not shrunk. It was still bigger than he could ever be, with more obstacles, tangles, confusion, and dark, dark, dark!

When he broke into a meadow where the stars were visible and a waning moon was finally rising, he collapsed to the ground with a quiet whimper, limp and totally spent, head hanging, conflicting thoughts bantering in his head.

She's gone.

No, no, she isn't. Just have to find her, that's all.

Where? Where could you even start looking?

Well, some daylight would sure help.

She'll be somebody's dinner by then.

No. God won't let that happen.

Look at what He's already let happen! Remember where you are! There are different rules out here!

Reed's hands went to his head as if he could corral his thoughts. His aimless thrashing around in the woods for hours had accomplished nothing; a mad and frenzied mind would accomplish even less. He forced himself to lie still, breathing for breathing's sake until he could construct a coherent thought.

First coherent thought: He hadn't found his wife.

Second coherent thought: In all his mad scrambling and searching, he could have wandered farther from her, not closer.

Third coherent thought: He'd become part of the problem. He was lost, without provisions, without a weapon.

He still had his map and compass. If the sun ever came up again sometime in his life, he could take a look around and hopefully get his bearings. For now, he was too tired and emotionally spent to work it out, and any more wandering would only make things worse. Until he got some rest and some real light, he would be no help to Beck or himself.

The dying orange beam of his flashlight found an old fallen snag just a few feeble steps up the hill, with a hollow in the ground beneath it. His heart screamed against the decision, but his mind made it stick.

He would shelter himself under the snag to maintain his body heat, and rest until daylight.

■ ■ ■

"Beck . . . Beck . . . Beck!"

Beck was dreaming, far from fear in the dark, merely puzzled by her husband's anguished voice as he screamed her name.

Beyond her dream was a faraway pain, a dull throbbing, a dizzy world tipping and turning, a body aching, but she didn't wake up from the dream. She didn't want to. Waking would hurt; the dream didn't. In the dream she was floating as if in a stream, gliding past limbs and trees and leaves that went *swish*, with the ground so far below.

She was warm, as if cuddled in a furry blanket, but it was dark, like being in her bedroom at night.

Can't wake up, won't wake up, eyes won't open, staying in the dream, moving fast, can feel the breeze . . .

■ ■ ■

Monsters, snorting, drooling, stomping, invisible in the dark. All around, closer, closer. Beck! Beck! His legs wouldn't move—

"Reed! Beck!"

Reed awoke with a start.

"Reed!" That sounded like Cap.

He stirred, unclear as to where he was, but willing his legs and arms to move, to pull, push, and claw his way into the open, through tangled exposed roots and crumbled rocks into eye-stinging daylight.

The distant call came again: "Reed! Beck!"

Reed rolled out into the grass, the dew soaking through his clothes. Everything looked so different. "Hello!" he cried.

He heard Sing's voice call, "Reed! Where are you?"

"Up here!" he called.

He leaped to his feet, but his head emptied of blood and he fell, reminded of how weak and shaken he was. They shouted again, he answered again, and that was all he was good for until his friends reached him, snapping and rustling their way through the thick undergrowth until they emerged into the clearing.

They looked prepared for a week in the wilderness, with packs on their backs, hats, boots, jackets. Reed figured he must look pretty horrible, judging from their expressions.

"Reed! We found your pack down by the creek. What happened?" Cap asked.

"Where's Beck?"

■ ■ ■

By that afternoon, the Tall Pine Resort began to see more activity than it had all season. Two squad cars from the Whitcomb County Sheriff's Department were angled in against the meandering, up-and-down porch. On either side of them were the pickup trucks, SUVs, cars, and motorcycles that had brought the Search and Rescue volunteers. The volunteers, more than a dozen strong, wasted no time unloading and filling backpacks with needed gear, testing portable radios, and organizing survival equipment and medical supplies. Some of the guys prepared high-powered rifles and stowed cases of ammunition. A van arrived and lurched into a space at the far end of the parking lot, an eager German shepherd barking and whining in the back. Across the parking lot, hooked to an RV power outlet, was the Search and Rescue command vehicle, a converted school bus now crammed with equipment, supplies, a computer, and radios. Close to the main door was a sharp-looking King Cab pickup with an Idaho Department of Fish and Game insignia on the side.

Deputy Sheriff Dave Saunders, in green field jacket and billed cap, walked briskly out the main door, reporting into a handheld radio, "Yeah, Jimmy Clark's here debriefing the witness. We'll all get rolling when he's done. It's a probable bear attack, so we're lining up some hunters—"

Sheriff Patrick Mills signaled a halt right in front of Dave's mouth and whispered sharply, "Dave, let's not say it so loud, shall we?"

The deputy followed the sheriff's glance to where Reed Shelton sat on a wooden bench farther up the meandering porch, just outside Room 105. He was haggard, dazed, and dirty, apparently trying to make sense to Jimmy Clark, the conservation officer who asked him questions.

"Oh, man, sorry," the deputy said.

Sheriff Mills, a tall man weathered by experience and sporting a graying mustache, went back to a conversation he'd been having with Cap and Sing on the slapped-together porch near the main door. He was dressed for wilderness work, in the standard-issue green jacket with *SHERIFF* in large yellow letters on the back, but instead of a policeman's hat, he wore a cowboy hat with a county sheriff insignia on its front.

"Sorry," the sheriff said to Cap. "Now, you were saying?"

Cap stood nervously, taking deep breaths, shifting his weight, grasping the porch post as if to steady himself. The college professor's words raced and his voice seemed weak. "We found—it was on the rocks below the waterfall."

"Blood," Mills refreshed him.

"Yeah. We checked all around the creek area, both sides of the trail, up and down the slope . . ."

"How wide a radius?"

Cap shrugged. "I don't know, maybe forty feet, maybe fifty . . ." He looked at Sing, passing her the question.

She was sitting on a hand-hewn bench against the old log wall, her face troubled as she studied the LCD of Reed Shelton's camera. She was reviewing the digital photographs Reed had taken of the splintered cabin and the shots of Beck sitting in their campsite, her cheeks plump with a mouthful of sandwich. Sing and Cap's backpacks rested against the wall next to her, packed to bulging but never opened. Leaves and needles clung to her clothing and her braids. "I would say a hundred-foot radius. But it was difficult. The brush is thick in that area."

Mills looked over Sing's shoulder at the small camera screen. "Did he get any shots of Thompson's body?"

Sing came to the end of the pictures in the camera's memory. "No. Apparently Reed was in no picture-taking mood when he and Beck were running for their lives."

"And you never got back to the cabin to check it out?"

Cap was obviously on edge, tiring of the questions. He wagged his head. "We only wanted to find Beck, that was all."

"So you didn't see whether or not there was a body up there?"

"No!" Cap lowered his voice. "Reed said Randy was dead, and that was good enough for us. Beck was the one we were concerned about."

Sing stroked her forehead. "We weren't getting anywhere. Reed didn't want to leave, but we had to get back here; we had to get some help."

Mills regarded the folks gathering in the parking lot, well trained, some specialized, all there to find Beck Shelton no matter what. "You made the right decision. Sing, you've been our forensics specialist for five years now. You've teamed up with some of these people before. You know they're good at what they do."

Sing nodded and gave a wave to the dog handler, who was sharing a piece of breakfast toast with Caesar, the German shepherd. "I never thought I'd be part of the case we're working on."

Sheriff Mills looked past Cap and Sing to where Reed was still being questioned by Jimmy Clark. "So how clear do you think Reed's head is right now?"

Cap stole a glance. "I don't know. He's in some sort of shock, like he's having waking nightmares. If he tells Jimmy what he told us . . ."

Sing shivered, putting the camera in its case. "Reed was right about the cabin. If we find Randy Thompson thrown up in a tree, we might have to believe the rest of his story."

"Being in the dark, in the woods, can make things seem a lot worse than they are," the sheriff suggested.

"Maybe finding Randy's body was the thing that shocked him," Cap offered, "and after that, well, then, Beck gets grabbed . . . I don't know, I'd probably be seeing some pretty horrible things by then."

"Reed's a deputy sheriff!" Sing's voice was edgy. "Let's not underestimate him!"

Awkward silence followed.

"Duly noted," Mills finally said. "Sing, take Reed's camera over to Marsha in the command vehicle. See if she can download those shots of Beck and print 'em up."

Sing got to her feet, as if eager to do something, anything. "And then can we please get up there?"

Mills looked at his watch. "Pete said he'd be about ten minutes."

Cap started to say, "We don't *have* ten—" when tires growled on the gravel.

An older brown pickup with a rumbling muffler pulled in and nosed up against the building four vehicles down. The fellow who got out looked as though he'd already been in the woods most of his life and would be out of place anywhere else. He was dressed in tired jeans, a frayed leather coat, and a drooping, wide-brimmed hat with a rattlesnake skin for a hatband. He may have had a haircut three or four months ago but obviously hadn't thought much about it since then.

"Ah," said Mills, "there he is."

Pete Henderson, search manager and tracker, was already sizing up the situation when Mills met him in the center of the parking lot. "Huh. Jimmy's here," Pete said, "so it was a bear. You're here, so somebody's dead. You've got me and my searchers here, so you can't find whoever it is."

"Come on." As they crossed the parking lot, Mills gave Pete an abridged version of Reed's account.

"You are kidding me—Reed said that?"

"Let's hope his head starts to clear up."

They walked quietly, unobtrusively, up to where Jimmy was finishing up with Reed. The conservation officer sat on the edge of the porch, pen and notepad in his hands, questioning, almost grilling Reed in his eagerness to get the information and get going. His conservation officer's uniform spoke well of his manner, meant for the wilderness, not the town or city; no creased trousers with a stripe, but tough, forest-green Levi's; no spit-polished shoes, but oiled boots for slogging through rough and often muddy terrain; his gray shirt had a shoulder insignia, but it was rugged enough for the wilderness and had obviously been there. His billed cap with the Idaho Department of Fish and Game insignia rested on the porch nearby.

Reed was sitting on the bench against the building, seemingly immovable as if he were a fungus that had grown there. His hair was matted from sweat; his face and clothes were those of a desperate man who'd lost his wife and spent the night under a fallen tree. Reed's voice was barely audible as he said, "It had to be Randy. He had a long black braid, I saw that clearly."

Jimmy looked up at Sheriff Mills and Pete. They knew that described Randy Thompson.

When Reed lifted his face, a tiny hint of hope came to his eyes. "Hey, Pete!"

"We're here for you, partner," Pete said.

"We're almost finished," said Jimmy. He prodded, "How did he look to you, Reed? Was there anything about his condition that would indicate an attack by a—"

"He was thrown up in the tree!" Reed insisted as if he'd said it before. "His head was practically torn off!"

"But he could have been climbing the tree, trying to get away from a bear, right?"

Reed thought a moment, then nodded. "Yeah. That makes sense, if that's what you want to think."

Jimmy looked around, apparently for the right words. "Reed, I'm hating this. You know that."

Reed's head sank. Tears filled his eyes. "If we hadn't camped there that night, if we'd only buried that garbage, if I hadn't forgotten to hang up those stupid sandwich containers . . . !"

"Was Beck having her period?"

"No."

"Did she bring any makeup along?"

Reed looked at him blankly.

Jimmy explained, "To a bear, the smell means food."

"I didn't see a bear," Reed emphasized as if for the hundredth time.

Jimmy just looked at his notes. "There could have been any number of factors, Reed. You don't need to blame yourself."

"Are we through?"

Jimmy nodded. "Yeah, Reed. We're through. We're gonna get on this, right now."

Reed bolted to his feet. "I've got to get my gear ready." He ducked into Room 105 and slammed the door, not looking back.

Jimmy rose from the porch and drew in close to Sheriff Mills and Pete.

"Pete."

"Hi."

Jimmy reviewed his notes and spoke in secretive tones. "Guess you've heard the story by now."

"Has it changed any?" Mills asked.

Jimmy stole a furtive glance at Reed's door. "Don't think so, so I can't tell you what happened up there besides the obvious. Reed's so shook up right now he's hallucinating, talking about a woman screaming and big monsters fighting in the dark. He insists something really big and foul-smelling chased him and Beck along the trail and then grabbed her." Jimmy's expression said, *Need I say more?*

Mills asked, "Did he say anything about Beck falling over a waterfall?"

"Yeah, right before the attack. If it really happened, I'd guess that's where the Abney Trail cuts across Scatter Creek."

"Cap and Sing can show us the spot. They just came from there."

Jimmy consulted his notes again. "Reed drew a map to show where he and Beck found Randy's body. It's up the creek a little, on a knoll above the cabin."

Mills spoke to Pete, "Looks like we'll need two teams, one to work the cabin site and one to work the creek."

"We'll most likely be picking up the pieces," Pete muttered, bitterness in his tone as he peered over his shoulder toward the volunteers.

Jimmy leaned close to Mills. "Sheriff Mills, I can't let Reed go on this hunt."

"Good luck holding him back."

"He's gonna be a liability."

"*If* he's crazy," said Pete.

"Guys, I can't allow it, even if he is my friend," Jimmy insisted.

"I'll talk to him," said Mills, "and we'll take it from there."

Jimmy's glare was unmistakable. "Sheriff. This is a bear attack. It's my jurisdiction."

Mills didn't get ruffled. He'd been sheriff—and known Jimmy Clark—too long for that. "Jimmy. We don't know what it is, not yet. Let's see if we can be a team until we get it sorted out."

"There's nothing to sort out!"

"Okay, try this: Anything having to do with the bear, that's your jurisdiction. Anything having to do with bodies, living or dead, that's mine. Can you work with that?"

Jimmy sighed through his nose, his face still defiant. "I'll work with it. For now."

"That's right. You will." Mills let that settle the matter and moved on. "So tell me where you want to start hunting your bear."

"The cabin's the most likely center of the bear's foraging range right now. I'll start there."

"Okay, Dave and I'll go with you. Pete, I'd like two or three searchers."

Pete was counting noses. "I've got 'em."

"And we're gonna need weapons on both teams," said Jimmy.

"My regular guys are here, and . . ." He scanned the crowd some more. "Looks like we've got a few more I haven't met yet."

Mills instructed Pete, "Your team'll be looking for Beck, starting at the Scatter Creek waterfall. Take the search dog. Jimmy, I want Sing to have a good look around that cabin area before anybody contaminates it."

Jimmy smirked in Sing's direction and did not succeed in keeping his voice down. "So now you're trying to make this a crime scene?"

"I get the bodies, remember?"

Jimmy waved it off. "Whatever." To Pete, "Just hurry up with the dog."

"Don't worry," said Pete. "Are we about ready?"

"Pete, one more thing," said the sheriff, detaining the search manager a moment. "Forget any tales or theories you've heard thus far. You find whatever you find and let it speak for itself, you got it?"

Pete gave a nod and adjusted his hat. "I'll get the volunteers assigned."

The sheriff and Jimmy Clark watched Pete head into the parking lot, his volunteers gathering to him like Israelites to Moses.

"He's right about one thing," said Jimmy. "There won't be much left to find."

"We'll know when we know," said Mills.

They went to join him.

■ ■ ■

Pete craned his neck, hands on hips, and looked over the small and willing crowd. They were his neighbors: a carpenter, a housewife, two firemen, a schoolteacher, a machinist, a dental assistant, a heavy equipment operator, and several others, all away from their jobs, geared up and ready to trek into the wilderness, even sleep there if necessary, for no pay. They'd been together many times before, in every season, in every kind of weather, because someone was lost or in trouble. If anyone were to ask them why, they'd just say it was the thing to do.

Pete spoke out, "Okay, everybody, listen up. You all know the situation. We've got a three-way problem: a possible bear attack with two possible victims who need to be found. Anybody working the bear issue, you're gonna be following Jimmy Clark's lead. Anybody searching for the victims, you get your orders from me. If you can't stand me or Jimmy, you can grouse to Sheriff Mills here. We all take our orders from him. Now, Sing—where are you, Sing?"

Sing and Cap were just stepping out of the command vehicle, fresh computer-generated fact sheets in hand. Sing waved the papers in the air for all to see.

"Okay, Sing's gonna hand out photographs and detailed descriptions of the missing persons. Give these papers a good looking over."

The listeners stood quiet and grim, receiving the quickly compiled information sheets from Sing's hand. Most of them already knew Randy or Beck or both.

Jimmy took his turn, his voice trumpeting over the crowd, "We're going to be working two teams from two locations in the Lost Creek drainage. We need people who are capable in tracking, hunting, and—don't miss this, now—recovering human remains. This is a bear attack. It's serious business." That caused a stir. "Pete knows what your skills are, so he'll select the teams. Pete, go ahead."

Pete Henderson addressed the crowd again. "You medical folks stick around, and let's see, how many marksmen do we have? Okay, the two of you go with Jimmy; you two come with me. Don, you'll work with me at flank. Tyler, you here? Okay, Tyler, you be the other flanker."

■ ■ ■

Cap stood on the edge of the crowd, hanging on every word.

"Hi there."

Cap winced at the greeting. This was not the time for idle chat. He turned only half his attention to a buzz-cut man somewhere in his thirties, dressed in camouflage like a hunter—or a marine. He was carrying a rifle, obviously one of the marksmen.

"Hi," Cap said.

"Steve Thorne. I understand you found one of the victims?"

Cap shook his hand. "Michael Capella. Yeah. We're friends of Reed and Beck Shelton. This is my wife, Sing."

The man whispered a greeting to her. She returned it with a quick smile, trying to listen to Pete's organizing.

"I'm really sorry," said Thorne.

Cap said, "Thanks," his eyes on Pete.

Thorne didn't go away but pressed with another question. "So what was it your friend saw?"

What kind of a question was that? Cap gave the man a long look, then, deciding he was trying to be helpful, said, "I don't know what he saw. We're trying to find that out."

"I suppose it had to be a bear. Is that what he said it was?"

"I don't know. The whole thing happened in the pitch black, and . . . I don't know. It was a horrible experience, and he's still very shook up about it."

Now Pete was calling, "The rest of you folks, talk to Marsha. She'll get you working support and communications here at the command post."

"So he didn't see anything," the guy pressed.

Cap was trying not to be abrupt. "Not that he's been able to say for sure."

Thorne gave him a gentle pat on the back. "Thanks. Just wondering."

Cap turned his full attention back to Pete Henderson, who caught his look. "Cap—is that what they call you?"

"Cap'll do."

"Nice to meet you. Which team you want to go with?"

"I want the waterfall," he answered.

"Who was that guy?" Sing asked.

Cap shrugged, impatient. "One of the hunters. Some thrill seeker, if you ask me."

■　■　■

Reed had yanked off his dirty clothes and pulled a fresh shirt and jeans from his backpack—and then put on the dirty jeans with the clean shirt. He took off the shirt. No, it was the clean one. He put it back on and tried to take off the pants—he forgot he'd put on his boots. He unlaced them and pulled them off. Now, where were the clean pants? He'd thrown them into the pile of dirty clothes. He fished them out and put them on. Now if he could find his belt—

There was a knock at the door. "Reed?" It was Sheriff Mills. "Yeah, come in."

Mills stepped inside and closed the door quietly behind him. "How you doing?"

Reed didn't answer because he didn't want to lie. He only hurried to pull on a boot as he sat in one of the room's two chairs.

Mills grabbed the other chair and set it down directly opposite Reed, almost in his way as he tried to pull on the other boot. "I said, how you doing?"

It felt like an interrogation. Mills pressed into Reed's space big time, and Reed didn't like it. He met Mills's gaze deliberately, angrily. "With all due respect, sir, that's a stupid question."

"I need a firm answer, Reed—"

"Are we heading out?"

"—or you don't go."

"Arrest me!" Reed said.

Mills whacked Reed on the side of the head. Reed froze in disbelief, staring into the eyes of his superior officer, who still held that hand close to his face, forbidding Reed's eyes to stray.

"You can thank me later," said Mills. "In the meantime, you'd better listen. There are more than a dozen trained volunteers out there who just might be risking their lives on your behalf, so before I let you out that door, you'd better decide what role you're playing. We need men on this job, not victims. Not basket cases. If you need time to work this through and pull yourself together, I'll grant you that, no questions, no shame, but I need to know."

Reed gave some thought to his attitude and tried to ease down. "Sure didn't turn out right."

Mills was listening.

"It was supposed to be good for her, supposed to get her out of the house, get her out where she could just, just live a little without having to talk to anybody. Out in those woods, there aren't any social rules, you know? No expectations." He looked Mills squarely in the eye. "She would have aced it. She would have done great. I knew she had it in her. I don't think people give her credit."

Mills nodded. "She would have aced it. You're right."

Reed's eyes teared up again. He looked away to clear them, to clear his mind. "I just didn't want her to be afraid anymore."

"Reed, look at me."

Reed met his eyes. The gaze coming from under that hat brim was kind but would not be trifled with.

"You and Beck signed up for a challenge. Well, now you've got one, only there's no teacher and there's no pretend, no trial run. There's just a truckload of real trouble, and Beck doesn't need you fumbling around and getting in the way because you're wallowing in what should have been. She needs you to get your mind cleared up and on the problem. She needs you to do your job. We all do." He rose and went for the door. "We're pulling out of here in about five minutes. Let me know what you decide."

■ ■ ■

Mills stepped out onto the porch, caught a breath, then signaled for Sing's attention. She joined him near the main door.

"Don't imagine you have any of your gear with you?" he asked.

"I was on vacation!"

"Got your camera, though."

"Yes. And my notepad. I was supposed to be taking survival training this week."

"I want you to come along with Deputy Saunders and me to the cabin area. We'll treat it like a crime scene, document everything so we can figure out what happened up there—and what didn't." He saw the question in her eyes. "Reed's got a wild story, one that people won't want to believe, and that means they'll start believing other things. Let's get that door closed right away, first thing."

■ ■ ■

Reed emerged from Room 105 correctly dressed, his backpack slung over one shoulder, but walking like a drunk man, his face reddened with emotion, his hand against the wall to steady himself.

Jimmy was finishing the briefing in the parking lot. His voice carried well enough for Reed to hear the gist of it: ". . . the bear could still be around guarding its kill, so, hunters, be sure to take point position and secure the area. Prepare for the worst, and by the way . . ." He lowered his voice, but Reed still heard him admonish, "Let's be careful what we say. Reed's a little crazy right now, and I would be too."

Several folks noticed Reed and nodded a greeting or even gave a little wave. Some were jerking their heads, pointing, shifting their gaze, trying to let Jimmy know of Reed's presence, but Jimmy, with his back toward the resort, just kept going. "Bears usually go for the soft organs, but any fresh meat will do; they'll eat arms and legs too. Let's be sure to bring several body bags, because she may not be in one piece."

Reed's feet wouldn't move. All he could do was stare at Jimmy's back and wonder why he couldn't find the strength to deck the guy. Jimmy finally got a clue from his listeners and looked over his shoulder. Jimmy's face flamed with embarrassment. Too late. Reed felt worse.

Reed ducked inside the lobby, clumsily closing the door behind him. The floor reeled as if he were on a ship in a storm. He staggered to the counter, stomach churning, as the pack fell forgotten and unnoticed to the floor. With elbows on the countertop and his face in his hands, he tried one more time to pull himself together, to be the man Beck needed, to do his job.

Now even the countertop seemed to be moving, but at least the room was empty, and he was so thankful for that. He drank in the silence, waiting one moment, one breath at a time for his mind to settle on some workable scheme of reality, just one simple pathway to sorting this whole thing out.

Maybe I am crazy.

A simple conclusion of insanity was pretty tempting right now. It would be so much easier. It would explain away everything, and he could dismiss his nightmarish memories like any other outlandish dream.

But he found no comfort in such thoughts. Even if his mind was creating nightmarish memories of hellish things that never happened, it was probably to replace worse memories of even more hellish things.

Either way, here he was with only the counter to keep him from collapsing to the floor, an official basket case. Wasn't that what Sheriff Mills said they didn't need?

He breathed a moment. He prayed, and his mind cleared just enough for him to realize he was too messed up to be safe out there. He could never survive or be any help to the search teams or to Beck when he couldn't trust his own senses.

So, looks like I won't be going, he thought.

He rubbed his face, partly because it expressed his pain and confusion, mostly because his face was a tangible reality he could be sure of. It was still there. He could feel it. He guessed he still had elbows too; they were holding him up.

What else was real around here? He let his eyes drift around the lobby, taking in the trophies—the moose head, the elk head, the deer head, the big bearskin, the many sets of antlers. So it seemed *somebody* knew his way around out there and had come back the winner, somebody way out of Reed's league.

His eyes drifted down the wall and almost passed over a yellowing poster—

His gaze returned and parked there. The dark, two-legged creature striding along a log-strewn riverbed was blurry and grainy, but it was looking his way. A shiver coursed through Reed's limbs. He saw no silvery-green retinas glowing in the dark, but something about that image brought back the same nerve-jangling, hand-trembling terror.

His eyes went to a glass case below the poster and focused on a plaster cast of a huge footprint. As he leaned close to the glass, the sound a foot like that could make in the soft earth of the forest came back to him. Suddenly the speed and mobility of the shadow he'd seen did not seem impossible.

His heartbeat quickened. His hands trembled. He looked around the lobby, through the windows at the people gearing up for the search after Jimmy's lecture on how to handle dismembered bodies and fear-crazed, delusional family members. Hadn't any of these people seen this stuff in the glass case or that picture on the wall? Had it never occurred to them that it might not be a bear, that it might be—

Caution took hold, and Reed didn't run anywhere to yell anything.

Of course they'd seen it. They'd heard his story too. He tried to understand why their minds would only go one direction, locked on only one explanation, and he could settle on only one answer: they weren't there last night.

He looked at the poster again, trying to imagine that thing in the dark—

"I don't know if you ought to be looking at that."

Arlen Peak, the owner of the place, had come into the lobby from the souvenir shop. Worry in his eyes, he stood beneath the huge, clawed bearskin, watching Reed.

Reed looked toward the glass case. "I never saw one before."

"It's hard to find anybody who has, and anybody who has usually won't talk about it."

"Have you ever seen one?"

The old man shook his head, almost sadly. "No."

Reed knew it would be safe to tell this man. "I think I have."

Peak approached and spoke gently. "Son, you need to be sure about that. I don't want anybody thinking I've put ideas in your head."

Reed gazed at the big footprint. "Do they . . . make a crying sound like a woman? Not screaming, but, you know, wailing and crying?"

The innkeeper half-smiled and shook his head.

"How do you know?"

"Let's just say nobody's ever heard one do that."

"Do they smell bad, like the worst armpit in the world?"

Peak hesitated just a moment, then answered, "Only when they're frightened or upset. It's what a lot of apes do. It's a defense mechanism."

"Do they howl and scream like, well, like apes?"

The old man's silver fillings twinkled in the windows' light. "Now, *that* I've heard."

"Do they whistle?" Reed tried to mimic what he'd heard, the long, soaring whistle with the little warbles in it.

Now Peak actually straightened, staring at him.

∎ ∎ ∎

Outside, the teams were ready to trek into the woods. Jimmy Clark and Sheriff Mills, rifles slung on their backs, exchanged a look with Pete Henderson, then glanced toward the front door.

"You saw him, didn't you?" Jimmy asked. "He was so wiped out he looked like he was *on* something."

Sheriff Mills waited only a moment, looked at the folks gathered for the search, then sighed through his mustache. "Let's do it." He shouted, "Okay, everybody, let's go!"

The front door opened. Everyone froze on the same cue.

Reed stepped out, a little pale, just a little wobbly, but standing tall, his pack on his back, his deputy sheriff's cap on his head. He was ready with an answer and spoke in strained tones to Sheriff Mills, "Ready when you are, sir."

∎ ∎ ∎

Beck heard a long, soaring whistle with little warbles in it. Then a deep-throated, disgusting grunt, like a gigantic old sow in the mud. Another low grunt. Another soaring whistle.

And then Beck was aware of gook in her mouth—clumpy like gooey raisins and tart like wild berries—and someone wearing big leathery gloves shoving more gook into her mouth.

She gagged, then coughed, then spit it all out—

And the whole world shook.

Beck opened her eyes. They were still slimy from a long sleep, and her vision was blurred. Nothing was real, not yet.

Someone was holding her, cradling her in a smelly brown blanket.

Rescue! I've been rescued!

There came that whistle again, like a boiling teakettle.

Shmoosh! More gooky berries in her mouth, and she could feel some of them smeared on her face. She jerked her head away, spit them out, blinked to clear her vision.

The world came into focus, and she gathered she wasn't home. All she could see were tangled branches and green leaves. The cool breeze told her she was still outside, somewhere in the mountains, somewhere in the shelter of thick bushes. Bushes with berries. Huckleberries?

She looked up—

NO!

Her lungs pulled in a long, quaking gasp and held it there as her mouth hung open and her jaw began to quiver. Though her hands began to shake on their own, she dared not move or utter a sound. She could only lie there, stiff with terror, and gape at the deep, monstrous eyes looking back at her.

The eyes were dark amber, with muddy brown around the iris instead of the usual white. They were intense and probing— studying her as if she were a specimen under a microscope—deep set under a prominent brow. The face was reddish brown, leathery like an old saddle, bordered by thick, straggly hair.

Beck felt hot breath passing by her face in sour little puffs. The bulging lips tightened against a row of white teeth and the thing whistled at her.

The same whistle Beck heard in the dark when glowing eyes bored into her and a dead man dangled from a tree.

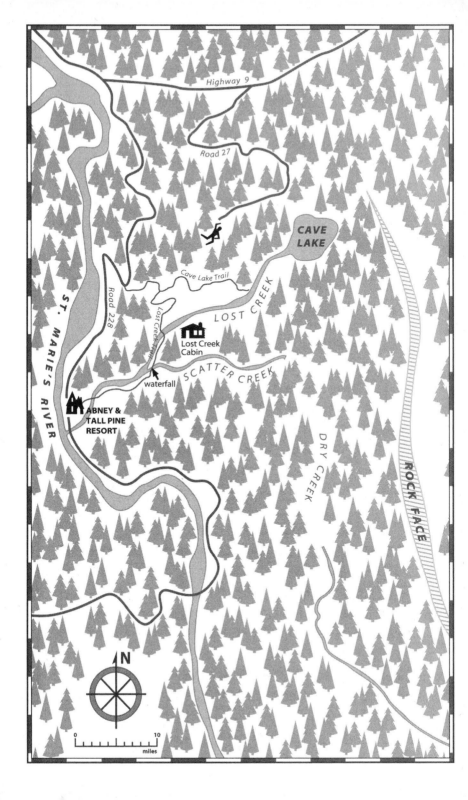

FOUR

Unthinking, her mind paralyzed by fear, Beck responded as she was taught to respond to hornets, bees, rattlesnakes, and assorted monsters of childhood: she froze—except for the trembling in her hands, which she couldn't help.

The thing shoved more berries into her mouth with fingers the size of sausages. Beck forgot her mouth was already open, and now suddenly it was full again. She closed her mouth, an unconscious reflex, and the berries remained inside, an unchewed mass. The beastly eyes locked on her, waiting, the face stern under a heavy, furrowed brow. The thing grunted again, then tapped on Beck's mouth with thick, berry-stained fingers.

Somehow, it occurred to Beck to chew. The berries burst in her mouth, filling it with juice, half-sweet, half-tart. The wizened face waited and watched, huge volumes of air rushing in and out through the broad, flat nose.

Still chewing, and just now remembering to breathe herself, Beck let her eyes drop enough to see another huge hand with dirty black fingernails curled around her, pressing her against a mountain of dark, reddish-brown hair. The hair was coarse and oily, the body beneath it warm and moist, with a familiar—and unpleasant—sweaty smell. She could feel the rib cage expanding, pressing against her, then easing away as the mountain breathed. She'd never been this close to anything with lungs this big.

Oh, please, don't kill me . . .

Could she run? Where? As near as she could tell, she was in the woods somewhere. Beyond the tangle of the huckleberry bushes, she could see the thick forest, and through its canopy, a blue sky.

A powerful, hairy arm reached up and grabbed another cluster of berries from a branch.

When the hand that was bigger than her whole head descended to deliver the berries, Beck didn't dare argue. She opened up, let the berries tumble in, and started chewing.

With the taste of the berries and her ability to chew them came a conscious realization that she was still alive—quite notable, given the circumstances. How long she would remain that way she had no idea and no encouraging thoughts.

She turned her head just enough to study her situation. She was being held by what appeared to be a huge ape, similar to a gorilla, but not quite a gorilla. The crown of its head extended to a narrow crest like a gorilla's, and it had a prominent brow ridge over the eyes, but the jaws didn't protrude as much and the lips were more flexible and expressive. As near as Beck could tell, the creature's legs were folded beneath it, but one large, hairy foot jutted out, with a wrinkled, hairless sole and all five toes aligned in a row. By its ample, fur-covered bosom, Beck concluded it was a female. They were now sitting in a cavity created when a tree upended, pulling the root ball out of the ground. Thick bushes, most of them huckleberries, had since moved in and now provided a blind that hid them from the outside world. The female held Beck inescapably in her lap with her left arm while feeding Beck with her right.

Another load of berries was on the way. Beck couldn't take much more of this, but unless she wanted more berries smeared all over her face . . .

She opened up and let the beast dump them in. She chewed but did not move, did not stir, did not make a sound. Her hands were still trembling.

Suddenly the big arm loosened and the creature let her go. She slid down that big hairy body to the ground.

Run! her instincts screamed at her. It didn't matter which direction. *Run for the trees!*

All it took was the slightest weight on her right ankle. "Oww!" With a shriek of agony, she fell in the tangled limbs and stalks, grabbing her ankle, grimacing. She checked for a break, for—"Awww!" The pain flashed up her entire leg, red-hot and lingering. She settled backward on a bush, bending and crumpling branches, gasping. She thought of crawling, pulling herself out of the woods with two hands and one good leg.

Not good enough. The beast lunged forward faster than Beck could pull to get away. It overshadowed Beck like a rust-red thundercloud, nudging her, poking her with a big finger, nearly flipping her body over. Terror in combination with her stutter took away Beck's ability to speak, even to scream. The creature backed off, resting on all fours, and gave her some space.

Daring to move, Beck felt her ankle again under the creature's sentrylike stare. The ankle wasn't broken as near as she could tell, but she did have a cruel souvenir from her tumble over the falls— a bad sprain. She wouldn't be walking, much less running, anytime soon.

Beck lifted her eyes to the creature. Was it possible to make peace with this beast? A cluster of berries was within reach. This beast seemed to want Beck to eat them. If it would make it happy . . .

Daringly, her hand still quaking, Beck reached halfway to the berries, hoping such personal initiative would not seem threatening.

There was no violent reaction. The thing didn't growl or bite her.

Slowly, inch by trembling inch, she reached the rest of the way and grabbed them. The ape-thing let her, making strange, guttural rumblings and a clicking sound like wood hitting bamboo: *Tok! Tok! Tok!*

Beck placed the berries in her mouth and reached for more, eating them slowly. The beast's expression softened. She eased back onto her haunches and watched. From this slight distance Beck got a first full look at her. She was very much like a gorilla, but with a body like a barrel and a neck so broad it blended with her shoulders. Her legs, thick as tree trunks and covered with hair, were longer than one would expect in an ape, but the arms were definitely ape arms, long enough to reach Beck's neck and wring the life out of her.

As Beck lay still, chewing berries, the pain in her ankle subsided enough for her to notice a dull ache in her head. She touched the side of her forehead, felt a bump—Ouch! *Another spot that hurt!*—then found dark, flaking blood on her fingers.

Ohhh . . . dear Lord, what happened? She remembered falling, but after that, nothing. If she was this beat up, what had happened to Reed? Was he lying somewhere in worse shape than she was? Her backpack was missing. Maybe this monster tried to raid their backpacks for food and Reed had tried to resist, tried to save Beck, gotten the brunt of this monster's rage—

She dared not think it.

But then came more bad news. A further inventory revealed a large smear of blood on her leather jacket where she'd been pressed against the creature's side. She looked and found a corresponding dark stain on the big ape's shoulder and left flank.

If her fear had ebbed even slightly, now it returned. She met the creature's eyes and thought, *What have you done?*

The monster stiffened, suddenly alert and alarmed. The lips pulled back slightly, revealing the edges of the teeth—sharp, white incisors between an imposing set of canines.

Beck cowered. *Oh no, I've made it angry.*

But the big female wasn't angry. It wasn't even looking at her. It was listening. The look on its face, the piercing stare of its eyes, its motionless body reminded Beck of their dog, Jonah, and how he reacted whenever he heard a distant coyote or the UPS truck approaching a half mile away. And there was that foul smell again, a new, sickening wave of it.

It happened so fast Beck didn't have time to object or resist. Before she could even scream, the big hands enfolded her and snatched her from the ground, shaking her insides and nearly giving her whiplash. Limbs, leaves, and berries blurred past her eyes and whipped her head and shoulders. She covered her face.

There was a burst of acceleration so fast that the wind swept her hair from her face. She lifted her eyes.

She was flying, lunging through the forest at an altitude of six feet, her body held fast against that abundant bosom by two muscular arms. Tree limbs blurred by like fence posts on a freeway. She curled her legs up as her hands grabbed fistfuls of red hair in a death grip. Beneath her, the creature's big feet pounded the ground as she leaped over logs and dodged thickets and brush with incredible agility, slowed by nothing.

■ ■ ■

With a little whine, Caesar the German shepherd balked only a
few yards into the trees, turned back, looked down the hill at
Agnes, his handler, tried again, whined again, and finally, at a
timid trot, ran to his master and cowered behind her legs. Agnes,
whose dogs had served the county sheriff's department, the state
patrol, and local police departments for the past twelve years,
looked puzzled to say the least as she stroked the shy dog's neck.
"Caesar, what is it? What's the matter, boy?"

Reed did not find the dog's behavior one bit surprising. He
felt that way himself—he just wasn't going to whine about it.

Pete Henderson and his team of searchers looked as mystified
as Agnes, gawking up into the woods from a small clearing on the
mountainside. Scatter Creek ran through this clearing, cutting
across the trail just below them and cascading over a ten-foot waterfall. Agnes had taken Caesar to the base of the waterfall, the spot
search teams call the "LKP," the Last Known Place Beck had been,
and let him go. He'd hesitated, whined, followed a scent up to the
trail, spun in circles, followed it across the trail and up the clearing,
turned back at the trees, and then, with some goading from Agnes,
continued into the trees. A few yards in, he'd had enough.

Pete's radio squawked. "Team 1 in position at the campsite."

Pete spoke into the handheld, "Team 2 above the waterfall at
the LKP." He gazed curiously at the dog. "We're, uh, working
the K-9 right now. Good hunting."

He clipped the handheld to his belt and looked down toward
the trail where Reed and the others waited for further orders.

Reed tried to keep his impatience in check. He knew all these
people were as eager and on edge as he was: the two Search and
Rescue volunteers, one the dental assistant and the other the

heavy equipment operator, both tracking apprentices; the two marksmen, one of them a newcomer named Thorne who looked like a marine; two medical technicians with emergency kits and a stretcher; Don Nelson and Tyler Jones, experienced trackers, who would form the three-man tracking team with Pete; Agnes Hastings, the K-9 handler; and Cap Capella, there because he was a friend. All were dressed for the job and grim with the business at hand, but any hasty move at this point could destroy important signs and evidence. Pete had to make the calls.

Pete was obviously troubled over the dog. He asked the handler, "Has he ever done this before?"

She was still petting Caesar, who refused to budge from her side. "No. Never."

"But he has tracked bears before?"

"Nine times in the past two years."

Pete gestured toward the trees from which Caesar had fled. "Well, he found something. It turned him back, but it's something." He reached for a set of short aluminum poles that hung on his tracker's vest and began to screw them together into one five-foot length. This was his tracking stick, a rod marked in one-inch increments, with movable rubber O-rings for marking on the stick the size of prints and the stride length between them. "Don and Tyler, I'll take point; you flank. We'll start where Caesar's afraid to go. Reed and Cap, you follow the flank men. You step where they step and don't disturb anything. Agnes, I know Jimmy's real eager to have Caesar help out at the other location. Want to head up there?"

The dog handler gave a resigned shrug, put Caesar's leash on him, and led him up the trail toward the cabin. Caesar was more than happy to go.

Pete took a moment to focus on Reed. "Reed, buddy, you ready?"

Reed knew he didn't know what he was saying, but he answered, "I'm ready."

Pete told Cap, "You stay close to him." He directed his attention downhill. "Joanie and Chris, stand by. When we find the trail, we'll need you to cross-track. And you guys with the guns, guard our flanks. Everybody keep quiet. That bear could still be around. Medics, stand by on the radios."

Pete led the way up the hill. The flank men took positions just behind him, one on his left and one on his right, forming a triangle with Pete at the "point." Reed fell in behind the man on the left, Cap behind the man on the right. The marksmen, guns ready, eyes and ears alert, followed wide to the sides. When Pete moved, they all moved as one body.

Pete led the train slowly, eyes scanning back and forth as they all moved into the trees, his tracking stick ready in his hand. Only a few steps in, he used the stick to point out bent grass and crushed twigs where an animal—or a human—had passed through. "Had a lot of traffic through here this morning," he said in a quiet, stealthy voice, "so the trick is gonna be telling the difference between everybody else's sign and the sign we're looking for."

Reed and Cap exchanged a look. Yes, they and Sing had spent quite a while thrashing through these trees and thickets, leaving their own disturbances everywhere and possibly obliterating everything Pete needed to find now. Reed didn't know whether to feel sheepish at the blunder or just plain aggravated at life's unfairness.

"Boot print on the right," said the right flank man, pointing with his own stick.

Pete saw it. "It's coming your way, Tyler."

The flanker to the left inched forward, carefully checking for more prints. "Okay. Got it." He pointed out a depression in the pine needles at Pete's eleven o'clock.

Pete held his tracking stick between the two tracks, measuring the distance between them, then straightened and asked, "Reed, Cap, either one of you come through here?"

Reed and Cap exchanged a look. Cap wagged his head. Reed answered, "I think I did."

"Let me see the bottom of your left boot."

Reed grabbed Cap's shoulder to steady himself and stuck up his foot.

Pete studied and measured the boot sole while Tyler pulled out a pencil and a preprinted diagram of a footprint. Pete dictated, "Okay, three-point waffle tread, section 4, thumbnail pattern on right side, center to lower right corner; section 10, sliver in lower right corner."

"It's him," said Don, looking at the track on the right.

Tyler drew the wear patterns on the diagram and labeled it "Reed Shelton."

"I suppose you were in a big hurry last night?" Pete asked.

"I was," Reed admitted.

"Well, it's you, all right. Thanks."

They moved farther into the trees, as far as the dog had gone. They could see his sign as Pete pointed it out—paw prints, a bent pine needle, a toe and claw mark on a rotting log—a trail left by a very hesitant canine who didn't know which way to turn next. This was the spot. Whatever was troubling Caesar had to have left something here.

Pete sank carefully to one knee and remained still, as if listening. His eyes began to sweep across the cluttered forest floor as he studied the twigs, the pine cones, the fallen needles, the scattered pebbles, the blades of grass and tiny, broad-leaved weeds. Reed saw his jaw tense. Then Pete pointed with his stick.

Tyler replied, "Yeah, you've got it."

Reed peered over Tyler's shoulder but couldn't see a thing except the cluttered, busy, infinitely detailed forest floor.

Pete removed his hat and went down on his belly, the side of his head to the ground, his open eye next to the ground, the other winked shut. "Yeah."

He raised up on his side and carefully pressed his thumb into the soil, leaving a small oval indentation. Then he went in close, his nose only inches from the tiny leaves and grass. "Yeah, maybe half a day old. Could've come through last night, easy."

Tyler whispered to Reed, pointing carefully with his tracking stick. "See the shine on that leaf right there? And the dip in the needles underneath?"

Reed looked a long time, but finally he saw it—he thought.

"Rear foot?" Don asked.

"I wanna see another one," Pete answered as he measured the impression with a tape measure. "Got about five . . . and one-half inches across. Whew! That makes him one for the record books. *Heavy* son of a gun too." While Don flagged the impression with a pink ribbon on a Popsicle stick, Pete pivoted the tracking stick forward, holding the handle over the impression and swinging the tip in a slow, careful arc. "C'mon now, let me see a heel print."

Pete—and so the whole group—inched forward.

Don pointed with his stick. "Got some snapped branches at one o'clock."

They all looked and saw the spindly, mostly dead branches on the lower trunk of a pine either bent or snapped in an uphill direction.

"Ehh, bingo," said Pete, selecting some tweezers from his pocket and plucking a long reddish hair from the jagged stump of a limb. The hair gave him pause. He handed it back to Don. "That look like bear to you?"

Don held the specimen up to the light. "Well, maybe. Kind of long."

Pete asked Reed, "What color is Beck's hair these days?"

Reed examined the hair Don held in the tweezers. "Reddish brown."

Pete exhaled a half whistle. "Hoo, lordy."

Don carefully placed the hair in a Ziploc bag.

Pete stood still, probing ahead with narrowed eyes. Finally, he let out a held breath. "Okay," he said, pointing. "We've got another one."

The body of trackers inched forward again.

This one was more visible, a roundish impression in some humus. To Reed it looked as though someone had knelt there and left a knee print.

Pete went on his belly again, eyeing the print carefully, then measuring it. He straightened up, still on one knee. He was troubled, eyeing the area between the two prints. "Where are the *front* feet?"

"We've missed something," Don agreed as he flagged the print.

"Well, we'll find 'em," said Pete. He stretched out his tracking stick to measure the distance between the two tracks, but it wouldn't reach. He chuckled. "Either that, or this bear has one heck of a stride."

They moved ahead, this time according to the length they'd found between the first two tracks. The third one, nothing more than a scuff on a rotting log, was where it should have been, the same distance from the second as the second was from the first. They had a pattern.

■ ■ ■

Sing crouched in the doorway of the sorrowful old cabin and took one last shot of the destruction inside. She was amazed. In her line of work, she'd photographed and reconstructed crime scenes involving hoodlums and vandals, domestic spats, drug-related murders, and meth lab explosions, but they were nothing like this. For one thing, the beast that made this mess was far, far outside the human category. Certainly, human scum could show this kind of disregard for property, but to snap support posts like toothpicks and tear whole walls open required an inestimable strength she had never encountered. For another thing—and this still felt a little odd to her—according to the rules out here, this wasn't even a crime scene but made perfect sense: bear gets hungry, bear finds food, bear does what is necessary to get it. Tearing the windows out of a building, smashing cots and shelves, and splintering a door were shocking, destructive acts to civilized perceptions, but to a bear's way of thinking, no different from clawing the termites out of an old stump.

It was frightening and fascinating, and not hard to understand.

If it was a bear.

"How's it going?" Jimmy, the conservation officer, called from the bridge.

He was obviously impatient, and she couldn't blame him. Agnes the dog handler had arrived with Caesar, and Jimmy and the hunters were ready to move, so the only thing holding them up was Sing's directive from Sheriff Mills. She'd photographed Reed and Beck's campsite, their food stash, the log bridge, and the littered area around the cabin. She'd paced off distances and made notes. Everything that was directly knowable she'd recorded on several pages. She'd worked expeditiously, but the process took precious time. Jimmy had somehow managed to defer to the sheriff on this one, but she could feel him breathing down her neck with each passing minute.

With great relief she called back, "I'm through," and stowed her camera and notebook in her backpack.

Jimmy immediately turned his attention to Agnes. "All right.

Let's get a scent and track that baby!" The hunting party, with sniffing Caesar in the lead, nearly stampeded off the bridge and down the trail.

They jostled past Sing as if she were an obstacle. She hurried up the trail, relieved with every step that put distance between them.

The other team members were now covering the surrounding area in widening quadrants. She could hear them calling to each other, maintaining voice contact as they worked their way among the trees like fleas in a hairbrush. At certain moments she spotted some of them, but she hadn't caught sight of Sheriff Mills to fill him in on—

"Sing! Up here!"

Ah. He was waving to her from the hillside above the trail. She selected a route up the embankment with sufficient footholds and branches to grab, and worked her way to him. At the top, Mills and Deputy Saunders were waiting for her. They were examining the campsite, two sleeping bags on a ground cloth, cloistered in a tight pocket among some trees. It wasn't an instant find; as Reed had warned, it was hard to see from the trail.

"Find anything unusual down there?" Mills asked her.

"Besides everything?" She looked down into the draw where Jimmy and his hunting party lurked near the cabin, waiting for Caesar to show them the way. "That bear was very hungry or very angry at being so hungry, or . . . Well, let's just say he was highly motivated."

"But no sign of Randy?"

She hated to tell him, "No sir."

Mills's expression was troubled as he scanned the forest in wide arcs, his eyes landing on the searchers below. "We need to find a body, Sing."

The deputy suggested, "Why don't we get Reed over here so he can show us where he saw it?"

"He won't leave the search for Beck," Sing cautioned.

Mills gazed at the rough map Reed had drawn. "We've located the campsite and the stash of food containers between the two trees . . . but this tree right here, the big cedar tree where the body is supposed to be . . . Well, maybe it's the right tree, maybe it isn't, but there's no body."

Then Jimmy cursed so loudly it startled them.

Agnes started hollering, "Caesar! Caesar, come, boy! Come, Caesar!"

Of course they had to watch. From up here the view was quite good.

Caesar was trying to run up the trail away from the cabin, and Agnes was hot on his heels, leash in hand. The dog stopped at her command, shied away again, answered her command again, then fidgeted, obviously wanting nothing but to get out of there. When Agnes finally snapped the leash onto his collar, he tugged at it, jerking in little circles, trembling and dribbling urine.

"What's his problem?" Jimmy demanded, rifle in hand but with nothing to shoot. "I said, *what's his problem?*"

"I don't know!" the handler shouted back. "I'm about to retire him! He's just never acted this way!" Her legs were getting snarled in the leash.

"Well, does he track bears or doesn't he?" Jimmy asked.

"He tracks bears! Black bears, grizzly bears, any kind of bears!"

"Well, he's not doing us much good now, is he?" Jimmy turned toward the marksman behind him. "What did you say?"

The marksman was not the kind to be intimidated. "I said, 'Maybe this ain't a bear.'"

Now Jimmy was simmering at a temperature even Sing could feel from the hill. He pointed his finger at the man. "Excuse me, Janson! If you're going to be on this team, you're going to handle yourself and your mouth with professionalism, you got that?"

"Yes sir, I got that."

Now Jimmy addressed all three people in a voice suitable for a hundred: "This is a rogue bear we're after. It's serious business. We're going to keep our minds clear and straight ahead so we get the job done without anyone getting hurt, is that understood?"

Janson nodded, the other hunter said yes, and Agnes just petted Caesar.

Jimmy leaned in on her. "Agnes, we need a dog that'll track this bear, and if your dog can't do that, we need another dog. Are we clear on that?"

"Clear enough." Agnes steamed a moment, then led Caesar back up the trail toward Abney. "C'mon, boy. We don't need any more of this!"

Caesar led her, only too eager to go.

Jimmy watched her go, then stomped around a bit, then conferred with his hunters, saying something about bait and bear stands.

The show was over. Sheriff Mills turned back to Sing and Deputy Saunders. "We'll give the searchers a few more minutes, and then we'll have to get Reed and Pete over here."

Sing thought it wise to remind him, "Sheriff, every other aspect of Reed's account holds up."

Sheriff Mills regarded the cabin below. "So you don't think one man could do that kind of damage to the cabin?"

She almost laughed. "Not even remotely. And if you'll remember, Reed's camera recorded pictures of the demolished cabin before it recorded pictures of Beck, alive and well."

Mills nodded but asked, "I don't suppose you've spotted any bear prints anywhere?"

She felt the strange sensation of thin ice under her feet—and maybe Reed's. "Well, it is loose ground around here, lots of rock, lots of humus and pine needles that don't register a print, at least to someone who isn't a tracker."

"We'll see what Pete says."

"Sure. We'll see what Pete says. But, sir . . ." She felt nervous. "Reed never said anything about a bear. He provided no bear scenario. If there was foul play, if he had planned this—"

Mills held up his hand. "You don't have to sell me."

"I'm glad to hear it, sir."

Mills only responded, "But we'd better pray they find Beck."

■ ■ ■

Pete's team was picking up some speed now that they knew what to look for. They'd worked their way up the hill another hundred feet while two trackers, accompanied by the marksman named Thorne, started crisscrossing their path a shouting distance ahead of them, hoping to encounter signs farther up.

For Reed, it was all too tedious. Beck could die in the dirt somewhere long before they would ever find her. Cap must've sensed his mood, because he kept whispering, "Easy, now, we're moving okay; we'll find her. Got to do it right."

"What'd this thing do, have its claws cut?" Pete muttered.

Then came a shout from one of the trackers far up the hill. "We've got something!"

Pete told Reed and Cap, "Better stay here." He and his men went on ahead.

Time stretched into an eternity, but Reed had no hurry left in him. He could only stand there and take frightened, furtive glances as Pete and his men disappeared into the forest. For a long time—such a long time—Reed heard them pushing through the limbs and brush as they spoke in hushed, clipped phrases and moved in a wide arc. When they finally came into sight again, they were far away, their outlines broken by a jittery web of branches and limbs. He could just barely see them approaching the other team members and whatever the object was.

Pete circled the object, then called out, "Come on up, Reed."

Reed drew a deep breath and wiped his eyes clear.

"C'mon," said Cap, touching his arm.

They pressed through the pines and firs, approximating the path the others had taken. When they finally emerged from the insistent, aggravating, view-blocking fingers of the forest, Reed could see the others gathered in a wide circle in front of a huge fallen log, the two marksmen warily standing guard. In the center of the circle was a blue backpack, not set there but dropped. It was dirty and the frame was bent—as if it had fallen over a waterfall. Every eye focused on Reed, waiting for the verdict.

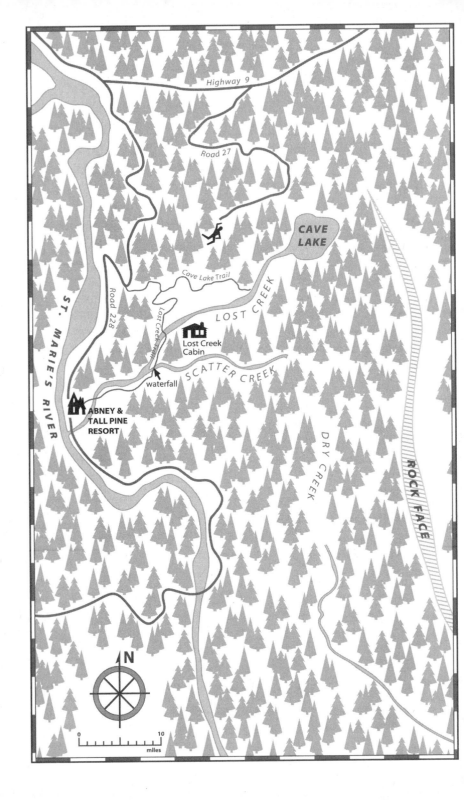

FIVE

Reed's voice quavered though he tried to control it. "It's hers. She picked out the color."

"Don't touch it," said Pete, looking around the area and at his two flankers, visibly bothered about something. He asked Reed, "Do you know if there's any food in there?"

"We packed some granola bars, and she may have had some of her lunch left over."

Pete went down on all fours for a closer look, studying the pack on all sides. "If I were a camp-raiding kind of bear, I'd be interested in that. This one wasn't. This pack doesn't have a mark on it." Then he pulled out his tweezers again and probed at one of the flaps. "Got some more of that hair here, tangled up in the Velcro. Tyler? Let's get those medics up here with one of those . . . you know, those bags. We need to bag the whole thing up."

Body bags, Reed thought. Pete wasn't very clever at talking in code.

Tyler got on his radio.

"May I see the hairs?" Cap asked, leaning over the pack. Pete pointed them out and Cap looked at them closely. He even sniffed them, then sniffed the pack.

"Any thoughts?" Reed asked.

Cap backed away as if caught in an illegal act. "Oh no, no, no thoughts. Just curious."

"Got a pretty good toe print here," Don reported from near the log.

"We're on him now," said Pete, showing a hint of excitement despite himself.

Cap went to have a look, hands clasped behind his back, unobtrusive.

"Check that log," Pete told his guys. "See if he went over it." Then he sniffed the pack himself and made a face. "Reed? Come smell this."

Reed approached carefully, dropping to his knees, then all fours, crouching down to get his nose close enough to the blue fabric.

It was a defining moment he hadn't expected: a reassuring horror, a dreadful relief, an encouraging fear. He knew this odor; for him, it was the stench of Beck's abduction, the reek of the creature that had chased them and taken her. It had filled the air the previous night and become a suppressed and forgotten ingredient in what he'd taken for madness, a crazed illusion he'd come to doubt. But that was then. Now, among friends and objective observers in broad daylight, it was real—horribly, reassuringly real! "This is what we smelled last night. The smell was everywhere!"

"No wonder Caesar had a problem," Pete mused.

The flank men had reached the other side of the log and were checking the ground. "Got a heel print over here, deep compression," Don reported.

Tyler checked the top of the log, his head low, eyeing the aged, crumbling grain.

"What do you see, Tyler?" Pete urged.

Tyler looked at the heel print again, then at the top of the log again. "Looks like he jumped over."

That brought Pete to his feet. "Over *that*? Doggone, Tyler, I don't need any more surprises!"

Tyler explained, "We've got a deep push-off in that toe print and a deep compression on the heel over here, and nothing on top of the log."

Pete examined the toe print, then checked the top of the log with his light. "Don, I want you to tell me you've got some claw marks."

Don knelt and studied the print from several directions. "Can't say I do."

"No claw marks," Pete muttered, obviously fed up.

"That thing jumped," Tyler repeated.

Pete looked back. "And that's when Beck lost her backpack."

"We're missing something," Don objected.

"A bear would've torn some pretty good claw marks in this log going over, especially if it was carrying a . . . carrying somebody."

"What are you talking about, 'carried'?" Tyler said. "A bear doesn't carry a body; it drags it in its teeth."

Reed gave up trying to contain himself. "It didn't drag her. It carried her. I saw it lift her off the ground." They all stared at him, so he threw back a challenge. "Have you found any sign that says different?"

The trackers looked at each other, waiting for one of them to answer.

"We're . . . we're missing something," Don said again.

"No, we aren't," said Pete, and Tyler agreed with a wag of his head. "Nobody got dragged. The sign says what it says."

"And what is that?" Reed demanded.

No answer.

"Tell me!" he shouted.

Pete was thinking when his radio squawked, "Pete. Pete, this is Mills."

"This is Pete. Go ahead."

"We can't find a body up here."

Pete made a curious face. "Say again?"

Mills came back, speaking with forced clarity. "We cannot find a body. Do you copy?"

Pete looked at Reed, but Reed was dumbstruck. "Uh, we copy that you cannot find a body."

"We need you and Reed to come and help us out for a few minutes."

First one blow, then another! Reed shook his head.

Pete spoke into his radio, "We've found Beck's backpack. We could be close."

There was a pause, apparently while Mills thought it over, and then Mills replied, "Pete, hand off to your flank men, let Reed stay there, but give him a radio so we can talk to him, and you come up."

Pete checked visually with Don and Tyler. They were ready to take over. He reassured Reed, "You can trust these guys."

"I'd rather you were here," Reed protested.

Pete sighed and spoke into his radio again. "Can it wait?"

Mills came back immediately: "No, it can't."

■ ■ ■

Beck's head throbbed, her ankle shrieked, everything in between hurt, and it was getting hard to breathe with those huge arms squeezing her. She'd been hanging on to fistfuls of fur, ducking her head as branches swept close, and praying for an end to this for what seemed hours. The big female had climbed, galloped, strode, reversed course, run, reversed again, and run some more, penetrating miles of forestland and covering vast stretches of mountain slope to the point where Beck hadn't the foggiest clue where on the planet they were. Everything—trees, gullies, ridges, boulders— looked the same. She couldn't even be sure she was still in Idaho.

But the creature was hurting too. She hobbled and wheezed, swaying unsteadily as she walked. Beck had the uneasy feeling she was sitting high in a tree that was about to fall over.

She was right.

With her last feeble steps, the big female pushed into a scrubby clump of trees, spun a few dizzying turns, then collapsed like a condemned building imploding, her legs giving way beneath her, her nostrils huffing clouds of steam. She bumped on her behind, teetered there a moment, and then, with a long, breathy groan, slumped onto her side. Her arms wilted like dying plants and Beck rolled onto the moss and uneven rock. Her clothes were dampened with the creature's sweat, and she ached in every muscle, wincing from the pain in her ankle, and amazed she was still alive.

Her hair-covered captor sounded like a locomotive leaving a station, chugging and laboring for every breath, holding her side. Her eyes were watery, filled with pain and unmistakable fear.

Beck stared, unable to make sense of it. *The* beast *is afraid? What could a beast of such power and size be afraid of?*

The female looked back at her, never breaking her gaze, until her expansive rib cage began to settle into a quieter, more restful rhythm and her eyes softened from fear to a kind of resignation. With a deep sigh and a swallow, she pushed herself into a sitting

position and began peering through the trees like a soldier in a
bunker, scanning the expansive landscape below, the deep amber
eyes searching, searching, searching.

Beck sat up as well and followed the creature's gaze. The view
was spectacular from here. Below them stretched a vast valley
under a thin veil of blue haze, and beyond that, so clear it seemed
one could touch them, a range of granite peaks took a jagged bite
out of the sky. It even *sounded* vast up here: dead quiet except for
the all-surrounding whisper of air moving through the trees and
the trickle of a stream nearby. If Beck wasn't so miserable, fearful
for her life, and occupied with trying to think of the "right" thing
to do, she could be enjoying this.

The right thing to do? She wanted to cry. The right thing
would have been to stay home where she had a warm bed, a latte
machine, fuzzy slippers, and a nice shower with brass handles.
This was unthinkable!

The shadows were long now, the mossy rubble outside their
hiding place almost entirely in shade. Not comforting. She'd
learned the hard way what to expect in this weird, wild world at
night, and she did not relish facing that alone and lost.

She looked at her smelly, unknowable, unpredictable host,
who was still looking out over the valley as if expecting an enemy.
What were her plans? *Had* she captured Beck for a meal? Beck
remembered something she learned at a zoo once, something
about gorillas being vegetarians. This creature seemed to like
berries.

But so did bears.

Keep thinking, Beck; keep thinking!

Okay. What was it going to take to survive? Shelter. Water.
Food. In that order.

She considered shelter. If she could move, if she had some
tools, if there was anything with which to build a shelter . . .

Well, what about the next one? She hadn't had any water since last night, and that stream was calling to her. She craned her neck but couldn't see where—

Whooa! Hands wrapped around her like a big sling, and she was in the air again. No freight-train speed this time, though. As the creature ambled with smooth, bent-kneed strides through the trees, over rocks, and down a shallow draw, Beck felt a sensation much like floating over the ground on a ski lift.

They found the stream, sparkling and splashing over broken rocks and forming pools from which to dip water. The big female set her down on a large, flat stone and then squatted next to her, dipping up bucket-sized helpings in her hands, slurping them down. Beck watched, wondering if it was safe to move, to take a drink herself. She leaned over the water, then checked with a sideways glance. The creature didn't seem to mind; it may have been expecting it. Beck prayed silently, *Oh Lord, don't let me get beaver fever—whatever that is,* and then started dipping and drinking.

After only a few gulps, she heard a familiar whistle and froze to listen. Her furry captor heard it too and became alert, cocking her head one way, then another. When the whistle came again, she pressed her lips against her teeth and returned a whistle of her own. Its piercing sound made Beck flinch.

The whistle answered, closer this time, and now Beck heard rustling and saw movement in the brush on the other side of the draw. She backed away from the stream on one knee and two hands, looking about for a hiding place.

The beast reached with her inescapably long arm and pulled Beck in, half-dragging her, pressing her close against her furry, sweaty side. Beck felt like a trophy, a prize, a fresh kill about to be shared. Playing dead occurred to her, but the beast's big arm wouldn't let her fall down.

Across the stream, from somewhere in the trees and thick brush, a low whistle sounded, and then a pig grunt.

The beast whistled back and gave a soft pig grunt of her own.

There was an interval, a strange moment when nothing happened—no sound, no stirrings, no whistles or calls. Beck searched the bushes, but all she could see across the creek was a sea of leaves, motionless except for an occasional flickering in the breeze. She had the distinct feeling she wasn't just being watched—she was being *studied*.

Then, so slowly, so silently that it almost escaped notice, a gray, hairy dome rose like a dark moon out of the brush. Beck looked directly at it—

It vanished as if it was never there.

The big female whistled again and then made that strange guttural noise with the loud tongue clicking. *Tok! Tok!*

The gray dome rose again, and this time, two steely, amber eyes glared at Beck, narrow with suspicion.

Beck could only hang there motionless, expressionless, without the first thought of what she could do.

With its eyes darting from Beck to the big female and back, the second creature moved forward, only the head and shoulders visible above the brush, until it emerged, stooped over, stealing, sneaking, edging closer.

Beck looked it in the eye again. It leaped back several paces, almost vanishing in the brush, hissing through clenched teeth.

Don't look it in the eye, Beck thought to herself. *It doesn't like that.*

She looked down at the water instead and watched the beast's rippling reflection as it relaxed enough to approach again. It came closer, one furtive step at a time, until it reached the other edge of the stream, and then stood there, still making a nervous, hissing noise with every breath. Beck ventured a look at the feet. All five toes were up front, in a row, but the bone structure was somehow different from human. The feet had a funny way of flexing in the middle, conforming to the streambed, curving over the rocks.

Beck let her eyes move up a little more. The creature was standing nearly upright now, almost seven feet tall by Beck's estimate. It was another female, a mass of muscle covered in dark gray fur and a little thinner than the first one, although at the moment its fur stood out and bristled, making it appear larger and anything but friendly.

It uttered some pig grunts that could have been an inquiry. Beck's female gave some pig grunts that could have been an answer, then extended an open hand. The other female ignored it, eyeing Beck with vicious suspicion.

There was another stirring in the brush, and a third creature appeared. It was steely gray in color and, judging from its size, a youngster. It sidled up to the big gray, gripped her leg, and joined her in staring at Beck. This one appeared to be a male. Beck stole one quick little glance at its eyes; he was unflinching. He stood at least five feet tall. The face was pale, like a baby chimp's, and the hair on its head stuck out in wild directions. If she'd seen this thing in a zoo from a safe distance with bars between them, she probably would have thought it was cute.

She ventured one more look in its eyes—

"Roargghh!" The little beast exploded like a bomb going off, leaping into the stream, sending up a spray of water that doused her. Terrified, Beck squirmed, kicked, and tried to get free while the juvenile roared from the middle of the stream, arms flexing, fists clenched, fur on end, teeth bared in a vicious display. Then his mother got into it, roaring and putting on a horrific show of anger.

The big red female pulled Beck in close and turned her back to the onslaught. Beck was glad for the shield, but the female was cowering, and Beck could feel her tremble.

With just one eye peering through red fur, Beck saw the other female standing her ground on the opposite bank, teeth bared and growling, while the youngster, emboldened by his mother, splashed across the stream, grabbed up pine cones, and threw them. The hurled cones bounced off the big female. Beck leaned out a little too far and one glanced off her shoulder. It smarted. Another pine cone whizzed by her ear and she ducked.

The big gray stepped into the stream. In only a few long strides, she loomed over them, eyes burning with anger—particularly at Beck.

Shaking with terror, Beck buried herself against the red female's chest.

The female toppled forward.

"Nooo!" Beck cried.

Suddenly Beck was buried under an avalanche of muscle, fat, and fur, nearly smothering in the coarse hair, her back pinned against the rocks, in total darkness. On top of her, the mountain trembled and quaked, the heart pounding like a huge drum. Beck couldn't breathe. She couldn't move either. She cried out to God. Things got quiet. The mountain lifted slightly and daylight trickled in through the hair, along with breathable air. A pine cone bounced on the ground just outside, but it landed lightly, so it had to have been tossed, not hurled.

Beck heard feet sloshing back across the stream as the mountain sat up. She dared to peek. The youngster and his mother were returning across the stream. He clung to a fistful of fur on her side, and she stroked his head. He looked back over his shoulder as they left, bared his teeth, and huffed at Beck and her keeper.

With one parting, spiteful grunt, mother and son hurried into the brush, then barked one more loud insult before they vanished from sight.

So there were *three* of them.

. . .

Reed sat on the bed in Room 105, Beck's bent and soiled backpack in front of him. Carefully, solemnly, he removed the contents, handing each article to Cap. As Cap arranged everything on the floor, Sing listed each in her notebook: dry changes of clothes, an extra pair of long underwear, rain gear, matches, dehydrated snacks, a first aid kit, a tool kit, a compact tube tent, a compass, a Swiss Army knife. Reed wept when he found two rolls of toilet paper and a small pouch containing makeup, but he kept going. He couldn't allow his emotions to keep him from this task. Next came a thermal blanket, some containers of food, and—Reed paused to look at it—a crumpled, bent book, *Wilderness Survival*, by Randy Thompson. Several pages were marked and paragraphs highlighted.

"She read it," he marveled. "She actually read all this stuff."

With so much precious time lost and Beck not found, Reed felt as if he were in a torturous limbo between faith that they would find her and cold reason that insisted she couldn't be alive. He dared not voice such things, for he wasn't ready to face them, not yet.

"I'm proud of her," he said, withered by emotion. "I'm really proud that she tried. You know she never finished a painting? She did finish one novel, but she was afraid to send it to any publishers. She was afraid of what they'd think."

"It was a great book!" Sing affirmed. "And listen, Reed, for the record, the survival vacation was a great idea. Sure, Beck needed it, but I think we all could have gotten something out of it."

"You did the right thing," Cap agreed.

Reed gazed down at the pack. It was empty now. Cap took it off his hands and he sat quietly, trying to fathom the day's

disappointments. The two teams had returned for the night, some
to stay at the Tall Pine, some to catch a few winks at home. What
little hope there was, was fading. Reed wondered if they would all
return the next morning. "They don't believe me, do they?"

"It's tough to get a read on some of them," said Cap. "I think
Pete and the trackers are with you, but as for the others, there's
some talk starting up."

Sing tried to reassure him, "You have to expect that, Reed.
You know this business. It's all you can do to keep faith in
people."

"I saw Randy's body. Beck saw it. We both *saw* it!"

Sing put out a hand to halt any more of that. "Reed, let's
move on. Something happened to it. What—that's the question
now."

"Pete did find the tree, right?"

Sing answered, "As near as we could tell from your map and
directions. He thinks he found your and Beck's footprints around
it, and that bush you say she fell into. That all lined up."

"But no body."

"No body. Anywhere."

"But no bear tracks either, right?"

"There may have been tracks—"

"But not *bear* tracks!"

"Pete wouldn't say one way or another."

"That's because this isn't a bear and he knows it!"

Cap objected, "He doesn't know it!"

"He found more of the same prints he found above the waterfall, am I right?"

Sing tossed up a hand. "He found some prints. Some of them
could have been Randy's, and some of them were just—I'll tell
you what I think: I think Pete does have some doubts about the
bear theory, but he's waiting before he says anything."

"Nobody knows what the real story is here," said Cap.

"So what were you sniffing the pack for?" Reed said.

"What?"

"You were sniffing the backpack! You were looking at the hairs! What were you thinking?"

"Reed, I wasn't thinking anything." Reed and Sing locked eyes with him. "Well, nothing *serious*!"

Sing leaned toward her husband, emphatic. "We need to identify those hairs, Cap."

Cap looked cornered. "Why look at me?"

"You have friends at the university who can do it."

"They're not my friends!" They locked eyes with him again. "Well, okay, some of them are. They *might* be."

Sing reached into her backpack and pulled out a plastic Ziploc bag, sealed with red "evidence" tape. The hairs were in it. She tossed it to her husband.

He tossed it back. "I am *not* going back there! I *can't*!" He felt their gaze again. "All right, give me more reason and I'll think about it!"

■ ■ ■

It took a long moment of stillness before the big red female relaxed her grip and Beck could move a little. Beck allowed herself a small bit of relief, a calming breath or two, but her heart was racing and the trembling wouldn't go away.

A hand with the texture of a baseball glove wrapped around her face and forced her to look directly into the creature's face, mere inches away.

Beck couldn't even scream, her silent throat betraying her yet again.

With long, slimy strokes, a big pink tongue began mopping

the berry stains and blood from Beck's face. She raised her hand
to push the big mouth away—*lick*—but then realized—*lick, lick*—
that this disgusting, smelly, slimy act could be—*lick*—an act of
kindness—*lick, lick*—and she'd better not mess with it.

The creature licked her some more, then inspected her face
like a mother inspecting her child. Satisfied, she set Beck down
and went to the stream for another drink.

Nauseous, Beck wasted no time crawling and hobbling to the
stream, where she flopped on her belly and splashed water on her
face. She could feel the slime on her skin, in her hair, on her neck,
even in her ears. She kept splashing, frantically washing, longing
for some soap and cleansing moisturizer, that wonderful, good-
smelling stuff that came out of the quaint, decorative pump
bottle by her sink in her nice, warm, clean house—

A string of slime hung from her fingers as she brought them
up out of the water. When she stopped to stare at it, she heard an
explosive spitting noise upstream.

The big female was drinking, then spitting huge, stringy
mouthfuls of water. Apparently she wasn't too pleased with how
Beck's face tasted.

Beck stopped, too insulted to continue washing. How could
that disgusting monster find *Beck* disgusting?

The lady finished drinking, rolled back onto her haunches,
and gave Beck a relentless, studious look, a gaze so unbroken it
put Beck's nerves on edge.

A cold wind whipped across the mountainside, swaying the
trees and leaching heat from Beck's body. The sun had dipped
behind the mountain and a worrisome chill was moving in. So
what to do? Was there anywhere she could curl up out of the
wind? What if the other two creatures came back?

She eyed the big red female and tried to weigh disgust against
wisdom. It seemed the big gal *was* intent on protecting her, some-

thing Beck couldn't figure out but had to consider. With night coming on, she might do well to reconsider that big, warm body. She immediately looked elsewhere. There had to be another way.

The beast grabbed her again.

"Noo!" Beck screeched.

She pulled Beck close.

The smell was enough to make Beck gag, the fur was oily and sweaty, and there was still that frightful streak of blood.

But the body was warm.

The beast's big hands held her close, cuddling her. The coarse fur poked her in the eye and tickled her nose. The blood was turning sour; it gave off a smell like a dead mouse.

But Beck was warm. The cold wind would not reach her tonight.

She pushed the creature's hair out of her eyes, then tried to relax and, of all things, accept the situation—if she could only breathe.

Reed was right about one thing: the rules were different out here. How different? How would she learn them other than one mistake at a time, and what if a mistake turned out to be fatal? She wished Reed were here to help her.

A cold breeze interrupted her thoughts and reminded her that there were more immediate things to worry about—like staying alive right now. Cringing, she pressed in close to the odorous, furry body and drew in the warmth. The beast cradled her with a big arm. More warmth.

■ ■ ■

Not far south of Abney, in a small meadow about ten miles back on a logging road, Ted and Melanie Brooks, a couple in their twenties, were "roughing it," cooking up a meal over the open fire in front of their two-person tent. Several beer bottles lay empty in the grass, and they were working on two more. A boom box kept them company, preventing any unwanted quiet with the steady pulsing of bass and drums and the angry wailings of a lead guitar.

Ted was frying up the hamburgers. In the light of a camp lantern, Melanie was chopping up some bananas, apples, and melons for a fruit salad. Nearby was their camp cooler, the lid open, full of drinks, fresh eggs, and raw bacon for the morning's breakfast. They'd eaten lunch in the early afternoon and burned their paper plates, but the leftover McDonald's French fries and half of a Caesar salad still remained, resting on a stump, waiting to be part of tonight's meal.

"Hey, babe," Ted said, turning his face away from the heat of the fire. "You want to take a hike later? Nothing like a walk in the dark in the woods."

"I'm up to it if you are," Melanie teased back, her perfect smile lighting her face.

It felt good to get away from the big-city grind. Ted sang along with the CD now playing, a Hendrix tune he'd sung along with from his youth, as he flipped the patties in an iron frying pan.

"Almost done," he announced, excessively happy. He reached for another beer.

"Salad's about ready," Melanie answered, cutting crookedly as the beer metabolized.

A reflection appeared in the trees at the edge of the meadow. It glimmered, moved, then winked out. Ted *thought* he saw it. "What was that?"

Melanie looked up. "What was what?"

Ted took the iron pan off the fire and set it on a nearby stump where the grease and burgers continued to steam and sizzle.

Then he stood away from the fire, watching the darkness. "I thought I saw something."

Melanie stood very still, though a little unsteady. "I think I *heard* something."

Ted hurried over and shut off the boom box.

The sudden quiet was jarring, eerie. Except for the crackle of the fire and the steady breath of the camp lantern, there wasn't a sound.

Then there was.

Snap! Crunch!

Melanie grabbed Ted's arm, hard.

They both peered into the darkness beyond the reach of the lantern, frightened by the shadows—even their own.

A rustling and another twig breaking.

"Something's out there," Ted whispered.

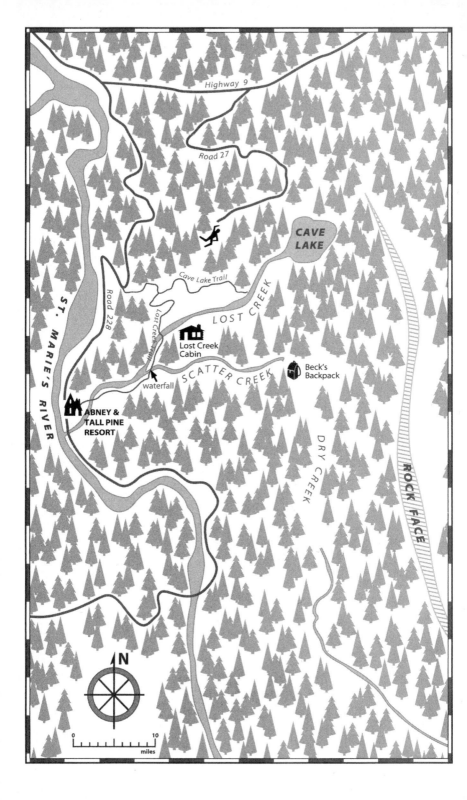

SIX

D id we bring a gun?" Melanie whispered in fear.
"No, no gun," Ted answered, eyes fixed on the darkness beyond
the dimly lit trees. Something was still moving out there. He heard
the thumping of feet on a log. "Hello? Hey!" he shouted.

"Don't yell. It might—"

The scream sent a shock through their nerves, jolting their
muscles, turning their stomachs, quaking their hands.

"It's . . . it's a . . . there's a woman out there!" Ted blurted, his
voice high and trembling.

The mournful wail was still going, rising, falling, rising again.

"Who is it?" Melanie asked no one in particular.

"Hello? Are you all right?" Ted yelled into the dark, then
rebuked himself, "That's a dumb question." He stepped forward.

"Where are you going?" Melanie said.

"I'm going to see who it is."

"Don't go out there!"

Ted walked cautiously, shakily, toward the sound, just now falling away. "Hello? You hurt?" He ventured beyond the reach of the light. His form was dim, broken into segments by the shadows. He stumbled on some fallen branches he didn't see.

"Ted! Come back here! I'm scared!"

He turned to look back, his face illumined like a lone planet in the dark of space. "Can you see anything?" he said.

She could see only his face and his right shoulder.

Just beyond his right shoulder, two silvery-green retinas turned into the light.

Melanie screamed the scream of her life, backing away, hands to her face.

Ted spun around just in time to take a blow to his head that nearly snapped his neck. He tumbled like a rag doll out of sight. Branches snapped and Melanie heard hissing through the leaves.

"Ted!"

Something big was moving out there. It screamed like a woman being stabbed. Melanie found a rock and threw it into the blackness. It glanced off a tree.

"Melanie!" Ted's voice was muffled as if he was yelling into the ground.

The shadow moved that direction.

"Ted, run! *Run!*"

She heard him screaming, thrashing in the brush, moving right, falling again, screaming again.

The woman screamed just above him.

Melanie grabbed the hot frying pan with a pot holder and bolted crazily into the dark, her own shadow a black demon dancing on the trees before her. She caught a glimpse of Ted high-stepping, grappling, pushing through the woods on her right, trying to make it to some light.

"Melanie, it's behind you!"

She spun, swinging the frying pan like a baseball bat. The pan tilted vertically and contacted a black, furry mass with a dull *bong* and the hiss of hot grease.

The thing screamed and spun away. Melanie dropped the pan and ran toward the light.

Ted was ahead of her now, his body a silhouette against the camp lantern, his shadow a man-shaped tunnel through the campfire smoke. She ran down that tunnel, stumbling on the uneven ground.

The thing was behind her, screaming in pain and rage.

Ted had reached the car. "Come on, Melanie, come on!"

She got there as he started up the engine. She dove inside, slammed the door, then groped, slapped for the lock button until she found it and pounded it down.

Ted hit the gas and the car lurched forward.

The thing leaped through the headlights, its coarse, black flank absorbing the light, then glanced off the right fender. For an instant, Melanie saw a face in her window: crazed, glowing eyes, a gaping mouth, glistening fangs.

They roared down the logging road so fast that debris from the potholes and ruts hit them like flak.

Melanie twisted and looked through the rear window. The light of the camp lantern was quickly receding, and against that circle of light, in a backlit haze of campfire smoke, a monstrous, hulking shadow was ravaging their camp.

■　■　■

Arlen Peak stabbed two remaining slabs of beef brisket, lifted them off the open-pit grill, and dropped them onto a platter. "Okay, when they cool down, stick 'em in the freezer."

His wife, his daughter, and his two granddaughters were cleaning up dishes and tables after the barbecue buffet, the Tall Pine's contribution to the search effort. Most of the search crew had stuck around for the free meal, but it wasn't a festive occasion. The meal passed quickly, and now the courtyard and tables were empty under the floodlights, the haze from the barbecue thinning with the evening breeze.

Reed poked his head out of Room 105 and surveyed the courtyard and parking lot. Not too many folks still up and around. Most of the search crew had either gone home or were settling in for the night in the RVs neatly parked at the hookups across the parking lot. Satisfied, he stepped out, an empty plate and silverware in his hand. He'd eaten because he knew he had to, but he'd eaten in solitude. With a little luck, he could return his plate and utensils and maybe get some air without seeing anyone.

I'm acting just like Beck, he thought, wagging his head at the irony. This had to be how she felt most of the time: awkward, stared at, discredited for no good reason. No wonder she avoided people—as he was doing right now.

He'd often been asked, "How in the world did you ever get to know each other?" It wasn't easy. They first crossed paths in St. Maries, Idaho, when he was a well-established high-school senior and she was the new girl in school. He'd seen her at school but actually met her in church, which, he'd often reflected, was a good place to meet a girl. She was a shy, awkward, introverted newcomer to the youth group, devastated the first time the youth pastor called on her to read a scripture aloud, terrified of conversation, and slow to make friends. Nevertheless, he'd already eliminated most of the other girls from his field of interest, and though he could never explain it, he found her fascinating. Their first date was a movie—they just watched the movie and didn't have to talk. Then, after he promised that talking wouldn't be required, she took a pleasant afternoon walk with him along the St. Joe River. After that, he took her bicycling, which they enjoyed in silence. When he took her out to dinner, she pointed at what she wanted on the menu and he ordered for them both. The silence between them took getting used to, and he often caught himself babbling to fill the dead space. Nevertheless, it was in those quiet times that she could be amazingly articulate with her eyes and playful, even teasing, with the corners of her mouth.

Without a word, she had him hooked.

It was the evening they played Scrabble with her folks that he first heard her put an articulate sentence together, word after word, and he was astounded. When she was at home, in a safe and familiar world, her speech impediment nearly vanished. She won the game that night, and after that she started talking, in halting phrases at first, and later in fluid sentences, but only to him. It was like striking oil, a real gusher of information, her soul in words.

But she could only speak if she was comfortable, and that became *the* ongoing problem. At their wedding, her maid of honor repeated her vows for her and she nodded in agreement. His friends at the Sheriff's Academy never saw his wife, not even at graduation. She met Sing Capella only because Sing went out of her way to meet *her*, prepared with things to do and share without a word being spoken. The two were chattering with each other within a week, but talking with Cap took longer.

So Cap and Sing became their closest friends, but Beck still had *few* friends, and that was troubling. Cap, Sing, and Reed had often had their little talks in Beck's absence about what they could or should do to help her. If only Beck could get a little confidence, they'd said. If we could just help her come out of her shell and face life head-on, just a *little* . . .

Reed stacked his plate with the others in the kitchen pass-through and dropped his silverware into the big can of soapy water. Arlen's granddaughter looked at him, smiled a bit, and kept on stacking the dishes in the dishwasher. He passed two search volunteers on his way to the parking lot, but they didn't bother him; they didn't even look him in the eye.

Cap and Sing had already said their good nights. Sheriff Mills had left to catch up on loose ends at the department. Pete Henderson had gone home to crash, planning to start fresh at first light. And Jimmy Clark was . . . well, Reed didn't much care where Jimmy was so long as he was elsewhere, at least for the night.

All Reed wanted right now was a little space, a little air, a little time to think—or not think, which would be even better. A walk around the town might feel good—

He heard voices from the other side of the RVs, over in the picnic area.

"But did you see that cabin? One guy couldn't have done that."

"One guy with a good-sized hammer—"

"Oh, get real!"

Reed turned and drew closer, not sneaking, but not making his presence known either. From the shadows among the trees, he recognized two Search and Rescue volunteers sitting at a table, conversing with another man who leaned against a tree. The two at the table had worked with Team 1 at the cabin that day; the guy standing, with hair in a ponytail and so blond it was nearly white, was a newcomer Reed hadn't seen before.

"I've done search and rescue after a bear attack before, up in Glacier," said the newcomer, "and let me tell you two things: number one, the victim isn't drug very far, so it doesn't take that long to find him, and number two, the victim's dead. He isn't wandering off."

"That's how it's gonna turn out," said the bald guy.

"That's how it *should* have turned out, but it didn't. We're still here."

"Well, Jimmy's setting out bait tomorrow. We'll bag the bear, and that'll be the end of it."

"Hey, wait a minute!" said the younger man in the Mariners cap. "What if Thompson and Shelton's wife staged the whole thing so they could run off together?"

"You've seen way too much TV!" said the bald one.

They were laughing.

The newcomer wasn't laughing when he said, "What if Shelton turns up with another woman?"

Reed's hands balled into fists.

The other two quit laughing.

"You serious?" the bald guy asked.

"Why not?" The newcomer took a drag on a cigarette, the orange tip glowing in the dark. "Like that cop in Spokane who shot his wife and blamed some black guy that didn't exist. These things happen."

"But what about the cabin? You think Shelton tore it all up?"

"What if a *bear* wrecked the cabin and Shelton saw an opportunity? Took out his wife *and* Randy Thompson because Thompson could have been a witness?"

The two were silent as they thought about it.

"I guess Shelton's wife was a little strange, kind of a retard," said the bald one.

"Yeah," the young one agreed. "If he's got another babe somewhere . . ."

"So what'd he do with the bodies?"

"Put 'em where we'll never find 'em," said the newcomer. He took another drag and the smoke puffed out with his words. "That way nobody will find out how they really died."

"You're sick, you know that?" the bald one replied.

"Think what you want. My money's on Shelton."

Reed wanted to meet this guy, introduce himself, share a few words of understanding, and put him on the ground. Maybe he could even acquaint the man with the natural taste and crispy texture of pine cones stuffed in that big mouth. He took a step forward—

"Reed!" It was Cap, hollering from the inn. "Reed!"

Good old Cap. Reed hurried back across the parking lot with eyes and thoughts forward.

Cap was on the porch in tee shirt and jeans. His boots were still untied. "Reed, there's been another attack!"

Shock. Relief. Horror. I-told-you-so. "Where?" Reed breathed.

Sing burst out the front door in blouse and jeans, barefoot, her hair unbraided and billowing down her back, a handheld radio close to her ear. "Two campers were attacked an hour and a half ago, six miles up Service Road 19, north of Kamayah."

"Kamayah. That's—what?—about ten miles southeast of here?" Reed said.

"Ten miles southeast," Sing confirmed, "then six miles north up that service road . . . it'd be within four to six miles of the first attack."

Cap finished tying his boots. "That thing's moving."

"Does Sheriff Mills know?"

"He and Jimmy are on their way now," Sing answered.

"What about Pete?"

Sing traded her radio for her cell phone. "I'm going to rouse him out of bed."

Reed spun around, counting vehicles and RVs, trying to guess the number of available bodies still around. "We can't give up the search *here!*"

"We won't."

Cap was insistent, excited. "We've got to see this. It could explain everything!"

Reed looked directly, boldly, at the three men having their little whodunit discussion around the picnic table. "It sure could."

· · ·

Flash! Sing, in warm coat and cap, photographed the empty frying pan lying facedown where the woods bordered the meadow. Cap was her light man; he held a strong floodlight so Sing could see what she was doing. It was close to midnight. Ground fog and campfire smoke hung along the ground and shrouded the trees in a ghostly haze.

Jimmy was shining his flashlight around the devastated campsite and counting the empty beer bottles scattered in the grass. From the breath and demeanor of the two campers huddled by the revived fire, there was no question in his mind where all the suds had gone. "Guess you've had a few beers, huh?" Jimmy said.

Apparently, Ted became obstinate and easily offended when drunk. "So what? We weren't driving!"

"You drove out of here, didn't you?"

Melanie, when drunk, became gushy and emotional. "Well, wouldn't you? Wouldn't you wanna get away if some big monster was coming after you?"

Flash! Sing captured the beer bottles, a shattered camp lantern, and a broken camp cooler.

Jimmy swept the edge of the woods with his light. "That the frying pan you hit him with?"

"That's it!" said Melanie. "He got the message!"

"I think he ate the hamburgers," said Ted.

"Looks like he ate a lot of things," Jimmy observed. "You had fruit salad lying out, hamburgers frying, eggs and bacon . . ." He walked to where the remains of a paper plate lay in the grass alongside scattered remnants of lettuce and tomato. "What was this, a salad?"

"My dinner salad," Melanie replied. "With French fries."

Flash! Sing took a shot to show the location of the ravaged salad in relation to the campsite.

Jimmy drew a breath, as if gathering patience. "Folks, you should know better than to have food like this lying around your camp. Fried foods, greasy foods, garbage like this putting out all that smell, it's a wonder you didn't attract every bear within fifty miles!"

"This-s wasn't a bear!" Ted countered, his voice slurred and unsteady. "It was a big, hairy thing! It was like K-king Kong or . . . something!"

Sing went blind in the dark. "Cap. The light."

"Oh. Sorry."

Flash! She captured a field of debris: a jacket, a paperback novel, a punctured thermos, shredded food packaging.

"What else have you had tonight?" Jimmy asked the two campers. "Any mushrooms, by chance?"

"Hey, whaddaya trying to—"

"Just be careful what you say. You don't want to get in trouble with the law."

Sheriff Mills picked up an edge of the flattened tent and looked underneath, probing with his light. Two sleeping bags were spread out; a hot rod magazine and a gardening magazine were undisturbed. There were no mushrooms.

Flash! As the sheriff held the fallen tent up, Sing captured the tent's interior.

■ ■ ■

Reed tried to keep his voice calm as he questioned Ted and Melanie Brooks. "Did it make a sound like a woman screaming?"

Their eyes got wide with the recollection. "Yeah," said Ted. "Scared us to death!"

"We thought it was somebody in trouble!" said Melanie.

"Did it walk upright?"

"Sure looked like it!"

Jimmy asked, "Was it about twenty feet tall?"

Ted and Melanie looked at each other, and then Ted answered, "Coulda been!"

"Big hairy hands?"

"I saw it using its hands, yeah! They were real hairy," said Melanie.

Jimmy nodded to himself, then called toward some flashlights sweeping and winking only a foot from the ground near the edge of the meadow, "Pete, you got anything?"

"Not yet," came Pete's voice through the murk.

"Sing, did you get a shot of this cooler here?"

"Got it," she replied, working her way toward the woods.

Mills met her with the punctured thermos in his hand. "Better bag this." The thermos had been nearly bitten in half, the tooth marks forming a jagged, saw-toothed rift.

Sing pulled a Ziploc bag from her pocket and dropped the thermos inside. "Mr. Teeth again, just like the can of beans I found at the cabin." She placed the bagged thermos in her shoulder bag.

Mills called, "Jimmy! Pete!"

"Yeah?"

"We're raising the caution level. Searchers go out in twos from now on, with at least one rifle or a sidearm between them."

"Understood," said Pete, his voice muffled by his nearness to the ground.

"You got it," said Jimmy, having a further look around. "Good idea."

Reed took hold of Jimmy's arm to get his attention. "Jimmy, you heard 'em, right? They saw the same thing we did!"

"Reed," Jimmy said, "didn't you hear the questions you were asking? You were leading the witnesses. Give me a break!"

"Jimmy! What's it gonna take to—"

Jimmy put his hand on Reed just to hold him steady—and quiet. "Reed, listen," he whispered, "you don't want to get lumped in with those people. They're drunk, they might be on drugs—"

"But they—"

"Reed! They're bad for you. They're two fruitcakes who did everything a stupid camper can do to attract a bear!"

"But it wasn't a bear!"

"Shh! *Don't!*" Jimmy looked around, clearly afraid that someone may have heard that. "Reed. Look at me. I'm talking as your friend. This could be a real break. This has to be the same bear, which means we have a fresh trail. We might even be able to backtrack from here and get some kind of lead on Beck. Now . . ." He put his finger in Reed's face to hold him in check. "Reed, I'm telling you—don't ruin it. We've got plenty of volunteers ready to work with us *as long as* they're good and clear on what it is they're doing. If there's a bear to be tracked down and killed, they're with us. But if you start going on about some big, hairy . . ." He looked around again. "They're talking already. Some of them are having some real doubts about what we're doing and about you, and you don't want that. You want them on your side."

Headlights illumined the camp as a truck pulled up.

Jimmy searched Reed's face a moment. "Reed, am I getting through?"

Reed whispered hurriedly, "You don't believe me, do you?"

"What difference does it make as long as we find Beck?"

The blinding headlights obliterated anything and everything

behind them until the engine quit, the lights winked out, and four men walked into the dull orange glow of the campfire. All four were armed with rifles. The first two were Steve Thorne, the buzz-cut "marine," and a close partner Reed recognized right away, the man with the near-white hair, whose "money was on Shelton." Ol' White Hair had one of his picnic-table buddies with him, the kid in the Mariners cap, Sam Marlowe. The fourth was the hunter named Janson.

"Hey, guys," said Jimmy. "Probably won't need you till we get some light."

"Couldn't wait," said White Hair. "We brought the overnight gear. We can camp out here 'til morning."

Reed eyed him steadily but did not offer his hand. "I'm Reed Shelton."

The man just eyed him back with a wry smile on his face. "Wiley Kane, from Missoula. Glad to be along."

Reed shot a glance at Jimmy, then engaged Wiley Kane one more time. "Looks like it's happened again."

Kane nodded emphatically. "Oh, yeah. It's a rogue bear all right. I've seen this kind of thing before."

"Yeah. Right. A bear." Reed stole one more look at Jimmy, who returned his look approvingly.

"Reed?" It was Sing's voice, coming from behind Cap's light near the edge of the woods. "Can we see you a second?"

"Excuse me." He was more than glad to be somewhere else. He made his way through the grass to where Sing and Cap awaited him, dark shapes against the white, wiggling background of flashlight beams in the fog.

"Come on," said Sing, "and step where we step."

He followed them, his flashlight on their feet, as they moved through the grass in a single file toward Pete Henderson and the man helping him. Immediately to their left, peeking through the creeping fog and smoke, a trail of bent-over grass skirted the edge of the woods and then broke into clear ground.

Pete was on his knees and bent over, measuring a print while his assistant held a light at a low angle along the ground, bringing out the shadows. Without looking up, he said, "Reed, I think it's your critter."

They encircled a patch of bare ground next to a dry streambed, flooding it with their flashlight beams. When the stream ran during the rainy months, this patch of ground was a shallow eddy of standing water, the bottom lined with a thick layer of silt. The water had receded for the summer, leaving the silt in a smooth, moist state, perfect for registering a footprint—which it had done.

"This is big medicine," said the assistant, holding his light steady as Pete measured and sketched in his pocket notebook.

Pete looked up. "Reed Shelton, this is Marty Elkhorn. He runs the store down in Kamayah. The campers used his phone to call us."

Reed offered his hand. "Have you met Cap and Sing?"

Elkhorn nodded, his face grim, his wrinkles deep in the bouning light of the flashlights. He looked up at Sing. "Pete tells me you're Coeur d'Alene."

She nodded.

"Shoshone," he replied. He gazed at the print that was starkly lit like a feature on the moon. "So you must know the warnings, the things our fathers taught us."

Sing gazed over Pete's shoulder at the print, her face eerily cold and statuesque in the weak light. "*Tsiatko?*"

Elkhorn nodded, the fear in his eyes chilling. "The wild men."

Pete looked up from his work. "Marty, I do appreciate your traditions, but this is an *animal*."

"No! Don't think that! The Indians didn't make up the *tsiatko*. They were here before we were! We knew about them before the white man came, and they have always been with us! Every tribe has its own name for them. *Oh-Mah*, the hairy giants. *Skookum*, the evil wood-spirits."

Sing offered, "And I believe the Salish word is *sess-ketch*."

Elkhorn nodded. "When the white man came, he pronounced it his own way: *Sasquatch*."

The mist crawled on their skin and the darkness closed in on them as every eye focused on the print, deeply impressed in the black silt. The heel was distinct, with clear dermal ridges, but the forward half of the foot had shifted in the track, leaving a smeared impression.

Reed was just as mesmerized as the others but had to be sure, at long last, that he could accept his own memories. "Pete, what in the world is it?"

Pete finished jotting down his measurements. "Fifteen inches long, six wide. It's not a perfect match with the other prints we found, but those prints were nowhere as clear as this one, so we might allow for that." He pointed. "Four clear toe impressions, and this dip here must be the fifth. No claws. I'm gonna figure he was at the cabin last night, and at the waterfall." He glanced toward the wrecked camp where Jimmy and the hunters were combing through the mess. "This ol' boy's temper is sure a match."

Elkhorn was getting more agitated the more they talked about it. He finally rose to his feet. "We can't stay here. This is big medicine. *Tsiatko* has taken this ground."

"It has my wife!" Reed objected.

"Of course it does! That's what *tsiatko* does when it finds men on his ground." He looked at the others, then pointed at the print. "And you think this is the only one? There are more.

They've come to these woods, and you won't see them either, not before they come in the night and take you!"

Sing tried to explain to the others, "Many of our parents raised us to believe that, if we weren't good, the giants would come and take us away." She added, as politely as possible, "For some of us, these traditions are ingrained in our thinking."

Elkhorn, all the more resolute and fearful, stood eye to eye, nose to nose with Reed. "It has your wife. What more do I need to say?" Suddenly, in what seemed an act of madness, Elkhorn dropped the flashlight, threw up both his hands, and shouted to the forest in a shrill voice, "Elkhorn is leaving! Do you hear me? Elkhorn will never set foot on this land again! His wife and his children will never set foot here! Do you hear me?"

Now the campers, hunters, Jimmy, and Sheriff Mills were looking.

Elkhorn bolted and ran across the meadow, through the tattered campsite, and to his old car. He opened the driver's door but stood to shout one more time, his arm upraised, "Elkhorn is gone, do you hear? He will never come here again!" Then, with his engine roaring and his wheels spewing gravel, he got out of there.

Jimmy hollered to Pete, "Where'd you get *him*?"

"Crazy Injun," said Kane.

"Pete! What are you looking at over there?"

"Prints," Pete answered.

"Okay," Jimmy said. "This bear's a regular camp raider. Tomorrow we put up some bear stands and put out some bait."

"Good idea," said the white-haired Kane. "I'll take the first shift."

"I'll back you up," said Thorne.

Jimmy rubbed his hands together briskly. "Okay, you two guys set up at the cabin. Janson and Sam, you take this site. We'll have both locations covered. It'll be a shooting gallery."

Pete waited, but Jimmy's attention was elsewhere. "Won't even look at 'em," Pete muttered. "Reed, maybe you can hold the light."

Reed picked up the flashlight and stooped down, once again illuminating the print in the silt. "Pete, what is it?"

Pete had to consider a moment before answering. "Could I please not have to answer that—at least 'til an answer comes to me? I've been tracking in and around this county for fifteen years, and I've never seen a track like this one. No question, though: whatever it is, it's one mean critter and we've gotta find it."

Sing snapped some photos and then said in an aside to her husband, "Cap . . ."

"What?" Then he wagged his head. "No, no, I'm not jumping to any conclusions—and neither should you."

"Conclusions about what?" Reed asked, impatient.

"I've seen how it works," Cap said. "People believe what they want to believe, and if they want to believe something badly enough, they can see things that aren't there or not see things that are."

"So what are you saying?"

"I'm saying . . ." Reed could tell that Cap was trying to be careful. "I'm saying we really, *really* want Beck to be alive. It's *the* driving force in our minds right now; it's dominating our emotions."

"So?"

"So . . . what if we just don't *want* it to be a bear?"

Now Reed stood to face him. "Now *you* think I'm seeing things, is that it?"

"Reed, maybe we *all* are because we *want* to. I admit, I really *want* to believe that something just picked Beck up and carried her off, because that opens up limitless possibilities, even fantasies that are a whole lot easier to handle than—" His sentence hit a wall. "See? I can't even say it."

Pete broke in, his hand outstretched. "Reed, I need that light."

Still looking testily at Cap, Reed slapped the flashlight into Pete's hand.

Sing intervened. "Cap, unless I'm wrong, you have it backward." He looked as though he would have come back with something if he *had* something. "You believe it, Cap, and not because you want to; you *don't* want to! You've been arguing with yourself ever since this whole thing started."

"Now I know it wasn't a bear," said Pete. He shone his flashlight farther up the dry streambed, illuminating a strange, lumpy pile. He approached the new discovery and they semicircled around him like a nature class, flashlights centered on a pile of fresh droppings—lobed lumps loosely connected in a chain by strands of leaves, grass, rodent hair, and paper food packaging.

"It's only a few hours old," said Pete. "But no bear leaves scat like this."

Sing looked at Cap and said softly, "Does it look familiar at all?" She gave him time to ponder while she aimed her camera and took some more pictures.

Cap studied the droppings. From the look on his face, the news was bad, and the longer he looked, the worse it seemed to get. The others fell silent, waiting for his answer.

Finally, after a fleeting glimpse at Sing, he asked Pete, "Can I get a sample?"

"Take the whole thing," said Pete.

Sing was already pulling out a Ziploc bag. The droppings were soft, loose, and messy; it was difficult to preserve their original shape as she spooned them up. "I'll get you those hairs as well. And I've got a thermos here you should take along. Saliva."

"Let me get some sleep and I'll leave for Spokane tomorrow— or is it today?"

"It's today," said Sing.

Reed was speechless for a moment, but finally he met Cap's eyes and said, "You're the one, Cap. Any help you can give us . . ."

Cap made sure the bag was properly sealed as he replied, "Well, it's a chance to sleep in my own bed again. But this is a long shot. They may not even let me in the door."

"Try the back," said Sing.

Cap weighed that a moment. "If they catch me, I'll tell them you said it was okay."

"You do that." She winked at him.

"So what do we tell Jimmy?" Reed asked.

"Aw," said Pete, rubbing his tired eyes, "just let him and his boys hunt their doggone bear. Cap's right; people believe what they want—but it's gonna be the weirdest bear they've ever seen." He shoved his notebook back in his pocket. "I gotta crawl into my truck and get some sleep. Don't let anybody mess up these tracks. And, Reed?"

"Yeah?"

"You're not crazy, so get to work."

"What do you want me to do?"

"Do . . . cop stuff. Find a pattern or something, one of those whatchamacallits . . . an MO. Any information's useful." Pete trudged on by. "It's time somebody else did some of the work around here."

Reed watched Pete disappear into the darkness and fog, and then met the eyes of Cap and Sing.

Cap looked away a moment, taking in the trashed campsite, the mysterious footprint, and the plastic bag in his hand, then met Reed's eyes again. "There *is* a chance you're not crazy."

"Far from it," said Sing.

Suddenly Reed had only a vague memory of feeling helpless and despondent in another time, another place. He could recall

feeling like a liar even though he'd never lied, but now he had
friends who believed. His mind began to turn over like an old car
out of mothballs. "So . . . we really do have two occurrences, in
two different places—No! *Three* attacks: Randy on Monday—we
need to verify from Arlen Peak just when Randy went up there.
Did somebody ask him that already? Then Beck on Monday
night—and I can place that at about 11:30. Now we have this one,
Ted and Melanie . . . ?"

"Brooks," said Sing.

"Brooks. Okay, you've got their contact information?"

"Got it."

"Cap, you'll stay in touch, right?"

"I'll have my cell phone," he answered, "or you can just leave
a message at the house."

"If we all stay in regular contact, we can swap any new
information. Sing, what about your mobile lab? Think we can
use it?"

"We'll head home and I can bring it in the morning," she
replied.

Reed was actually thinking, and it felt good. "Load it up. We
need your computer, all your forensic stuff, and let's get a batch
of GPS transceivers with peer-to-peer positioning, one for each
of us."

Sing raised an eyebrow. "With satellite feed to a master con-
sole on a PC?"

Reed liked that. "That'll work."

Sing wrote it down.

Reed began to fidget and pace. "There might be a pattern
here, something we can extrapolate both directions, past and
future. We've seen three attacks, but there could have been
more." He stopped abruptly, afraid he was getting ahead of himself. "Does that make sense?"

Cap smiled. "Just keep going, Reed. You're doing fine."

He needed that. "Okay. I'll get on it." He took off for the cars. "Can you drop me by the Cave Lake trailhead to get my car?"

Sing and Cap exchanged an arched look and followed close on his heels. "You got it," said Cap.

"Sheriff Mills!" Reed said.

Mills was finishing up, tossing garbage bags into the trunk of his car. "Yeah?"

"Is the office open? I need the computer."

Mills didn't ask why. Something in Reed's manner and tone must have answered that question. He just smiled the faintest hint of a smile, dug in his pocket, and tossed Reed the key.

SEVEN

Beck couldn't sleep. Lying against the beast's immense body provided plenty of heat, but Beck's slender rib cage, shoulders, and hips—not to mention her constantly complaining ankle—could only endure the bumpy, rocky ground for a minute or two before she had to wriggle, reposition, roll, curl, and search for some other way to get comfortable. The beast must have been uncomfortable too. She was squirming and rolling as much as Beck was, which gave Beck one more concern to keep her awake: making sure the big female didn't roll on top of her.

Finally, one brief moment of sleep came when the female lay on her back, her forearm over her eyes, and Beck found a way to lie against that big stomach with her head on the female's breast. Now, that worked—

Until the beast rolled and sat up, dumping Beck onto the ground again.

"Oww!" A rock jabbed Beck in her rump, her elbow took a gouge from another hard spot, and, of course, her ankle gave her a sharp reminder. Sitting there on the rocks, in the cold light of a half-moon, Beck whimpered. Anywhere else it may have seemed childish, but out here, who would fault her? Certainly not the ape, who seemed to be ignoring her anyway, lumbering over to a grove of young firs and inspecting them, first one, then another, then another. She tugged at their branches, sniffed them, yanked them hard enough to make their branches quake and their tops whip about.

She found a ten-footer she liked. With one hand and one lazy, apish move, she tore it out of the ground, looked around for a good spot, and flopped it down. She then probed and poked around in the grove like a woman at a yard sale until she found another one she liked. With no apparent strain, she plucked it up and laid it next to the first. Starting at one end, she moved along, removing the branches with deft little twists of her hands, and laid the branches side by side across the two tree trunks.

Beck watched in amazement—this big ape was actually building a nest to sleep on. Beck wondered why it had taken her half a night of sleeping on rocks to think of it.

Now the beast was gathering leafy limbs from surrounding undergrowth and laying them on top of the framework she'd made, mashing them down with her hands. She was quite absorbed in her work, which presented Beck an opportunity she knew would not last long. Of course, judging from the urgent signals she was getting from her bladder and bowels, she would not *need* long.

The squashed roll of toilet paper Beck found in her coat pocket was nothing short of manna from heaven. The two smooth logs, with a comfortable gap between them, lying in an enclosure of maple and syringa bushes, were like a tabernacle in the wilderness.

It went well. It was worth staying up half the night for. Never, ever in her life did she imagine herself doing such a thing, but now, as she began to unroll a length of toilet paper, she breathed a prayer of thanks.

The leaves rustled and she looked up.

The big female was watching her, head cocked in fascination. *Different rules,* Beck reminded herself. *Different rules!*

The female came right in, pushing through the limbs and leaves and settling in front of Beck to see how the whole process worked. The toilet paper held special fascination for her. She reached out tentatively to touch it.

Beck tore off one little piece and gave it to her. She sniffed it, then put a corner on her tongue. Unimpressed, she tried to spit it out. It stuck to her tongue, so she tried again, then finally rolled it off against her upper lip and blew it away.

Having completed her task, Beck quickly pocketed the roll, reassembled herself, and rose gingerly. She hobbled out of the enclosure, hand-over-handing along the logs, expecting the female would follow her.

But the female didn't follow her.

Beck turned, curious, just as the bushes opposite the enclosure quaked, then parted, and the big gray female and her son burst headlong into the clearing like children after tossed candy.

How? She'd had no idea they were there, no indication, and—

And apparently Beck's female had not been the only one watching! Beck was mortified, and even more so to see how fascinated these creatures were with her most recent accomplishment. They probed and sniffed. They were almost fighting over it.

Since Beck was on their turf, and even the young ape outweighed her at least three to one, she backed off and gave them all the space they needed. Hopefully they would like whatever it was they were learning.

Then the juvenile's eyes darted elsewhere, his attention cut short by an eerie, faraway whistle. The two females became alert and silent, heads erect, eyes shifting. Beck was more than alert; so far, whistles had not brought good news.

From somewhere in the dark, far beyond the enclosure, an animal was calling, first in a low whistle and then in a low, guttural rumble like boulders tumbling.

The gray female answered in a whistle and then a low-pitched, subdued moan, chin jutting, lips pursed in a tight little O. When a rumbling reply came back, the three apes huddled, grudges apparently put on hold, eyes searching beyond the enclosure, anticipating something as they grunted and snuffed at each other.

For Beck, dread had become normal, changing only in degree. She peered through the trees, side-glancing at the others for any clues about which way to look. Part of her, like a hopeful child, wondered if it might be a team of rescuers come to take her back, but the rest of her knew better.

The forest on the mountainside was broken into smaller, struggling clumps of stunted firs and pines: black, saw-toothed cones against a moon-washed sky. A soft, distant rustling directed Beck's attention to a black mass of trees that swelled sideways until one tree separated from the others, walking, spreading in size as it approached. Beck perceived the shape of this new shadow from the stars and sky vanishing behind it: broad, lumbering shoulders; thick neck; high, crested head; huge arms, with hair like Spanish moss.

Like little kids caught in mischief, the females and the juvenile scurried out of Beck's makeshift outhouse, looking over their shoulders and panting little exclamations to each other. Beck's female, with typical surprising speed, swept Beck up in her arms, and Beck, in typical fashion, rode along, like it or not. They dove into the stand of young firs and sat on the female's nest as if they'd all built it, the other female overtly fascinated with her own fingernails; the juvenile cuddling up against his mother; and Beck's female doting on Beck, first dropping her onto the nest as if she could handle being dropped, then nudging her this way and that way as if to make Beck comfortable. Beck did not appreciate the poking and prodding. There was so much of it, it was sure to draw the big male's attention.

The big newcomer sensed—most likely *smelled*—something outside of normal before he even got there. He had been moving swiftly, silently, like a spirit through the broken forest and over the rocks, but now, just outside the grove of firs, he moved one careful, exploratory step at a time, sniffing and huffing suspiciously, looking about for whatever was wrong.

This had to be the daddy, all eight feet of him. He was covered in coarse black hair; his face was one big scowl in a leathery mask, and Beck had never seen such piercing eyes, each cornea reflecting the moon in a diamond of light. He carried a slain deer in his left arm, its head dangling on a broken neck. Preoccupied, he dropped it.

Beck knew what was wrong—*she* was wrong—but she hadn't a clue what to do about it. All she could do was cower behind the red female's big frame and—

That option vanished. Abruptly, the other female dropped facedown to the ground, bowing on all fours with her head low, rumbling and clicking her tongue in homage. Beck's female, as if reminded of her manners, dove to the ground and did the same. The young one, because he was a male, or because he was still a juvenile and not expected to know any better, did not participate in the ritual but sat where he was, glancing in Beck's direction as if to guide the alpha male to the proper target.

Beck, now on open display, had never felt so caught-and-in-trouble in her life. Her hand went unconsciously to her neck, as the images of both Randy Thompson and the dead deer flashed through her mind.

And she *was* in trouble. The male leaped backward in shock, eyes wide, a raspy huff gushing from his throat and his hair bristling on end. With steamy breath rushing through his nostrils, he glared at Beck and then at the two females, muscles tense, teeth bared.

He thinks I'm a threat!

Learning—fast—from the other two females, Beck flopped to the ground and bowed.

The thing didn't move. After three or four seconds, Beck was still alive.

The other female moved aside and enfolded her son, leaving the big red female to explain.

Beck's female rose to her knees and reached for Beck—

The male shot forward, took the female by the scruff of the neck, and threw her into a row of young firs, bending them over like field grass. She screamed, arms covering her face, white teeth glinting in the moonlight, as she slid down the bent trunks—

He grabbed her before she reached the ground and threw her again, this time into a larger tree that shuddered as she bounced off its furrowed trunk and thudded to the ground. She cried in pain.

Beck didn't have to think long or hard. There was absolutely no safety here, no hope of living. She pushed herself from the ground and hobbled and hopped out of the grove, dragging one foot while she jumped with the other, fleeing from one branch to another, stumbling from trunk to trunk, groping for anything that would bear her up and keep her moving. She could still hear the female screaming and the alpha male roaring; she heard the blows and felt the ground shake. It didn't matter that she had no idea where she was; the only thing that mattered was being else-where, anywhere but here. She pulled herself, pushed herself, counting the inches, desperate for distance.

The screaming stopped. Beck could easily imagine the big female's head nearly twisted off, her tongue hanging, her eyes rolling. So much for Beck's protector. Their strange, unnatural interlude was over, leaving Beck lost and unwelcome in a scratching, entangling, tripping darkness with nowhere to go that was anywhere. She fell against a tree—she didn't find it; it found her, and it hurt. She remained still, just breathing, waiting for the pain in her ankle to subside enough for her to take one more step.

Now that she was quiet, she realized that the woods were not. Somewhere behind her came a crashing, a crackling, and the thudding of heavy footfalls.

"N-n-n-no . . . no . . ." She forced herself onward, tripped over a log, and rolled among fallen branches, clenching her teeth to stifle a scream. She reached, groped, tried to sit up and get her legs under her. Her good leg moved. The sprained one was stuck and punished her severely for pulling. She pulled anyway and couldn't help a whimper of pain. She was free.

The thing was coming closer, moving through the tangle with unbelievable speed.

Randy Thompson. This was how it was for him!

She tried to climb the tree but found no handholds. She lunged forward, leaping on her one good leg, groping for any branch, any tree trunk—

Huge hairy arms grabbed her around her middle and jerked her backward, knocking the wind out of her. She screamed, she kicked, she tried to wriggle free.

The arms were like iron.

■ ■ ■

Willard, Idaho, was a loosely arranged, quiet little town of red brick storefronts, older farmhouses on hillsides, and scattered modular homes on weedy lots. It was like many in Idaho, built in a day when timber and mining were sure to make money and folks thought there would be some point in living there. Today it survived as the Whitcomb County seat with a proud, pillared courthouse. Down this old building's tight corridors and behind its many doors with the frosted windows were all the entities that held the county together: the district court and judge, the prosecuting attorney, the county commissioners, Planning and Zoning, Disaster Services, County Assessor, Social Services, and on and on, enough to fill the building directory on the wall just inside the front door.

If someone wished to find the county sheriff, the directory would send that person next door to the newer building meant to serve as an expansion of the old one. This building was white concrete block, one story, plain and practical, intended for a specific purpose, which was to house the county sheriff's office and the county jail. Inside the front door was a reception counter; behind that were four desks, a fairly neat one for the secretary and three generally cluttered ones for the deputies; to the right was Sheriff Patrick Mills's private office, a separate room with a door he usually kept open. To the left and through an archway was the examining station for driver's licenses, complete with two testing booths, an eye chart, a camera, and two green footprints painted on the floor to show the applicant where to stand for his or her photo.

In a corner behind the counter and past the four desks was the computer station. There were other computers in the building, but this was the "department" computer, the one strictly devoted to law enforcement, available to any member of the staff for the performance of his or her duty. Some months ago, a flight simulator and a commando game had cropped up in a coded folder on the computer's desktop, but these were not openly discussed and only discreetly used.

Right now, with everyone gone but the night jailer and all calls forwarded to the central dispatcher, Reed sat at the computer in the light of a single desk lamp, the blue glow from the monitor on his face, an overlapped clutter of windows and boxes on the screen. He was tapping and clicking his way through the multiple levels and links of the National Center for the Analysis of Violent Crime, a networking tool used by law-enforcement agencies all around the country in tracking criminals and sharing investigative information. The program had subgroups for different categories of crime, regions of the country, and types of criminals, with subgroups under those, and side links from those. Sifting downward through all the levels could have been tough for someone who hadn't slept in more than twenty-four hours, but Reed knew what he was after and pushed away sleep as he pushed through the program.

Maybe Jimmy and the others—including bigmouth Kane from Missoula—did know the woods and had good reason for their opinions. They were outdoorsmen and Reed was a cop; so maybe Reed was a little out of his realm of competence.

He tapped the keys, hammered the backspace and tried again, clicking the mouse.

But then again, maybe they didn't know everything, and maybe he did know something. Just standing around and letting them tell him what to think wasn't going to resolve the question, nor was it going to expedite the process. Enough of that. Reed had a brain and skills of his own. He was going to do cop stuff, whatever it took to find Beck.

Was there a pattern? Whatever this beast was, had it attacked anyone else, anywhere else? If so, when? Where had it come from, and which way was it going? Was there anything more they could find out about it?

Reed finally clicked his way into a subgroup that linked and compared known homicides with unexplained deaths, a program intended to help law enforcement detect homicides that may not have been recognized as such. In a few more mouse clicks, he narrowed the time frame down to the last two weeks, and the region to his own and the three neighboring counties. The pickings were slim: a hit-and-run outside a tavern, and a logging accident. The tavern was far to the west, in another county, and took place a week ago.

The logging accident . . .

Reed read the entry again, carefully noted the location, and then checked a map.

Ooookayyy. He clicked, nearly *banged,* the "print" command and then fidgeted while the paper slowly rolled out of the printer. By the time it had finished, he had his coat on. With the printout in his hand, he turned off the lamp and got out of there.

■ ■ ■

With a slightly gentler drop than the last time, Beck landed back on the nest in the grove, limp and despondent. She'd given up trying to understand. The big red female, moving stiffly from her own bruises, had brought her back and now hunched over her, nudging, stroking, fussing.

Beck grunted and pushed her hand away. *I'm going to die anyway, thanks to you. What's left to fuss about?*

Her eye was on the alpha male as he shared the dead deer with the other two just outside the grove. He slurped blood, ripped flesh from hide, tore the meat with his teeth and hands, and chewed, his mouth and chin bloodied. He looked her way only once as he chewed, just long and intensely enough to send a message of loathing, making sure she knew she didn't belong. After that, for as long as Beck watched him, he paid her no mind; he just kept eating.

Beck looked away. Maybe that was the end of it. Maybe for now, her captor "mother" had gotten her way and the male had relented—grudgingly, of course. But he'd sent his message loud and clear.

All things considered, this should be bearable. It beat being thrown against a tree or having her head ripped off. Beck glanced at her aching feet and the recent scratches on her hands from all those dry, prickly branches in the dark. This was the worst that had happened to her. She was alive for one more moment, maybe one more night. She should be glad.

She broke down and cried.

The big female sank onto the nest beside her with a quiet groan and pulled her in close, an act of affection that only worsened Beck's despair. Beck was too upset to say it; she could only think it: *Why can't you just let me go?*

The beast got a message—the wrong message. She immediately extended her hand toward the others and pig grunted.

They ignored her, so she grunted more insistently, rocking back and forth.

The male finally looked her way as if doing her one more additional, very troublesome favor, then regarded what was left of the deer. With indifference, he took hold of the head in one hand and the shoulder in the other, and wrenched the head and neck from the body. When the female grunted imploringly one more time, he tossed it to her.

It flopped at her feet, throwing blood. She picked it up, obviously glad to get it. With slow, lazy-fingered deliberation, she turned it over and over, sniffing and studying as if she'd never seen one before, and then, breaking the jaw open, she yanked out the tongue and bit the end off.

Beck looked the other way, feeling sick. How could God create such creatures? And even worse, how could He throw her in with them? She never asked for this. She wouldn't have been able to conceive such a horror to ask for.

The female grunted and nudged her. She winced and would not turn her head. The female nudged her again, grunting, and Beck ventured a timid look with one eye.

The ape was offering her a string of meat. Beck couldn't recognize where it had come from, which was a good thing. She shook her head, her mouth clamped shut.

The lady dangled the meat in front of her face and wiggled it so it thumped against her lips. It reminded Beck of when she tried to feed worms to a baby robin. The robin wouldn't eat and soon died.

Thump! The meat hit her face again. Beck reached up and took it as the female intensely, relentlessly watched.

It's a strip of bacon, Beck told herself. *It's like sushi. It's rack of lamb without the rack*, really *rare. It's steak on the platter right before the barbecue.*

Building up to the moment, Beck put the slightest tip of the meat between her teeth and nipped it off. As she pressed it against her tongue, the flavor came through, and really, it wasn't half bad. It was raw and tasted a little "wild," but it was meat. A little salt would have helped, she supposed, but . . .

She bit off another piece and chewed it slowly on one side of her mouth and then the other. She swallowed it, and then, of all things, she wondered if there might be more. She was hungry.

Her female captor was still working on the tongue but found a nice strip from the back of the neck and bit it off to give to her.

I'm eating, Beck thought. That was nothing unusual in itself, but it taxed her sanity to think she was taking part in this meal, in this setting, with these creatures. They were bloody, fearsome carnivores who were sharing a deer's head with her, but she was eating it. They had blood and grease on their fingers, but so did she. They were disgusting to watch, but she was gaining an appreciation for how hunger could supplant politeness; she could relate—sort of.

The female handed her another strip of flesh, and Beck received it gladly, chewing it down. That seemed to please the beast. She reached down and fingered the fringes on Beck's brown buckskin coat. Then with her index finger, she hooked and twirled a strand of Beck's reddish-brown hair.

Beck dared to take hold of the hand and give it a furtive stroke, an action she knew worked on dogs, cats, and horses.

It communicated. The lady gave a grunt, then another. The tone wasn't angry, but seemed comforting.

Beck couldn't speak it, but the big red lady—and her hot-tempered gray rival—reminded Beck of Rachel and Leah, Jacob's two wives in the Bible. Leah could bear children, but Rachel could not. Beck didn't know if that was the case here, but she felt sorry for the red lady anyway. She gave the hand a little pat and looked up into that quizzical, leathery face. "R-roo-Rachel."

"Hmmph," Rachel replied, rotating the deer's head in search of another bite.

Beck watched the others who were still eating, wolfing down the heart and liver and gnawing on the ribs. She'd made their acquaintance, she realized—they'd sniffed and studied her excreta and she'd eaten from their deer's head. Naming them would be appropriate. The other female's name would have to be Leah, the biblical Rachel's rival for the favor and attention of . . . Jacob. And the brat? Well, the biblical Jacob's firstborn son was named Reuben. It was difficult to give a name she liked to a creature she didn't like, but it would have to do.

As for what these creatures were, the time had come to settle on that as well. Like most anyone else, Beck had heard some snippets of the Bigfoot legend; she'd heard some of the stories, seen a poster for a Sasquatch monster movie, even recalled seeing Bigfoot as a cartoon character. In close-up reality, these creatures were so different from their legend that it was difficult to relate the two, but legend and myth weren't difficult to discard when sharing a meal with the real thing.

These were Sasquatches—real ones.

Beck accepted another string of venison from Rachel's hand and chewed on it thoughtfully, feeling just a little more oriented now that she'd named and identified everybody. The group almost felt like a big, hairy family, not entirely dysfunctional, but having some issues, to be sure, and Beck was one of them.

Had she been observing all this from her own little world at home, it would have been entirely too bizarre.

■ ■ ■

Wednesday morning, Jimmy Clark stood beside the sorry, splintered cabin and took a 360-degree look around the ravine, nodding to himself. "Yeah. He's out there, and we're gonna bring him in." He unknotted the top of the black plastic garbage bag he'd brought all the way up the trail from Abney and let the contents—four dozen day-old doughnuts—rumble and tumble into the bottom of a sawed-off steel drum.

"Okay, let's mix in the scraps."

That was Steve Thorne's job. He, Jimmy, and Wiley Kane had tossed coins that morning, and Steve was the odd man. That gave him the privilege of packing in the bacon grease, kitchen scraps, and dish scrapings from Arlen Peak's café, sealed inside a five-gallon plastic pickle bucket. Steve poured the mixture in with the doughnuts.

Jimmy spoke to the forest, "Okay, big guy, come and get it!"

"So what now?" Kane asked while Steve trotted in search of breathable air.

Jimmy pointed up the hill to a spot not far from where Reed and Beck had camped that first horrible night. "As long as the air's moving up the draw, you take that ledge. It'll make a good blind, and the angle ought to give you a clear shot through the heart and lungs. When night comes and things cool down . . ." He pointed to another high spot down the ravine from the cabin. "I'd set up in there and break out the night scope."

Thorne asked, "Aren't we gonna get relieved?"

Jimmy wasn't happy about his answer. "Some of the guys have gone home. I've got four hunters left to man the bear stands, and the sheriff has whoever's left going with the trackers."

Kane ventured, "It wouldn't have anything to do with all that 'Bigfoot' talk, would it?"

"What do you think? No man with better things to do wants to be out here day and night on a snipe hunt, and some of them think that's what this is."

"Should have brought a book to read," Thorne muttered.

"Well, the other two are no better off—no, they're *worse* off. That campsite's on level ground, so they have to sit up in a tree all day and all night, just the two of them."

"Well, all the more bear for us four," said Kane.

"*If* the search crews don't scare the thing off." Jimmy shook his head. "Well, that's none of your concern. Take turns relieving each other and sleep when you can. You've got your radios. Check in every even-numbered hour."

■ ■ ■

Pete and his whittled-down crew worked their way slowly up the drainage from the site of last night's camp raid, somewhat refreshed from a short night's sleep but not encouraged by today's progress.

They did have a plan: Joanie and Chris, with two armed searchers, were working the area above where they found the backpack, hoping to pick up a trail again. Pete and his crew were tracking backwards from the campsite, hoping to meet up with them coming the other way. If it worked, the two teams would have covered the creature's trail from the first location to the second. It was along that trail that they hoped to find whatever remained of Beck Shelton.

But the plan wasn't coming together. Some of the hunters had bowed out—for no good reason, as far as Pete was concerned—and because of the apparent danger and Sheriff Mills's order to carry firearms, the searchers who weren't comfortable with weapons had to stand down. Don, one of his key flankers, had called early that morning to express his disinterest in tracking "Indian legends" and to tell Pete that he was staying home. Medical personnel were on standby.

That left Tyler to help with the tracking, one searcher—Benny—to keep an eye out for any signs of Beck, and only one designated hunter, the bald guy named Max Johnson. Both Pete and Tyler had to carry rifles on their backs, which were becoming a real nuisance during the bending, crawling, and crouching that tracking required.

On top of all that, the trail of this creature, whatever it was, was unpredictable and rambling, cutting through thick serviceberry, syringa, and bracken fern that cluttered and confused everything. Sometimes the trail joined with established game trails, where it became obliterated by elk and deer prints. Unlike hoofed animals, this creature moved about on soft, padded feet that left little disturbance and no claw marks. An occasional impression in soft soil helped, but trying to find the next track, and then the next, and then the next, in constantly changing environments, was exhausting.

The searchers were feeling it too. Pete could tell by their conversation in the trees just a few yards downhill.

"Can't they make this hill any steeper?" Benny asked, puffing a little.

"I hope we don't have to go clear to the top," said Max. "I mean, just between you and me, we're never going to find her. She's table scraps by now."

"So what about the bear? How are Fish and Game going to bag that thing if we're up here chasing it off?"

Pete was wearing out from the tracking and wearing thin from the whining. "Gentlemen, let's keep the noise to a minimum, shall we?"

■ ■ ■

Beck didn't realize she was asleep until Rachel stirred, rolled, and woke her up. At first Beck groped for that same comfortable spot on Rachel's belly so she could rest her head there, but daylight hit her eyes and she realized it was midmorning. She and Rachel had slept quite a while, considering they were on the ground again and having to cope with rocks, bumps, and a limited menu of not-quite-comfortable positions. A few feet away, the rest of the family lay fast asleep on Rachel's nest, awkwardly entangled but clearly comfortable, enjoying the fruits of her labor.

Rachel rolled again, then sat up, alert, silent, sniffing the air and listening.

From the hairy, leggy mass on the nest, Jacob raised his head, eyes stern, nostrils flaring as he sampled the air. Whatever was bothering Rachel was bothering him.

■ ■ ■

Max said something funny, and Benny started laughing.

Pete straightened up, not wanting to be a babysitter. "Tyler, perhaps you can clue these guys in?"

Tyler faded back to have a word with them.

■ ■ ■

Jacob rolled off the nest with liquid grace, his hands and feet contacting tree trunks, branches, and the ground with a silent, cushioned sureness, bearing him through space as if he weighed nothing. Remaining crouched in the shadows of the grove, he peered down the slope, nostrils still sampling.

Rachel had found her own little window through the firs to the outside. She crouched in that spot, riveted to whatever was happening below. Beck copied her, finding another gap in the branches.

Was that a voice she heard in the valley? It could have been a coyote, or maybe a bird.

Or maybe a human.

■ ■ ■

Benny slipped on a smooth log and fell over, hollering as he went down.

Whoosh! Up the slope, a dozen finches fluttered out of a tree.

■ ■ ■

Beck saw birds flying just above the trees in the valley below. So that's what it was.

Unless something else had scared them.

Jacob didn't make a sound, nor did he move from where he was crouching; he only turned and, with long and powerful arms, reached and yanked Leah and Reuben off the nest and slapped the sleep out of them. Leah muttered and Reuben whined, but their first focused look at Jacob's face stung them silent.

Leah squatted, and Reuben leaped upon her back. She rose to her feet and followed Jacob stealthily, hurriedly, out of the grove.

Beck wasn't ready to leave, not at all. She pushed forward through the trees for a better view of the valley.

Rachel, seeing she was left behind, was so alarmed she couldn't remember how to pick Beck up. With a sudden lurch that knocked Beck's wind out, she grabbed Beck from behind and snatched her out of the trees.

Beck wanted to scream but struggled to breathe first. Rachel had her around the hips instead of her torso, and Beck, despite a frantic effort to remain upright, flipped over, head down, her legs kicking in Rachel's face. Rachel let go of Beck's hips to grab one kicking leg, fumbled that leg in her effort to grab the other, and finally dropped Beck altogether.

Beck landed in Rachel's nest and rolled right side up, her stomach reeling as if someone had punched it. Shadows of a blackout clouded her vision. *Rachel, you klutz!*

Rachel began to whine, rotating and stamping in one place, flustered.

Beck finally found a precious breath, then another. Not wanting to die of manhandling, she waited until Rachel turned her back toward her, then she grabbed onto fistfuls of hair and pulled herself up, pushing with her good leg, until she could get her arms around Rachel's neck as she'd seen Reuben do.

Rachel finally quit stamping and turning and bolted out of the grove, racing to catch up with the others.

Had Beck heard a human voice in the valley? Wondering about it would drive her crazy.

■ ■ ■

By now, Pete's crew had made enough noise to alert every creature on the mountainside. Pete paused to breathe, to rest and calm himself.

Tyler offered, "Well, it's not like we're actually hunting . . ."

Pete responded, "Not today, we aren't."

■ ■ ■

When Sing returned with her mobile lab—a thirty-foot motor home outfitted for remote forensic and crime-scene work—she didn't drive to Abney. Reed caught her on her cell phone while she was still en route from Spokane and gave her a new place to rendezvous: behind the Chapel of Peace funeral home in Three Rivers, a lumber town about thirty miles of winding highway to the northwest of Abney, just outside the national forest. The side trip took her an extra hour and a half.

She arrived in Three Rivers just as the whistle at the sawmill signaled the end of lunch break. She drove past the big yard where sprinklers sprayed acres of stacked logs, and the sweet smell of sawdust came through the RV's air vents. The funeral home was right where Reed said it would be, on the main drag, one block down from the grade school and kitty-corner from the Three Rivers Grocery and Laundromat. It was an attractive, cedar-sided structure with a shake roof, stained-glass windows, tall firs all around, and a decorative totem pole out front, obviously carved by a white man.

"Turn in where you see the brown hearse," Reed had told her.

She swung a wide, easy turn into the parking lot, coasted past the hearse, and came to a stop at the end of a long row marked on the blacktop with white paint: *FAMILY*. Had there been a funeral, she would have been first in the procession.

When she swung the RV door open, Reed was standing right there waiting for her, far more awake than he should have been. She couldn't imagine that he'd slept much, but he had obviously showered, shaved, and gotten into his uniform. He carried a Forest Service map in his hand and some big, exciting notion in his eyes. "Sing! You've got to take a look at this guy!"

She looked around. "What guy?"

Reed was already walking. Sing assumed she was supposed to follow, and she did. They were heading for the rear entrance. "Allen Arnold. He was a logging foreman working a clear-cut up Road 27 off Highway 9." Reed unfolded the map and stopped so abruptly Sing almost ran into him. "Look at this."

She looked as he pointed.

"Okay. Here's Three Rivers. Now here's Abney, right in the middle of the national forest, about thirty, thirty-five miles southeast of here. Here's the Abney trail up to the cabin, here's Lost Creek, and here's about where the cabin is. Now: Here's Kamayah, and here's the location of the young couple's campsite."

Sing easily followed the marks Reed had made on the map. "Right. The campsite is about six miles southeast of Abney."

"So check this out." Reed traced a line with his finger, moving northwest from the campsite attack, through the cabin attack, and to an X he'd marked near a squiggly, dashed line labeled 27. "Start at the campsite above Kamayah, go northwest ten miles, and you've got the cabin at Lost Creek. From there, go another eight miles northwest and you've got the logging operation where Allen Arnold was found dead—Monday morning."

Sing studied the map, tracing the line the other direction.

"Monday morning," Sing said, "Allen Arnold the logger is found dead . . . about sixteen miles southeast of here. Monday afternoon, by our best guess, Randy Thompson is killed at the cabin on Lost Creek, about twenty-four miles southeast of here. Monday night in the same place, Beck is attacked . . ."

Reed jumped in, "Tuesday night, the campers get raided another ten miles southeast. What do you think?"

Sing cocked an eyebrow and nodded, impressed. "Is Mr. Arnold inside the funeral home?"

"He is."

"Then I think we'd better see him."

■ ■ ■

Cap watched, smiling but impatient, as the brown capuchin— commonly recognized as an "organ grinder's monkey"—ran after the rubber baton and brought it back to Nick Claybuckle, the trainer, or rather, the researcher.

"Good boy," Nick exclaimed in a pet lover's tone of voice, handing him a grape through the bars of the cage. "That's my Sparky!"

The little monkey gobbled the grape down, shooting little side glances at his cage mate, a male of similar size, age, and appearance.

"Now watch this," Nick said over his shoulder to Cap.

He said to the second capuchin, "Okay, Cyrus, go get it! Go get it!" He tossed the baton to the far end of the cage.

Cyrus sat on his haunches, his eyes shifting unhappily from Nick to Sparky and back again.

Nick held out a slice of cucumber as an incentive. "Bring me the baton and you get a cucumber!"

Cyrus turned, walked away, and sat against the wall, pouting.

Nick looked at Cap, sharing the landmark moment. "Do you see that, Dr. Capella? Inequity aversion, pure and simple!" He straightened, beaming at the results, and grabbed his clipboard to jot some notes. "You know how it is with capuchins. Cucumbers are, ehhh, okay, but grapes, wow, they're to die for! Cyrus'll trade the baton for a cucumber if Sparky gets a cucumber, but if Sparky gets a grape, hey, *No fair. I'm not playing!*"

Nick, rotund and bespectacled, would have made a great nerd in high school. Come to think of it, he made a great nerd as a graduate student.

Cap smiled and hinted, "Should I have brought a grape?"

"Huh?" He caught on. "Oh, sorry. I was just, you know, the experiment, I was really into it. Yeah, I turned in your samples."

"And?"

Nick casually scanned the room, his fingers drumming his clipboard. Halfway down the row of cages, within earshot, a young female undergraduate was observing how a capuchin reacted to its reflection in a mirror.

Nick whispered, "Um, that's Carol. She's doing a perception analysis—you know, cognitive processing of nontypical sensory inputs."

Cap whispered, "So?"

"Does she know you?"

Cap stole another look. "I don't believe so."

"Eh, let's walk around anyway."

They turned and walked casually out of Primate Lab 1, went one door down the hall, and peeked into Primate Lab 2. This room was like the other—long, clean, and well lit, with a bank of cages along each side. These cages housed rhesus monkeys, some playing, some sleeping, some just staring through the bars. There were no humans in the room at the time, so Nick stepped inside and Cap followed.

When the door clicked shut, Nick took a CD from his pocket and handed it over. "The bottom line is the results came back inconclusive."

Cap winced. "That was quick."

"No, no, I think the lab really did the sequencing, but the sample was contaminated."

"Oh, come on! I brought a whole truckload of hair samples. There would have been more than enough DNA present—not to mention the PCR amplification."

"Hey, I'm a behaviorist. All I know is what they told me."

"Well, can I get the samples back?"

"They tossed 'em." Cap was incredulous. "Hey, Dr. Capella, come on, that's what they do!"

"I told you I wanted the surplus returned. Don't you ever listen? No. You don't. That's why I almost flunked you."

"Hey, I was having problems with Maribeth back then. You remember that."

"So is that your problem now, your love life?"

Nick brightened at the very thought of it. "Aw, no, it's just great. It's Susie Barton, remember her? She—"

"Did you tell them the samples came from me?"

Nick had to return to this world. "Well, yeah—"

"Nick!"

"They *asked* me. What was I supposed to do, lie?"

That cooled Cap's jets. "No. No, don't start doing that. There's enough of that around here."

Nick's face held that same imploring look Cap used to see in biology class, right around midterms. "Listen, Dr. Capella, it was primate poop. No question. I ought to know. I got my bachelor's cleaning out the monkey cages. I know my poop."

"That's quite a distinction, Nick."

"Proud of it."

Cap softened, smiled, and patted him on the arm. "I owe you one."

"Eh, you did a lot for me, Doc. I wouldn't have gotten into the graduate program without you. Hey. The droppings were diarrhetic. Did you notice that?"

"Yes."

"Your ape was ticked off about something."

"He has a bit of a temper."

"What are you working on, anyway?"

Cap patted him on the shoulder. "I need you to help me find out." He turned to leave.

"Are you spying on Burkhardt?"

That made Cap stop and turn. "Should I be?"

"Well, somebody ought to do something. I don't like having to cut back when he's—" He shrugged it off—poorly. "Aw, never mind."

"Never mind what?"

Nick backed away with a head shake of regret. "Nothing. Really. I mean, with all due respect, sir, if you're going to make a bunch of waves again, I don't want to get sucked into it. I've got a nice job here."

Cap cracked the door and looked to be sure no former associates would see him. "Well, I can't tell a lie either, and you deserve to know: there are going to be some waves."

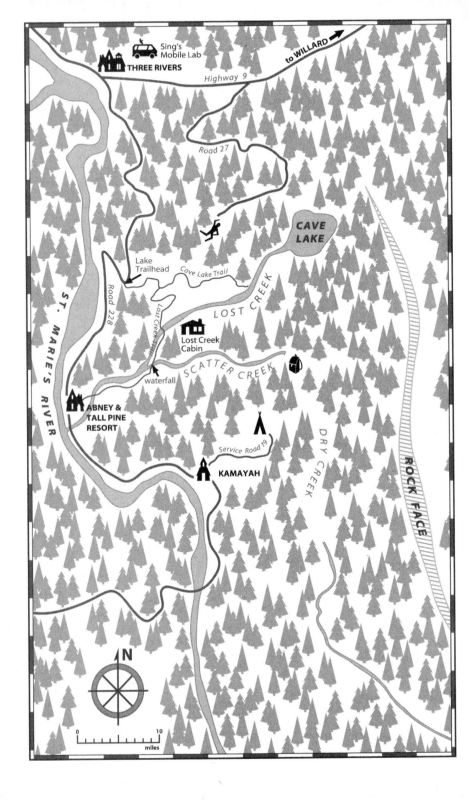

EIGHT

D r. Arnold was well respected in the community, and certainly he had no enemies. I had no reason to suspect any foul play, but of course I had to be curious." Milton Tidewater was an amiable, older gentleman, soft-spoken, highly cordial, well suited to his profession. A man of proper procedure, he'd already put on his green apron and surgical gloves before opening the cold, walk-in storage locker.

The first thing Reed and Sing saw were the soles of Mr. Arnold's feet, jutting from under a white sheet on a wheeled worktable.

"Oh, dear," said Tidewater, readjusting the sheet, "I am sorry, Mr. Arnold." He said to Reed, "Could you take that side?"

Reed gave Tidewater a hand rolling the table out into the workroom.

"Mrs. Capella, you may help yourself to Mrs. Tidewater's apron and gloves, right over there."

Sing took a second green apron from a wall hook and put it on. She found a box of surgical gloves, size small, exactly one inch from, and parallel to, a box of gloves, size large, on the shelf above the work counter.

Tidewater carefully, respectfully removed the sheet from Mr. Arnold, fold by neat fold, revealing the remains. "Now, you understand that I've already begun some restoration, so you'll have to allow for that. Just imagine what he used to look like, right after the accident."

Reed didn't have to do a lot of imagining. It was a good thing this guy was going to be wearing a suit and tie. "How'd this happen?"

"A stack of logs rolled on top of him, just piled on top of him like jackstraws. It took his crew several hours to uncover him. Of course, he was long dead."

Sing spoke quietly, commenting as she observed. "Punctures and lacerations all along the front of the body. Bits of bark and pine needles embedded in the skin." She took hold of the left arm and lifted it gently. The upper arm bent as if it were made of rubber. "Fracture of the humerus."

"You'll find plenty of fractures," said Tidewater.

Sing rotated the arm for a closer view of some puncture wounds. "What do you think caused these?"

"Sharp rocks on the ground? Perhaps the jagged stumps of branches on the logs."

"Uh-huh. Any evidence of bleeding?"

"Oh yes. Certainly."

"What about these other injuries, these lacerations from the logs? Any evidence of bleeding before you cleaned them up?"

Tidewater was struck by his own answer. "Um, now that you ask, no, I don't think so. The blood was congealed for the most part."

Sing looked closely at a gouge on the left chest. "I don't see any bruising either."

"No, it's a little surprising."

"What about the lividity on his front side?"

"Hmm?"

"Well, the injuries tell me he was faceup when the logs fell on him. Was that the case?"

Tidewater fumbled. "Um . . . I believe he was faceup, yes."

Sing grabbed her camera. "Is it okay if we . . . ?"

"Oh, certainly," said Tidewater.

She handed the camera to Reed, who started snapping pictures, following Sing as she worked her way around the body. His first shots were of the puncture wounds on the left arm.

Sing pressed down on the rib cage with both hands. It sank easily beneath the pressure. "Rib cage is flailed." She pressed on the hips and made a painful face. "Iliac wings are entirely mobile! The pelvis is crushed!"

Tidewater wagged his head. "Oh, you don't know the half of it. It took hours to reshape him, and the rigor mortis certainly didn't help. The suit will cover a lot of it, of course. But the neck—that has me a little puzzled, especially the bruising. What do you make of it?"

Sing stood at the head of the table and gently cradled Mr. Arnold's head in her hands. She tilted the head this way and that, observing the neck. She pulled a little, and the neck stretched. She rotated the head to one side and the neck didn't resist; it just went *squish*. "I see what you mean."

"I've seen some broken necks, but nothing like this."

Sing felt along the neck, pinching, pressing, twisting. "No. It's a severe subluxation, a separation at the first and second cervical vertebrae. I would guess this hemorrhaging all around the neck is due to the vertebral arteries being severed." Her professional demeanor weakened as fear crept into her eyes. Reed wondered what it meant. She blinked the expression away and continued, "Of course, the spinal cord would have to be severed as well.

"Diffuse, circumferential ecchymosis around the neck." She held the head in an awkward, twisted position while Reed got some shots of the bruising on the neck, then she backed away, so troubled she couldn't hide it. She said to Reed, "Like Randy Thompson?"

Reed swallowed. "That's about how he looked."

She carefully returned Mr. Arnold's head to as near a natural position as the damage would allow. "Mr. Tidewater," she said, "this is what killed him, not the logs. The hemorrhaging and bruising around the neck are well spread. That means Mr. Arnold was alive when it happened. He still had a beating heart and blood pressure. The lacerations, the tears, and the punctures from the falling logs show no bleeding or bruising, which means there was no blood pressure when they occurred. Mr. Arnold was already dead.

"To make matters worse . . ." She pointed out large darkened regions on the man's chest and belly. "This discoloration you see is fixed lividity. When a person is dead, the blood settles by gravity to whichever side or part of the body is lowest. In this case, the lividity tells us that Mr. Arnold was lying on his stomach after he died, not on his back, the way he was found. The fact that the lividity is fixed—see here? When I press on it, it doesn't displace; the blood has congealed—that means he was dead at least eight to twelve hours before he was moved."

"So he died Sunday night," said Reed.

Sing nodded. "And the logs fell on him Monday morning."

Tidewater stood there, mouth half open, nonplussed. "I understand, but then again, I don't."

■ ■ ■

Reed and Sing did not discuss Mr. Arnold until they were alone at a picnic table near a playground on the edge of town.

Even though they were well out of earshot of anyone, Sing still spoke in lowered tones. "Those punctures on the left arm have the same arrangement and spacing as the punctures in that thermos from the campsite. This thing has teeth, and it isn't afraid to use them."

"It doesn't mind wringing necks either."

"No. In fact, I think it prefers it. The bruises on the head and neck weren't from teeth or claws, but fingers," Sing reviewed. "Somebody or something wrung that man's neck, just wrenched it, and then left the body facedown."

"And then someone else moved the body."

"And left it on its back, not on its stomach."

"And dumped the logs on him to make it look like an accident."

Sing shivered at the thought. "Which doesn't bode well for Cap."

"Excuse me?"

She waved it off. "Oh, just thinking out loud."

"But we have some patterns now, don't we? A line of attacks running southeast, two dead guys killed the same way, one hidden under logs, one . . ." Reed's voice trailed off.

"Hidden. We just haven't found him yet."

Reed nodded. "So I'd better get up to that logging site and see for myself. You took pictures of that cabin, right?"

"Took plenty."

"So did I. I want to see them. All of them, right next to each other."

Sing checked her watch. "Meet you back in Abney?"

Reed rose from the table. "Let's roll."

■ ■ ■

As Rachel plunged into the woods, barreled through pine and fir boughs, leaped over logs, and snapped off dry, obstinate branches, Beck found that riding on her back was a definite improvement over hanging, clinging, and dangling every which way in her arms. Rachel seemed perfectly suited to taking the brunt of the branches and limbs that whipped past. Riding her was much like riding a lean, well-bred horse.

So Sasquatches did have a practical and efficient way to transport their young. Rachel just needed someone to remind her.

Rachel and Beck were dropping down the mountainside into a shady draw where the trunks of ancient cedars and cottonwoods supported the forest canopy like pillars in a dark cathedral. Beck had no idea where they were geographically but guessed from the occasional flashes of sunlight that they were still heading south.

As they entered a boggy bottomland among the cottonwoods, Rachel slowed to a cautious, furtive walk, padding quietly over the black, rotting leaves, turning in quick little circles, looking this way and that, sniffing and listening. The fear was there again; Beck could sense it in Rachel's demeanor, in her eyes, in her movements, and in the fear odor that intensified when Rachel was alarmed. It made Beck wary, and she began rubbernecking in all directions, not knowing what to look for but wanting to be sure it wasn't there.

Rachel let out a soft whistle.

Another whistle came back immediately, and Rachel bolted forward, through the grove, through a stand of young cedars, and into a small meadow where sunlight showcased wildflowers and cattails grew in tall clumps at the edge of a pond.

Rachel sank to her haunches, disappearing up to her waist in the meadow grass. Beck alighted on the ground beside her. Taking one deep, calming breath, Rachel fingered the leaves of a dandelion, then plucked them up and put them in her mouth, her eyes scanning casually as she chewed.

She grunted, "Hmph!"

"Hmph!" came a reply among the cattails as a gray shadow came alive, moving but still hiding. Beck saw one coffee-and-amber eye gazing at her, then the other eye, then the first again as the breeze opened and closed the gaps in the leaves. Leah's gaze was icy and suspicious.

Rachel rose lazily, strode to the cattails, and with Leah's grudging indulgence, began fingering through them like a woman shopping for a blouse. When she found one she liked, she yanked it out, roots and all, and set it in the grass. She plucked up another, nibbled on it, plucked still another, nibbled on it, decided she preferred the first one, and put the second one back.

Rachel returned with her arms full and sat down, setting the plants between her and Beck, enough to get sick on. From past experience, Beck knew her future: she was going to have to bite off, taste, chew, and force down every raw, chewy, stringy bit while Rachel watched. And watched. And watched.

Rachel had already grabbed a cattail and was making quick work of it, chomping down the brown, cylindrical head as if it were a soft carrot and making it look delicious. She eyed Beck, waiting for her to do the same.

Beck followed her example and reached for one, wondering where she should start biting into it.

A whistle!

Leah was the first to reply, emerging from behind the cattails and whistling back. Then Reuben popped up out of the pond, streaked with slime and excited, mud flying from his feet. Even Rachel paused with a cattail hanging from her mouth and gazed toward the old cottonwoods.

Jacob emerged, looking tired from a long trek but still awesome in the light of day, his black hair gleaming, his sagittal crest a priestly miter atop his head. His hands and arms cradled something against his belly.

Beck actually felt glad to see him—he was carrying fruit! Apples and pears! Real food! *People* food! Nothing ever looked so wonderful!

Leah and Reuben were there in an instant, bowed low with hands outstretched, groveling like beggars before a noble, catching the luscious fruit as it fell from Jacob's hands.

Rachel stared and fidgeted, whining, clearly wanting to be invited to the party but too timid to ask.

Hey, come on! Don't just sit there! "Roo-r-Rachel!" Beck pointed at the fruit with one hand, poked at Rachel with the other, and gave a plaintive cry, as near as she could get to an apelike "Ooh! Ooohh!" The sound made her throat hurt.

Leah and Reuben bothered to send her a scowl and went back to consuming the fruit—an apple, a pear, another apple, not slowing, slamming them into their mouths, making them disappear with alarming speed.

Beck bounced up and down for emphasis, reaching toward the fruit and making whatever apelike sounds she thought would register. She felt ridiculous, but she was hungry.

Rachel lifted a lazy finger toward Jacob and grunted.

Jacob glanced her way and took several precious seconds to think it over. He looked down at an apple he held in one hand and a pear he held in the other.

Leah and Reuben had their eyes on the pear and apple too, their greedy hands outstretched.

Jacob reached a decision somewhat grudgingly and all too slowly took three steps toward Rachel. He tossed the pear and apple the rest of the distance. Rachel caught the pear with the skill of an outfielder. The apple bounced on the ground and Beck grabbed it up. Rachel chomped and mashed the pear like a fruit grinder until it was gone. Beck took a bite from her apple—

And then stared at it. *Wait a minute. An apple.* A domestic fruit from a tree someone had planted.

She lifted her eyes to Jacob, who was settling down in the grass for a much-needed rest. Then Beck scanned all around as if she might catch a glimpse, a clue, a hint of where Jacob had been.

Wherever he'd been, people had to have been nearby. It had to have been a farm, a homestead, an orchard, something owned and operated by people with roads, houses, and telephones.

She examined the apple again. *What kind was it? Was this kind of apple ripe in July, or did someone buy this at a grocery store? Where did—*

She didn't hear or see Reuben coming until his big, filthy fist appeared over her shoulder and grabbed the apple.

"Nooo!" Instinctively, in desperation, Beck clamped her hands around the apple, clutched it close to her body, and held on for sheer survival.

Reuben's grip was like an iron vise, and Beck's body was a feather as he flipped her on her back and tried to pry the apple from her hands. Screaming, hoping for help, wondering where in the world Rachel was, she slipped from his muddy grip, then wriggled and squirmed until she was on her belly, the apple under her.

Through the blades of grass, she saw Rachel come running,

screaming and displaying, until Leah, growling and showing her teeth, tackled her to the ground and pummeled her.

Reuben clearly felt no qualms. He took Beck by the hair and yanked her off the ground. She was twisting, dangling by her scalp, which brought a roar of pain from where she'd hit her head, but she didn't let go. Reuben groped for the apple, and Beck turned, holding it from him. She saw an opportunity and kicked him in the stomach with her good foot. The stomach didn't even give. Reuben dropped her, then grabbed at the apple with both hands. Beck tried to run.

One step and her ankle punished her. She screamed in pain, nearly fell, then recovered her balance—

So suddenly she scarcely saw it happening, the apple was gone. She yelped at the sight of her empty hands, and her eyes went immediately to the ground, searching, searching, darting everywhere.

But Reuben had left her, and she could easily see why. He walked away with a triumphant, head-high gait, his hand to his mouth. She heard the apple's flesh snapping and crunching deliciously between his teeth.

Leah punished Rachel with one more slap across her shoulders, and then she retreated, gathering up her thieving son.

Oh God, where are you? Beck cried. *How could you leave me like this?*

She collapsed to the ground, whimpering. It just wasn't fair!

She heard a familiar pig grunt above her, and for a moment a huge silhouette blocked the sun. Rachel sat beside her, sniffing, panting, and moaning little sounds of comfort. Leaning so close Beck could smell her breath—a scent of pear still lingered—she gently groomed the hair that fell across Beck's face and then, leaning back, offered Beck the only consolation she had: a cattail.

■ ■ ■

One chain saw was noisy. Four chain saws were very noisy. Four chain saws, a bulldozer, and an occasionally falling tree were more than enough to make conversation difficult. The clear-cut on Road 27 was going to be a noisy place, at least until the six-man crew quit for the day. Reed, wearing the required hard hat, felt a little silly yelling at the man who stood only a few feet away, but the new foreman, a beer-bellied man in his forties, yelled as if he was used to yelling, so yelling had to be okay.

"So where was the truck?" Reed asked.

A huge fir came down right on top of his question, and the foreman shouted, "What?"

"The truck! Where was the truck parked?"

The foreman turned his head to look toward the clearing, and that's where most of his answer went. "Oh, I theeni was ritovther supplace!" He was pointing to the center of the clearing, now a field of stumps, slash, dozer ruts, and sawdust.

Reed pointed to where the bulldozer was piling up a fresh batch of logs. "Was that where you found him?"

The foreman pointed at the pile and hollered something. Reed caught the words "Found . . . under there . . . morning . . . flat like a bug."

"Uh-huh."

"Duz mega bitta sense." The foreman finally turned and shouted in his face. "Those logs don't dump over that way, not without some real help. But you oughta think about this: that dozer had an extra tenth of an hour on it when we got here."

Another tree came down like an avalanche, sending a cloud of dust, pollen, and needles into the air. Reed waited for things to settle before asking, "Another tenth? Uh, could you explain that?"

The foreman turned his head to look and point at the bulldozer as it came by, the stack rumbling, the treads rattling and
shrieking. " . . . ev day we ridown thours . . ."

Reed hurried around to yell into his face. "You keep track of
the hours on the bulldozer?"

The foreman looked at him as if he were dense. "Yeah, that's
what I said. Clocked it out when we left Friday night, and when
we came back Monday morning, Al was squished and the dozer
had an extra tenth of an hour on the clock."

"So how do you explain that?"

The foreman shook his head. "Can't—'cept, if I wanted to
dump over a pile of logs, I'd need a bulldozer to do it."

"You mean somebody could have purposely dumped the logs
on him?"

"I dunno. None of us do."

"Well, if they did, how'd they get him to hold still?"

The foreman arched an eyebrow under his hard hat. "So *now*
the police are interested, is that it?" He signaled Reed to follow and
walked toward the road where the crew's vehicles were parked.

Reed came alongside him, relieved to get farther from the
noise. When the foreman reached his old pickup, he reached
through the window and brought out a jagged metal object.

It was a thermos, crushed and bearing a familiar pattern of
teeth marks.

"Found that behind a stump near the truck, not too far from
Allen's hard hat. Allen always liked to come up on Sunday night
and stand by his truck, have a little coffee, plan out the week. And
he always wore his hard hat. Whatever got him, got him over
there. He wasn't anywhere near the logs."

■ ■ ■

Sing was only half her calm self. "We were looking for a pattern in the animal's behavior, but we weren't expecting *this*!"

Cap was listening over his cell phone while seated at a computer station in the University Research Library. From this spot in the library's Internet Center, he could see most of the main floor; if he slouched enough, the computer's screen hid most of his face. "Why would the perp dump all those logs but leave the thermos for somebody to find?"

"He didn't see it. It was thrown behind a stump."

"What about fingerprints on the dozer?"

"Obliterated. The dozer was handled and operated for two days after the incident."

"Sounds to me like you'd better be careful."

"*You'd* better be careful!" Sing said.

He smiled wryly. "Hey, I'm at an institute of higher learning, surrounded by knowledge's elite. What's to be afraid of?"

"That's not funny."

"It's incisive and satirical."

She chuckled. "We'll both be careful, won't we?"

"We will."

He said good-bye and folded his cell phone, feeling *careful*. Discreetly, he rotated his head and got a visual on who might be working—or lurking—at the other computer stations, and then eyed the flow of patrons on the main floor. Absolutely nothing appeared out of the ordinary, and he'd worked on this campus long enough to recognize ordinary when he saw it.

The University Research Library was a modern, inexhaustible depository of knowledge, six floors, miles of stacks, and millions of bound volumes. It was the haunt, the second home, of graduate students and doctoral candidates who created their own offices in the study booths along the walls and maintained a steady flow of traffic in the elevators. It was a quiet, somber place where great minds could meet and challenge new frontiers—as long as they did it quietly and brought in no food or drinks. There hadn't been any murders here lately—maybe a flasher or two up in the stacks, but certainly no spies or killers.

Cap relaxed and smiled to himself. *Okay*, he thought, *I've been careful.*

He directed his attention back to the computer screen, trying to sort out, make sense of, and interpret the "inconclusive" findings Nick had brought back from the Judy Lab—the campus nickname for the Judith Fairfax DNA Sequencing Core Facility. The files on the CD Nick had given him were burgeoned with row upon row of the same four letters—A, C, T, and G—in a myriad of combinations, all representing specific strands of DNA from the hair, stool, and saliva samples. These were the clues, the indicators that would tell him what creature the samples came from, if the specific strands could be matched with those of a known creature.

Fortunately, DNA sequencing had reached such a level of sophistication that, using Internet resources such as GenBank and the calculating power of a high-speed computer, Cap could access vast archives of known strands, request comparisons, and find a match.

At least, that was the way it was supposed to work. So far he'd found plenty of matches but plenty of confusion as well. To most anyone, including the folks at the Judy Lab, the data would have to be ruled inconclusive; Cap's samples had to have been contaminated.

Contamination was the classic "wrench in the works" as far as DNA sequencing was concerned. Even though much of the sequencing was now automated, eliminating most of the usual errors, contamination was one determined little gremlin, constantly waiting for a chance to mess things up. The field was full of stories of misidentification due to foreign DNA somehow getting into the mix. DNA from a triceratops was once found to be 100 percent identical to DNA from a turkey, but the researchers could never be sure whether the dinosaur was really identical to turkeys or whether someone eating a turkey sandwich during the sequencing contaminated the sample.

To most anyone, Cap's samples indicated that kind of contamination, foreign DNA somehow mixed in with known DNA.

To most anyone, that was the end of the matter.

For Cap, it didn't end there. Of course, he wished that it did. It would have been so much better than having to deal with another possible explanation and what that could mean.

Cap leaned back in his chair, hands interlocked in his lap, as he stared at the screen. *What now?*

Well. A paunchy man in a sagging wool sweater walked into the library's comfortable, chair-and-sofa study lounge.

Dr. Mort Eisenbaum, just the man Cap needed to see.

Eisenbaum was an unmarried, socially inept genius who preferred huddling and communing with organic molecules, amino acids, and proteins to living in the complicated world of people. He and Cap weren't close, but they'd often consulted on projects and compared notes on particular students. This man was a pioneer in DNA sequencing and usually liked being consulted about it. Cap had all the data laid out systematically on the computer. It wouldn't take much of Eisenbaum's time.

Cap ventured out of hiding and into the study lounge. Eisenbaum had settled into a favorite spot at a large oak table and was leafing through a stack of research volumes, obviously on the trail of something.

"Excuse me. Mort?"

Eisenbaum looked up over his reading glasses. A cloud fell over his face. "Dr. Capella. How are you?"

"Pretty good, pretty good. I was working on something when I saw you come in. It's got me a little baffled."

Eisenbaum closed the volume he was reading, stacked it on top of the others, and rose from his chair. "I'm afraid I can't help you."

Cap groped for some words as Eisenbaum brushed past him. "Um, well, it's just over here on the computer. It would only take a moment, I'm sure."

Eisenbaum kept walking, not looking back.

"Well, what about—we don't have to meet *here*. What if we went someplace private, had some coffee or something?" Cap followed him, trying not to look desperate. "The agreement doesn't say we can't talk to each other, just outsiders—" He stopped. *I am an outsider.*

Eisenbaum went out the door as if he and Cap had never met.

Cap was disappointed. Eisenbaum had always struck him as a lone eccentric, not affected that much by department politics.

Back to square one. Cap returned to his computer station and slouched in his chair, staring at the computer screen in case God might send a revelation. Did these results really make sense in their own bizarre way?

Many of the sequences from the stool, hair, and saliva samples matched chimpanzee DNA, but there were just as many sequences that matched up with human DNA. At first glance, one would think that either the chimp DNA was contaminated with human DNA, or the other way around—except for an entirely distinct third group that seemed to be an odd hybrid of both. It closely matched chimp, and where it didn't match chimp, it closely matched human. Contamination couldn't have caused that.

To make matters worse, mixed in through it all were weird sequences that didn't match up with anything; they were "junk" DNA, unidentified contaminants with no explanation for how they got there.

Unless . . .

Cap saved all his findings to a fresh CD and tucked the disk away in his pocket with the CD he'd gotten from Nick. He had a hunch, but he needed someone to test it and hopefully tell him he was wrong. He needed someone who loved to tell him how wrong he was about virtually everything, someone who would pull no punches.

He immediately thought of just the person. Judging from the cold reception Cap got from Eisenbaum, it might be tough getting through to him, but no matter. Cap was desperate enough.

■ ■ ■

Pete set down his rifle, shed his tracking gear, and dropped onto a bench on the porch of the Tall Pine with a deep, tired sigh. He removed his hat, ran his fingers over his scalp, and allowed himself a moment of staring at the plank floor with his mind a blank.

Tyler had set his gear down near the porch rail. For some reason the young flank man still had enough energy to remain standing. "You guys want something to drink?"

"Coffee," said Max, lying on his back on the floor. "Nothing in it."

"I'll take a Coke," said Benny, plopping down next to Pete.

Tyler waited, but Pete said nothing. "Pete?"

Pete returned to this world long enough to answer, "Just some water. Thanks, Tyler."

Tyler went after the drinks.

There was about a three-second moment of silence, which was apparently all Benny could stand. "Well, we made it back. Still got about an hour of daylight left."

Pete could not be cheered. "There wasn't much left to do anyway."

Jimmy Clark walked over. He looked fresh enough. His clothes weren't even dirty. "Everybody down?"

Benny answered, "Yeah, we're calling it quits. Joanie and Chris have gone home already. They're the smart ones."

Pete took his turn after Benny—he'd been doing it all day. "The woods are clear. Your guys can have at it, and I really do wish you the best."

"Thanks, Pete, I appreciate it."

Pete rubbed his tired eyes. "I wanted out of there anyway. I don't want my crews up there in the dark when that critter has all the advantage."

"It'll all be over by tonight. I've got a feeling."

"Yeah, you'd better hope so," said Benny. "Not all of us are happy how things are going."

A voice called from across the parking lot. "Pete!"

"Speak of the devil," said Benny.

It was Reed, in uniform, coming from a big motor home Pete recognized as Sing's mobile crime lab. Pete gave a weak smile. The young man was brewing up something, he could tell.

"So where've you been?" asked Benny. "Out chasing Bigfoot?"

"Benny!" Pete's voice was strained. He then said quietly, "I think it's time for you to go home."

"Well, I'd just like to know what he's been up to while we've been busting our butts up there looking for his wife." He challenged Reed, "You *do* have a wife, don't you, or would you rather not discuss that?"

Reed smiled at him. "I appreciate all your hard work, but I think Pete's right—you need to go."

"Well, there's more going on here than meets the eye, I'll bet on that!"

Pete barked, "Go home, Benny!"

Benny glared at Pete, then at Reed, then grabbed up his gear. "I'm not coming back."

"I won't expect you," Pete said.

Benny stomped across the parking lot to his truck, muttering how he should have been paid, but no amount of money was worth it anyway.

Reed watched him go, strangely calm, then looked at Pete, the question in his eyes. Pete answered, "We didn't find her. Didn't find a thing."

Tyler returned with drinks in a cardboard holder. "Where's Benny?"

Max took his coffee and Pete took his water. Pete said to Reed, "Help yourself to a Coke."

Reed took it. "Sing and I would like a meeting with you over in the rig."

Pete was already interested before Reed even said anything. "You got it."

■ ■ ■

The sun was low and the ravine was in shadow. The forlorn, dismembered cabin was fading, becoming indistinct in a premature dusk. The white-haired Wiley Kane and Steve Thorne, the marine, had moved to the downwind location above the ravine, thankful for a change in the view and the tedium. They'd spent the afternoon bored out of their minds, whispering jokes to each other, expecting no action until darkness came.

Now, darkness approached, and as the light faded, their interest revived. Each checked his rifle one last time, sighting through the scope and drawing a bead on that half drum of doughnuts and greasy goo. Soon they would need the night-vision goggles. Wiley Kane, who would have the first shift, tried his out.

■ ■ ■

Sam Marlowe, the young Mariners fan, checked his watch. He hadn't slept much, but he'd gotten some reading done, and now it was time to relieve his partner. He rose quietly, rifle on his back, and moved out.

Janson carefully climbed down from the bear stand that was hidden among the limbs. They said nothing to each other. Marlowe simply gave Janson a pat on the shoulder and started climbing, limb by limb.

The bear stand was a device suitable only for the durable and patient. A precarious-looking platform clamped to the trunk of the tree about twenty feet off the ground, the bear stand was not much more than a foldable chair with footrests to keep the hunter's legs from dangling and a safety harness to keep him from killing himself should he doze off. Marlowe eased himself off the limbs and onto the platform and strapped himself in. The campsite of Ted and Melanie Brooks lay just below, deserted, but tantalizingly baited. Jimmy Clark had called for the old standby, a half drum full of doughnuts and bacon grease, but Marlowe and Janson had added their own enticements based on what the campers had been eating: a paper plate with a wilting salad and three fried hamburger patties on a small card table.

Come on, fella, Marlowe thought as he prepared his night goggles. *Let's get it over with.*

■ ■ ■

Sing's mobile lab was cramped, tightly furnished with two lab benches, drawers and shelves, flasks, test tubes, pipettes, cameras and tripods, a microscope, charts and maps, rulers and tape measures, a laser level, a drawing table, and now the radio and GPS gear Reed had ordered. Sing sat at her compact computer station, clicking and opening digital photos on her laptop while Reed and Pete, squeezed into two folding chairs, looked over her shoulder.

"Check this out," said Reed, finishing his Coke. "Exhibit 1. I took this picture when Beck and I first got to the cabin."

Sing opened the window on the computer screen.

It was a shot of the cabin interior, torn apart, shelves broken, with shredded packaging thrown everywhere and a white dusting of flour on everything.

"Huh," said Pete. "No tracks."

"I was shooting the area in front of me before I stepped on it," said Reed.

"And note this," Sing said, selecting and enlarging a detail with the mouse. "The shovel on the floor near the upper left corner."

"All right," said Pete.

"And now Exhibit 2," said Reed.

"I took this one the next day." She brought up another photo and positioned the two photos beside each other.

"Okay, right," said Pete. "That's how it looked when I was there." The second photo showed the same cabin interior, this time with several boot prints clearly visible in the flour, and another difference Pete saw immediately. "Hm. No shovel."

"And note the boot prints," Reed added.

Pete nodded. "Right. Two sets." He pulled some footprint diagram cards from his pocket and studied them one by one. "I recorded three different prints up there." He pointed at the tracks on the screen. "These are Reed's. Same size, same sole, same wear patterns. But these others, up in the corner where the shovel was . . . I thought they belonged to Randy." He leaned back, stroking the back of his neck. "But they sure don't."

Reed spoke what Pete had to be thinking. "By the time those other prints were made, Randy was dead and Beck and I were . . . having our trouble. Our campsite was hidden up in those trees. Whoever it was must have thought my prints were Randy's—until he found Randy dead."

"Our guess is our third person buried Randy's body, hoping no one would find it," said Sing.

"So we have two men killed the same way," said Reed, "and both deaths concealed. First, Allen Arnold was buried under a pile of logs, and then Randy Thompson was buried somewhere with the shovel from the cabin."

"The shovel was discarded, maybe hidden with the body so there wouldn't be any fingerprints or clues—out of sight, out of mind," Sing added. "This is all an educated theory, of course."

"What do you think?" Reed asked Pete. "Do you think we could be right?"

Pete leaned back and clasped his hands behind his head. "If you ever find Randy's body, you'll know for sure. Does Sheriff Mills know about this?"

"He will when he gets here tomorrow morning," said Reed. "I'm hoping he'll either buy our idea or come up with a better one, but *do* something either way." Reed drew a breath, his emotions close to the surface. "None of this says Beck is alive, but I'm still believing."

"And we're ready for new ideas, that's for sure," said Pete. "So what about Jimmy? You gonna let him in on this?"

"I'll leave that up to Sheriff Mills. Jimmy still thinks I'm crazy."

Pete stared at the computer screen. He ran a hand across his forehead. "As if that fool critter wasn't enough, now he's got helpers!"

■ ■ ■

There was something about the coming of night that changed things. As the sun turned bloody red, then winked out behind a distant ridge; as the sky faded from blue to black; as the night voices of the forest began to mourn, click, yelp, and chatter, Beck felt *another* fear returning like a slow-working potion, spreading through her in perfect cadence with the deepening of the night. Though she and Reed had tried to talk themselves out of it that first night above the cabin on Lost Creek, she now had a name for it—Night Fear—and believed in it, even trusted it. It never came invited, but it was there for a reason: there was something *out there* to be afraid of.

Strangely, chillingly, the Sasquatches seemed to feel it too. These wild animals, clearly capable of traveling and foraging at night, were afraid. Beck could sense it in the nervous darting of their eyes, the overcaution of their gait, their strange, stealthy silence, and, of course, the fear scent that thickened as darkness came. They were moving again, *fleeing* by the looks of it, winding and dodging through old-growth forest on a steep mountainside, stumbling and tired, short on sleep and hungry, driven by something *out there*.

They broke out of the cover of the forest to cross a vast field—*acres*—of broken, angular rocks. The sky was open above them, and directly ahead, Sagittarius and Scorpius twinkled close to the horizon. They were going south. The apes' soft, flexible feet conformed and gripped the rocks. With speed and silence, they made it across and back into the trees.

The clash in the trees was like a bomb going off—sudden, deafening, jolting. Beck lurched, gripped Rachel's neck, tried to see what was happening. It was too dark to tell exactly, but Leah had run into something, had disturbed something, or was being attacked by something. There was a terrible thrashing in the brush and branches. Leah screamed; Reuben bawled; Jacob roared.

Rachel, trying to look in every direction for what the problem might be, spun so fast she threw Beck from her back. Beck landed on one foot, hopped to favor the other, and stumbled backward into a thicket. She rolled, wrestled, tried to get up. Branches, leaves, vines, and twigs entangled her. She couldn't get her legs under her.

The ground was quivering. Jacob was still roaring. Reuben was screaming. Rachel was huffing, terrified.

Lost Creek. For a moment, Beck was back at the forlorn little cabin, hearing the same sounds, mad with the same terror. She let out a cry as her arms flailed in the thicket, trying to find a handhold.

Leah had encountered something big, powerful, and fast, but apparently she'd scared it. It was now smashing and crashing through the tangle to get away from her—and coming Beck's way. When the thing raced through a shaft of light, Beck saw an immense round body galloping toward her, leaping over logs and pushing through limbs. She knew immediately it was a bear. She also knew that in just a second or two, it was going to run right over her. She struggled to get up. She slipped, then tripped and got nowhere.

She screamed.

Was that Rachel? Just above her, something let out a roar so deep and loud she felt it in her chest. She wriggled and looked up just in time to see Rachel leap over her and land directly in the bear's path. Rachel's hair bristled like a brush, enlarging her outline.

The two huge bodies collided like a thunderclap, then rolled and grappled, impacting tree trunks, shattering limbs, throwing leaves and dirt, pounding and gouging the ground. Beck heard it and only partially saw it until Rachel stood in a shaft of ghostly moonlight, hefting the huge black mass as it kicked and flailed. With skill, quickness, and astonishing power, Rachel took the bear's head in both hands and whipped its massive body about until the neck bones crackled and the bear went limp. She whipped the body again. It hung like a sack of lead from her hands, motionless. She shook it to be sure, then dashed it to the ground, heavy, contorted, and dead.

Reuben was still bawling. Leah was moaning and clicking at him, no doubt trying to calm him down. Jacob huffed from somewhere close, pushing toward them through the undergrowth.

Rachel was still angry, her hair bristling, her nostrils steaming, her canines flashing in the dim light. She reached down, grabbed two handfuls of bear hide, hefted the bear over her head, and dashed it to the ground again. The guts tore loose with a mashing sound that made Beck wince.

Beck ventured only one look. She couldn't see the bear's eyes, only its tongue protruding from its mouth and glistening in the dim light, a row of white teeth—and the head grotesquely twisted and dangling, nearly severed.

Rachel breathed heavily as she came toward Beck, hands extended to gather her up.

Beck cowered, shied away. *Don't. Don't touch me.*

She'd heard terrible screams before and been terrified. She'd seen Randy Thompson's brutally murdered body and wondered what hideous monster could have done such a thing.

Now, looking up into Rachel's dark and wrinkled face, she knew.

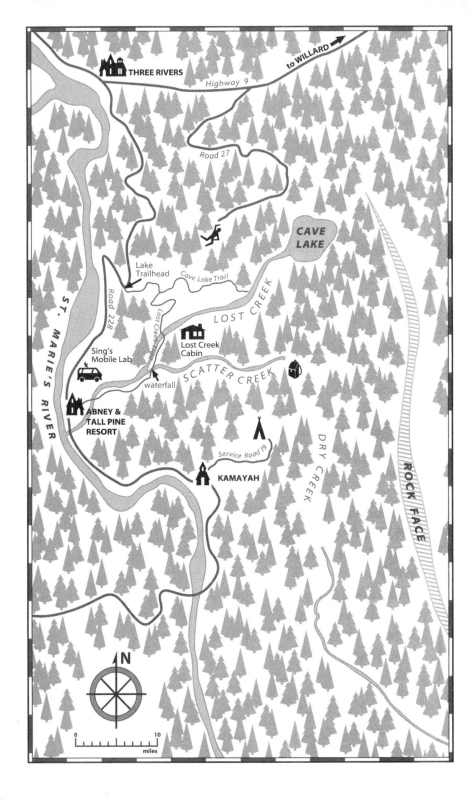

NINE

The cold of the night was creeping into Sam Marlowe's feet, but since he was strapped into the bear stand on the side of a tree, there wasn't much he could do other than wiggle his toes and flex his ankles. The rifle was cold and heavy. Dew formed on the barrel, and his hands complained, threatening to cramp. He held the rifle in one hand while he flexed the other, then traded hands and flexed again.

The woods were alive; the night shift was on duty. Leopard frogs in the nearby streambed called each other at regular intervals; a crowd of coyotes howled and yapped in their usual, ghostly fashion, never *there* as much as *out there somewhere*. Every few seconds, a bat flickered like a giant, ghostly moth across the field of his night goggles.

Below him, the half drum of rotting refuse sent up its stench, but so far, no visitors.

. . .

Wiley Kane almost dozed off, but one tiny snore brought a quick elbow from Steve Thorne, the only one allowed to sleep at the moment. Kane lifted his night goggles long enough to rub his eyes, then went back to scanning the woods.

Movement down by the cabin caught his eye immediately, but he was disappointed. The half drum of grease and doughnuts had attracted its first visitor: a skunk.

Well. *Somebody* was bound to show up.

. . .

Beck held on, her arms around Rachel's thick neck, her legs wrapped around Rachel's middle, as Rachel hurried once again through the forest, floating in her strange, bent-kneed gait, back slightly stooped, long arms gently, silently moving tree limbs aside as they passed through. Leah strode about thirty feet ahead of them with Reuben on her back, a vague, cloudy shape in the dark that melted in and out of the shadows and hardly made a sound. Somewhere in the enfolding web of forest and thicket ahead of Leah, Jacob was leading, and somehow, Leah could see him. Where they were going, only Jacob knew.

They broke out of the forest and followed a dry streambed awash in cold, silver-blue moonlight. The path was littered with deadwood and crisscrossed with the weather-checked remnants of fallen trees. Mountain slopes formed black walls on either side, and directly above, Lyra twinkled beneath the Milky Way. Now Beck could see Jacob far ahead, a silhouette in light but invisible in shadows. He strode across the river rocks and leaped over fallen logs, maintaining a demanding pace the two females were expected to keep up with, even with heavy children on their backs.

The image was hauntingly familiar. Men. Always showing off. She could have named Jacob *Reed* instead.

Oh, Beck, such thoughts! Jacob was a bloodthirsty, flesh-tearing beast; Reed was a man, and what she wouldn't give to be home with that man right now! Sure, he was one-upping and offending her at every turn in the trail, but that was just his clumsy, male way of helping her grow. He'd pushed himself and her before, and she'd been offended before, but it was his way. He was a man who relished strength and youth, but still a boy tripping over himself trying to grow up. He meant well, and sometimes, like right now, she could see it that way.

She laid her head on Rachel's shoulder. She missed Reed, ached for him.

Rachel's pace, once steady, now slowed. Beck glanced ahead. Jacob had stolen to the opposite side of the streambed and become a dark extension of a dead snag's shadow. He remained still as Leah and Rachel, trudging and tired, caught up. Leah moved silently to where a tall hemlock and a hollow stump stood side by side and became one of them, standing still, dark, and massive. Reuben dropped silently from his mother's back and became a stump. Rachel located herself in a thicket and became a bush, blending her own outline with the shapes around her. Beck settled into the bushes beside Rachel and remained still, satisfied that the leaves would hide her.

Now only the forest made sounds—the barely noticeable whisper of the breeze, the occasional squeaking of a tiny creature under a rock, the faraway screech of an owl. As far as the forest knew, even as near as Beck could tell, the Sasquatches weren't there.

So what was happening? What was this all about? The only

information Beck could glean came from Rachel, who peered intently toward a clearing beside the streambed. Beck searched the clearing, shifting as stealthily as she could to peer through the leaves and branches.

Her heart quickened at the same time her mind balked with uncertainty. Just beyond the tops of some obscuring grasses, she saw a patch of bare ground, and in the middle of that ground, an incongruous pile of roundish objects.

It was fruit. Apples, pears, even some bananas.

So this was where Jacob was taking them. He had to have been here before.

But fruit meant humans, so what was this really? It was hard to imagine someone had placed all the fruit there just to be nice to animals. It had to be bait, and if so, for what purpose? Were hunters in the trees, waiting for some unsuspecting animal to walk into their gun sights?

The Sasquatches must have been wondering the same thing. They remained still, watching, listening, sniffing, wanting to know all there was to know about this place. If Jacob had been here before, it hadn't lessened his caution.

Should I call out? Should I make some noise?

She thought better of it. Silence and stealth were the rule now, and she was freshly aware that violating the rules could get her killed. Fear had become a given, never gone, seldom lessened, but she couldn't let it control her or make her do something stupid. She had to think, plan, learn, and wait. There would be another way, sometime, somewhere.

After another long moment of silent watching, listening, and smelling, Jacob finally broke off from his concealing shadow and moved forward into the clearing. Leah followed next, and behind her, like a half-sized copy, came Reuben.

Rachel sighed as if with relief and rose slowly from the thicket.

She took one more look and listen, then slipped into the clearing. Beck followed close behind her, limping but standing on her own, trying to step where Rachel stepped and be just as quiet about it.

The others reached the fruit first and wasted no time grabbing it up and gobbling it down. Rachel hesitated at the edge of the bare ground, then took a step. When she didn't get growled at or clobbered, she took another. Jacob tossed an apple her way, which she immediately grabbed up, but that was the only toss she got. She drew closer.

Hungry as she was, Beck was still more interested in the surroundings. She was unable to see anything amiss in the black wall of the forest. She heard no gun bolts sliding, no camera shutters clicking. She saw no blinking red lights from camcorders. Even so, this whole thing had to be a setup. Domestic, store-bought fruit didn't appear in the middle of the wilderness without some human with a plan.

Then she realized the ground under her feet felt different. Peering down, she saw that it looked different too. She reached down to touch it; her finger sank to the second joint in loose soil. The ground had been tilled and raked, much like a garden prepared for planting. Her boots sank in, making impressions.

It hit her.

Footprints. She and the beasts were leaving them everywhere—which was precisely the idea.

Rachel nudged her, but Beck paid no mind.

Footprints! She saw this once on a TV nature show, and now here it was for real. Some nature lovers were hoping to capture the footprints of wild animals. They'd prepared this site with loose soil and bait, and whether they were here now or would return later, they were keeping an eye on it! Beck looked for a trail somewhere, some path the humans had used to get here. She had to find it and remember it.

Rachel nudged her again, and Beck took a pear from her hand.

Footprints. Beck started stepping and limping around the site in any loose soil she could find. *Got to leave some footprints!*

Rachel followed her, offering her a banana and obliterating every footprint Beck left.

She took the banana and retraced her steps, trying to put her footprints back, but they were much shallower this time. Rachel kept following her, curious, flattening the impressions under her big, soft feet.

"Rachel, don't!"

"Mmm."

Beck stopped to eat the banana just so Rachel wouldn't follow. Rachel stopped and ate her apple.

While hurriedly eating the banana, Beck spotted some unstomped soil near the edge of the tilled circle. With the empty banana peel in her hand, she limped to the place. Rachel followed, protective and fascinated.

With her finger, Beck began scratching numbers in the ground. 2. 0. 8 . . .

Rachel squatted beside her and watched in the same way she watched everything Beck did, with utmost, unbroken attention. She reached down herself and ran her finger along the ground, leaving one furrow, then another, captivated by the activity.

Beck could only hope Rachel would remain distracted so she could complete the number. 9. 6.

She heard the others stirring behind her, rising to leave. *Please, just two more seconds!* 9. 2—

Jacob huffed. The party was over.

The banana peel tumbled to the ground. Beck's finger was still extended to write as she lurched into the air and flopped over Rachel's shoulder—Rachel's best attempt so far at loading up her kid.

"Nooo! L-l-l-leh . . ." *Let me finish!*

Rachel was already trotting out of the clearing, following the others. Beck hung on, gripping, grappling, trying to get right side up. She finally got one hand around Rachel's neck, then the other, and then her legs astride Rachel's middle, resting on the hips, as the whole family vanished into the woods again.

Hope. Beck hadn't gained as much as she wanted, but at least she had a start on it.

■ ■ ■

The gorilla was doing a clumsy line dance without a line, the tops of its running shoes plainly visible above its phony, slip-on feet. It carried a placard that read "Apes Have Rights," and from under the plastic ape-faced mask, a young man's voice chanted in a monotonous cadence, "Freedom for our brothers; freedom for the apes! Freedom for our brothers; freedom for the apes!"

He was one of about a dozen chanting protestors gathered for their Thursday morning demonstration outside the York Primate Center, an old but renovated brick structure on the Corzine University campus. The gorilla suit was a new feature Cap hadn't seen before.

On the other hand, Cap, in a loud, tropical shirt, straw hat, Bermuda shorts, and sunglasses, was a sight the *protestors* hadn't seen before. Not that he was that unusual; the protestors, most of them students with too few causes and too much time, liked to dress in outrageous ways to draw attention. Besides the gorilla, there was a cheap, K-Mart version of the orangutan from Disney's *Jungle Book*, an overweight Tarzan in a loincloth and fright wig, and a scientist in a white lab coat spattered with red paint. When Cap joined them and took up their chant, they were happy enough to count him as one of their own.

It was mostly during the summer months that these folks displayed themselves at the Primate Center's gated parking entrance, waiting for the "ape killers, torturers, and exploiters" to venture in or out. Any car arriving or leaving would have to run the gauntlet and endure the latest chant of outrage. Cap had driven this gauntlet on many a Thursday himself.

Someone had given Cap a sign to wave: "Where Have All The Primates Gone?" He held it high, utilized a few dance steps of his own, and tried to blend in as the chant broke apart and abated in the lull between cars.

"Hey! You're new here." He was being addressed by the group's leader, a brassy-voiced young woman with garish purple hair and enough metal in her face to set off an airport alarm.

"Not really. I used to work here."

"At the Primate Center?"

"Yeah, a little bit, but mostly in Bioscience. I taught biology."

Tarzan quit talking to the gorilla and they turned to listen.

"Why don't you work here anymore?" the leader said.

"I was fired."

"Cool," said Tarzan.

"How come?" asked the gorilla.

"I kept finding problems with Darwinism," said Cap.

The response was predictable: the little gasps, the incredulity, the wagging heads, the side glances and snickers.

"You're kidding!" the young woman in the lab coat cried. "I thought you were a biology prof!"

"Mm-hm, molecular biology."

"How can a biology prof have a problem with Darwinism?"

"How can a Darwinist have a problem with *anything*?"

"So what are you doing here?" She sounded just a little suspicious. "Do you care about our brothers?"

"You mean the apes?"

"*Yeah*, the apes! They're our brothers, our closest relatives!"

The gorilla added, "We're 98 percent chimpanzee."

Cap tried not to sneer. "*We* taught you that."

"So they have rights just like we do," said the woman, "and we're gonna stay here until those rights are recognized!"

That was a prompt. The others all cheered, "Yeah!"

"Rights for the chimps!"

"Set 'em free!"

Cap countered, "Have you ever been in there? The primates aren't being abused. This is noninvasive research, strictly behavioral. The worst they do is give the primates cucumbers instead of grapes."

Some moaned, others wagged their heads, some rolled their eyes. Tarzan even got hostile: "Hey, don't lie to us, man!"

"They're being held in cages, aren't they?" said the orangutan.

The woman got right in Cap's face. "That's what they want us to think! Sure, maybe the apes here on campus aren't being abused, but what about the ones they take *off* campus?"

"Off campus?" Cap asked. "How do you—?"

A girl decked out like a tree with a toy chimp in one of her branches—her arm—shouted, "Car coming!"

They scrambled into lines on either side of the driveway and took up the chant, waving their signs. "Freedom for our brothers; freedom for the apes!" The gorilla broke into his line dance; Tarzan yodeled a yell; the orangutan spun in circles, waving his arms; and the little tree swayed in the wind as the gate lifted and a car rolled through.

Cap bolted from the curb and stood in front of the car. "Hey! Hey, Baumgartner!"

The driver braked abruptly, then honked.

"You're gonna get arrested!" the little tree cried out to Cap.

Cap raised his sunglasses as he leaned over the hood of the car. "Baumgartner! It's me, Capella!"

The driver quit honking and stared through the windshield.

Cap took off his straw hat.

"Cap! Michael Capella!" The driver rolled down his window and stuck out his head. "Cap! Are you crazy?"

Cap handed his sign to the gorilla and ran around to the passenger's side, shouting through the closed window. "We've gotta talk!"

Baumgartner anguished a moment, then reached over and opened the door.

Cap settled into the passenger's seat and closed the door behind him, blocking out the din of the chants. "Sorry for the getup, but they wouldn't let me in to see you."

Dr. Emile Baumgartner hit the gas. "Well, let's get out of here before anybody sees *you*."

■ ■ ■

Fleming Cryncovich, twenty-three-year-old, unemployed son of an unemployed miner, stood there and stared, his head wiggling back and forth in tiny, unconscious expressions of awe and amazement. His spidery hands shook, awaiting orders for an appropriate gesture from his stupefied brain. Words wouldn't come to his lips, only little gasps and *Ohhhhs*.

It was early morning. The shadows were still long, which brought out the footprints in stark relief. He'd been hoping for years to capture just one Bigfoot print, pressing on and wasting bait while the world laughed and his parents shook their heads. Sometime since yesterday morning, it all became worth it.

His hands shook so badly he had trouble pulling his camera from its case. He forgot for a moment how to turn it on. He nearly dropped it trying to focus.

Click! He shot from one side.

Click! He shot from the other.

Click! From high above.

ClickClick! Close-ups.

ClickClickClick! A montage he would paste together on his computer.

Click. A human print.

His finger froze on the shutter button. He stared over the top of his camera.

There wasn't just one, but several boot prints, some stepped on by a big Sasquatch foot, some on top of the Sasquatch prints, some by themselves. It was a small print, perhaps that of a woman.

He'd read about this, something about a missing woman up near Abney.

Arlen. He had to call Arlen! Fleming ran in a circle, excited, nervous.

Numbers. Those were numbers scratched in the dirt!

He yanked out his pen, dropped it, picked it up, wrote the numbers on his hand.

Then he ran up the trail, jamming his camera back into its case. He needed casting plaster too, and a ruler, and he had to call Arlen!

■　■　■

"We just need another day!" Jimmy was adamant.

"It's moving. It's gone," said Pete. "Doesn't matter how long your guys—"

"Listen! You've had your people tramping through the woods, stirring things up and making noise and leaving their scent everywhere. It's no wonder we didn't bag this bear!"

"I can't call the search off," said Sheriff Mills. "Not 'til we—"

"You've covered all eight zones. Where are you going to search next, the rest of the world?"

Pete, Sheriff Mills, and Jimmy stood nose to nose on the front porch of the Tall Pine, refreshed from some sleep and ready to lock horns.

Pete held up his hand, hoping to keep the floor for at least one complete sentence. "Whatever that thing is, it's moving south. It doesn't care about your bear stands and your doughnuts."

"You don't know that!"

"Well, Reed's worked up a pretty good theory—"

Jimmy rolled his eyes. "So you're listening to *him* now?"

"He's got a good case if you'd just listen!"

"I'd like to hear it," said Sheriff Mills.

"You'll lose credibility!" Jimmy warned. "You're losing people already, or haven't you noticed?"

Kane and Max stood to the side, having slept little and accomplished less. They weren't invited to be part of the discussion, but Kane spoke up anyway, "Sheriff, pardon me, but a lot of us need to know we're not wasting our time. Do we have a good, clear mission or don't we?"

Max piped in, "Are we still searching for somebody, or are we hunting a bear, or Bigfoot, or what?"

Jimmy jumped on him. "We're not hunting Bigfoot!" He returned to Mills. "See? That right there is the kind of fire I'm constantly having to put out, and I'm getting sick of it!"

"Just tell us what the mission is, once and for all," said Kane.

The sheriff looked at Pete. "Maybe you'd better tell me what's happening."

Pete had to admit, "It's been tough holding the crew together. Joanie and Chris cashed it in. Don's out. I had to let Benny go. The medical folks aren't waiting by the phone, we all know that."

Kane offered, "Nobody trusts this Shelton fellow, that's the problem. How do we know he didn't off his wife and he's just making everything else up?"

Pete bristled. "Kane, why don't you just shut up?"

"Well, I'm not the only one who thinks so!"

"Shut up anyway," said Sheriff Mills.

"Sheriff," Jimmy said with a sigh, "the search is over. Beck Shelton is dead, and so's Randy Thompson. We need to deal with the hazard that's still out there—we need to get that bear. It won't happen with everyone traipsing around."

The sheriff looked at Pete as if trying to read him.

Pete was struggling. "Sheriff, there *is* more to this. You haven't seen all the cards yet. You just have to trust me."

"What about the search? Are we done?"

Pete looked down at the ground. "I know some folks don't see much point in going out there again, and maybe they're right. I'm going back out there, even if I'm alone."

Jimmy sighed. "Pete, we all feel that way."

"Do we?" Mills asked.

"Patrick—Sheriff. You know the score here. I don't have to tell you the chances of finding Beck or Randy alive."

"So now I suppose you want some big decision from me."

Mills drew a deep breath and took a moment to weigh his words. When he had all four of them by the eyes, he answered, "It's easy enough to tell me—heck, even tell yourselves—that Beck Shelton is dead. But which one of you wants to tell Reed?" He didn't wait long for an answer; he just kept going. "When you can look Reed Shelton in the eye and tell him his wife is dead even though you can't prove it; when you're ready to watch his hope lie right down and die; if any of you can come away from breaking the heart of a friend and still call him your friend . . ." Now it was his turn to struggle. "Then, all right. I'll accept that and say we did our best."

They were silent and would no longer meet his eye.

"Sheriff Mills!" It was Reed, in hunting garb, bursting from his room.

Mills shot a warning glare at every one of them, and then he waited.

Reed strode up, papers in his hand: maps, charts, some blown-up photographs. "Good morning, sir. I have something to show you—" He noted the group. "What?"

"Reed . . ." Mills met Reed's eyes, then directed his attention toward Pete and Jimmy.

Reed looked at them. Jimmy drew a breath—

"Sheriff! Sheriff!" Arlen Peak burst out the front door of the inn, a scrap of paper in his hand. "Somebody's found her!"

Reed was all over that. "Where? *Where!* Is she alive?"

"No. I *mean* . . . I don't mean no; I mean, no, he doesn't know. Am I making any sense?"

Sheriff Mills looked about ready to grab the innkeeper by the scruff of the neck, but his tone was enough. "We're listening, Arlen!"

Arlen referred to his scribbled notes and tried to recap things in a logical order. He got a call from a friend of his—

"Who?" Mills demanded. "What's his name?"

"Uh, Flem Cryncovich."

"Come again?" said Jimmy.

Arlen repeated the name and told how he'd come to know the kid, then went on to explain the baiting site, the fruit, the soft ground—

"This isn't another nut case, is it?" Jimmy barked.

"Will you let him talk?" Reed scolded.

The footprints in the soft ground, the—

"Bigfoot?" Jimmy asked. He folded his arms over his chest.

Arlen ran a hand through his hair. "Uh, well, yes, if you really must know!"

Jimmy cursed and turned away. "I knew it!"

"But there were other prints!" Arlen went on. "Boot prints, uh, you know, people prints, a small size, like a woman's!"

Jimmy's face completed the transition from pale with shock to red with rage. "That is the most insidious, most despicable, most insulting pile of crap I have ever heard!"

"Jimmy," Mills cautioned.

"It's a hoax! This guy's read the papers! He's nothing but a sadistic wacko!"

"No!" Arlen insisted. "No, he's . . . he's a little different, but he's no wacko. He's honest. He tells the truth."

Reed was about to grab the paper from Arlen's hand. "I'm *waiting*, Arlen!"

Arlen showed him the numbers Fleming had given him.

"What are these?"

"They were scratched in the dirt right next to the prints."

Reed read them, then half cried, half laughed.

"What is it?" Sheriff Mills demanded.

Tears filled Reed's eyes. "That's . . . It's my cell phone number! The area code and the first four digits!"

They gathered around as Reed held the paper up for them to see.

"Beck's running around with Sasquatches and leaving her phone number?" Jimmy said, disdain in his tone. "Guys, come on!"

Mills had to cover the question: "Is there any way this Fleming What's-his-name could have had your cell number?"

Reed was trembling. "Are you kidding?"

Pete asked, "Where is this place?"

Arlen answered, tapping the paper. "Whitetail, up one of the gulches. I can take you there."

Pete nodded. "Whitetail. That's farther south, Reed. It's south of Kamayah."

Reed caught his meaning. "South! I'm outta here."

"Whoa, wait a minute!" Jimmy stood in Reed's path. "Reed, listen—"

"Jimmy!" Mills's big index finger filled Jimmy's vision. "Now *you* shut up." He followed that up with an arch of his eyebrow, and Jimmy held his peace. "The search crews pick up where they left off, and if they've covered the zones, they'll start over again at the first ones. Pete, give 'em their assignments, put Tyler on the tracking, and then grab your gear. Jimmy, if you want to come along on this—"

"No thanks. I've got a bear, a *real* bear—"

"Hunt your bear, any way you want. Pete, we need a fourth man."

Pete looked at Max, who shot a quick sneer in Kane's direction and said, "I'm in."

Pete tapped Reed. "Hey, maybe Sing oughta bring her mobile lab—" He halted when he saw the hope in Reed's eyes.

"What?" Reed asked.

Pete wished he could answer, but he had neither the words nor the time. "Nothing. Let's go have a look."

■ ■ ■

"Cap, it's impossible." Dr. Emile Baumgartner, jacket and tie removed and shirt collar open, sipped from his coffee cup, then smiled with amusement. "Oh, it's all very intriguing. It would make a great story, but it's impossible."

Baumgartner had driven them to his home, a comfortable Victorian on the south side of Spokane. They were seated at a wrought iron table on Baumgartner's patio, enjoying a latte while a timed sprinkler *chit-chit-chitted* in rainbowed arcs across the lawn. Cap's notebook computer rested on the table between them, its screen filled with the data from the Judith Fairfax DNA Sequencing Core Facility.

"Impossible?" Cap loved hearing that word coming from an evolutionist; especially Baumgartner, an esteemed anthropologist and research associate at the York Center. Over the years, he'd been Cap's kindest opponent in the evolution debate. They'd had many discussions in many places, some private, some public, at various volume levels, but still they managed to stay friends. "Are you sure you want to say that word?"

Baumgartner laughed. "I'm not afraid of it. I *think* it all the time."

Cap laughed along, out of courtesy. "And then you leave it to poor stooges like me to say it—or write it."

"That was your choice. But that's what amazes me now—that you, of all people, would think it possible when you've basically ended your career arguing that it isn't."

"Burkhardt thought he could prove it," Cap said.

Baumgartner rolled his eyes and snickered. "Still does, so Merrill thinks he can do it because Burkhardt says so, but I'm sure you'll agree, blind devotion to a theory sometimes supplants real science."

"*Merrill's* backing him?"

Baumgartner held up a hand. "Ah, tut-tut-tut. The agreement, remember. We go no further on that."

"All right."

"Suffice it to say, Burkhardt may be pitifully myopic in his area of expertise, but far-reaching in his ability to work the system. He has the respect of the scientific community; he has friends with money; he's published some amazing theories. The university brass dote on him as if he's the next Watson or Crick, and he may well be—if he ever, *ever* succeeds in proving anything he's proposed."

"Jealous?" Cap said.

Baumgartner sniffed a chuckle. "Of course. But he's starting with an entirely faulty premise, as you pointed out."

"Really? You're saying I was right?"

Baumgartner laughed. "Oh, come on! You're not always wrong, no matter what I've said!"

"But where am I right?"

"You want to hear it from *me*!"

"You bet I do!"

"All right, all right." Baumgartner took another sip of coffee and set the cup down, pensively watching the lawn sprinkler. "When you argued that an organism is much more than the sum of its DNA sequences, you were right. I agree with you on that."

"So you also agree that we can't find specific genes that govern particular behaviors like swinging from trees or preferring grapes to cucumbers."

"Or that make Homo sapiens walk upright or even read Shakespeare. Agreed."

"But Burkhardt seems to think you can."

"He's wasting a lot of money." The anthropologist caught himself again. "I didn't say that." He continued, "Anyone can lay human DNA beside chimp DNA and sort out the similarities and differences, even quantify them."

"As in, 'We're 98 percent chimpanzee'?"

"You can't embarrass me, Cap. I didn't coin that phrase, though I'd be a richer man if I did. But as you pointed out—and I agree with you—we can find patterns in the DNA. We can even ascertain what creature or plant the DNA came from, but we can't create the code in the first place, nor can we rewrite it. It's far, far too complex."

Cap was surprised to find Baumgartner so full of concessions. "Wait a minute. No argument in favor of site-directed mutagenesis?"

Baumgartner laughed. "Do I detect sarcasm?"

"You've argued for it, remember?"

"In *reverse*, Cap. *Reverse* mutations. If we can identify the mutation that knocked out a healthy gene, we can use site-directed mutagenesis to restore the original gene and rescue the mutant, returning it to normal. You've seen that for yourself."

"Okay. That's one for you."

"Thank you. For that you get a bonus." He lowered his voice as if enemies might be listening. "*However*: In all the years of mutating, we have never actually *improved* anything. We have never produced an individual more fit than the original."

"Another concession?"

"Delivered in private, in confidence."

"Well, given that, what about the argument that insects mutate and develop resistance to insecticides?"

Baumgartner glared at him in mock anger. "So this is how you return my generosity!"

Cap lifted an eyebrow. "You've used that argument on me in public. Now that we're off the record . . ."

Baumgartner took a prolonged sip of his latte, apparently trying to build up the willingness to say it. "You're right about that too. As long as the toxin is present, then of course selective pressure is going to favor those mutants that are resistant, at which point it's tempting to cut short all observation and conclude a beneficial mutation. But all you have to do is remove the toxin and keep observing, and you'll find that the resistant mutant has so many other weaknesses that it can't compete with the normal insects and it dies out. It's a bad trade, like someone with sickle-cell anemia being immune to malaria but dying from the anemia. There's no real benefit." He flopped back in his chair, smarting from his own words. "If you were still the least bit respected in the scientific community, I would never have given you that. But since no one will listen to you . . ."

"I've always appreciated your honesty."

Baumgartner relaxed, the worst over, then he said, "Tampering with DNA is like a child trying to fix a high-tech computer with a toy hammer. It's always an injury, never an improvement, and we have boxcar loads of dead, mutated fruit flies and lab mice to prove it."

Cap paused and watched the sprinklers for a moment himself. "You understand what you're saying?"

Baumgartner nodded. "Something I would never attempt to publish."

"That mutations are not beneficial?"

"No, that would be plagiarizing *your* work. I'm only saying that tampering with DNA would be injurious. If you try to alter the genetic code of a chimp, for example, you would get one of three results: a normal, unchanged chimp; a deformed, retarded chimp; or a dead chimp."

Cap was startled. "Why would you concede that?"

"Because we achieved all three." He sipped from his coffee cup, effectively hiding behind it.

For Cap, that was news. "You tried to alter chimpanzee DNA?"

Baumgartner squirmed as if he'd overstepped. "We tried it; we learned; and we abandoned the project. For professional and legal reasons, there's nothing more to be said about that."

"What about Burkhardt?"

"I won't go there either."

"I suspect he didn't abandon the project," Cap offered.

Baumgartner shot him a correcting look.

"Okay. Okay." Cap lifted his hands in the air.

Baumgartner finished his coffee. "By the same token, I have nothing to say about your DNA results, except to repeat my position: what you're suggesting is impossible—and I think we've proved that, at great cost."

"So would you care to comment on the scuttlebutt I got from the protestors—" Baumgartner laughed derisively. "Well, they said that some chimps were being taken off campus, away from the Center—"

"Cap. We can pretend that you never had a clue as to how things are run on that campus. We can pretend that you hung yourself in total innocence, that you didn't know the damage you could do to science. We can pretend you haven't noticed that you are now, for all intents and purposes, unemployable, but, Cap, make no mistake: I have noticed. All your former colleagues have noticed, and there is, of course, the confidentiality agreement. I can't help you any further."

Cap took the blow, then nodded. "It's a matter of survival, I suppose."

Baumgartner agreed with Cap one last time. "I suppose." Then he looked away, seemingly interested in the rest of the world beyond their conversation—his way of signaling that the conversation was over.

"I'm just trying to find out why my best friend's wife is missing . . ." Cap shrugged. He knew it was a low blow, but it was the best he had. He reached to close down his computer.

Baumgartner put out a hand and stopped him. "However, I might pose a rhetorical question—and it is only that, a question."

Cap left the computer turned on. "Pose away."

Baumgartner looked away again, as if he were talking to someone else. "What if you were Burkhardt, and you had Merrill breathing down your neck demanding results, because *he* had big backers breathing down *his* neck demanding results? And what if a certain Dr. Capella's published contention that 'evolutionists have no ultimate basis for being honest' is in fact true?"

Cap didn't know quite how to answer. If Baumgartner was

cutting him a break, he didn't want to ruin it. "Could you, uh, expound on your question just a little?"

Baumgartner would not look at him—apparently his way of having the conversation without really having it. "Well, just for the sake of discussion, if you were expected to, say, bridge that 2 percent gap between humans and chimpanzees to demonstrate how we originally diverged from a common ancestor through mutations, how many base pairs would you have to change, rearrange, correct, or mutate, in precisely the right order, using site-directed mutagenesis alone?"

Cap already knew the answer. He and Baumgartner had publicly debated this topic several times. "The human genome contains some three billion base pairs. Two percent of that would be sixty million."

Baumgartner nodded quietly, seemingly amused by the numbers. "Sixty million. That would be a lot of changes to make even if you had the four million years we all think we had, and of course every single change would have to be beneficial. Imagine how daunting that job would be to an ambitious anthropologist in his midforties."

Baumgartner finally turned his eyes to the computer screen as if to confirm something. "Given all this, if you were Burkhardt, would you attempt to cheat? Would you, perhaps, entertain the possibility of moving wholesale amounts of DNA, even whole genes, the quickest way possible?"

Suddenly Cap knew where Baumgartner was going, and it was so obvious it was embarrassing. He leaned toward the computer and began to see in those myriad, confusing lines a pattern he hadn't put together before. "Viral transfers."

Baumgartner pointed out some of the lines himself. "Your 'junk DNA' may not be the junk you thought it was." He leaned back in his chair again, acting aloof. "Then again, maybe it is.

Huge, horizontal transfers can get messy. You're never quite sure where the new information is going to land or how the organism is going to turn out."

Cap grabbed up his computer. "Emile, you just might be a real scientist one day, you know that?"

He waved it off. "I was only posing a *question!*"

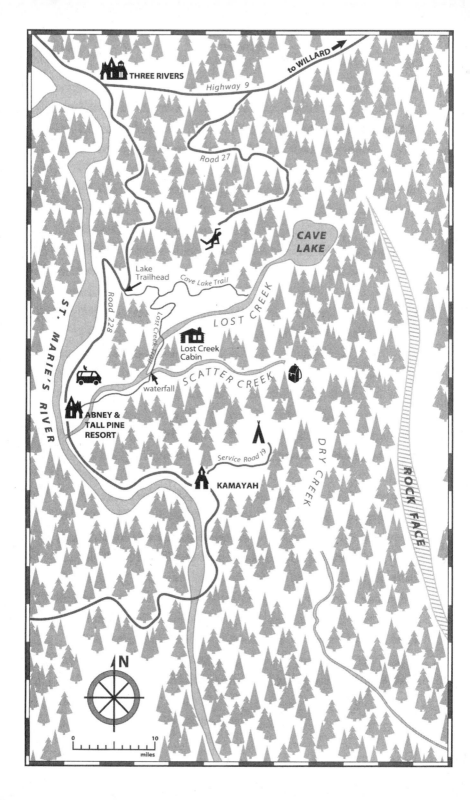

TEN

For one fleeting moment, Beck felt a sweet happiness. She was home with Reed and they were talking and laughing with each other in whole sentences. Sunlight streamed into their living room through an open front door, and strangely, she felt no urge to close it. Whether someone was coming to visit or she and Reed were going to venture out for a walk, either prospect was just fine, maybe for the first time in her life.

But that fleeting moment was in a dream, and when she jerked awake under a dark canopy of serviceberry, the dream slipped from her, image, by image though she struggled to keep it, until nothing remained but a sad sense of loss.

It was morning again. She couldn't remember what day it was or how many days she'd been lost in this place, wherever this place was. But as she shook off sleep, one thing felt different, enough to make her look around the thicket, searching for old and familiar company.

It seemed she was alone.

She looked about discreetly, stealthily. She listened. Were they gone? Had they left her?

She felt her ankle, then put some weight on it. With a crutch, or perhaps a brace of some kind, she could walk on it—for a while. She was on a mountain slope. They hadn't traveled very far since leaving their footprints at that baiting site. If she could make her way down the mountain and find that dry streambed, it might lead her to the baiting site and from there, to people.

It was now or never.

She crawled quietly, pressing through the fine and brittle branches, looking about, hopeful. So far, the forest was silent, as if—

"Hmph," came through the tangle to her right as the ground heaved into a reddish mound obscured by needles and leaves.

Beck stopped crawling, closed her eyes, and sighed, her head dropping. So much for that little hope. *I can't outrun her.*

A quiet stirring beyond the thicket drew her eye, and she saw Jacob sitting with his back against a pine tree, eyes half-open. He looked rather smug. Leah was combing and picking meticulously through the hair on his head and neck, pulling out pine needles, leaf fragments, and an occasional bug, which she ate, a tip for the beautician.

With no escaping in her immediate future, Beck thought of her own hair. Just trying to run her fingers through it told her it was a mess. She pushed free of the entangling undergrowth and settled down on the soft humus, taking the folding hairbrush from her jacket pocket. She brushed slowly, finding snags, tangles, twigs, and needles, but it felt great, almost spiritual. It was something she could do for herself because she wanted to, a way to restore a small measure of order to her ridiculous world—and it was something *human* for a change.

Having brushed out the last tangle, she pitched her head forward to gather her hair into one strand and deftly tied her hair into a neat knot on top of her head. There! Neat, brushed, and out of the way.

She thought she heard Rachel gasp. An ape, gasping? She looked toward the bushes. Rachel stared at her as if she were a stranger with two heads, antennae, and one big eye in the center of each forehead.

Beck's hand went to her head. "Hmmm?" *What's the matter? It's just me.*

Not good enough. Rachel approached in a cautious, sideways gait, head cocked with curiosity and alarm as if she couldn't believe what she was seeing. Gently, but with the firmness of a corrective mother, Rachel took hold of Beck's head—

Beck screamed and fought back, squirming, kicking, swatting, trying to free herself, struggling for her life.

Rachel didn't kill her. She examined Beck's head and then, with a gentle but irresistible cradling embrace, pulled Beck in close, sitting her down, like it or not, scolding her with pig grunts.

Still alive, with head and neck intact, Beck put her screams and kicks on hold, but she couldn't control her trembling. In scurrying thoughts she reminded herself that Rachel had never yet harmed her. Maybe if she went limp and played dead, Rachel would be satisfied. Maybe if she remained calm, Rachel would calm down as well. Maybe if—

With Beck properly positioned in front of her, Rachel went to work, poking, pulling, and yanking the knot on top of Beck's head. It hurt.

"Oww!" Beck dared to reach up.

Rachel huffed and batted her hands away.

Beck reached up again. Rachel batted her hands away more

sternly, then picked her up and sat her down with a bump as if to say, *You sit still, young lady!*

There was nothing to do but grimace until Rachel undid the knot. Beck's hair tumbled to her shoulders.

With the issue resolved, Beck's terrifying brush with death was over. Rachel gave Beck's hair several gentle combings with her fingers and let her go. Beck hobbled away, hair untangled, groomed, and free in the breeze. She sat in the grass, trying to calm herself.

It wasn't easy. What was the big problem? If Rachel was so obsessed with appearances, she could certainly give a little more attention to her own appearance!

Beck took a slow, deliberate breath and tried to remind herself that these were animals, and animals just did what they did. Rachel liked Beck's hair the way it was, and as for the reason—Beck snickered bitterly—did Rachel even need one? Was she even aware of one? Maybe appearances *were* important to Sasquatches; maybe they were unsettled by change; maybe Beck was projecting her own feelings into these animals and was totally wrong about everything.

Feeling grumpy, Beck took out her hairbrush. If she couldn't wear her hair up, at least she could brush it again, her way of having the last word. She ran her brush through her hair with strong, anger-driven strokes, purposely turning her eyes away from Rachel and devoting her attention to Leah and Jacob.

Leah seemed in no hurry as she combed Jacob with her fingers. She deftly scooped out bugs with her fingernails and neatly arranged his coat one section at a time, all the while stealing an occasional side glance to see if Rachel was watching. Beck marveled at Leah's expression. She reminded herself again that these were animals, but the more she watched, the more she had to wonder—Was it possible for an ape to be *catty*?

A movement from Rachel drew her attention—and held it. Beck stopped brushing, the brush poised in her hair at the top of a stroke.

In her slow, lazy way, and with her eyes focused on Beck's right hand, Rachel was stroking the left side of her head with her big fingers.

Beck switched and brushed the hair on her left side.

Rachel clumsily stroked the right side of her head with her right hand, a hairy mirror image.

Beck felt Leah looking their way and shot a glance back. Leah immediately went to work as if she hadn't been watching a thing.

Now, this was intriguing. Beck looked down at the brush in her hand. Was Rachel mimicking, or was she asking?

She rose carefully, tentatively. While gently touching Rachel's chest to soothe her, she placed the brush against Rachel's head and passed it lightly through the tangled hair.

Rachel sighed and relaxed. She was all for it, like a dog getting petted.

Beck brushed a little more, and Rachel leaned into it.

Well. Okay, then.

Beck kept going, brushing out the tangles, combing with her fingers, cleaning Rachel's coarse, oily coat. When she stopped to pull twigs, bugs, leaves, and loose hairs from the brush, Rachel nudged her to continue. She returned to her work, parting Rachel's hair neatly down the middle, coifing the sides and teasing the hair to give it body, blending the head and neck hair with the hair on Rachel's back. She had to pause frequently to clean debris from the brush, but Rachel finally accepted that part of the process once Beck gave her first choice of anything the brush found.

Before Beck realized it, she was having fun. She started humming to herself, no tune in particular.

Rachel stared off into space and made a deep-toned noise of her own. "Hmmmmhmmmmhmmm."

Beck smiled and kept humming, working on Rachel's right shoulder. Grooming the whole body was going to be a big job, like brushing down a vertical horse, but the hair was mostly cooperative, sorting itself out and falling into place as the brush passed through.

Rachel watched, obviously pleased, as Beck brushed her right arm. "Hmmmmmhmmm."

Beck started whistling just to see what would happen.

Rachel cocked her head, apparently surprised.

"Woo-w-whistle!" Beck said, and did it.

Rachel had to think about it and then tightened her lips against her teeth and made her playful teakettle sound. Beck laughed and whistled with her. It was just like getting their dog, Jonah, to "sing" by making high, howling sounds. Beck whistled, Rachel whistled; Beck whistled, Rachel whistled. Now for that left shoulder—

"Rooarr!" Rachel flinched so violently she sent Beck tumbling.

Beck righted herself, poised to run, expecting to die, thoroughly, shakingly terrified. *I've broken the rules!*

But Rachel wasn't angry. She looked down at her left shoulder, gingerly touching the place Beck had tried to brush.

Still trembling, and making sure she had Rachel's permission for each step, Beck dared to come back.

Now that the caked blood was broken up by the brushing, Beck could see for the first time where the blood had come from. The wounds were recent and just beginning to heal—two large tears near the top of the shoulder with smaller cuts between and on either side. The curved pattern suggested the obvious: Rachel had been viciously attacked and bitten.

Beck backed away, the brush at her side, and stole a fearful glance in Jacob's direction. He was still sitting against the tree, basking in all the attention he was getting from Leah. He met her eyes only once, then looked straight ahead as if he didn't care to discuss it.

. . .

Cap, in billed cap and blue coveralls he borrowed from the caretaker's garage, carried a bag of garbage on one shoulder to obscure his face as he walked down an alley to check out the rear of a particular building. During the summer quarter, many of the labs and classrooms were not in constant use, meaning the lab he needed might be empty. At least the alley was empty. He tossed the bag into a Dumpster, looked around as casually as he could, then walked briskly up the alley to a back door.

This was Corzine University's Bioscience building, his old stomping ground, a modern, three-story structure with lots of glass, state-of-the-art labs and classrooms, and what used to be his office. Access through the front door would mean signing in and making his presence known, which would bring questions and permission denial, things he couldn't afford. This door in the back, known only to maintenance staff and professors trying to avoid squabbles with student protestors, required only a key.

He pulled a key from his pocket, the one he'd unknowingly left in another pair of pants when the administrator told him to turn in all his keys. He'd planned to bring it back or maybe just mail it. If things didn't go well today, they'd get it anyway.

The key worked. The door opened. He ducked inside.

He was in the combination office and locker room of the maintenance department. Against one wall was a row of lockers; opposite the lockers were the desk and cot of the head custodian, Louis. The desk calendar was filled with Louis's usual notes and reminders in blue felt-tip pen. Good. Things were still the same.

Hopefully, Louis kept the same schedule. He always arrived for work at eight in the evening, after everyone else had gone home—except for intensely occupied molecular biologists who had a habit of working late. He and Louis had gotten to know each other pretty well.

Cap even knew which locker was Louis's, and that Louis never bothered to lock it. Inside, he found the custodian's coveralls and, most important, an access card that operated the doors in the rest of the building. Louis lost that card once, and another time his youngest daughter had used it for making motor sounds in the spokes of her bicycle. Ever since, Louis kept it in his locker, strung on a lanyard.

Cap hung the access card around his neck. He checked his watch. Most of the staff and students were probably at lunch right now. This was going to be tight, but doable.

He hurried into the next room, where supply shelves reached to the ceiling and the cleaning carts were parked evenly spaced in a straight row. The trash cans on board were emptied and relined, cleaning solutions replenished, clean dust cloths in place, mops beaten and ready to go again. He picked a cart, added two more dust mops with big heads to the cart's broom rack—in case he needed to hide his face—and wheeled the cart up to the metal-clad fire door that stood between him and the rest of the building.

Without waiting to rethink this or bolster his courage, he swiped the card through the slot of the keypad. The lock clicked open, and he pushed through.

It felt odd sneaking into a place where he felt so much at home. He'd been up and down these clean, off-white halls and through these department doors so many times he almost knew this place better than his own house. He hurried down the hall, avoided the eyes of a few students who passed by, came to a T—

A man with perfectly coifed hair and wearing a tailored suit stood at the end of the hall to the right; he was straightening a few pages that had gone crooked in a notebook he carried.

It was Dr. Philip Merrill, formerly the department chair of Molecular Biology, recently promoted to dean of the College of Sciences. He was more than well entrenched in the system—he practically *was* the system—and he and Cap had never been on good terms.

Cap turned down the hall to the left, ducking around to the front of his cart and pulling it behind him, keeping his back to Merrill and the cart with the big mops between them.

He rolled past an informal lounge area with chairs, a couch, and some *Science*, *Nature*, and *Cell* magazines, and then through some heavy double doors marked Authorized Personnel Only Beyond This Point.

Immediately to the right was a door with a large glass window. A placard on the wall to the left read Molecular Biology Research Center, and under that was a blank space where his name used to be. Cap swiped Louis's card through the keypad, and once again, the lock clicked open.

Inside was a wondrous place, his former world. His micropipettes and PCR thermal cycler waited faithfully on the bench where he preferred them, although the electrophoresis gel boxes and power supply had been rearranged to someone else's liking. The reagents inside the glass storage cabinets were exactly as he'd left them, so they would be available if he needed them. Joy of all joys, the fluorescent microscope was still in place and operational, its video camera still interfaced with a computer.

There was no time to waste. Cap parked the cart against the door, adjusting the mop heads to block the window. Then he pulled the blinds on the outside windows. He reached inside his coveralls for a paper bag, and from the paper bag he pulled three plastic bags—one containing the rest of the hair samples, one containing the rest of the stool samples, and one containing the squashed thermos that still held dried saliva. The folks at the Judy Lab were good people, but Cap knew they also had professional considerations, especially where former biology professors were concerned. Holding back a portion of the samples and keeping them safely tucked away was a planned precaution.

He'd already made a trip back to the Internet, asked the right questions, and gotten a positive ID on that "junk" DNA. Now he knew what to look for, and he had a very good idea where to find it. The procedure would only take a few hours, and he could do it alone. If Baumgartner's not-so-subtle hint was correct, he would soon know.

■ ■ ■

As long as Beck was slow and careful, Rachel let her brush out the blood-encrusted hair around the wounds and even helped by licking the area with her tongue. It was tedious work, sometimes hair by hair—Beck didn't want to get decked again—but they made it through the task together. The perilous area groomed, Beck stepped back to clean her brush, admire her work, and enjoy the feeling.

Rachel grunted, reaching for the hairbrush. Beck let her take it to sniff it for treats while Beck removed her jacket. Rachel sniffed the brush and probed it with her fingers, but better treats could easily be found for less work. She lost interest.

"Hmm?" Beck prompted, her hand extended.

Rachel gave the brush back.

Beck worked her way down Rachel's expansive back and around her waist, nudging that big body one way and then the other so she could reach every side. Rachel was looking good, the dandiest Sasquatch in the forest.

She sent looks Leah's direction. *Hey, Leah!* I'm *getting* groomed! *What do you think about* that?

Jacob abandoned Leah, disappearing into the forest in his usual, mysterious way. With no source of glory, Leah sank against a tree and moodily examined her fingernails.

Rachel jutted out her jaw and wiggled it at her competitor.

Apparently, Leah reached some kind of limit. A plaintive expression came over her face; she actually fussed a little and then started to rise as if she would come their way.

Rachel lurched and barked at her, teeth bared, a display so abrupt and loud it made Beck jump. Leah sat back down, her eyes averted.

Beck wasn't sure she could believe what she saw. "M-my, my!"

Rachel snuffed in Leah's direction, an assertive postscript, then heaved a deep sigh and relaxed, looking lovely.

"Woo-w-well! It's about time!" Beck touched the side of Rachel's face and looked her in the eye, something only safe between friends. "See? You're not so bad." A cluster of mountain bluebells grew within reach. Beck plucked them up, twisted them together, and stuck them in Rachel's hair. "The ugly duckling is now a princess!"

Rachel pulled the bluebells from her hair, sniffed them, and ate them.

Oh well.

When Beck heard a sickening, ripping sound, she knew what it was—and who was responsible—before she leaped lopsidedly to her feet to look.

"No, noo!"

She'd wondered where Reuben was, and of course, all it took to bring him out of hiding were Beck's eyes averted and her jacket unguarded. He had her buckskin jacket in his teeth; he bit and yanked pieces of leather as if it were beef jerky. A sleeve was already torn off and lying on the ground by itself.

Beck limped toward him, yelling, screaming, waving her arms.

He found a pocket and pulled out Beck's precious roll of toilet paper.

"N-n-noo! P-p-p-!" *Please!*

She took one step too many toward Leah's child. Leah exploded from the ground and became a fearsome wall between them, teeth bared, hands ready to break Beck in half. Beck lurched away to save her life, and Rachel caught her, growling, but moving to their safe zone.

Reuben discovered that the toilet paper could unroll.

Beck wailed in anguish and disbelief. This couldn't be happening. God wouldn't let a thing like this happen. This was worse than losing the jacket.

When Reuben pulled on the streamer of toilet paper, the dwindling roll danced and tumbled. He leaped with delight and pulled it again, getting another loop of streamer as a reward.

Beck sank to her knees, defeated, insulted, and violated, watching the last vestige of her cherished world unravel in the hands of a savage beast.

With his body draped and looped in white streamers, Reuben grabbed the jacket again and, like a dog slinking away to chew on a treat, bolted into the woods and out of sight.

God, did You *make him do that? You couldn't allow me just one little comfort?*

And just when she was feeling better. She'd even spoken a few sentences.

It wasn't fair.

■ ■ ■

It was unbelievable, but the evidence was clear, recent, and right in front of them, not more than an hour's hike from Whitetail.

The roughly twelve-by-twelve patch of tilled and raked earth now abounded in tracks unlike any they'd ever seen before.

"Never in my life," said Arlen Peak, in total awe.

Fleming Cryncovich, still burdened with heavy bags of casting plaster and clanging mixing bowls, was the sort whose excitement went straight to his mouth. "Hey, forget Bluff Creek and the Skookum Cast, I mean, this is something, this is really something, this is four of 'em all at once! This oughta change some minds, don't you think? My mom and dad, you know, they don't believe in Bigfoot, but I always knew . . . It's patience, right? Patience is what it takes. Let's cast 'em, man, before they erode."

Sheriff Mills, unabashedly staring, visibly shaken, put up his hand. "Slow. Slow down. And stay back, please. We have no idea what we've got here, not even the half of it."

Fleming backed up a few steps, his impatience showing. Max Johnson and Arlen Peak stayed close to make sure Fleming wouldn't be a problem. That didn't mean they could keep him quiet. "I've tried to stick with local fruits, the kind that grow around here. But I guess somebody liked the bananas too. Listen, there's a running creek right over there. I can bring water for the plaster; it'd be easy."

Pete, with Reed at his shoulder, had worked his way around the perimeter, measuring boot prints near the edge and comparing them to a drawing he'd made near the Lost Creek cabin. He placed his tape measure in his pocket and looked one more time at his drawing. Finally, he reported, "It's her."

Reed exhaled a held breath and locked his knees to keep from collapsing. He couldn't hold back his tears, but he resolved he would remain standing, whatever it took.

Pete pointed as he spoke. "Same boot sole, same wear pattern. See there? She's favoring her right foot, putting most of her weight on the left. She's injured, but she's alive and walking. Can't explain it; can't explain any of this, but that's how it is."

"Well," Fleming piped in, "Bigfoot are not known for violence against humans, except maybe the Ape Canyon incident, but that's grown into a legend by now—but there have been reports that they don't like dogs very much . . ."

Sing kneeled on the opposite side of the tilled area, glasses perched on her nose, magnifying glass hovering over the largest print. "It's explaining itself, *if* we can believe it." She rested back, sitting on the grass at the edge, more shaken than Reed had ever seen her. She brushed some hair away from her face and looked at Arlen. "This footprint has a scar on the ball of the foot. It's an old injury that's healed, with the dermal ridges turned inward." She sighed, overcome. "Arlen, you know that casting you have back at the inn? That footprint and this one were made by the same animal."

Arlen was stunned, then beaming. He and Fleming high-fived each other.

Pete nodded. "Most likely a male." He turned to Reed and Mills, "The *alpha* male, if that's how these animals operate. We've got four of 'em: one big male, two smaller adults that are probably females, and one juvenile, can't guess what sex it is."

"And Beck," said Reed.

"And Beck," Pete agreed.

Sing was still looking at the big print. "This print's a full eighteen inches long, and—Pete, what do you make of this?"

Pete circled around, along with Reed and Mills, and knelt close. "Yeah, lookie there. See the outside edge of the print?" He pointed it out to Reed and Mills. "The dermal ridges—you know, the crinkles in the skin like fingerprints—they're running along the length of the foot, not across it, like human prints."

"So tell me what we're looking at," said the sheriff.

All eyes went to Pete. He scanned the prints one more time. "I may as well admit the obvious." He paused and gave a deep sigh. "I'd say we've got ourselves a Bigfoot." He cast a questioning glance at each of them.

Reed had thought so all along, and now he let his face show it. Sing nodded acceptance. Mills stared back, stern as a rock.

"Which one has Beck?" Reed asked.

"Not the camp raider." Pete pointed to one of the midsized prints. "I'd say this one here. It's the closest match with the size we found above the waterfall, and look at that pressure ridge in the middle of the print."

Sing was still amazed about it. "Right behind the midtarsal joint. These feet flex in the middle."

"That's how she fooled me. She pushes off from the whole front half of the foot. We couldn't tell what in the world we were tracking. But look there; figure that one out." He directed their attention to where the first digits of Reed's cell phone number were scratched in the dirt—two sets of prints seemed to be playing tag with each other. "When Beck tried to carve out your phone number, that big gal was following her." He sniffed a chuckle. "Looks like she even tried to write herself."

Sing grabbed the camera from her backpack and snapped pictures. Among her shots of the footprints, she also captured a few group shots, careful to include close shots of Fleming Cryncovich, Arlen Peak, and Max Johnson. She and Reed were compiling a record of every name, every face, no exceptions.

"How fresh are these tracks?" Mills asked.

Fleming blurted proudly, "I raked this area early yesterday. Found the tracks this morning."

Pete nodded. Apparently, what he saw matched that scenario. Still on one knee, his gaze sweeping slowly, he scanned the trail of tracks leading back across the coarse sand and into the streambed. "Could I have everybody stay put, and no noise, please?" He got to his feet and followed the tracks, taking one carefully chosen step at a time, staying well to the side. As the others waited and watched, the tracks took him clear across the smooth, dry river rocks of the streambed and to a narrow stand of river grass on the other side. Just beyond the grass, the forest began and the mountainside rose sharply, the trees rising one behind the other, tree above tree above tree, until the green mat of the forest ended abruptly against a jagged and near-vertical rock face. He stood very still in the grass, reading the sign, looking, listening, maybe even *smelling* for all the others knew.

Fleming piped up, his whisper loud and grating, "Can we do the casting now?"

Mills picked up his rifle as he answered, "When Pete gives the okay."

"I brought some more plaster," said Arlen, "but I don't think it'll be enough."

"I brought some too," said Sing. "We'll try to stretch it."

Mills looked at the field of footprints and gave his head a barely discernible wag. "Nobody's ever gonna believe this."

When Pete finally returned, his walk was brisk. He didn't speak until he was close enough to do it quietly. "They didn't follow the streambed." He pointed as the others gathered around. "They cut straight across and headed up the mountain. If they're still up there and we can push them up against that rock face . . ."

Mills nodded and whispered, "We can hem them in."

Reed got a grip on his apprehension by sheer force of will. His stomach was tight to the point of nausea, and even his whisper quaked: "What if Beck's with them?"

They all exchanged nervous looks.

"If Beck's with them," the sheriff finally answered, "then we can't let them leave."

Max sighted through his rifle scope a little too calmly, as if he wasn't buying any of this.

Pete walked to his backpack and dug out some small plastic spray bottles. "Better spray this on. The air's moving up that slope like a brush fire." He tossed a bottle to each hunter. It was scent shield, rather unpleasant stuff that covered up human scent. They sprayed it on their clothing and boots, then smeared it on their hands and faces. "There're only four of us, but maybe that's better," Pete said. "No dogs, no mobs, no racket. I want to get close this time." He pulled his shirt open and sprayed his armpits. The others did the same.

"Can we cast the prints now?" Fleming nagged.

"You may," said Pete. He studied the mountainside as he addressed Mills. "If we push 'em, they're gonna break left or right. If I can get you and Reed to handle the left and right flanks, Max and I can sew up the middle."

Max seemed unconvinced. "So how do we even know they're up there?"

"Right now it's a good guess," said Pete. "But we're gonna find out real quick."

■ ■ ■

The big metal door swung open and Cap came through, shoving the cleaning cart ahead of him, brooms swaying, bottles sloshing. He checked his watch. Louis wouldn't be arriving for several hours. So far, so good. He pushed the door shut and wheeled the cleaning cart back into its parking place. Now. Which mops did he add? He pulled one out—

A key rattled in the back door.

I'm dead!

He never danced so quickly in his life as he spun and swivel-necked, trying to spot a place to hide.

Behind the carts. It was his only choice.

He yanked the cart out of its parking place, dove into the space behind, and pulled the cart in after him. It didn't fit all the way in, but maybe Louis wouldn't notice.

The back door opened and somebody big came in, work shoes thudding and shuffling heavily on the floor. It was Louis, all right. Cap knew that familiar whistle. The tune was "Georgia." Louis was a big Ray Charles fan.

And he was ever-so-inconveniently early!

Cap looked down and noticed he still had Louis's access card around his neck. *Oh, please, Louis, don't go to your locker.*

He heard the locker door open and the rustle of Louis's coveralls as Louis pulled them on.

Then the whistling stopped. Louis was rummaging around in the locker. The big footfalls went to the desk. Papers shuffled. A drawer opened and shut again.

The huge footsteps came into the supply room and stopped. Louis was looking around. The silence suggested he was being cautious.

I'm deader than dead. Louis had to weigh 270, 280 pounds, and he was all muscle. If he wanted to detain Cap—and that was putting it nicely—it would happen, absolutely.

Cap prayed, his heart pounding. *Dear Lord, don't let him worry about one of his carts being crooked—*

Louis came straight to the cart and pulled it out.

The light streamed in on Cap, cowering like a frightened mouse against the back wall.

Louis, a towering African American with a lineman's body and a shaved head, gawked at Cap for a protracted moment. Cap considered trying to explain, but this ridiculous situation and the sight of this huge man struck him stupid and he couldn't find the first word.

The big man sighed through his nose, rubbed his lips together thoughtfully, and finally asked, "Should I come back later?"

Cap struggled to his feet, never breaking eye contact and trying to smile. "Uh, no. I'm all through." Once on his feet, he still had to look up to meet Louis's gaze.

Louis reached and with one finger gave the card hanging from Cap's neck a little jiggle. Cap took it off hurriedly and handed it to him. Louis looked it over as if checking for damage, then put it around his own neck.

"You better get out of here," he said. "I got some crew comin' in, and I don't wanna be stuck explainin' you."

Cap inched around the big man's frame and made a beeline for the back door. "Louis, uh, thanks."

Louis followed him at a distance, watching him. "You get what you needed?"

Cap paused at the door, considering the question and the data printout he'd stuffed in his pocket. "I'm afraid so."

He got out of there.

■ ■ ■

Reed worked his way carefully up the incline, searching and selecting a firm, hopefully silent place to plant each step, weaving and dodging from tree to tree, his pulse pounding, his rifle slick in his sweating hands. The GPS receiver strapped to his left forearm showed him he'd come halfway up the slope; the four numbered blips on the moving map indicated he was maintaining formation with the others. They were moving up the hill in a semicircular arrangement, like the bottom half of a clock: Reed was at three o'clock; Pete was downhill and to Reed's left at five o'clock; Max was coming up the middle to Pete's left at seven o'clock; Sheriff Mills was directly opposite Reed at nine o'clock. The rock face was directly above them.

The GPS doubled as a two-way radio, and now Pete's voice whispered in Reed's earpiece, "The tracks are veering south a little. Let's add another ten degrees."

Reed spotted a big fir about fifty yards up the bank and ten degrees to his right. He headed for it. The blips on his map made the same correction. The half circle warped, lagged, caught up, overtightened, then loosened again as each man struggled with the terrain, but so far they were holding the dragnet together.

Reed held his rifle in one hand while he dried the other on his pant leg, then switched hands and dried again. Part of him—the part with the weak knees, pounding pulse, and sweaty palms—couldn't help dwelling on the flaws in the plan. There were only four hunters forming this semicircle, and they were spread out over half a mile. Any creature brave and wily enough could slip through the huge gaps between them and be long gone before they knew it. The success of Pete's plan rested on these animals being either very shy or very deadly. If they were shy, they would back away until the hunters could tighten the circle and hem them in against the rocks; if they were deadly, then at least one of the hunters was bound to encounter them sooner or later. Pete didn't mention how even shy animals could become deadly if cornered, but it did occur to Reed that, given what they were attempting, they were going to be dealing with a deadly wild animal either way. Pete's only admonition for whenever that happened was "Don't let them get past you."

Right. No problem. Those eighteen-inch footprints had given Reed a whole new way of looking at shadowy trees, obscured stumps, and breeze-rippled bushes. He'd already chambered a round. The safety was off. Thinking of Beck was the only thing that kept him pushing into this madness. Pete had said she was injured, limping most likely. Reed hoped it wasn't more serious. How had she managed to survive this long when two strong men had died at the hands of these beasts? That was the question no one had asked, and yet it bothered Reed. Was she living in a terror that far outpaced the hell he'd been living in?

There were only three blips on his GPS screen. "Sheriff Mills? I don't have you on-screen."

". . . I'm . . . on the . . . here," Mills came back, his voice breaking up.

■ ■ ■

Sing had returned to her mobile lab, parked next to a trailer-turned-tavern in the obscure, almost-town of Whitetail. She could see all four blips on her computer screen via the satellite dish on her roof. "The satellite's picking up everybody," she reported over her headset. "It's the peer-to-peer radio signal between the units. Sometimes terrain and distance can block it."

"Yeah, I'm down in a hollow," Mills reported.

"It happens. Max? Better add another ten degrees; you're drifting left."

"Ten more degrees," Max replied.

"Everybody, I copy you about a quarter mile below the rocks."

The blips kept moving, inch by inch.

"Whoa!" Max whispered.

Pete radioed, "Hold up!"

The radios went silent. The blips on the screen stopped moving.

■ ■ ■

Reed merged with an elderly hemlock, nothing moving but his eyes, and then, as slowly as the sweep hand on a clock, his head. The forest around him was thick enough to hide anything. Apart from the chirping of a bird somewhere, he heard nothing. No movement. No twigs snapping, no rustling. He waited.

Pete came on the radio, his whisper barely audible. "Max, I heard some movement your direction."

Max reported in a tense, hushed voice, "Yeah. There's something up there, my eleven o'clock."

Pete replied, "Any visual?"

"No."

■ ■ ■

Sing leaned toward her computer monitor, her hand pressing her earpiece against her ear, her mind leaping into the map she saw on the screen. The blips were motionless, still in a rough semicircle on steep terrain.

"Sheriff?" came Pete's voice.

"I heard it. My two o'clock."

■ ■ ■

Reed scanned the forest to his left, inside the semicircle. His gaze locked onto a brown mass behind some elderberry. It didn't move. After a blink, a look away, and a return, he saw that it was a stump.

He carefully stole a step, then another, then four up the hill where he merged with another hemlock.

"Yeah," came the sheriff's muffled voice. "There it was again, two o'clock."

Pete replied, "Sheriff, move up toward the rocks. Max, fill in. I'm up the middle. Reed, move left, close in, quick and quiet."

Reed separated from the hemlock and moved left, his eyes on the trees, the tangled brush, the ferns, the obscuring broad leaves. He stopped short at the sight of a shadow behind some devil's club. When he was sure it was an upturned root ball, he stepped again, carefully placing his foot on soft earth or solid log, anything silent.

"I'm getting closer," said Mills. "I can hear it moving, still to my right."

"Move in, everybody," said Pete. "Move in. Tighten the circle."

Reed checked the screen on his GPS. All four numbered blips were visible now, but the semicircle didn't look much tighter than before. He tried to move faster.

He froze. His finger wrapped around the trigger.

Something uphill, to his right, caught his eye. Something white, flickering, waving. A whitetail deer? No. It wasn't moving from that spot.

"Did you hear that?" Mills asked.

"Yeah," Max replied.

Reed checked his GPS. Mills was moving in, tightening the top of the semicircle. Max and Pete moved up the hill, flattening the pattern. He could see his blip still lingering out on the right flank.

The strange white thing was there, moving in the slight breeze. Reed quickened his pace, eyes alert, as he closed the distance. It appeared to be a ribbon of some kind, but what surveyor would have been clear up here?

"Heads up, heads up," Mills whispered. "It's coming down the hill."

"Max, eyes open!" said Pete.

A quick run across the open grass, and Reed came to an elder-berry bush sporting the white ornament. It looked like—

He reached it, even touched it.

A string of toilet paper.

"I think I saw it!" said Mills. "Huh. I think it's a bear. It's black."

Reed did not remove the toilet paper from the bush but stood by it, surveying in all directions for any other sign. There! Only fifteen feet away, a small scrap of white lay like a fallen leaf on a patch of brown pine needles. Nervously, quickly, keeping an eye open for anything approaching, he entered his present location as a waypoint on the GPS. He was about to report when—

"I don't have it," said Max.

"I don't either," said Mills. "It's quit moving."

"Pete, Reed, where are you?"

Sing responded, "Pete's on his way, about a thousand feet at your five o'clock. Reed, how're you doing?"

"I've found something," he said. For some silly reason he didn't want to say he'd found toilet paper. "I'm going to—"

He heard it, and time stopped. His thoughts, his breath, maybe even his heart, stopped. That ghostlike cry of anguish, though echoing and distant, chilled his blood even more than when he'd first heard it in the dark near the cabin on Lost Creek.

■ ■ ■

Beck barely had time to flinch before Rachel grabbed her up and dove into a sheltering clump of elderberry and maple, huffing in alarm. Clamped against Rachel's chest, Beck looked backward over Rachel's shoulder and saw Leah crouching in the open, call-ing for Reuben with faint, high-pitched yelps, until the leaves closed in and she saw nothing.

She didn't have to. With the jolting surprise over and the

brush settling back to stillness, she heard the distant sound that so alarmed her captors. Her hands became trembling fists as she clamped onto Rachel's fur.

■ ■ ■

Reed was about to call, but Mills spoke first.

"It's her!" said Mills. "Reed, I can hear Beck!"

No. *No!*

"Sounds like she's hurting," said Max.

Reed tried to control his voice as he radioed, "It's not Beck! Repeat, it is *not* Beck. Do you copy?"

"Reed, you're breaking up," said Pete.

Faint in the distance, Sheriff Mills was shouting, "Beck! Beck Shelton!"

Reed broke into a run, ducking and veering around trees, thrashing through thick brush. He radioed as he ran, "Mills, get out of there!"

"Max, let's move!" Pete ordered.

The blips on Reed's GPS crawled steadily toward each other, tightening the pattern.

"I've got it," said Mills. "It's a—" A drawn breath. The squeak of leather, the rattle of metal. The sheriff was fumbling with his rifle. "Man, oh man, I don't believe it!" His signal cut out.

A rifle shot!

"Mills! *Mills!*" Reed cried.

Mills came back on the air, breathing heavily as if running. "Get up here; you hear me? Get up here!"

Another rifle shot.

Pete demanded, "Sheriff, are you all right?"

"God help me, that thing's *walking!*"

ELEVEN

For a microsecond, Reed forced himself to stop against every raging need to plunge forward. He gripped his rifle high, ready to sight down the barrel at so much as a squirrel if it dared to move. Between gasps for air, he listened for any sound, no matter how insignificant. Whatever Mills had encountered, it wasn't the only one.

Pete was yelling, his voice distorted in the earpiece, "*Mills!* Just shoot. Draw a bead and shoot."

"I can't see him!" Then came a scream of alarm. Another shot.

Reed was moving again, eyes wide open, rifle ready. He came to a clearing, swept it visually, and dashed across.

"Mills?" Pete called. "Mills! Max, do you see him?"

Max didn't answer. Reed checked his GPS as he plunged into the trees again. Mills was moving north, obviously running. Max's blip had stalled. "Max, Sheriff Mills is northeast of you. Move northeast."

Max finally answered, "I can't get there from here. I've got to go around—"

They heard a scream, first piercing, then garbled, then muffled—

Then cut short. Silent.

A second scream followed: the woman—that same invisible banshee of Lost Creek—screamed as if she'd been cut open, the echoes of her voice layering one upon the other as the barren rocks sent the sound back and forth, back and forth, back and forth across the valley. Reed froze in terror, his back against a tree, his eyes darting, his hands nearly dropping the rifle.

The nightmare had returned in daylight. From *out there*, a legion of demons answered the woman from their haunts and hiding places, their guttural howls long and mournful like ghostly sirens following one upon the other, rising, fading, notes clashing, echoing, echoing, echoing.

The radios were silent as every man went speechless. Reed was petrified, wishing he could meld into the tree at his back. These were no strangers; he'd heard this eerie dirge before, and it was no less terrifying now.

■ ■ ■

Beck clamped her hands over her ears and cowered, unable to squirm out of Rachel's iron grasp as the Sasquatch, head raised and jaws agape, howled with the power of a ship's horn. Rachel was trembling, stinking. Her eyes swept about the brush canopy as if death hovered over their heads.

I heard shots, Beck thought. But still the woman screamed. *What's happening?*

■ ■ ■

Just outside their hiding place in the brush, Leah crouched in the undergrowth and howled just as loudly, still anxiously looking for her son.

Reuben came bounding out of the trees, tattered shreds of toilet paper streaming behind him. Leah scooped him up; he clung to her, a frightened child, and Leah immediately plunged into the elderberry thicket, nearly trampling Rachel and Beck in her haste.

■ ■ ■

Pete called, "Mills? Sheriff Mills, can you hear me?"

No answer.

Reed checked his GPS. Max and Pete were moving again. Max would reach Mills first.

But Mills's blip wasn't moving.

Reed called, "Sing, are you getting anything from Sheriff Mills?"

Sing's voice was tight with emotion. "His GPS is still working and I'm getting his radio signal, but he isn't moving. He isn't responding."

Reed checked his bearings, dried his hands on his jacket, and plunged ahead, knees weak. "Hello, this is Reed. Somebody out there talk to me."

Pete came back, "We're closing on Mills. Watch yourself. That critter's still out here."

Reed was watching, all right. These woods were full of shadows and dark places to hide. His rifle barrel went anywhere his eyes went. A raven flew from a dead branch above him and he almost shot it.

Sing came on the radio. "Max? Are you all right? Can you talk to me?"

Max didn't answer. Reed checked his screen. Max was moving, so he was alive. He was getting close to Mills's location.

Sing asked again, "Max?"

Reed kept moving, pushing through the brush, clambering over rocks and logs, eyes darting, dread closing over him like a cloud.

Pete radioed, "I have Max. He's okay." Movement. Branches snapping. Pete's laboring breath and footsteps came over the radio. "Max? I'm coming up behind you." Pete's voice became strangely quiet, cautious. "Max, I don't see your rifle. Point it in the air for me, will you, bud? Okay. Good. Now just keep it there, okay? I'm coming up behind you. You see me? Max? Just look over your right shoulder. It's okay; it's me."

Now Reed heard movement ahead of him. "Pete? I'm coming your way from slightly uphill."

"I hear you, Reed."

"What's the story?"

"Stand by. I'm gonna check on Max. He's—"

Silence.

Reed didn't like silence, not now. "Pete?"

"Uh . . ."

Reed could see a small break in the forest canopy ahead of him. Light was penetrating to the forest floor. A few more steps through the undergrowth and he saw Pete, looking his way.

Pete waved at him, weakly at first, but then urgently. "Get out of those trees, Reed. We've got a casualty."

Those were the words none of them wanted to hear. Reed carefully chose some short leaps down the grade and broke into the clearing.

Max was sitting awkwardly on the ground, teetering as if he'd collapsed there, his face pale, his body quivering and palsied with shock, his eyes staring, then averting, then staring again. Reed thought he was injured, even shot.

Pete stood by Max, alert, rifle following his eyes as he continuously scanned the forest on all sides. He gestured for Reed to close in. Reed crossed quickly and stood by him, guarding Pete's back as Pete guarded his.

The question had only formed in Reed's mind when the answer assaulted him from across the clearing. He lurched, looking away, flooded with shock and revulsion.

"Sorry," said Pete in a hoarse whisper. "Should've warned you."

Reed forced himself to look again.

Sheriff Mills's body had been hurled against a tree and now lay wrapped around the trunk, crumpled and contorted like a broken doll. The earpiece lay in the grass, still connected by wire to the GPS on his left arm. Mills's rifle lay in the grass, the stock broken off. Except for a few remaining sinews and dripping arteries, the head was all but separated from the body.

Reed's mind was paralyzed, but only for a moment. Without a conscious thought, he positioned his rifle and turned his full attention to the surrounding forest.

For several seconds, with tendons tightened to their limit, sweat dripping down their faces, and every breath controlled, Reed and Pete rotated slowly about a common center, back to back, eyes, ears, and rifles on the dark, concealing forest that encircled them.

At their feet, Max slumped to the ground, vomiting and moaning.

"Max, shh," Pete whispered.

Max tried to finish as silently as he could.

Sing came over the radio. Her voice was frantic. "Pete? Reed? Please report."

Without taking his eyes off the forest or his hand away from the trigger, Reed spoke quietly, slowly, and deliberately, the way Sheriff Mills would have. "Sing, get hold of yourself. Sheriff Mills is dead, same as Allen Arnold and Randy Thompson." He thought he heard a faint "Oh *no*," but after that, nothing. "Sing? Acknowledge."

Her voice was controlled. "I'm here. Sheriff Mills is dead."

"Call Deputy Saunders. Tell him to evacuate all the search teams, every last one of them. And have him contact the Forest Service. No civilians go into the woods, not campers, hikers, anybody—and that's by order of . . . well, me. Guess I'm the county sheriff for now."

"What are you going to do?"

Reed kept his voice steady. "I want you to get hold of Jimmy. Tell him we need him and all of his hunters up here, and if he can scare up any more from the Forest Service, we can use them too."

"Reed, are you secure until they arrive?"

"Get us the medical crew, somebody to take Sheriff Mills out of here."

"Reed!"

He got firm. "Sing, are you copying this down?"

■ ■ ■

She was trying to. Her hand shook so badly her writing was nearly illegible. "Dave Saunders, evacuate the search parties. Jimmy Clark, relocate the hunters. Get the medics here to take out . . ." Emotion overcame her.

Reed's voice was so steady it was almost mechanical. "Remain where you are so you can meet them. I'll leave Sheriff Mills's GPS with his body so you can guide them in."

"Got it." She listened to several seconds of radio silence and finally asked, "Reed. What are your intentions?"

Reed exchanged a look with Pete, who gave him a slight but definite nod. "This is as close as we've ever been to finding her since Lost Creek."

"We'll be all right," Pete concurred.

Sing asked, "What about Max?"

Max lay on the ground, still recovering from shock and nausea. Discreetly, while Max wasn't looking, Pete crouched to examine the soles of Max's boots, quickly referring to the blue cards in his vest pocket. With a quick look and a barely discernible head shake in Reed's direction, he radioed Sing, "Max can come with us if he's up to it."

Max pushed himself off the ground and breathed a moment. He nodded at Pete and Reed, then slowly struggled to his feet. "I'm in." He was still shaking, and he kept his back toward Mills's body.

Reed and Max stood guard as Pete quickly found signs: scuffed earth, bent grass, broken twigs, one impression, and a few drops of blood. "He took off south again, uphill. If we can keep him up against those rocks, we'll have half the battle."

Reed radioed, "Sing, you got us on your screen?"

"Good to go," she replied.

"Pete, I'll check this out," Reed said. He showed Pete the waypoint he'd entered and told him about the toilet paper.

Pete shook his head in wonder. "Either Beck was there or something she had a run-in with. It'd be a good place to start; you're right about that." He then suggested, "If I were you, I'd duck downhill to that open country where you can make better time and get south of there. Then you can climb uphill again and

close in from the south, maybe head 'em off. Max, you work your
way from here, parallel to those rocks, and do whatever it takes
to keep 'em up there." Pete nodded toward Mills's grotesque
form. "It only took one of 'em to do this, so don't wait to shoot.
I'll try to put the cork in the bottle, come in from the north. And,
Reed . . ."

Reed knew what Pete was going to say. Pete eyed the mountains above. "Those footprints down below told a story, and I
thought we had it right. But this . . ." He looked—unwillingly—
at Mills's twisted body. "This is the real story. There's no mistaking this."

Reed was more direct. "You're saying Beck is dead?"

Pete glanced away a moment, waiting for words. "This might
be more of a hunt than a search."

Reed weighed that, then replied, "So don't let them get past
you."

Pete answered, "You neither."

That was enough for now.

■ ■ ■

Cap was considering, only *considering*, his next move, when Sing
called and told him of Sheriff Mills's death. Her last words before
"I love you" were, "Cap, we *really* need to know what this is.
Please."

That locked his decision and his resolve. After a quick trip
home to change into presentable clothing—black slacks, a plain
almond shirt, conservative tie, navy sports coat—Cap drove
back to the Corzine campus and went straight to the
Bioscience building. He used the front door this time and
walked boldly down the hall to the cherry-paneled office of Dr.
Philip Merrill, dean of the College of Sciences, former depart-

ment chair of Molecular Biology, an ice sculpture in a suit—
and Cap's former boss.

"Do you have an appointment with Dr. Merrill?" his secretary asked.

Cap glared down at Judy Wayne, the same lady Cap had said
good morning to and mooched doughnuts from for the entire six
years he worked there. "Judy? You know I don't need an appointment. I need to talk to Phil."

She tilted her head condescendingly. "If it's about your sever-
ance package, you need to talk to accounting."

"What if I told you it's a matter of life and death?"

"I wouldn't believe you."

"Is he here?"

"I'm sure he's busy."

"You can tell him you tried to stop me." He skirted around
her desk and went to Merrill's door. She ran after him, of course,
protesting, citing policy, afraid for her job.

He knocked gently, then turned the big brass knob and opened
the door.

Merrill was still Merrill: hair combed straight back and in place,
suit jacket neatly hung on a wood valet in the corner, necktie conservative and tightly knotted under his Adam's apple. His desk was
a squeaky-clean battleship, and he was the admiral. He was on the
phone, which was actually a good thing because it forced him to
watch his language when he saw who barged in. His eyes went
frosty cold, but he held his demeanor, putting his hand over the
receiver. "Cap, you must know this meeting isn't going to happen!"

"I tried to stop him!" Judy squeaked.

Cap held up two fingers. "Two minutes. Please."

Merrill glared at him for a long moment, then spoke to the
phone, "Uh, got a snafu here at the office. Can I call you back?"
He hung up.

"Shall I call security?" Judy asked.

Cap gawked at her in disbelief but told Merrill, "Phil, this concerns you, not me. It's in your interest."

Merrill processed that, then waved Judy away. "Hold off on that. Just, uh, just leave us alone—for two minutes."

Judy walked out.

"And close the door."

She closed the door.

Merrill leaned back in his chair and silently gestured, *Well?*

Cap expended a few precious seconds taking a seat on the fancy leather couch. This wasn't going to be easy, but what the heck, he was already fired. "I thought you'd want to know that the Whitcomb County sheriff was just found up in the national forest with most of his bones broken and his head nearly torn off, just like a logging foreman from Three Rivers who died in exactly the same way on Monday morning."

Merrill showed no reaction. He simply said, "And why would I need to know that?"

"There's a trail guide missing, and then there's also a woman missing, a gal who's married to a friend of mine—a deputy sheriff. Sing and I have been trying to help out, trying to track down the *animal* responsible."

Merrill steepled his fingers under his chin. "I thought you said this concerns me."

"I ran a Fluorescent In Situ Hybridization on stool, saliva, and hair samples from the thing. I found chimpanzee DNA with human DNA present."

"Hm. Contamination. Too bad."

"The human DNA was juxtaposed with adenovirus."

Merrill processed a little more and then tried not to laugh. "You can't be going where I think you're going."

"I just thought you'd be interested."

"And you were hoping to get a reaction, I suppose."

"Considering what Adam Burkhardt's been working on all these years, and—hey, you know what? He isn't even around. I checked at his office and he's on sabbatical . . . again. How can he possibly make any money for the university when he's never here?"

Merrill's gaze was mocking. "By producing results, Cap. He produces results."

Cap nodded. "And that's why the department gets all that funding, all that money from those big corporations . . . uh, Euro-Atlantic Oil, the Carlisle Foundation—"

"So you've done some homework."

"American Geographic and Public Broadcasting's got their fingers in it too. He's worth a lot of money to you, isn't he? Come to think of it, you might owe him a debt of thanks for your promotion."

"Jealous?"

"Bothered, for the same old reasons: it's not *results* that get the funding—it's *correct* results. Give 'em what they *want* and they'll send the money. *Question* what they want and—"

"What they want is *science*, Cap. I could never get you to understand that."

"But science prides itself on being self-correcting."

Merrill looked at his watch. "I'm waiting for you to make your point!"

Cap leaned forward. "What if something went wrong? What if Burkhardt's results weren't 'correct'? What if people got hurt? What if people got *killed*?"

"I must warn you, if you are in any way considering a violation of your confidentiality agreement—"

"What do you suppose would happen to the funding—or even your job?"

That hit home—finally. An old, cold look returned to

Merrill's eyes. "As you may expect, I will not abide what you're suggesting, nor will I dignify it with a response."

Cap knew this man; he was familiar with Merrill's style of lying. He rose from the fancy couch and leaned closely over Merrill's desk. "Self-correcting. I've brought you data of great interest, I'm sure—if you're a *scientist*."

Cap had what he came for. He walked out, leaving the door wide open.

Merrill followed just a few seconds behind and watched him go down the hall toward the front door. The dean was not quite as poised as before.

Judy looked up from her desk. "Everything okay?"

"He's leaving."

Merrill returned to his office, circled behind his expansive desk, unconsciously checked his hair, then consciously checked his desk, his way of assuring himself that his world was still stable, predictable, and under his control.

His eye was immediately drawn to a void in the fastidious arrangement of calendar, telephone, desk caddy, and pen set on his desktop. An allotment of desk space was now empty where he usually kept—

He burst from his office. "Call security!"

Judy got on the phone.

Merrill was trembling with indignity, looking up and down the hallway. "That weasel just stole my master keys!"

■ ■ ■

Sheriff Patrick Mills's lifeless eyes gawked at the sky one last time as a paramedic placed Mills's cowboy hat on his chest and zipped the black body bag shut.

Jimmy Clark respectfully removed his own hat as two paramedics carried the body out of the clearing. Wiley Kane did the same, exposing his long white mane. Steve Thorne, looking tough and military as ever, watched grimly, camouflage cap in place. Young Mariners fan Sam Marlowe tried to concentrate on familiarizing himself with a GPS unit. Janson—no one ever asked Janson his first name—chose not to watch at all. Not one man set down his rifle for any reason.

Jimmy had already strapped Mills's GPS to his arm—a most regrettable task, but it had to be done. He carefully washed the blood off the earpiece with a handkerchief and water from his canteen, then put the earpiece in his ear and pressed the talk button. "Sing, this is Jimmy. How do you read?"

■ ■ ■

"Loud and clear."

Sing was at her computer in the mobile lab, watching the same GPS blips in a new arrangement: Reed was south of his toilet paper waypoint and doubling back; Pete lingered to the north, waiting to hear from Reed. Max was roughly halfway between them and a quarter mile below the stone face of the mountain. They formed a very large triangle, and each man looked pitifully, frighteningly alone out there. Jimmy, now represented by Mills's old blip, was still in the clearing where Mills had died, but that would change—soon, she hoped.

The hamlet of Whitetail had gotten busy. Two Forest Service vehicles, Jimmy's Fish and Game rig, a medical emergency vehicle, and two private cars were now clustered around Sing's mobile lab. A lot of firepower had gone into the woods, meaning there was a major chance something was going to come out dead. Sing was feeling hope and fear in equal proportions.

Another blip appeared on her screen right next to Jimmy's. A voice crackled in her headset: "Sing, this is Thorne."

About time!

"I have you on-screen, voice is loud and clear."

■ ■ ■

Steve Thorne was satisfied he'd figured things out. He positioned the GPS on the underside of his left forearm so he could read it while holding his rifle, and he was ready.

Sam Marlowe just did what Thorne did and he was ready in half the time. "Sing? This is Sam Marlowe."

"Okay," she came back. "You're number 6, on-screen, loud and clear."

Jimmy greeted the four armed forest rangers who had just arrived, then called via his earpiece, "Reed? Pete? We're ready down here."

■ ■ ■

Reed hurried up the hill through thick woods, homing in on his waypoint, eyes and ears wary. Under the circumstances, he was glad to hear Jimmy's voice.

Pete radioed, "Let's fill in the circle, guys, quick as you can. I think we can work within a quarter-mile radius; we're that close."

■ ■ ■

With all the grimness of a platoon leader leading his men into combat, Jimmy divided his hunters into three teams headed by himself, Steve Thorne, and Sam Marlowe. "Sam, you and your

guys fill in around Pete's position; Steve, spread your guys along
that west side and help Max. My team'll take the south end and
do what we can to help Reed. We don't have GPS units for everybody, so the rest of you stay within earshot of your team leader.
Let's go." As they dispersed into the woods, he radioed, "Sing,
we're moving."

■ ■ ■

Beck tried moving once, just raising her head enough to peer out
of the thicket, but Rachel held her back with a firm hand, clamp-
ing her like a child against her bosom and holding her still. Beck
settled—for the moment—and became like Rachel, Leah, and
Reuben: a shadow, a dark, indistinct area within the elderberry
thicket, obscured by a web of stalks, branches, limbs, and leaves.
This was hiding as Beck had never experienced it—as an animal:
motionless, silent, part of the darkness. Like ogres in a dim, odorous underworld, they'd become as dead things while the forest
lived, stirred, and chattered above them.

I heard shots.

Moving only her eyes, Beck tried to meet theirs. None would
look back, but she could tell they knew what was happening:
something terrible, something frightening—to them.

And hopeful—for her.

Maybe Jacob was in the middle of another grisly killing when
he encountered something he wasn't expecting: Hunters.
Humans. Big burly guys in camouflage, looking for a lost woman
of her description, toting rifles and ready to blow away any hairy
monsters that gave them guff.

Maybe someone found her footprints and made some sense of
Reed's cell phone number. Maybe Reed was still alive and leading
the search. Maybe, at long last, the rules were changing in her favor!

She had to know.

Fighting back a rising quiver of excitement, she tried to be still, like her captors, and hear what they might be hearing. The forest above was still speaking in its everyday way, in a language she didn't know. Were the birds concerned about something, or just gossiping? Was that quiet rustling a passing creature, the wind in the branches, or a hunter?

Then she noticed—and felt—something, only because it changed. Rachel's heart and the slow, steamy flow of air through her nostrils had quickened. For the first time, Rachel's head turned. The other heads turned. Beck turned her head.

The birds took flight, sounding alarms. Footfalls approached through the undergrowth—two feet, not four. There was a soft, rumbling grunt as they passed by and continued on.

Abruptly, and so typically, Rachel rose to her feet without warning and burst out of the thicket, heaving Beck over her shoulder. Leah, with Reuben on her back, followed directly behind. Beck hooked an arm around Rachel's neck and swung down into a manageable straddle, but she was looking back, to the sides, anywhere else she could catch a view of the forest. *Were* there hunters out there?

Rachel and Leah ran south in a nearly straight line as if they knew exactly where they were going, and then, so quickly Beck missed when it happened, Jacob was with them, leading the way. His gait was hurried and cautious, his hair bristling. His fear scent trailed behind him like smoke from an old locomotive, and he kept glancing over his shoulder, not at all the haughty kingpin he'd been before.

Beck was afraid to assume too much, to hope too much, but from all appearances, they were being chased. Jacob was leading a getaway.

■ ■ ■

Cap knew he wouldn't have much time and wasted none of it getting down a flight of steel stairs and into the subterranean world under Bioscience. The main hallway was narrow, its ceiling cluttered with conduit, plumbing, and ductwork. The walls were a monotonous gray, undecorated except for frequent red signs on imposing doors that shouted, Danger: High Voltage, This Door to Remain Closed at All Times, and Authorized Personnel Only. He came to a sign that read Blue Clearance Only Beyond This Point. He kept going, his shoes clicking on the bare concrete. He'd been stripped of his blue clearance badge along with everything else, but maybe no one would notice—if he even encountered anyone. So far, the whole floor seemed strangely deserted.

He did feel a pang of conscience, as if he were a spy or even a burglar, but he kept telling himself he was down here because (a) he was a scientist, (b) he had a theory, and (c) a scientist tested his theories through experimentation and observation.

Following up on Baumgartner's "question" and that second trip to the Internet, he'd used a fluorescent tagging method to check the human DNA in the samples for adenovirus sequences, and bingo! Knowing what to look for, he'd found them everywhere.

Adenovirus was a tool commonly used in gene splicing because, being a virus, it naturally spliced its own DNA into the DNA of a cell it infected, making it an ideal delivery system. It was a matter of using an enzyme to cut a DNA sequence from a donor cell, splicing that sequence into the virus, and then infecting the recipient cell with the virus. Once in the recipient cell, the virus spliced the donor DNA into the recipient's DNA along with its own, making the desired addition but also leaving its own detectable sequence.

In the case of the DNA from the stool and the saliva, meticulous rearranging of base pairs through site-directed mutagenesis—SDM—was clearly evident but, predictably, too slow for the genetic engineer's schedule. Whoever it was resorted to viral transfer, using adenovirus to transfer, splice, and mix human with chimpanzee DNA whole sequences at a time, a much faster process but haphazard. In SDM, the genetic engineer controlled what base pairs were being changed, switched, and moved. In viral transfer, the *virus* decided, potentially doing more harm than good.

So Cap had a theory to explain the strange sequences the Judy Lab had revealed: chimpanzee, human, and hybrid all in the same animal, laced with sequences from the adenovirus that did most of the splicing. It was no accident, and there was no contamination. The presence of human DNA was intentional.

But of course, it was still a theory, and incomplete at that. He had the *what* and the *how*; but he needed to confirm the *who*, and while the possible answer was a no-brainer as far as he was concerned, it was necessary to test that answer through observation.

That observation was going to begin on the other side of a plain door marked with nothing but a number: 102.

He pulled a small cedar box from his jacket pocket, a nice keepsake Merrill had received from the American Geographic Society in recognition of his contribution to the field of evolutionary biology. It bore his name and the society's logo, laser-etched on the lid. Cap flipped it open and took out Merrill's master keys to the department's labs and classrooms.

The third key Cap tried opened the door. With a quick glance up and down the hall—so far, he was still the only one here—he slipped inside, closing the door behind him.

He knew where to find the light switch because he knew this place well. This was the lab of Dr. Adam Burkhardt, the unsung and secretive pioneer—*poster child*, Cap had often thought derisively—of molecular anthropology. In Cap's early years at the university, and at the very strong suggestion of Merrill, Baumgartner, and other department colleagues, Cap had spent many hours in this room working side by side with Burkhardt, supposedly to restore Cap's faith in beneficial mutations and keep him on the right path as a professor of biology. If anyone could prove that mutations really worked as the mechanism for evolving new species, it had to be Burkhardt. He'd spent his whole life trying—and as Cap kept pointing out, failing. That, of course, wasn't the conclusion Cap was supposed to reach. After two years of working together, their respective positions became so polarized that they parted company, Burkhardt to his secretive, high-priority research, and Cap to his role as the outspoken, question-asking department pariah.

But Cap had no time to dwell on unpleasant memories. Right now he had to deal with the fact that he was carrying stolen keys, would soon be caught if he didn't move quickly, and was standing in a lab that was, by all appearances, vacant. The workbenches, once cluttered with a dozen different projects in various stages, were now clear and unused except for a few cardboard boxes that were lined up near the door. The biology posters were gone from the walls, the specimen jars were gone from the shelves, the lab mice were gone from the cages.

Burkhardt's old desk was bare. Cap set down the box of keys and pulled out the drawers; they were all empty. The bulletin board above the desk carried a calendar still flipped to January even though it was July, announcements of events that had long passed, and a few snapshots held in place with pushpins: a pretty grad student holding a lab rat as she injected it; rats with mottled colors in their fur; four male students grinning as they held a trophy they'd won at a regional collegiate science fair. Burkhardt's

PhD diploma had been removed from the wall, but the square of unfaded paint still marked where it once hung. A "Teacher of the Year" plaque remained, dusty and forgotten. Cap remembered Burkhardt losing interest in teaching over the years, and now it seemed Burkhardt didn't care much for the memories either, nor for the young lives he'd influenced, considering he'd left their pictures behind.

Cap went to the cardboard boxes and folded back the top flaps of the first. Ah, here was at least one vestige of Burkhardt's presence. Inside, wrapped in several layers of newspaper to protect from breakage, were some of Burkhardt's glass specimen jars. Burkhardt always prided himself on his vast collection of evolutionary icons in formaldehyde, a display that once took up several shelves along the front of the room and caught the eye of anyone who dropped in. He'd bought, borrowed, and swapped with other biologists around the world to collect Galapagos finches with different-sized beaks, peppered moths both white and gray, coelacanths that were regarded as living fossils, bats whose wing bones bore a homologous similarity to the human hand, lizards that had supposedly evolved from snakes, and a boa constrictor that had supposedly evolved from lizards, all part of Burkhardt's sideshow of the dead. These remaining jars must have been the last ones packed, still waiting to make the move, wherever it was they were going.

Cap pulled out one of the jars and carefully removed the newspaper wrapping. He'd no doubt seen this specimen before—

No. He hadn't. This one was new, and from its appearance, Cap decided, Burkhardt hadn't bought or traded for it— Burkhardt had *produced* this one.

It was a lab rat floating in amber preservative, a pitiful animal with a twisted spine and—Cap counted them twice to be sure— six legs.

He pulled out and unwrapped the second jar. It was another lab rat, this one with mottled fur and no eyes.

The third jar contained a rat with no legs at all.

Cap felt his face flush and his stomach grow queasy. He rewrapped and placed the jars back in their box, not looking at the contents, trying to sell himself a foolish, vain hope that Burkhardt had gotten the message and stopped with rats—or at the very worst, chimpanzees. Burkhardt *was* a scientist, after all. Surely he knew how to read the indications of the data, especially at such a high level—

At the far end of the room, a solitary animal cage caught Cap's attention. He paused in wrapping the last jar and stared at the cage a moment, frozen in time, one hand on the jar and the other holding the box lid open.

He couldn't be seeing what he thought he was seeing. He wasn't ready for things to get worse.

He lowered the last jar into the box, then hurried down the aisle between the workbenches for a closer look.

The cage was similar to a large pet carrier, a rectangular box of tough plastic with a swinging, barred gate at one end. It had come on tough times. The opening all around the gate had been chewed as if by an enormous rat trying to escape. The slot for the latch was nearly gouged out. The gate was tooth marked and bulged outward as if pushed with incredible strength from the inside.

Whatever Burkhardt had kept in this cage, it was bigger than a rat; apparently—*hopefully*—Burkhardt had found a bigger, tougher cage.

"Dr. Capella!"

He'd stayed too long. Turning, he saw Merrill come into the room, flanked by two campus police in gray uniforms, the university's best and biggest.

Merrill was strong and confident between his two-man army. He extended his palm. "My keys?"

Cap nodded toward Burkhardt's empty desk. "They're on the desk."

Merrill retrieved them. "Cap, you have a choice: leave this campus immediately and do not come back, *ever*, or be placed under arrest right here, right now."

Cap walked slowly forward, hands half-raised in surrender. "Hi, Tim."

The first cop, lanky and bespectacled, said, "Hi."

"Kenny, how's it going?"

The second cop, arms crossed over his barrel chest, nodded and replied, "It's going all right."

Cap addressed Merrill. "Looks like more than a sabbatical. Looks like Burkhardt's pulled up and moved altogether."

"Which is no concern of yours."

Cap nodded at the damaged cage. "What happened? Did things get a little tough to contain?"

Merrill smirked. "A word to the *wise*, Dr. Capella—if that term means anything to you: we are all scientists here, and that means we deal in facts. You are a *creationist*, and now have the added liability of being a trespasser and a burglar. Before you say anything to anyone, please give careful regard to which of us has the credibility—and the power to destroy the other."

Creationist. Merrill used that word as an insult. Cap had seen this power trip before, and he was fed up with it. "Is this a *scientist* I hear talking?"

Merrill smiled. "In every way, Dr. Capella; in the eyes of my peers and, most of all, in the eyes of the public. I have my responsibilities, foremost among them, not allowing science to be undermined by detractors like you."

"Science? Wouldn't it be more accurate to call it 'the only game in town'?"

Merrill turned to his cops. "Get him out of here."

■ ■ ■

Rachel was in a full run, her legs blurring in a shock-free, fluid stride, her weight forward, her arms swinging in wide arcs. Beck hung on, head down, cringing close to Rachel's body and wincing as tree trunks and branches missed them by inches. She looked over her shoulder but saw no hunters, no friends, only rapidly retreating forest and distance building by powerful leaps. No hunter on foot could hope to catch them.

Though it terrified her, she looked down at Rachel's blurred feet, then the huge tree trunks that raced by, and tried to envision herself letting go, leaping into space, landing and rolling safely enough to live and limp away. What if she could drop into that clump of young firs? Would they soften her fall? Would Rachel realize she was gone? What if—

Suddenly, shockingly, Rachel dug in and lurched to a stop, nearly throwing Beck off.

Jacob burst out of the brush, stinking and huffing, so close he and Rachel almost collided. Leah followed, more frightened than Beck had ever seen her, carrying a whimpering Reuben on her back. The train was turning around. Rachel spun and moved into a run again, last in line. They were heading north, the way they'd come.

Beck looked behind and saw nothing but forest, but she'd read Jacob's face; something was back there—or some*one*.

Jacob turned down the slope, Leah and Rachel followed, and Rachel's fluid stride became a rocking, heaving lope as she leaped and landed, leaped and landed her way down the mountain.

Beck's stomach reacted immediately, and her grip began to weaken. She started sizing up landing spots again.

Rachel stumbled! Landing after a leap, she was trying to stop, heeling in, staggering, grabbing and snapping off branches. She danced several yards farther down the slope, finally gripped a tree trunk with one hand, and whipped around to a quick halt.

Beck couldn't have held on if she wanted to. She sailed backward, floating as the ground dropped away, then landing cleanly, tumbling through a struggling patch of Oregon grape until she found a stump to grab. It occurred to her not to stop, to keep going downhill. She let go of the stump and let herself roll until her feet came under her and she stood, bracing herself against a small pine.

Downhill and to her right, Leah clambered back up the hill with Reuben on the ground beside her, four-wheeling up the rocks. Beck veered left and half-limped down to the next tree, buying just a little time, a little more distance from Rachel.

Now she saw Jacob groping his way up the hill; he looked panicked, drooling and slow with exhaustion. Something had turned him back again.

A shock went through Beck like electricity. She caught only a glimpse, only a fleeting image through a gap in the trees far below, but she knew what it was.

A man's camouflage cap. Had it not been moving, and had she not seen one before, she would have missed it, but there was no mistaking it.

"Ohhh!" escaped her, a cry of hope *and* disbelief.

Rachel pounded down the hill toward her, snapping off branches and upsetting loose rock.

Beck hobbled downhill to the next tree and cried out again, not bothering with consonants or pronunciation but just making a noise, any noise she could.

A man's voice answered from far below, "Hello? Somebody up there?"

Beck had just opened her mouth to answer when Rachel caught her in midair, jarring her, stealing her breath, muffling her cry. Beck wriggled, squirmed, tried to get free. She screamed—

She saw nothing but fiery eyes, bristling black hair, flaring nostrils, and glistening teeth. Jacob never came this close to anything except to kill it. His throaty roar erased her brain; his foul breath paralyzed her will.

"Hello!" the man called.

Beck didn't answer.

■ ■ ■

Reed was closing in on his waypoint well ahead of Jimmy's team, when Steve Thorne's voice crackled in his earpiece, "I've got something above me! It's heading back up the hill!"

"Any visual?" he heard Jimmy ask.

"No, but I heard a woman scream."

"Max's team, tighten up!" Pete ordered. "Give us a wall down there!"

Reed looked at his GPS. He could see Max and Thorne tightening formation and inching uphill. Pete was moving south along the stone face, with Sam about five hundred feet below him. The other two guys were filling in between.

Reed got on the radio. "Heads up, everybody! Don't let the screaming fool you. That's not a woman! That's the target!" He didn't like the silence he got in response. "Jimmy, I've got you and Sam behind and below."

"Yeah, that's us," Jimmy replied.

"Can you get a man above me, between me and the rocks?"

"Give him a few minutes."

"Did everybody hear my heads-up about the screaming sound?"

Several answered that they had. Steve Thorne radioed, "You're sure that's not your wife?"

No, he wasn't sure and it was killing him. "Did she say anything?"

"No, she just screamed."

A hunt, and not a search. Reed fought down his fear. "Don't let that thing sucker you in. That's what happened to Mills."

"What the heck are we hunting, anyway?" Thorne asked.

Jimmy cut in, "I told you not to ask."

Reed paused to breathe deeply and gather himself. He glanced at his GPS. He was close now, only forty yards or so. The circle of hunters was closing in. Something inside that circle was going to be really ticked off.

▪ ▪ ▪

Beck's world was a cruel kaleidoscope of blurred images—powerful, grappling arms, brush and tree limbs whipping past, her own arms and legs kicking and flailing, the total, choking darkness of Rachel's bosom. In quick, intermittent flashes between grabs, holds, slaps, and kicks, she saw Jacob leading, ascending the slope, his flexible feet grabbing the ground and his legs pushing relentlessly upward.

Rachel was just too strong, and Beck's ribs, arms, legs, and sprained ankle were sending her warnings: *Much more of this, and you're going to break something.* With a whimper muffled in Rachel's hairy body, Beck gave up the struggle, if only to live one moment longer.

The climb continued. Beck pushed herself up just far enough to look backward over Rachel's shoulder. More forest, thicket, and impenetrable tangle. How these beasts could pass so easily through that stuff, she couldn't fathom. No hunter could ever get through there.

Ahead, she caught a glimpse of Jacob as he plunged into a tangle of honeysuckle and elderberry that had formed a living dome over a fallen aspen. Leah and Reuben followed, dropping through the tangled web of leaves and into a hollow beneath. Without slowing, Rachel lowered her head and shoulders and stormed through.

It was like falling through a roof into a dark cellar, but the landing was soft—there were three hot, hairy bodies to cushion their fall. One of them, possibly Leah, gave a painful grunt on impact.

The hollow was tight and confining, stabbed through with limbs from the fallen aspen, obscured on all sides by vines and brush, packed solid with steaming apes. It got hot right away. Jacob's scent glands were working overtime.

They were hiding again, motionless, eyes intense, breathing in quiet puffs. Listening. Peering through the myriad tiny gaps in the leaves, vines, and branches.

It made Beck afraid, as if the monster were lurking outside and not on both sides of her.

She could see through the curtain, a slot here, a chink there, tiny windows blurrily framing puzzle pieces of the forest outside. Other than the troubled forest chatter, she heard nothing. Something moved, and she gasped before she could catch herself. She leaned closer to the tangle, peering through a vertical hole between twisting vines. Something white dangled from a nearby elderberry bush, moving lazily in the breeze.

They had come full circle. Obnoxious, raiding Reuben had already been here.

Of course, Reuben's escapade with her toilet paper was not going to help the Sasquatches' cause. A streamer of white toilet paper would stand out like a surveyor's ribbon. One of the hunters was sure to spot it.

■ ■ ■

Reed took a moment to listen and watch before taking another step toward the white ribbon. He had his bearings now. He recognized everything. He whispered via his earpiece, "Pete, I see the toilet paper."

"We're closing on you," Pete replied.

"Still moving uphill," said Max.

"I've got a man above you," Jimmy said.

Reed didn't move. Maybe Pete Henderson was rubbing off on him, or maybe he'd been in these woods so long he was growing a whole new set of senses, but he *felt* something.

Steadying his rifle with his right hand, he flexed and stretched his left, then reversed the procedure, flexing his right. *A search or a hunt?* He checked the progress of the other hunters on his GPS. It was a search right now but would definitely be a hunt in a matter of minutes.

■ ■ ■

As one, Beck *and* her captors alerted, their muscles tensing, their eyes shifting about. When they heard a second step, their heads turned the same direction, toward the south, the broken bits of light painting speckles on their faces, glimmers on their eyes. Beck peered through an opening, saw nothing but leaves, peered through another, saw only forest, peered through a third—

At the sight of her husband, her diaphragm involuntarily leaped and a squeal escaped her throat. Rachel's arm nearly collapsed her rib cage; Jacob shot her a glance and a warning hiss;

Leah's glaring eyes cut through the dark. Beck clapped her hand over her mouth.

Reed took another step toward them. Beck craned her neck to steal a tiny, partial view of him through a gap in the leaves, her hand squeezing over her mouth ever more tightly as her emotions defied restraint.

■ ■ ■

Reed stole forward, one step at a time, ducking branches, stepping over twigs, hands welded to his rifle. He removed the earpiece from his ear, putting aside the other voices. He only wanted to hear what was around him, right here, right now. Two more steps, and he reached his waypoint. He was standing by the white toilet paper streamer.

■ ■ ■

He was so close that Beck could see only his legs.

Rachel's body had turned to iron. Her hair was bristling, stabbing Beck in the face and arms. Jacob breathed slowly but deeply, building strength in silence, his hair on end, ruthless murder in his eyes.

Beck put her other hand over her mouth but could not steady the quaking breath rushing in and out of her nostrils.

They're cornered. They have young: Reuben—and me. If I make a sound . . . If Reed comes any closer . . .

■ ■ ■

Reed stood still again and scanned around him, occupied first and foremost with staying alive, but driven by one irrepressible longing:

to see Beck, to hear her voice, to *know*, at long last, that she was alive. Maybe it was the *longing* that gave him the *feeling*; somehow—maybe it was that stupid toilet paper—but he felt she was close.

He remembered seeing another scrap of toilet paper the last time he was here, within sight of—

There! Fifteen feet away, the scrap of white lay on a patch of brown pine needles, right below a huge honeysuckle that grew over a fallen aspen. He took two small, careful steps. A leaf crackled under his boot and he froze.

Steady now.

One more step. Freeze. Listen. One more step.

A scent from an old nightmare reached his nostrils and his blood ran cold. Suddenly he wasn't just remembering that first horrible night; he felt he was *there*, hearing Beck scream and feeling helpless, so helpless. The *thing* was there too. Though he couldn't see it, he could feel it hiding, watching him.

Beck. He could think only of her and took one more step toward the terror.

It was one step farther than he'd ever gone before. One step ago, he was terrified. Now he was as good as dead, but he didn't care. His hands became steady. He had no urge to step back. This was his destination, exactly where he wanted to be, not just close, but *there*.

"Beck," he whispered. "I'm here, babe. I'm right here."

He could smell the *thing*. If he wasn't imagining that slow, steady, hissing sound, he could hear it too.

A search or a hunt? He'd come to do both. He swung his rifle about, daring that thing to move.

■ ■ ■

Reed stood just above the hollow. Beck heard a hiss crackling through saliva and teeth. Jacob's teeth were bared, his canines gleaming. He was crouching, poised, planning.

Reed, get out of here!

He didn't leave. He took another step toward them.

They're going to kill him. Honest to God, they're going to kill him!

TWELVE

Sing saw the circle tightening, closing in from the west, north, and south against the stone cliffs above. Inside the circle, toward the south end, Reed's blip wasn't moving. He wasn't answering his radio.

"Reed! Reed, talk to me! Jimmy, can you see him?"

"Negative," Jimmy whispered. "It's pretty thick in here."

"Do you have him on your screen?"

"Got him."

"Then what are you waiting for?"

Pete came on the radio. "Steady, everybody. Let's not get ourselves killed."

■ ■ ■

Reed could hear commotion from his earpiece. He replaced it, pressed the talk button, and spoke quietly, "This is Reed. I'm at the waypoint. I don't see the target, but I can smell it."

"Reed, fall back!" Sing cried. "Wait for the others."

"Negative. I'm not letting that thing get away again."

"Reed!"

He removed the earpiece.

■ ■ ■

Go away, Reed, Beck begged in her mind. *I love you. Please don't let them kill you. Go away.*

Jacob was waiting, ready to explode from the hollow. Beck couldn't even guess what would trigger him, but she knew the attack would only last an instant.

■ ■ ■

Reed moved slowly past the mound of vines, mentally mapping the area, looking for hiding places. An upended stump just below him could have hidden something. The fallen aspen looked suspicious, but could anything fit under there? Another step and he spotted an open space, just a little breathing room to his left. It might give him a half second more to react if anything charged him. He tried to catch that scent, tried to—

The sight made him jump. He calmed himself, looked around for danger, confirmed his grip on his rifle.

Brown leather.

At first he thought it was an animal, obscured by the wild grass and knapweed; then he thought it was a dead animal. It was bloody, torn, ripped.

Double-checking every direction, he carefully approached whatever it was, knowing what it was but not wanting to know.

■ ■ ■

Jacob eased back just a little, which eased Beck just a little, enough to think, *What can I do, what can I do?* No answers came.

She could see Reed through another gap in the overgrowth, moving into view in a small clearing. Apparently he'd found something, though for a moment she couldn't imagine what it could be.

Wait. Her jacket? She and the group had come full circle, back to where Reuben had raided her toilet paper. It might be her jacket.

Now her heart quickened with one spark of hope. If Reed found her jacket, he'd know she had to be around here somewhere. It would keep him looking, keep him hoping. It would be like a signal, a flare, a message in a bottle—

It *was* her jacket, or at least a piece of it. Reed picked it up, turned it over in his hands. Reuben had done quite a job on it, worse than a pup with a chew toy. It was chewed, shredded—

A foreboding hit her like a blow to the stomach; the fear—no, the certainty of death coursed through her like an electric shock. There was blood on that jacket, *Rachel's* blood from days ago. It was torn into pieces. It looked like—

A quaking, nearly dying breath passed through her lips as the words formed, "R-r-reed." *Don't think that, Reed. Don't think it. It's not my blood.*

■ ■ ■

The blood on the leather was days old by now, flaking and brown. The leather was tattered, tooth marked, and only a fragment of

Beck's jacket, a side panel and half of a sleeve. It spoke to Reed; it told him everything.

He sank to his knees, unaware of the forest, the search, the hunt, and even the danger. His rifle dropped to the grass. He gazed at the shredded garment and ran his thumb over the smear of blood. A shadow crept into his mind like black ink permeating a parchment, spreading, pushing away light and hope, stripping away every thought but one: Beck.

He raised his eyes. All he could see was Beck chewing on a cold sandwich and making a teasing face, a crooked, stuffed-cheek, half smile, while he took her picture. It was the last smile he could remember, and even as he tried to dwell on it, it faded, lost in the darkness of a night that would last forever. Though he tried to hear her laugh again, or even say his name, only silence answered.

■ ■ ■

If she screamed, he would die. She could only lie pilloried in Rachel's arms and watch in silent agony as Reed rose from the ground, weak as an old man, the tattered remnant of her jacket in his hand. He didn't think to pick up his rifle, but instead fumbled with an earpiece, his hand trembling, until he'd replaced it in his ear. She heard only the words, " . . . pulling out . . ." and then he started back the way he'd come.

Jacob tensed again. Reed would be passing by close.

Reed stopped, went back for his rifle, then passed by quickly, clumsily.

I'm not dead.

One last image through the vines: a trudging, wounded man, no longer alert or careful, in no hurry, stepping over a log, pushing aside a leafy branch . . .

I'M NOT DEAD!

He went out of sight. A quiet rustle followed, then the snap of a twig, then a very distant crunching.

Then there was no sound at all.

■ ■ ■

Sing threw open the door on her mobile lab and stood on the steps, gripping the handrail, watching the trail that climbed into the woods from the parking area. For the past forty minutes she had been not a human being but a stone, forbidding herself to feel, care, or cherish. There were hunters in the woods. Someone had to maintain contact and be their link to the outside world. Someone had to help them close up the circle in case the positioning signals winked out on their mobile units. She had to think of them, even while she watched one blip on her screen slowly make its way down the mountain, across the creek bed, past the site where Fleming Cryncovich found all the footprints, and back down the trail to Whitetail.

Now that the blip on her computer screen had reached the end of its journey, she expected to see Reed and Jimmy drawing near. When she did, she would release her heart. She would become a human being again.

But how she would ever bear the pain and loss, she didn't know.

Janson's voice crackled through her headset. "Hey, I need some help closing up the south end. A guy could drive a truck through here."

She shot a quick glance at her computer screen and replied, "Max? Steve? Do you have Janson's position?"

"No, I've lost him," said Thorne.

"He's bearing 135, about 800 feet. He's using Jimmy's GPS."

"One thirty-five, Roger."

"Janson, you're good. Stay where you are until they pick you up again."

Janson acknowledged grumpily.

And then she saw Reed and Jimmy emerge from the woods like tired soldiers returning from battle, eyes vacant, shoulders slumped, legs trudging, rifles slung on their shoulders. Jimmy stayed close to Reed, lending strength, as Reed managed to put one foot in front of the other. Reed caught her eye, but his face was hard to discern. He carried a bloodied piece of leather in both hands.

Now Sing's heart was free to grieve. Her hand went to her mouth as her body began to quake.

They met in the parking lot, embracing. Sing wept with no words. Reed seemed strangely empty, like a body without a spirit. He held her but did not cry.

"I'll, uh, I'll handle the radio," said Jimmy.

Sing watched him go to the motor home, recover the headset she'd left dangling by the door, and go inside.

■ ■ ■

When Jimmy's voice came over the radio, Pete had to turn down his volume. "Okay, guys, this is Jimmy. Just to let you know, Sheriff Mills and I had an agreement: as long as it was a search, the sheriff was in charge. When it became a hunt, Fish and Game would be in charge. Well, guys, like you've all heard, the search is over. We've got ourselves a full-blown hunt now, and that makes me the big kahuna. Thorne and Max, Reed and I are out of the game for now, so pull your line south and sew up the net before the big one gets away. Let's get ourselves a bear!"

Pete lost half his will to go on when he heard that Reed had pulled out. Now that it was clear there would be no finding Beck, he lost the rest of it. He checked his GPS. The north end was pretty tight now. Sam Marlowe was only ninety yards down the slope, with Wiley Kane and a forest ranger in between. They'd be able to carry on well enough without him. He got a bearing from his compass and started down.

■ ■ ■

Sing checked on Reed one last time. He'd shed his jacket and boots and left them on the floor by the bed, but he wouldn't part with the piece of Beck's jacket. He clutched it tightly as he lay on the bed in the back of the motor home, his face to the wall.

"I'll call Cap and let him know," she told him. "I've got some soup I can heat up. You need to have some."

He didn't answer. He didn't move.

"I'll be right here," she said.

Satisfied that he was comfortable—he would never be okay— she closed the door quietly and left him alone.

In the main room, Jimmy was at her computer, wearing her headset, still running things. "Pete, you need to move up the bank; you're slipping down too far. Say again?" He rolled his eyes. "Sam, head up the hill and push the other guys ahead of you. Close it up."

He looked over his shoulder at Sing. "How's he doing?"

"He's breathing. That's all I can tell you."

He stared at the rear bedroom door. "We were fools to let it go this long. I tried to tell him. I tried to tell Mills."

"But nobody ever listens to you." Her sarcasm was subtle but intentional.

"This isn't the time."

She picked up her cell phone. "No, it isn't."

"Have you called Dave Saunders?"

"I'm on it."

Jimmy turned to the computer screen, burying himself in the hunt. "Pete, can you hand off your GPS to Wiley on your way down? Thanks, guy, and hey, listen, we all understand."

Sing stepped out of the vehicle, closed the door behind her, and punched in a number. It was quiet out here—away from Jimmy.

She got Deputy Dave Saunders. "Hello, Dave? This is Sing Capella. Reed's calling off the search. Everybody can stand down." She listened to his question and fought back tears in order to answer. "No. Just a piece of her coat."

While he dealt with the news, Sing pulled herself together—for the moment. "Dave, are you there?" He was, full of condolences, wanting to help. "Reed would like you to contact the Forest Service; we have to close the woods to civilians until we hunt down the . . . until we get the problem cleared up. But, Dave, there's one more thing: the hunters have cleared out of the Lost Creek area, so you won't be in their way anymore. We still need to find Randy Thompson—I'm sure we're dealing with a body, or remains. If you could get a few deputies up there . . . Yeah, I know, but we have to try again, and this time, bring some metal detectors. You're going to be looking for a shovel."

■ ■ ■

Pete found Wiley Kane within minutes. All he had to do was follow the cigarette smoke.

"So," Kane said with a bit of a leer, "you've had enough, huh?"

Pete removed his GPS and handed it to him. "I was in this for Beck, not Jimmy."

Wiley dropped his cigarette and crushed it out in the dirt. He took the GPS and marveled at it. "Woo! So this has got all of us on there?"

Pete pointed out a few details: the available screens, the moving map, the zoom feature, and the various peer-to-peer blips. "You're gonna be me now, this dot right here. This one here is Sam, down the hill from you. You just put this earpiece in your ear and press this button to talk."

"Man, the toys these days!"

"Sometimes the terrain gets in the way and you wink out, but usually, as long as your unit's turned on, the other team leaders can see you and you can see them."

"Okay, my turn!" Wiley strapped it on his arm as he'd seen the others do.

"Just run that wire up the inside of your jacket. That'll keep it out of the way."

Wiley removed his jacket and started fiddling with the earpiece, trying to figure out where to route the wire.

Pete stayed at his back, acting as if he was helping, but all the while taking a good look at Wiley's boot print where he'd stamped out the cigarette. The print didn't match Pete's sketch from Lost Creek, but then again, Wiley Kane was wearing a brand-new pair of boots.

■　■　■

"Cap?"

"I'm here." No further words would come to him, but at the moment, he didn't care. It was enough for him to accept the news, bear the pain, and nurse the wound as he sat glum and alone in their living room in Spokane, the phone to his ear. The news didn't come as a shock, but more like the final, awaited outcome of a tragic story. From the outset, Cap and Sing knew it could end this way. Putting aside denial, a happy ending would have been more surprising.

"What are you feeling?" she asked.

He rested his forehead on his fingertips and closed his eyes. He was feeling so many things. "You mean, besides the sorrow? The loss?"

"I'm not sure what to do next."

"I got caught sneaking into Burkhardt's lab today. Merrill had me booted off the campus."

Now there was a silence on her end. Finally, "Is that it, then?"

He thought a moment, then answered, "Anger. I'm feeling anger; a close friend is dead and somebody's getting away with it."

"Do we have anything solid?"

"So far it's all circumstantial—and some of it could be imaginary. What about those photos?"

"I've photographed everybody within camera range. I took some more today when all the hunters came through."

"Why don't you e-mail those to me?"

"Will do."

"I've got one more lead I'm going to harass a little, and if that doesn't pan out . . . Maybe I should just get over there and, you know, be there."

"Reed could use you right now."

"Is he there?"

"He's sleeping."

"Oh. Well, give him my love, and get me those pictures, and . . . I'll take one more crack at it, for Beck's memory if for nothing else."

"You be careful."

"Oh, I think the worst is over—for me."

■ ■ ■

Sing closed her cell phone and climbed back inside the motor home. She found Jimmy still glued to the computer screen, not saying much and looking antsy. He nervously flexed his ankle with his toe planted, making his knee wiggle up and down like a jackhammer. It was a good sign he wouldn't be able to sit still much longer. She decided to let the tension build another few minutes before she said anything.

In those minutes, she used a second computer to go online through her cell phone, selected the folder containing her photos—some posed, some candid, some downright sneaky—of anyone and everyone who'd had anything to do with the search or the hunt. With a few quick taps on the computer's touch pad, the photos were on their way to Cap.

"How's everybody doing?" she asked Jimmy.

"Nothing so far." His voice was tense. "That south end was open a long time. The bear may have given us the slip."

"I can take over if you want to head up there again."

That turned his head from the screen. "You're sure?"

"Hey. You want to be stuck down here while somebody else bags that bear?"

He ripped the headset from his head, grabbed his coat and rifle, and went out the door, jamming the earpiece from Reed's GPS in his ear.

"You're welcome," she said, settling in front of the computer.

The first thing Sing noticed was Steve Thorne and Janson's GPS blips coming perilously close to Reed's waypoint, the place where he'd found part of Beck's jacket.

■ ■ ■

Jimmy's voice crackled in the earpieces, "Talk to me, Janson. What's happening?"

"We're at the location," Janson whispered back, "so everybody pipe down."

Janson stood guard while Thorne went first, keeping an eye out for any movement, any stirring. The streamer of white toilet paper was still there, hanging on the elderberry bush. It moved lightly in the breeze—as obvious and tempting as bait for a trap. Janson didn't like this place; there was just something about it.

Thorne moved slowly, carefully planting each step, sighting down his rifle as he checked out a dark stump amid a clump of young firs, a log within a thicket, a shadow under an upturned root ball. He was mindful that this was where the Shelton woman got chewed up, and he'd seen firsthand what happened to Sheriff Mills. He drew a sample of air through his nose. Didn't Reed Shelton say something about smelling the target? There did seem to be a certain odor about the place.

As a matter of fact, the odor could have been coming from a dome of vines that grew over a fallen aspen just a few yards away.

"Heads up," Thorne whispered, gesturing toward the dome.

Janson leveled his rifle at the mound. He nodded to Thorne. Ready.

Thorne approached slowly. The odor was getting stronger.

■ ■ ■

Sing watched intently. Thorne's GPS blip was dead centered on Reed's waypoint, apparently motionless, but probably stalking, sneaking. She couldn't imagine that that thing would still be there after all this time, but then again . . .

■ ■ ■

Thorne was close to the fallen aspen, and now he could tell that the tangled overgrowth had been disturbed, thrown open like a curtain and left to settle back in place. He shot a glance at Janson, nodded toward the tangled dome, held his rifle ready in his right hand, reached out slowly with his left, took hold of the vines, drew a breath, yanked the vines open—

Underneath the thick mat of vines, leaves, and branches was a dark hollow. A foul stench washed over him, making him flinch. His trigger finger tightened.

He relaxed.

Janson allowed himself to breathe again.

The hollow was empty.

■ ■ ■

The running, running, running finally came to an end in a secluded, soft-floored grove of pines and hemlocks somewhere in Idaho—or Montana, or maybe Canada for all Beck knew. Not that she cared anymore. When the adults finally stopped to rest and Rachel let Beck roll off onto the ground, Beck flopped and lay where she landed, face half buried in the moss and pine needles, too despondent to think about it.

Reed thinks I'm dead.

The image of him finding that tattered piece of jacket kept

playing, playing, and replaying in her mind. It wouldn't fade; it wouldn't turn off. It gave her no rest.

I'm alive and I can't tell him. He thinks I'm dead and that he can't save me.

I may as well be dead!

"Oooohhh!" She moaned and writhed from the pain and frustration, her voice muffled in the ground. *I may as well lie here until I rot, until trees start growing out of me. God hates me.*

Yeah. God hated her. He had to. Why else would He keep slapping her with nothing but lousy luck? Who else understood fairness enough to make sure she never got any good breaks? Who else could make her dead to the world and everyone she loved, and yet leave her alive to agonize in it? It was all too perfect. It had to be planned.

A rising anger gave her just enough strength to roll over onto her back, point her finger toward the converging treetops, and whine at God, "Y-y-yooo . . ."

Oh, right! She forgot. God gave her a stutter so she couldn't tell Him how ticked off she was!

She slapped the ground and growled at Him. Then she sat up and screamed at Him.

That upset Rachel, who'd been lying on her back in some maple bushes. She raised her head and looked over her belly. "Hmm."

Leah was half visible in another clump of maples, staring at Beck as she tore off the broad leaves and munched on them.

Beck just growled at them, waving them off. *I'm all right, don't trouble yourselves, don't get up, just leave me alone!*

Rachel's head sank to the ground again and she let out a tired sigh. Leah regurgitated a wad of chewed leaves into her palm and started eating them a second time.

Beck stared at the ground, angrily flicking tufts of moss with her fingertip. *What am I going to do? Everybody thinks I'm dead. They're not going to look for me anymore.* They're *going to get together and have a memorial service, and then they're going to eat chicken and potato salad and go home. Reed's going to cry for me every night, and I'm going to cry for him, and the only friends I have left are these . . . these . . .*

"Ooooohh!" Seething, she growled at Leah, who ignored her, and Rachel, snoring somewhere beyond those big feet and that round belly. She couldn't see Jacob or Reuben, but she growled at them anyway, wherever they were: *All right, so you hate me! Well, I hate you too! If you eat me, I hope you barf!*

Then she watched Leah, licking and nibbling her vomited wad as if it were coleslaw. These monsters *enjoyed* barfing! God thought of everything.

What am I going to do?

She sniffed derisively at her own thoughts. *Why do anything? God will only ruin it.*

She dug her hairbrush out of her pocket and began running it through her hair only because it made her feel better. Maybe God wouldn't notice and make all her hair fall out.

"Hmph." She heard a grunt from Leah. The big gray female was just finishing up her maple-leaf coleslaw and looking at her.

Beck looked back, angry enough to meet and match the gaze from those deep-set eyes. Direct staring was never polite in Sasquatch circles, and Beck could tell Leah didn't like it, but she stared anyway and kept brushing, not caring what Leah liked, disliked, thought, or wanted.

Leah swallowed the last of her green wad, licked her palm clean, and gave Beck's hairbrush her earnest, undivided attention. Then she extended her hand and grunted again. "Hmmph."

Beck quit brushing. She looked down at her hairbrush, then

at Leah, and the strangest and most unexpected thought came to her: *I have something she doesn't.*

It was uncanny. Had *God* thought of this yet? This huge, intimidating, massively strong animal could break Beck in half with no effort at all—but only Beck knew how to use a hairbrush, and Leah seemed to know it.

Leah's eyes glanced very quickly at the sleeping Rachel, then back at Beck, taking on an imploring expression, like a dog begging.

This is going to go wrong. Somehow, God's going to foul it up.

Then again, it could have been His idea. She looked toward the sky, didn't get an answer, and ventured a guess: *Maybe I'd better try it.*

She got up slowly, keeping her eye on Leah, who sat there next to the maple bush, eyeing her. Now she could see Rachel's face. "Mom" was asleep.

While the cat's away, the mice will play, is that it?

"Hmmph." Leah extended her hand again.

Looking around for Reuben and not seeing him, Beck stole forward, keeping the brush visible in her hand. She was about to enter Leah's space, so she hummed quietly, no tune in particular, and diverted her eyes from Leah's to be polite.

Leah sure looked big sitting there on her haunches, and those arms were all muscle, lots of it.

Beck came within a few feet—close enough to have her head swatted off—and thought of a safety tip: When approaching a Sasquatch, bow and try to make that low, guttural, rumbling noise. They seem to like that.

She bowed, knees bending, her hands almost touching the ground, and tried her best to make her throat rumble.

Leah looked puzzled.

Oh. Apparently, bows with rumbled greetings were only for the alpha male. Beck made a mental note.

"Hmmph," Leah grunted, leaning forward.

Beck reached out with the brush and touched Leah's head. Leah shuffled closer. Beck started brushing, stealing glances at the sleeping Rachel and feeling like a turncoat.

But she was doing Leah a service, maybe even gaining acceptance from Rachel's rival, and that seemed a smart thing to do. She continued, working more systematically, from Leah's head down to her neck and shoulders. Leah burped a green vegetation burp and sat still, looking pleased.

I don't know where this is going, but it just might keep me alive. After all, if Beck could be part of the group, maybe the group wouldn't eat her. Beck kept brushing, working her way down Leah's back, and Leah allowed her, letting out occasional hums of pleasure. Her gray hair was sensational, so soft and smooth, and once Beck got it all lying in the same direction, it became prismatic, reflecting a rainbow sheen.

So gross, and yet so lovely.

After that unfortunate death-flinch blunder with Rachel, Beck was careful to look before she brushed, and it was a good thing she did. Halfway down Leah's back, Beck spotted another anomaly and stopped brushing just in time.

Leah immediately noticed the pause and turned her head, grunting over her shoulder.

Beck hummed back at her pleasantly, finding a safe place to brush while she had a closer look.

Again, it was blood. Carefully parting the hairs, Beck recognized another bite wound, not as severe as Rachel's but just as recent. Beck gave a low, rumbling hum as if to ask, *What on earth happened? Did Jacob do this?*

Leah sighed, seemingly resigned to whatever the unfortunate situation was.

Beck kept brushing, carefully checking, then grooming Leah's

ribs. She found a shallow gash under the right arm, possibly a bite
that didn't quite land. Leah flinched when Beck brushed around
it, but she didn't get mad.

As Beck thought about it, it didn't make sense that Jacob
would do this. When Jacob punished Rachel the first night he
saw Beck, he was brutal and unforgivably abusive, but he never
used his teeth. Besides, Leah seemed to be the "alpha's pet" in
this group; she could do no wrong. Maybe Beck was seeing the
aftermath of a full-blown catfight between Leah and Rachel, with
Leah the winner and Rachel the cast-down loser. Either that, or
. . . she just couldn't imagine.

A shape moved through the pines, and Beck looked up to see
Mr. Bad News himself, Reuben, approaching in a wide, tentative
arc, head cocked in suspicion. He growled at her as if to say, *What
are you doing with my mother?*

Beck looked him in the eye and kept brushing.

He stepped closer, then started sidestepping, left and right,
left and right, making little waving, threatening gestures with his
arms as he growled.

Leah pig-grunted at him, which set him back slightly, but he
still wanted to fight about it and stared daggers at Beck.

Beck came to the brink of being frightened. She could feel
her stomach starting to tense, her hands starting to tremble, her
speech faculties starting to jumble—but strangely, surprisingly
even to her, she went only to the brink and no further. Standing
by Reuben's mother with her permission could have had something to do with it, but there was something else: for the first time
in her life, her penchant for being afraid had worn thin. After several days of terror and dread, terror and loathing, terror and
despair, she was tired of it.

And besides that, she was just plain mad. She'd lost her husband in a most enraging dilemma; she'd been a doormat to this

snotty-nosed throw rug from the day they met; even God was picking on her and wouldn't give her a break. "Aaargh!" she growled.

She met Reuben's stare, held her eyes steady, and didn't turn away. She growled again and even huffed through her nose at him. *Listen, kid, I'm somebody too!*

Leah grunted more loudly at him, her displeasure obvious.

Beck seconded that with an angry bark, her weight forward.

Reuben bought it. He backed off, gave her a look that was half dirty, half perplexed, and shuffled sulkingly into the pines to mind his own business.

Well! To Beck's amazement, things seemed to be going the right direction.

Leah nudged her, wanting more. Beck returned to her brushing and enjoyed every square inch of it, right down to Leah's toes. She finished with a soft hum and a flourish, then backed away passively, eyes diverted, honoring the custom with confidence.

Back in her own personal space amid the pines, she settled to the ground by herself with no one bothering her, feeling strangely unafraid.

And strangely alive.

■　■　■

"She's not dead."

Sing and Pete looked up from the dining table at a man not quite risen from the dead. Reed stood, his frame filling the rear bedroom door, but he didn't appear well rested, to put it mildly. He was still clutching the bloodied piece of jacket.

Sing rose from the table. "Can I fix you anything? I have some soup."

Reed stood there as if he hadn't heard the question, a weird, catatonic look on his face. "Uh, yeah. Please. And how about a sandwich or something?"

Sing rummaged in the tight refrigerator. "I've got pastrami and turkey breast."

"Okay. Please." He sat at the computer and looked at the screen, now dark. "So what happened?"

Pete answered, his fingers curled around a coffee cup, "Hunters are back down for the night. They'll regroup in the morning, go back to using bear stands and maybe some dogs. They found plenty of sign that something had been up there, but it's gone now."

Reed broke into a delirious grin and chuckled. "So they didn't get their bear." He chuckled some more, enjoying a demented laugh at a sorry situation. Pete stared into his coffee, and Sing sliced bread until he'd finished.

"I'm sorry, Reed," said Pete. "I wish to God things could've turned out different."

Reed gave him a curious look. "We don't know how they turned out."

Pete looked at Sing, who only looked down at the open sandwich.

Pete found words first. "Reed. You know I have the deepest respect for your feelings on this, but we've got to face it. Three violent deaths in a row don't line up with Beck just tagging along with a bunch of creatures, alive and well and leaving footprints. Now that piece of her jacket, *that's* consistent with what we've seen. That talks."

"So you're with Jimmy?"

Pete winced. "Oh, man, don't put me in Jimmy's camp . . ."

"He thought the Cryncovich footprints were a hoax. He thought Beck was dead a long time ago. Is that what you think?"

"We've been talking about that," said Sing.

"We've been going around and around about it," said Pete.

Sing still had a touch of fire in her eyes. "I'd like to know how those prints could be so accurately formed, and just what creatures were doing all that howling when Mills was killed."

Reed focused on the tired tracker. "Do you have another explanation?"

Pete could only give a slight throw-up-his-hands gesture. "Like I was telling her, I don't know, but what if Fleming Cryncovich is as nutty as he looks and just wants attention? He's a Sasquatch fanatic; he would've known how to fake footprints. And as far as Beck's boot prints, he could've found a size 6 boot with a matching sole. A boot is a boot."

Sing jumped on that. "With the same tread pattern you noted at Lost Creek? You *did* sketch it all out on one of your blue cards, didn't you?"

Reed added, "With the same wear pattern?"

"And what about the cell phone number scratched in the dirt?"

Pete countered, "I don't have it all figured out. I'm just trying to see this thing from all sides, that's all. Reed, isn't it possible that Arlen Peak could have gotten your cell phone number?"

Reed saw his point. "Yeah."

"And he's a Bigfoot nut too, isn't he? And he and Cryncovich are friends?"

Sing's temper was starting to show. "You know what you're saying about Arlen?"

Pete drilled her with his eyes. "Why'd you take his picture then?"

Sing got flustered. "Just . . . there's this whole cover-up thing. We can't rule out any possible suspect—"

"Well, there might be a cover-up and there might not be."

Sing was ready to grapple on that one. "Allen Arnold was moved."

"And Randy—was he moved?"

"Possibly."

"But you don't know that."

"Not really."

"And that's my point."

Reed asked, "So, what has Cap found out?"

Sing's discouragement was obvious. "Nothing solid. It's all conjecture."

Pete let his hand come down forcefully on the table. "There! Thank you! That's the word I've been looking for. Conjecture! I conject, then you conject, and that's all Cap has is conjecture. Reed, we've been at this all afternoon, talking about whether Beck's dead or alive, or somebody's fooling us, or we're just fooling ourselves, or whether there really are Sasquatches up there . . ."

Reed answered quietly, "And whether Sasquatches are killers, and whether it's a bear like Jimmy says, and why in the world somebody would want to protect those monsters with a cover-up—if there really are monsters and there really is a cover-up."

That gave them pause.

"I thought you were sleeping," said Sing.

"I was until you two started in on each other. But I've been thinking too."

"So help us out," said Pete.

Reed lightly stroked the remains of Beck's jacket as he spoke in a quiet, tired voice: "Considering how much we don't know, it might be early to say how things turned out."

Pete looked out the window to mull it over. Sing busied herself with lettuce, meat, pickles, and tomatoes.

"It's kind of funny, isn't it, how much this whole thing's been about what people think they know: it's a bear, it's a Bigfoot; I'm a wife-killer, I'm a crazy victim; Beck's dead, Beck's alive; it was a cover-up, it was an accident."

Sing finished making the sandwich, put it on a plate, and handed it to Reed. "Still want that soup?"

"That'd be great. Thanks." He set the sandwich on the computer bench, truly hungry but needing to speak. "I just keep thinking of Beck and me climbing up that trail before this all started, and how much I thought I knew, and how much I really didn't. Here I was, telling Beck her world was too small and if she didn't get out and stretch a bit, she'd quit learning and growing, and all along, I didn't know how small *my* world was. It's been one tough lesson."

He considered the tattered piece of leather in his lap, looking it over as he spoke, "Anyway, I guess it's never a bad idea to let your world get stretched once in a while, to just humble down and admit there might be something right in front of you that you haven't thought of before. So on the one hand, Pete, you're right about Beck's jacket. It talks."

He held it up for them to see, tooth marks, bloodstain, and all. "This bloodstain is several days old, isn't that right, Sing?"

Silently, she examined the stain, and then she nodded, knowing what it meant.

Reed spoke what the others realized: "It means Beck died several days ago, probably that very first night." He folded the leather carefully, solemnly, and set it on the dining table in the midst of them. "There's no way she could have made those footprints."

Sing and Pete stared at that tattered remnant. It did speak, without words.

Sing finally said, "It still doesn't answer everything."

Pete tried to say it calmly. "It answers enough. The rest of it . . . Maybe we'll never know."

Reed replied, "So that's one thing we can agree on, that we don't really know."

Pete and Sing silently checked with each other, then nodded.

"But on the other hand, maybe it's okay to *believe* a little? Instead of just accepting the way things look, maybe there's still room to stretch what we're so sure of just one more inch."

He leaned forward, confronting Pete eye to eye. "Pete, you ever had a feeling you couldn't explain?"

Pete understood. He nodded.

Reed looked at Sing. "How about you?"

"All the time," she said.

"When I was up there at the waypoint and I found this" —he nodded at the remnant on the table— "everything I saw told me that I'd finally gotten the answer, that I finally knew. But there was a part of me that *felt* something, like she was talking to me. I had every reason in the world to think—maybe even know—that she was dead, but still . . . There was some part of me that wouldn't let go, that still believed." He leaned back, eyeing the remnant on the table. "I could say I *know* Beck is dead, but I don't, not really. And as long as we don't know for sure, I can *believe* she's still out there." Then he added, "And I *believe* there's one last thing we haven't tried."

■ ■ ■

"No, no, now listen, I said I didn't want to get sucked into it!"

Nick Claybuckle was enjoying a relaxing jog around Manitow Park. He passed the big duck pond and the geometric rose gardens, pounded over the beautiful stone bridge and under the spreading maple trees—

Until he was overtaken by another jogger who could outrun him. "You heard me, kid! Pull over!"

"Doc, somebody's gonna see us talking!"

"Not if you get off the road," said Cap. He pointed. "How about in there? Nice benches, lots of hedges, nice and private."

Nick was huffing and puffing anyway, carrying too much extra poundage to get away. He hung a right and they ducked into a pleasant grove, sending a brown squirrel darting up a tree. Nick collapsed onto an ornate concrete bench with a brass plaque commemorating the donor. He was soaked with sweat and his glasses were foggy.

Cap sat down next to him, not even breathing hard. "Nick, my needs are very simple," Cap began. "We all know Burkhardt's been shifting his operation off campus for years, and now he's moved off campus altogether. I need to know where he went. I need to find him and his lab."

Nick gasped a few breaths and then answered, "Dr. Capella, you're one of the main reasons he moved!"

"Nick . . ."

"They're going to know I told you!"

Cap nudged him. "You said your department's having to cut back. Where's the money going?"

"Now, how would I know that?"

Cap hooked a finger under Nick's chin and forced him to meet his eyes. "Let me tell you about my ape. Remember him, the one who's ticked off about something? He's been killing people, Nick. He's been breaking their necks." Nick tried to look away. Cap used his whole hand to hold his attention. "He's killed a trail guide, a logger, the Whitcomb County sheriff, and now . . ." Cap came closer, nose to nose. "He's killed Beck Shelton, a close friend of mine—lots of bites, lots of blood, ripping, tearing, the whole nine yards. So, Nick, you have to understand, now *I* am ticked off. I am *not* a patient man!"

Nick's face went white; he was paying attention now. Cap let him go. A question began to form—

Cap intercepted it. "Chimpanzees, Nick, maybe as many as four, spliced so full of human DNA they're a patchwork quilt. Now, how do you suppose that happened?"

"The Judy Lab said it was contamination—"

"It was put there using viral transfers. That means human intervention, which means somebody's responsible, which means somebody's going to be in big trouble when the law sorts this all out. So who are you more afraid of?"

Nick stared, struggling to process it all.

"Where's the money going? Is Merrill diverting funds?"

Nick thought it over one more second, then gave in, nodding yes. "I checked on it. The college budget's gone up the last ten years, not down, but all the departments are being cut back, including the York Center. Merrill's got some kind of pet project going."

"With Burkhardt?" Nick hesitated and Cap nudged him again. "With Burkhardt?"

"That's the talk on the inside. Merrill's hoping for a big pay-off to make it all legit. I mean, you wouldn't believe the big people hovering around with grant money—"

"Like Euro-Atlantic Oil and the Carlisle Foundation."

"Yeah. And Mort Fernan."

Cap hadn't seen that name in his research. "The guy who owns the Evolution Channel?"

"Makes perfect sense, doesn't it? Whatever Burkhardt's working on, Fernan wants first dibs to put it on TV." He sniffed a bitter chuckle. "Must be pretty sexy stuff, a whole lot more exciting than inequity aversion in capuchins. But it's a gamble. The investors are holding back until they see results."

Cap nodded to himself. *Results.* There was that word again. "No results, no money."

"And Merrill will have some explaining to do."

"*Incorrect* results, no money," Cap mused.

"Same thing."

"So what about the chimpanzees being shipped off campus? Any truth to that?"

Nick nodded. "The York Center's turning away research proposals—which means we're turning away money—because we don't have new chimps. We have the old standbys, but they're getting too aggressive to be useful, and we're short on younger males."

"What about the females?"

"They're getting old too, and we don't have younger ones to replace them. The young ones get shipped out as soon as they're old enough to breed. Orders from Merrill's office."

"Where do they go?"

"Somewhere in Idaho. A place called Three Rivers."

That turned Cap's head. "Say again?"

■ ■ ■

Sing kept raking, loosening up the sand by the creek bank, cleaning out rocks and twigs that could prevent a clear footprint. Reed brought a gunnysack into the center of the tilled area and began setting apples, pears, and bananas on a short, sun-bleached log. Pete remained outside the circle, studying a map in the ebbing light.

"It's the right place," Reed assured him.

"Only if they come here," Pete answered, orienting the map to the surroundings. "They've got plenty of choices which way to go."

"But the food is here," said Reed, "alongside the same creek bed, and just a little farther south. If nothing else, Jimmy's hunters will drive them this way."

"We may have been driving them this way all along."

"That's what I've been thinking. If they were living in the forest around Abney all this time, why else would they move?"

"Then again, if they were living around Abney all this time, why haven't they attacked anyone before?"

Sing looked up from her raking. "I keep hearing the word 'they.'"

Pete grabbed up a second rake and directed a buddy's look at Reed. "It'll be 'they' as long as Reed wants it to be."

Sing smiled her gratitude at Pete.

"It won't be very long," said Reed, setting a few last items on the log. "I know this whole idea's ridiculous, but it's the only one I've got."

"Maybe just half ridiculous," Pete replied thoughtfully. "Look at it this way: Arlen and Fleming don't even know we're doing this, so if we get something this time . . ." He could only shake his head after that.

"It's either this or give up," said Sing. "So if you don't go through with it, I will."

"You write Beck a note?" Pete asked to make sure.

"I explained everything," Reed answered, taking long strides out of the circle, leaving a minimum of footprints for Pete to rake out.

Pete raked them all out, and then they stood there, gazing across a small circle of clear, carefully raked sand at what Reed had designated the Last-Ditch Attempt. It would be dark before they could make it back to Pete's truck, but they found it hard to leave.

"And I told her I loved her," Reed added. His gaze moved between his two friends. "Would you guys mind . . . praying with me? It would put my mind at ease."

Sing and Pete both nodded their consent. Reed put his arms around his two friends' shoulders and spoke softly. "God, wherever

Beck is, we know she's in Your hands. Hold her tight for me, will you? Keep her safe and bring her home soon. And . . . that's about it. Amen."

"We'd best get back," said Pete, and they grabbed up their gear.

THIRTEEN

Deputy Dave Saunders had spent Thursday evening on the phone, recalling any Search and Rescue volunteers he could find—four were ready, willing, available, and armed. Then he'd hunted around for metal detectors—two he borrowed from some hobbyist friends, one he rented, and one he bought with his own money. At first light Friday morning, he and his crew were at the cabin on Lost Creek. They would test Sing's theory by searching for something that was not necessarily there to be found.

"If you see, hear, or smell any belligerent creature in the area, I don't care if it's a bear or a Bigfoot or a raccoon on steroids, you get out of there," he told the faithful four. "If you find the shovel, then get on the radio and we'll all converge on the area. If there's a shovel, then chances are there's a grave, and that's what we're after. Any questions?"

The housewife, the fireman, the heavy equipment operator, and the machinist all looked back at him, silent.

"Okay, then, you know your quadrants. We'll take a snack break about ten. Let's go."

■ ■ ■

Cap drove east from Spokane. He planned to cut through Coeur d'Alene, Idaho, and then south into the timberlands. A highway map rested on the seat beside him, his destination represented by a small open dot.

"Three Rivers," he said into his cell phone. "I about fell off the bench when Nick said that. That's close to where Allen Arnold was killed, am I right?"

Sing replied, "Cap, I think you're heading into trouble."

"I remember Burkhardt talking about a vacation cabin in Idaho, and now Nick says the chimps are being sent to Three Rivers, right where all this trouble began, if the pattern means anything."

"That's exactly what I mean. I'd say call the police, but . . ."

"But what would we tell them?"

"Well, get something to tell them and then tell them!"

"Exactly my intentions."

"But tell me first—and be careful."

"Say hi to Reed."

■ ■ ■

Sing closed her cell phone and redirected her attention to the dozen camouflaged, rifle-toting hunters now gathered beside the mobile lab, planning, discussing, debating. Max Johnson, Steve Thorne, and Sam Marlowe were telling stories and expressing opinions about today's plan of action; Wiley Kane was having a smoke; Janson was repacking a backpack.

Jimmy and some forest rangers huddled around a map, pointing and muttering: "Set out bait here and here, but you can't have human presence pressuring from above," Jimmy said.

"How about a triangle? Just keep these guys in a triangle and make one big sweep," one offered.

"Dogs'll take care of that, really, if you want to wait," said a second.

Sing reached inside the motor home and brought out some briefcase-sized storage cases. "Here are the GPS units."

Jimmy was elated. "All right. I'll hand them out. Want to take the central command like yesterday?" He opened the first case and pulled out one of the units.

"I'll be here."

"Great. Now I need to know where Reed and Pete are."

Sing pressed through the huddle so she could see the map. She found the site of the Last-Ditch Attempt, along the same creek bed as the Fleming Cryncovich site, two miles south. "They're hiking back in there to look for any sign."

"Big footprints, I suppose?" Jimmy teased.

She only smiled. "We'll take anything we can get."

He gave her an encouraging pat on the back. Sing received it as such and stepped up into the motor home, settling in front of the computer.

"Okay, guys," she heard Jimmy saying, "here's the plan. Max and Janson, we'll start you guys up where Reed found that shred of jacket. You'll bait the area and then wait; you know the drill. Wiley and Thorne, I want you farther south, and take a look at the map here: Henderson and Shelton are in that area, so let's make sure we make contact with them and don't cross purposes; catch my drift?"

Jimmy's banter faded from Sing's awareness as she studied the computer screen, scrolling it south to reveal the terrain around the Last-Ditch Attempt. The map was clean—no activity.

"Hey, Sing?" Jimmy called. "We're short a GPS."

She called out the door, "Reed and Pete took it."

■ ■ ■

Reed and Pete were armed and cautious, working their way into the forest along a game trail that only the deer and elk used. There were no human trails here, no hikers, no trailside latrines, just thick, leafy forest and sun-starved undergrowth that swished and crackled despite their best efforts to keep quiet.

Pete led the way, setting his own pace, thinking, watching, moving stealthily, like an animal.

Reed's watch told him it was time to call in. He put a small handheld radio to his jaw and whispered, "Sing, we're half-way in."

Her voice came back, "Roger that. Jimmy's guys are moving in. Thorne and Kane are taking the south flank. They know where you'll be."

■ ■ ■

Leah sat on her haunches amid the Rocky Mountain Maples and wild roses, eyes half open as if she cared little about anything beyond her immediate, sweet little world, moaning and humming a song of pleasure.

Immediately behind her, Rachel hummed and grunted, busily, meticulously running her fingers through Leah's hair, making Sasquatch improvements in the grooming Beck had performed just the day before.

Immediately behind Rachel, Beck guided her brush carefully, maintaining the beauty of Rachel's full-body coiffure and humming quietly, constantly gauging how her behavior was being received and passed on.

The arrangement had fallen together spontaneously, like the revival of a forgotten routine. Rachel, as if desiring reconciliation, offered to groom Leah. Leah, having been groomed by the lowest member of the group, now seemed to find grooming from a slightly higher member acceptable, and allowed it. Beck, seeing a chance for just one more measure of acceptance—and possible influence—joined the party, and so it happened. She wasn't humming out of joy or pleasure, but to keep things calm and to keep appeasement flowing. This was a whole new social development, as precarious as a cease-fire between two mortal enemies, and she feared one wrong move could break the spell.

Either that, or one jealous little Sasquatch, obsessed with an ape's version of sibling rivalry. As Beck brushed, she kept a watchful eye on Reuben, fully expecting him to do *something*; she didn't know what. Right now he was sitting at a distance, his shoulder against a tree, contemplating his fingernails—a behavior he may have learned from his mother in a similar situation. Beck couldn't be sure just what it meant. He might be pouting or trying to act indifferent. Then again, he could be acting indifferent while plotting a vicious and wicked act. He was a wild card in this game.

He looked up, met Beck's eyes, and held the gaze—in this context, a challenge.

Leah gave a quiet, corrective grunt, and he looked down at his fingernails again.

Okay, Beck thought. *I just have to keep his momma on my side.*

As for Jacob, Beck didn't expect him to warm to her. He was a protector and provider, but every bit a beast, a cold and savage ruler. Even the gentle side she may have seen when Leah groomed him seemed a thin facade in light of the beating he gave Rachel and the brutal bite marks on his two women. The only reason Beck was a part of this grooming chain was because he wasn't around to render an opinion about it. If and when he ever showed up—

Suddenly the bushes quaked. Jacob was returning. Beck bolted away from the two females and hobbled to her spot in the pine grove, pocketing the hairbrush and plopping down, trying to appear passive.

Reuben was on his feet instantly, like a dog whose master had returned.

The two females rose at the same time, looked into the forest, and then flopped down to their hands and knees in formal greeting.

Beck got on her hands and knees as well, not wanting to challenge the patience of the king who now emerged through the trees, light and shadow, light and shadow blinking on his face and chest as he walked. He was clutching something against his stomach with his hands and arms.

Beck knew right away that he'd found more fruit, which brought a volley of questions to mind: Was it a farm, an orchard, or another baiting site? Were there humans around? Lastly, *Will I get any to eat?*

Jacob came to a small gap in the trees, sank to his knees, and let the fruit tumble to the ground. The selection was suspiciously familiar: apples, pears, and bananas.

Another baiting site, Beck thought.

■　■　■

Reed knelt in the sand, staring, at a loss for words except to say, "I don't know what to feel."

Pete was beside him, studying the huge footprints and needing a little time to become a believer again. "I've had my head turned around so many times it's about to come unscrewed." The similarity to recent horrors struck him. "Sorry."

"It's him, isn't it?"

Pete studied the tracks where they approached and then returned in a beeline across the creek bed. "It's him. Old alpha male, Mr. Scarfoot. He's still out there, like it or not."

"So Fleming's footprints weren't a hoax after all."

Pete didn't answer that but stood, scanning the area. "He took the bait, every piece of it."

Reed searched carefully around the perimeter of the raked ground. "*Every* piece?"

■ ■ ■

Beck held back, waiting to see what the rules might be this time around. Surprisingly, Leah and Rachel approached the fruit *almost* together, Leah first, but Rachel only a few steps behind. While Jacob sat back and watched without comment, Leah took an apple and allowed Rachel to take one after her. She didn't seem to mind Rachel sharing in the fruit as long as Leah chose first.

Reuben sidled up to his mother in his usual way and helped himself.

My turn? Beck wondered.

She waited, watching Jacob. He did not look at her, which could have meant a lingering hatred, prideful rejection, or total indifference. She tried to read his body language for any clues as to which it was, but she couldn't be sure.

She waited for Rachel to invite her, and after Rachel had downed two apples with the group's indulgence, she looked at Beck and pig grunted a call to supper.

Beck approached slowly, braced for some kind of reaction.

Jacob eyed her, his brow sinking slightly over his eyes, sending a warning, but just a warning.

She dropped her eyes and bowed slightly, trying to look small and submissive.

He glanced at the ground, scooped up a lump of his own dung, and popped it into his mouth, enjoying a fruit salad the second time around.

Beck came up behind Rachel, who moved over to give her room. Beck spotted a pear and leaned in to pick it up—

There was something lying next to it, and it was not a piece of fruit.

■ ■ ■

Reed found a crumpled shred of white paper snagged in a stunted pine. He carefully worked it loose. It had been chewed and was slimy with saliva, but he peeled the folds open enough to read what was left of his own writing: the last line of some instructions about batteries, the words "I love you," and his name. "I had this wrapped around the GPS with a rubber band."

Pete combed the surrounding ground with his eyes. "Well, obviously, it wasn't Beck who picked it up." He observed the chewed condition of the note. "Doesn't look good for the GPS, does it?"

■ ■ ■

Beck knew right away what it was. Reed, always the gadget nut, had shown her one in a sporting goods store. She'd managed to talk him out of buying it, but of course that reprieve only lasted a month before he brought home two. After they spent some quality time together learning how the gadgets worked, he put his in his car and she put hers back in its box.

But that was then. She felt no cynicism now, not the slightest tendency to brush it off as a "guy thing." That hand-sized device of yellow plastic with the LCD screen was nothing less than life itself. It spoke—no, it *yelled*—of Reed! This was so typical of him; he would have thought of this!

He's reaching for me! He hasn't given up!

Her hand trembled as she reached for it, reached for *him*—

Leah picked it up and sniffed it.

"Oh!" Beck stifled the squeal of alarm as soon as it escaped, her hand over her mouth. Leah shot a testy glance. Beck lowered her eyes—*Careful, careful, don't challenge her!* Now Jacob was watching, his piercing eyes focused on every detail, looking for trouble.

Beck tried to show interest in an apple, her hands shaking.

Leah went back to sniffing the GPS. She stuck out her tongue and tasted it.

Beck bit into the apple, trying not to look alarmed or interested, just letting her eyes pass over Leah without really looking. *Oh, please, Leah, please don't eat it!*

■ ■ ■

Reed and Pete stepped carefully, walking a square pattern around the baiting site, ten paces to a side, then twelve, then fourteen, probing and combing through the river grass, the flood-bent willows, and the knee-high pines, needing to know: Was it here? Did the beast pick it up and drop it? Eat it? Chew it and spit it out?

They needed to know.

∎ ∎ ∎

The GPS fell to the ground, and Leah picked up a pear instead.

Beck reached—

Rachel was curious and picked it up.

Beck jammed her tongue against the roof of her mouth, blocking a cry on its way out. Eye contact with Rachel was allowed. She tried it, her eyes imploring.

Rachel didn't notice; she was too fascinated with the strange object. She sniffed it, turned it over a few times, and then popped it into her mouth.

This time Beck took the risk and made a sound, extending her hand.

Snap! The plastic cracked between Rachel's teeth.

"Noo!" Beck took hold of Rachel's arm and got half her attention.

Rachel spit it out, flipping it off the end of her tongue.

Beck caught it before it hit the ground, hoping, praying it would still work. It was slimy now, slippery like a wet bar of soap, but she hung on, clutched it against her heart. The case was cracked, but maybe—*Oh dear God—maybe* the electronics were still intact. She looked for the on button as she wiped slime away from the keypad—

A hairy hand flashed over her shoulder and the GPS shot skyward.

With a shriek and without thinking, Beck took hold of Reuben's arm, reaching and grabbing with her free hand. His arm was impervious to her weight, like a thick tree branch, and as he stood he lifted her torso off the ground so that her feet were dragging. She groped for a foothold. He twisted, whipping her about. She hung on, fighting to wrest the device from his fist.

Words were impossible; she shrieked, she yelled, she growled, she hit him on his arm.

The females were on their feet, growling and barking, but not at each other. They were two mothers scolding their quarreling children.

Beck locked eyes with Reuben. *I won't give it up. No, not this time! This is my life!*

She got both hands on the GPS and pulled. It could have been embedded in concrete for all the good it did.

Her eyes were closed in a grimace when the blow came, a stunning haymaker across her face. She no longer felt the GPS in her hands; she no longer felt her hands. She went numb and oblivious, the world spinning before her eyes in a blur of sky, trees, grass, light, dark—

She slammed into the ground but felt no pain, only nausea, as the earth reeled beneath her and her vision wandered, then went black. As if in a dream, she heard Rachel barking and protesting while Leah growled and snarled, but they sounded so far away, so very far away . . .

■ ■ ■

Reed and Pete had walked and combed a square of fifty paces, an area that now included the creek bed and roughly 150 feet of creek bank and adjacent forest. Now they stood at the edge of the creek bed, the dry river rocks under their feet, and reached a consensus.

"It's gone," said Reed.

Pete removed his hat, wiped his brow with his shirtsleeve, and responded, "It'll make one heck of a scat pile."

Reed felt so numb, so empty. He'd been hoping for so long, and had that certain *feeling* so deeply, that he now hung in emotional space with nothing under him and nowhere to go. He couldn't believe Beck was dead, but he'd expended his last hope that she was alive. For several minutes, he and Pete stood silently on the barren river rocks, waiting for the next course of action—not just in their search but in life itself—to come to mind while no water flowed past, no squirrels chattered in the trees, and no birds took an interest in the place.

Pete finally suggested, "We can probably track it."

Reed didn't answer for a moment, then asked, "Do you think those tracks at the Cryncovich site could've been a few days older?"

"Could've been, but I doubt it."

"So Beck could have been alive then, but then she was killed soon after. Or maybe the Bigfoot tracks were real, but Beck's were faked."

"I don't think it much matters. I just remember what Sheriff Mills said before he was killed: 'God help me, that thing's walking.'"

Several seconds passed before Reed replied, "Sort of says it all, doesn't it?"

"I would say so, yeah."

Now, as Reed felt weak and his knees feeble, he didn't fight it. He sat down on an old gray log. Pete joined him. As the forest went on living, not mindful of them, they sat motionless, staring at nothing in particular, their eyes landing on those eighteen-inch tracks just once in a while.

"I suppose we ought to track it," Reed said at last.

"It's your call. If you're finished with all this, so am I."

Reed took another minute to fish around in the feelings he didn't seem to have anymore and concluded, "I guess I'm finished."

Pete rose from the log and offered Reed his hand. "Come on. Let's get you home."

Pow!

The rifle shot echoed upon itself, stretching out into a clattering roar that rippled through the hills.

Pow! There it was again.

■ ■ ■

Beck awoke as if from sleep, head throbbing, mind dopey, the world crazily sideways. Through the swaying, blurring, sideways blades of grass, she saw the Sasquatches huffing and stirring, alarmed by something. That was nothing new. They were always alarmed about something. Beck guessed they were going to run again.

Yeah, they were going to run. Rachel hovered over her, panting and grunting, taking hold of her arm, yanking, trying to rouse her.

She thought she might have heard something.

■ ■ ■

Pete borrowed the radio from Reed and called in. "Sing? We heard some shots."

Sing came back, "Where have you been?"

"What do you hear from the hunters?"

"Stand by. There's so much chatter I can't make it out."

Pete waited, exchanging a concerned look with Reed.

Sing returned. "Better get over there. They're close to the creek bed, bearing 175, about half a mile."

"They're south of us," said Reed.

"What've they shot?" Pete asked Sing.

"Jimmy doesn't know. Whoever did the shooting doesn't have a radio."

"Okay, we're heading over there." Pete handed back the radio. "Lordy! If they bagged that thing . . . !"

■ ■ ■

Beck saw the ground fall away, then start moving beneath her. She watched the grass and the Rocky Mountain Maple whisk by, then the trunks of trees and more trunks of trees and patches of light and shadow on the plant-cluttered ground, but all the while, search as she would, she saw nothing made of yellow plastic, kind of cracked, kind of slimy, maybe broken.

■ ■ ■

Reed and Pete rounded a bend in the creek bed and heard the voices of two hunters uphill in the trees, laughing and talking it up, all caution and stealth thrown to the wind. One of the voices was Jimmy's.

"Doesn't sound like they shot anything unexpected," Pete muttered.

The knowledge brought Reed no joy, but on the other hand, he didn't care much anymore.

They climbed into the forest, came over a rise, and found Kane down in a hollow, looking like a wild-eyed, white-haired mountain man as he knelt by the biggest black bear either of them had ever seen. He was holding up the head by the scruff of the neck and striking a pose while Jimmy Clark, in an unusually chipper mood, snapped his picture. When Wiley saw them he whooped long and loud. "Can you believe this?"

Another voice came from higher up the hill. "You get him, Wiley?"

"I got him!"

A vague, camouflaged shape wearing a matching cap wove its way downward through the spindly trunks. Only when it came close did they recognize Steve Thorne, all marine, looking ready for jungle combat. His teeth stood out brightly against the green and brown greasepaint he wore on his face, which put them off balance. They'd never seen him grin before. "Now, that's a record breaker, my friend!"

"That it is," said Jimmy, snapping another picture.

Kane probed the thick black fur until he found a bloody spot on the flank. "Perfect heart-and-lung shot! He dropped like a rock!"

Jimmy spoke into his earpiece. "Okay, everybody. We have a confirmed kill. Wiley Kane gets the trophy. Good work, and many thanks to all of you!" He laughed at the chatter coming back through the earpiece and relayed it, "Everybody says congratulations." He spoke to the earpiece, "Sam and Max, you're closest. I'd like to get you over here to help pack it out. Yeah, it's a monster."

"Gonna dress him out?" Pete asked.

Jimmy grinned up at them, jubilant. "Yeah, he's too big to take out whole."

Pete set down his rifle and backpack, then spoke softly to Reed, "They're gonna find out they shot a bear for nothing." Reed answered, "I'd better stay here."

Pete nodded and stepped down into the hollow.

Jimmy extended a hand, and Pete grasped it. "You were right," Jimmy said. "It was moving south. Sorry to get the jump on you, but hey, Wiley saw it first."

Kane just grinned.

Pete gave Kane a courteous smile. "For a minute I thought you may have shot something else."

Wiley knew what Pete was talking about. "Not today."

Pete took hold of the feet, studied the pads carefully, then looked up at Reed with a discreet wag of his head.

Jimmy saw it. "This is your culprit, Pete. I'll bank on it."

Pete kept his voice down. "I think the culprit's gotten clean away thanks to all your noise." He forced a smile Kane's direction again. "But congrats on your bear."

Jimmy took out his hunting knife. "You're welcome to watch."

Reed wasn't the least bit interested and found a small log a comfortable distance away. Pete circled around to stand by Kane and Thorne as they watched Jimmy open up the bear's abdomen with quick sawing motions of the knife. In just a few minutes, with a few quick cuts and a yank, the stomach rolled out on the ground. It was bulging. Jimmy sliced it open with one clean pass of the blade and it blossomed like a flower, the contents sending up a stench that made Kane back away.

Jimmy probed through the contents with the tip of his knife. "Lots of berries." He snagged some aluminum foil and food wrapping with familiar golden arches. "Robbed a garbage can somewhere." Under the mass of berry pulp, seeds, and garbage, something caught on his knife. He pulled it up, letting the other contents fall aside. He lifted his gaze to Pete's.

Pete reached down and, with deft fingers, worked the piece of leather loose and spread it out. It was brown, with a row of fringe. It was unmistakable.

■　■　■

Deputy Saunders's crew had not given up hope even though Dave never had much to begin with. They combed the woods, four people working four quadrants, weaving back and forth according to compass headings, numbers of paces, and red ribbon markers, metal detectors sweeping the ground.

The heavy equipment operator's detector let out a squeal that made him jump—he'd never heard his metal detector actually find something metal.

The sound was so loud and the man was so close that even Dave heard it. He ran to the spot even as the man dug hurriedly with his shovel.

Clink! His shovel hit something.

He probed farther, scraped, pried, dug some more, and finally wedged up—

An old ax head.

He got to keep it. The search continued.

■ ■ ■

Sing called Cap to let him know the hunt was over. The news was such a foregone conclusion that it didn't shock or surprise him. It only strengthened his resolve.

"Well, it may be over for Jimmy and his crew, but not for us," he said. "Get over here as soon as you can."

Sing said good-bye, closed her cell phone, and stood by her motor home, watching the final exodus.

Jimmy Clark secured the last bungee cord over his gear in the back of his Idaho Department of Fish and Game King Cab pickup, gave Sing a good-bye tip of his cap, and climbed inside. The four rangers from the forest service were already in their pale green vehicle, the engine running. When Jimmy started out, they followed, easing down the road through the hamlet of Whitetail until their taillights vanished around a far bend in the road and all was quiet.

Wiley Kane had taken great care in rolling and wrapping up his bearskin, setting it securely in the back of his old pickup so that only the bear's snout showed from under the canvas. He was whistling happily as Sing approached him.

"I want to thank you for your help, young lady," he said.

"I'm glad for you," she replied.

"Thanks. But I am sorry. All in all, this is not a happy day for you and your friends."

"Thank you."

"What's, uh, what's Officer Shelton going to do now?" he asked.

Sing looked toward the forest where Reed had gone walking alone. "He'll go on living."

"You figure he's convinced now? I mean, he's not going to be out there searching for his wife anymore, or hunting for Bigfoot?"

"No one could ever know that."

Kane smiled and offered his hand. "It's been nice meeting you."

She shook his hand. "May I ask for one small thing?"

"Yes, ma'am."

"May I have just a portion of your bear meat?" He looked quizzical, so she explained, "It would be for a remembrance, like flowers."

"Got twenty dollars?"

■　■　■

Pete stepped out of the motor home, feeling weighted down, dispirited, and twenty years older. He'd lain down to rest but hadn't slept. He wondered where Reed was, and how he was— alive, hopefully, which was the most one could expect for now. He wasn't sure where Sing might be. Most of the vehicles that had been parked along the road were gone, and Whitetail was nearly its old, mostly deserted self.

Jimmy had left without saying a so-long. Pete leaned against the motor home and took a moment to regret the less-than-friendly departure. He and Jimmy had had a discussion, then a disagreement, and then a pretty good shouting match over that piece of Beck's jacket in the bear's stomach. To Jimmy, it settled every doubt and answered every question. To Pete—and Reed—it was just another piece of garbage the bear had found, attractive because of the bloodstain and gulped down after Beck was no longer anywhere near it. Of course, bringing in the alpha male's footprints at the second baiting site did not serve well in resolving things but only made them worse.

Pete sighed, deeply impressed with how badly things could go sometimes, no matter what he did.

Smoke rose from a small campsite back in the trees. He headed that direction and found Sing seated on a log near a fire pit. She was wrapped in a warm Indian blanket, tending a fire in which a piece of bear meat was burning and sizzling, sending up smoke.

Max Johnson was there, carrying on a one-sided conversation. "So really, there's not a lot of point in prolonging this. I think you and Reed and Pete just need to settle this in your hearts and get on with your lives." He spotted Pete as he approached. "Oh, hi, Pete! How're you doing?"

"Beck Shelton is dead," he answered, matter-of-factly, as he stepped into the circle of logs placed around the fire. "How should I be doing?"

"I'm so sorry. But it's for the best, isn't it—that you finally know? It's closure. That's what you've been needing for days, and now . . ."

"Max." Pete looked at Sing, who said nothing, only watched the flames. "I think this is supposed to be a private moment."

Max looked at Sing as if really seeing her for the first time. He nodded and, without another word, left them.

Pete found a few more chunks of firewood and carefully placed them on the fire, keeping the flames hot around the burning meat. He sat on the log beside her, as close as a good friend.

Before long, alive, safe, and silent, Reed returned from the woods. Pete and Sing greeted him with their eyes, but there were no words. Reed observed the fire and the burning meat, then picked up two more pieces of firewood and added them to the fire. He sat on the other side of Sing, and all three watched the flames together.

When the meat was almost gone, Sing closed her eyes, releasing a trickle of tears, and began a plaintive lament from the old traditions, rocking gently as the flames crackled. First she sang in low, mournful tones without words, expressing a sorrow that only the soul could know. Then sorrow gave way to pain and the song rose in volume and pitch, the anguish lofting like the smoke from the fire toward the mountains where a friend had gone, never to return.

Tears came to Reed's eyes, blurring the flames, as the song wrapped itself around his heart, carrying his sorrow as if he were singing it himself. The song spoke for him. *This is me, who I am and where I am right now.*

Pete removed his hat and looked toward the mountains, not thinking much, just wondering, feeling the same old *why* that always came at times such as this. The song spoke for the wondering too, and fit this place so well. Maybe the mountains had taught it to her.

The song had no ending of its own. When Sing was finished, when she had delivered in full her complaint to the mountains and the God who made them, when she had cried out her last farewell, the song came to a quiet rest, closing like a door on the past. Sing was weary and drained, but just a little closer to peace.

The bear meat was consumed by the flames. She opened her eyes and wiped the tears away.

"Thank you," said Reed.

"Where'd you learn that?" Pete asked.

"My grandfather sang it when my grandmother died," she said softly. "I don't remember all the words—but I remember the feelings."

■ ■ ■

Beck flopped to the ground once again, delivered there by her exhausted, frightened, adoptive mother in the same old way. The flight through the tangled forest was a perfect copy of the last flight through the tangled forest. Jacob led the group relentlessly, with Leah and Reuben following behind and Rachel last in line carrying Beck. Halfway through the long, frantic run, Beck recovered her senses and climbed around to Rachel's back to ride conventionally, so even that was the same. As always, Beck had no idea where they were or where they were going, only that it was *away* from rescue, *away* from Reed and all she held dear.

She rolled onto her face in the undergrowth with her arms covering her head, trying to block out the sounds, sights, and smells of a wilderness obsessed with no better cause than tormenting her. It was so unfair! She couldn't get away from her overly possessive "mother" even when she wasn't welcome; she couldn't leave a cell phone number in the dirt; she couldn't let her grieving husband know she was still alive when he was inches away from her; and now—*Of course! Pardon me for even assuming that I could!*—she absolutely could not make use of a GPS she was certain Reed had left for her to find.

It was all so un—

"N-no!" Beck opened her eyes and forbade that thought to play through her mind. *No more.* She'd spent enough time and energy on it and gotten nothing but more unfairness for her trouble.

And what was she doing, lying in the weeds and bushes, feeling sorry for herself again? She'd done that before and, judging from how things were going, could easily be doing it the next day, or the next year, or even for the next twenty years, in the same weeds in the same woods at the whim and mercy of the same smelly, dung-eating, barf-chewing, power-struggling, upright-walking, run-from-everything pack of apes.

She sat up. Rachel lay next to her, her once-lovely coat reverting back to a walking dust mop for every type of forest debris. Jacob was perched on a mound with his back against a rotting stump, keeping watch like a lifeguard, looking tired and irritable. Only Leah's left knee and stomach were visible above the undergrowth, her diaphragm laboring as she tried to catch her breath. Reuben sat beyond Leah, preoccupied with his toes.

So how about it, Beck? Want some more? Ready for another lap around the merry-go-round?

There was nothing like a dumb question to make things clear. *No more for me, thanks.*

But what could she do?

It would help to have some idea where she was. They may have headed north again, judging by the location of the sun, but as always, nothing looked familiar.

She once heard Reed say that going downhill was always a good idea: every hill eventually drained into a stream, every stream eventually flowed into a river, and every river eventually crossed a road, wound through a town, or flowed by a settlement. It might work, except for . . .

When she tested her ankle, then looked at Rachel, who looked back at her with those watchful, motherly eyes, the outcome of such a plan became as predictable as night following day.

It made her want to kill Reuben—another plan with a predictable outcome that instantly ruled it out.

But she did give him a second look. She thought he'd been playing with his toes, but just now she thought she saw a glimmer of yellow.

Acting as lazy, uninterested, and detached as possible, she rose to her feet, stretched, faked a yawn, and double-checked.

He wasn't playing with his toes. He was playing with the GPS, lazily batting it back and forth between his feet.

FOURTEEN

The Lumberman Café was Cap's third stop in Three Rivers. The folks at the local filling station hadn't heard of a Dr. Adam Burkhardt; the lady at the Ace Hardware store knew him as an occasional customer but didn't know where he lived. Mr. Dinsley, owner/proprietor of the Lumberman, knew just enough.

"It's up the Skeel Gulch Road," he said, scribbling a map on a napkin. "You go up there about two miles. You go over a bridge—it's one of those little ones, you know, made of logs? It goes over the Skeel Creek up there. Then the road takes a left turn, runs along the creek . . ." He drew it as he said it. "And it's up in there somewhere."

Cap studied the map—three lines for the roads, a squiggle for the creek, and a little box for the bridge—and asked, "Uh, any sign out front, you know, house numbers or something?"

Dinsley shrugged. "Well, Burkhardt doesn't like to advertise.

But you oughta try Denny over at Ace Hardware and Lumber. He's done a few deliveries up there. Adam was building a big old shop a few years ago."

"Denny's on vacation."

"Oh, you've already been there!"

"Yeah. Claire told me."

"Oh, well, I haven't seen Adam for a week or so. Did you try calling him?"

"Lost his number."

"Oh. Well, since you're good friends, I guess he won't mind you dropping in. He is a private sort of person, isn't he?"

"He's that way."

Cap put the napkin in his shirt pocket, paid for his coffee and cinnamon roll, and went out to his car.

Down the street, in a pricey Mercedes that didn't fit in this town, four men with specific orders watched Cap's every move.

■ ■ ■

Beck sat quietly in the syringa and snowberry, invisibly tethered to Rachel, who appeared to be sleeping. She was watching Reuben with quick, careful glances, never a direct stare.

If she did nothing, Reuben would eventually destroy the GPS, probably chew it to smithereens. Even if he tired of it, all she had to do was show the slightest interest and it would become important to him again. If she tried to take it from him—well, she'd already tried that.

By now the sun and shadows told her the group was definitely heading north, and of course this was the wilderness; there were no boundaries here. The Canadian border wouldn't stop them. They could keep moving as far as there was forest, which meant she could wander in these woods forever, be given up for dead, and never be found.

But she had an idea. It wasn't a sure thing, but considering how the future looked if she did nothing, a failure wasn't going to set her back that much. She hated having to be the one to change things, but for all she knew, she was the only player left on her team. Any change, for better or worse, was going to be up to her.

She reached for the hairbrush in her back pocket. It had gotten her close to Leah once. If Beck could buy just a little more favor from Reuben's mother, then maybe . . .

She made sure Rachel was asleep, held the brush up in a wide gesture so Leah could see it, then ran it through her own hair a few times.

Leah sniffed and sat up straight. She was interested.

Beck set out before fear could catch up with her, quickly working her way through the brush toward Leah, head down, body language submissive, eyes lowered. For good measure, she added some quiet, conciliatory grunts and a little hum, a carefree, meandering sound.

Reuben saw her coming and immediately took a strong, protective interest in the GPS, clutching it close and eyeing her suspiciously. She ignored him, obvious about it, and held out the brush to Leah.

Leah grunted pleasantly. Beck met her eyes for a quick inquiry and found no fear or animosity there.

She began brushing, smoothing out the hair behind Leah's left ear. Leah leaned into it. Beck breathed easier. This just might work.

Then Rachel woke up.

Beck could understand the displaying, crying, and commotion. After all, Beck and her hairbrush were the only unique claim to power or pride that Rachel had, and though Beck was by no means joining up with Rachel's rival, how could Rachel understand that?

What to do? Commotion and disgruntlement she didn't need, but she had to have Leah's sympathy, and this was the only way she knew to get it. She kept brushing.

She hadn't considered how Jacob might feel about it. His eyes had narrowed as she approached Leah, but since Leah wasn't bothered but interested, Beck thought he wouldn't mind. When Reuben got upset, Jacob's hair began to bristle, but Beck wasn't about to challenge Reuben and hoped Jacob would see that. Then, when Beck started brushing Leah, he grunted a warning, but Beck felt it was only precautionary.

When Jacob came thundering down at her, roaring and threatening, she didn't think, hope, or feel anything, but leaped and rolled through the prickly undergrowth toward Rachel's protective arms. A gust of wind blew past her, generated by a deadly swat of his hand that barely missed. Falling into Rachel's enfolding arms was like running into a fortress, and fortunately, it worked.

Having returned Beck to her rightful place, Jacob backed off and sauntered back to his spot against the old stump, satisfied that he'd made his point—whatever it was.

Beck was shaking, very glad to let Rachel hold her and desperate to understand the rule she'd broken. Jacob had always made it clear that he was unhappy with Rachel's adoption of a human, but having punished her for such a dumb move, he seemed to be tolerating it. Apparently his tolerance ended when it came to the human making any further alliances with his females. Whether out of jealousy or feelings of threat, he wasn't going to allow it.

Beck set to work right away, brushing and grooming Rachel to be sure their relationship was intact. Rachel was forgiving, her same old doting self.

As for assuring support from Leah, that idea clearly wouldn't work.

■ ■ ■

Dave Saunders surprised himself. When the concentrated effort of his search team found only a rusty hunting knife with the handle rotted away, a cluster of spent rifle shells, a canteen, and a set of car keys, he didn't get discouraged, just more determined, even angry.

"Widen the search," he ordered. "Same quadrants, double the size."

The searchers had never met Beck Shelton, but they felt they knew her. They didn't grumble or question, but went right to it.

■ ■ ■

Sing turned her motor home into the parking lot of the Tall Pine Resort, eased into the same place she'd parked before, and shut down the engine. With her chin in her hand, she looked through the windshield at the tired old lodge with the patched-together add-ons, the rambling, up-and-down porch, and the big, blackened outdoor barbecue, and mused on how she and Cap first came here to get away from the struggles, the pain, the disappointment.

Yet all three had followed them here, more real and present than ever.

Less than a week ago, they thought they would learn to survive. They hoped they would hear from God.

She sighed. Maybe they had. It all seemed too much like life to be otherwise.

She shook off the sorrow and the weakness. As Cap said, it still wasn't over—and that was like life too. She straightened her spine and took a deep breath. *Eyes forward*, she told herself. She would join up with Cap in Three Rivers. Maybe the answers were there.

She set the parking brake and got out of the driver's seat, eager to empty their motel room, settle up with Arlen, and get rolling.

She noticed her computer was still on, listening for GPS signals that were no longer there. She'd forgotten to turn it off, maybe on purpose.

She left it on and went out the door.

"So you heading out?" came a voice from a few doors down the porch.

Thorne and Kane sat on a bench, kicked back and enjoying a beer.

Sing was surprised and knew it showed. "Aren't you?"

Kane took a swig from his bottle and wagged his head. "Got my bear in Arlen's cooler. It'll keep."

"Thought we'd stick around and do a little more hunting," said Thorne.

Then Max stuck his head out the door behind them. "Oh, you going now?"

Sing studied the three men only a moment and then replied, "Can't wait."

They seemed satisfied with that.

■ ■ ■

Reed and Pete pulled up behind the motor home in Pete's old truck. They had nothing new to say to each other and just a nod to give to the men on the porch. Someday they would talk about how badly things had gone, but they both needed time. With only a handshake, they parted company, Reed to his room to gather his things, Pete to the lobby to update Arlen and thank him for his help.

Room 105 was still in the pitiful, panicky mess Reed had left after Arlen got the call from Fleming Cryncovich. His uniform was draped over a chair where he'd left it. His computer printout regarding the logger's death and the photos of the mysterious unknown footprints in the Lost Creek cabin lay scattered on the bed. Leaning in the corner, carefully reassembled by Cap and Sing, was Beck's backpack. Looking at it, Reed remembered so clearly the moment she picked out the color. He remembered helping her get her arms through the straps as she wriggled into it at the bottom of the Cave Lake Trail.

He tossed his sheriff's deputy shoes off a chair—and stared at his gun, his radio, his handcuffs lying on the bedside stand. He snapped open the black leather case that held the handcuffs and drew them out. They were small enough to fit in the pocket of his flannel shirt, so he put them there, if only as a reminder. For Beck's sake, he would be strong and forever stand between innocent people and those who would take away their loved ones. He sat down, letting his eyes drift where they wanted, mostly toward the backpack, and letting his heart feel whatever it needed to feel. No words, no thoughts, no answers. Just feelings. Sing would be heading out to join up with Cap. Reed would catch up later, in uniform if the situation called for it. But this moment he wouldn't rush. It had waited for him patiently—the grief. He would give it its due.

■　■　■

With Rachel's indulgence, Beck stretched the limit of her invisible tether and reached a tiny crease in the terrain where a feeble stream trickled among rocks, aging logs, and moss-covered windfall. Crouching on all fours, one hand on a tuft of wild grass

and the other on a stick that bridged the stream, Beck sipped
with her lips just touching the surface so as not to stir up the
black mud on the bottom.

Survive, survive, survive, she thought. *Drink to live. Live to
hope. Hope for a miracle.*

The stick under her hand shifted, and she sat up before it gave
way and she got a face full of mud.

It didn't give way. It didn't crack either. With nothing better
to hold her attention, she closed her fist around it and lifted. It
came off the ground in her hand, about the size and weight of a
baseball bat. She wielded it just a moment, thinking of Reuben
and imagining what a good club it would make, but of course, she
was only venting her frustration.

She let the other end of the stick plop into the streambed but
still held on to her end, just for the feel of it. Thinking she should
return to the group before Rachel got nervous, she almost let it
go but didn't. Instead, she lifted it again, felt its weight, gave it a
few small swings. She tapped it against a rock. The stick hadn't
rotted. Years of sun had turned it hard and gray.

The stick had stirred up the bottom of the stream. She
reached in with just one finger and spooned up a sample of the
mud. It was fine and greasy between her fingers, like black paint.
She smeared it along the top of one finger. It coated the skin
evenly, turning it an impressive, smudgy black.

An outlandish thought crossed her mind: Displaying carried
a lot of weight in Sasquatch circles, didn't it? Stomping, hollering, threatening, throwing things, banging on things . . .

She studied the grass under her other hand, closed her fist
around it, and yanked it up. There was plenty of it. As a matter of
fact, there was plenty of other loose material around here, like
leaves, twigs, and moss. Her shirt was loose fitting. It could hold
a lot of this stuff.

No! She shook her head at herself, at God. *No! I'm not the one to do this!*

As if God Himself were saying it, the thought came to her, *Of course you are. Who else is there?*

She caught her reflection in the shallow water. There was only one face, one person looking back at her.

She smeared the black mud over another finger. Now two fingers were blackened—she *hated* getting dirty!

But it wouldn't be enough. If she was going to put on a show, it had to be a big one, something no Sasquatch—especially Reuben—had ever seen before or even knew to expect.

She dug for more mud and blackened her whole hand, grimacing with disgust. It felt awful. But it looked awful too, and awful was good. Awful might work.

She probed around the immediate area, looking for more ideas—and stalling a bit. That was when she found a real prize: a fresh pile of Sasquatch droppings, most likely Jacob's. The scent of that stuff would be quite alarming. If it was Jacob's, it might even be confusing. Confusion was good. The more the better.

She scrambled around the area on hands and knees, then on two hands and one and a half feet, gathering leaves, twigs, moss, and grass. The process gave her momentum, enough to forsake her hygienic world and move to the brink of the stream once again.

A thin barrier of disgust held her back for only a moment, and then she made a choice. With a dangerous, reckless resolve, she dug into the mud, brought up a sizable blob, and smeared her face.

■　■　■

Sing made her last trip from Room 104, carrying her backpack and a toiletry bag out to the motor home. She piled them into the rear bedroom along with the other camping gear and a well-read copy of Randy Thompson's book, the last vestiges of the vacation that never was. Arlen Peak had been a neighborly sort: he only charged for the first night, not the several days of searching.

She stepped into the motor home's overcrowded midsection where the bulk of her lab and crime scene reconstruction gear was stowed, hung, stuffed, and folded. The last thing to fold up and put away was the computer, still running.

She pressed the *Menu* key, arrowed down to the *Shut Down* option, clicked on it, and got a box with the final question, *What do you want your computer to do? Shut Down* was the highlighted option.

She hesitated, the little arrow poised over the *OK* button. With a sigh, and feeling just a little foolish, she closed that window and left the computer running.

The computer map of the mountains came on-screen again, with no activity indicated.

She would be having a last, parting consultation with Reed as soon as he was ready. Perhaps she would shut down the computer then.

■ ■ ■

Jacob was probing the old stump for grubs, breaking off chunks of red, rotten wood with his fingernails and removing the white larvae with flicks of his tongue.

Leah sat next to an elderberry bush, indulging in the leaves from a branch she'd pulled down.

Rachel was picking through the hair on any part of her body she could reach, removing seeds, twigs, and small leaves, sampling each find for flavor and edibility.

Reuben was discovering how to regurgitate into his hand, but he still wasn't sure what to do with the dripping contents. The intriguing yellow object was beside him on the ground, no longer an object of keen interest but a matter of territory nonetheless.

All four were aware of the female human's presence on the other side of a thicket, near the tiny stream. None could see her, but they could hear her rustling about, raking the ground, often splashing in the little bit of water there was. She'd puttered about before, feeding, drinking, grooming herself. They'd grown used to her ways.

But then came a strange silence that bothered them. She'd never behaved in quite this way before, standing still as if hiding, lurking like a predator, even stalking in the bushes.

Jacob flicked a grub into his mouth and watched the thicket, curious but not alarmed.

Rachel looked over her shoulder, mildly curious what her "child" was up to, and puzzled to see Jacob still eating grubs from the stump when she could detect his scent from her "child's" direction.

Leah shot a protective glance at Reuben, wary of danger.

Reuben was paying attention to nothing other than the green goo in his hand and wasn't expecting—

"*Aaaaaaiiiiiii!!!*"

They all jumped, even Jacob, as if a cannon had gone off in the midst of them, and then they stared, mouths gaping, as Beck exploded from the thicket, running lopsidedly on a weak ankle, shrieking like a cougar, brandishing a club, face, arms, and torso blackened with mud except for wide white areas around her eyes. She'd stuffed her shirt, sleeves and all, to the bursting point with leaves, twigs, and moss, expanding her outline. Grass shot out like bristling hair from her waist, her collar, her shirt cuffs, her pant legs. She'd even fashioned a headdress from her handkerchief and long spears of grass, creating a sunburst of grass and blowing reddish hair around her face.

Startling to hear, shocking to behold, she even smelled frightening, smeared with a liberal coat of dung that made her reek as if ejected from the bowels of the alpha male himself.

■ ■ ■

It was all or nothing. No turning back. No fear. No gentle, timid world. No mercy, no compassion, no propriety, no fairness. If this was how matters were settled out here, then this was how she would settle them. She ran headlong, her club raised, her eyes crazed, her mouth wide open in a permanent scream.

She closed in on Reuben, so focused and intense that he seemed to react in eerie slow motion—shyly jumping to his feet, gasping, and raising his arms in a singular moment that went on and on.

She would never get a second chance for that first blow, that first desperate grab for advantage. As she passed on his uphill side, she swung the club in a wide batter's arc and broke it in half against the back of his skull. He reeled, stumbled forward. Beck dug in, reversed direction, lunged at him, swatted him again on his head and shoulders with the half club still in her hand.

He ran for his mother, who was on her feet, screaming with shock and indignity.

The GPS, that precious GPS, lay on the ground, ripe for the picking. She pounced on it, got her hands around it. Precious yellow plastic, hope from home—

Reuben pounced on her and, with one powerful heave of his arms, threw her, head over heels, into the bushes. She floated, mashed the branches, tumbled into the tangle until the thick stalks near the ground bore her up. Her head was swimming, her world spinning, but she kicked, struggled, stayed alive. Still entangled and suspended, not knowing which way was up or whether her body was intact or what she could do next, she screamed, yelled, thrashed, and displayed, doing anything her body could do to show anger, defiance, and strength.

Rachel was coming her way, trying to save her. No. She couldn't let that happen. She had to stay in trouble. With a violent kick, a twist, and several strong yanks, she got out of the bushes and onto the clear ground.

Reuben was hunting for the GPS. She saw it the same time he did, in the grass, still intact.

She crawled, then got to her feet. *No fear. Show him who's boss. Bluff if you have to!*

She leaped, screamed, beat on her bulky, grass-and-moss-stuffed chest, waved her arms, slapped the ground. Her hand found a rock and she threw it, hitting him in the hip. He roared in pain.

Her entire field of vision suddenly filled with gray.

Leah.

■ ■ ■

"Tell you what," said Arlen, his voice gentle, like that of a friend. "Those trophies are probably the last I'll ever see. I would say you've paid enough. The room's on me."

Reed smiled, admiring the four new plaster casts in Arlen's Bigfoot display case. He could understand what a treasure they must be to a man with Arlen's perspective. "I do appreciate it," Reed said. He examined the grainy photo of the big female striding along a sandbar. "Think they'll stick around after all this?"

Arlen's smile slipped. "Maybe not. They've never been hunted before. If I were them, I'd probably move on."

"I hope you're right. I might be the interim sheriff, but I can't keep the trails closed forever, especially for a reason nobody's going to believe." Reed turned to go.

"Reed?"

"Yeah?"

"If I may speak on their behalf?" Arlen looked down at the casts for a moment, drumming the countertop with his fingers. "I can't explain what we found up there, other than that your wife was with them and she was alive. I'd like to think it was the bear that killed her."

Reed would never believe that, but there would be no point in bickering. "See you later, Arlen."

He quietly closed the front door behind him, leaving a sad old man at the counter.

■ ■ ■

Leah snarled, displaying, baring her teeth, arms upraised as if to strike—and then she looked up.

A savage roar came from over Beck's shoulder. Beck hugged the ground as the truck-sized mass of red fur sailed over her and plowed into Leah, knocking her backward. Leah recovered in only two steps, then shoved, slapped, and punched as Rachel returned blow for blow. They faced off, mirroring each other, circling, hair bristling, backs arched, fingers spread like talons, hissing and foaming through their teeth.

With Leah occupied, Beck half-crawled and limped forward, searching for that glint of yellow.

It was in Reuben's hands. He was slinking away with it.

Beck got to her feet, yelling, displaying, then loping toward him. She leaped with her good leg, then kicked him in the side. It was like kicking a wall. He flinched a little but didn't even lose his balance. She landed on the ground, got up again, faced him—

The slap sent her spinning. Her headdress disintegrated, the blades of grass falling like winnowed straw. The world was a blur until her hair blinded her. She hit the ground, her nose dripping, her face burning.

With one eye above the grass, she saw Rachel holding her own, not backing down, getting slapped, slapping back, exchanging threats, and circling. Leah showed no weakness. As for Jacob, he sat next to his stump, surprisingly aloof, a spectator.

Beck pushed against the ground, her body aching, nauseous. The ground reeled under her. Drops of blood glistened on the grass. She got to her feet, bent over to clear the dizziness, and wiped her face with her hands, streaking the mud, smearing the blood. She wiped her hands on her shirt and left red streaks. She straightened slowly—

Reuben's foot caught her in the back and she went down like a limp toy, tumbling in the brush, arms flailing, until a tree caught her in the side.

Half conscious, she thought she would never breathe again.

■ ■ ■

Reed poked his head in the door of the motor home. "Everything okay?"

Sing sat at the computer, scrolling the map up and down, back and forth, retracing old possibilities, exploring new ones. The GPS system was its cold and cruel self; it had nothing to say. "It's hard to leave," she said.

Reed looked back at the inn, at the bench on the porch, the front doors, the door to Room 105. There wasn't a pleasant memory anywhere, only sorrow and finality. "We have to."

She nodded but didn't turn the computer off. She only closed the lid, then went forward to the driver's station and pulled out a map. "So what's the best way to get to Three Rivers from here?"

■ ■ ■

Reuben stood a few yards up the hill, snuffing at her, acting superior and victorious, clutching the GPS in his hands, his snarl warning her to stay away, to stay on the ground, to remain subservient.

Beck rolled a painful quarter turn away from the tree, drew her first full breath, and pulled her knees up under her.

The two females faced off, daring each other to make a move. It wasn't so much a fight as a game, a war of wills.

Beck straightened, got one foot planted, rose on one leg—

And fell again, hurting in every limb, every fiber. Reuben must have opened her somewhere; she was leaving a trail of blood on the ground.

He displayed again, snarling, stomping, coming closer. She knew he would hit her, and this time it would probably kill her.

She could barely keep the females in focus. They weren't looking her way but glaring at each other.

If only she had won some favor. If only she was accepted.

She cried out, the best series of alarm screams she could muster, and extended her hand, crimson with her own blood, their way.

Rachel, facing Beck, saw her first. With a loud howl, she bolted Beck's direction.

Leah opposed her—

Rachel could have been fighting the bear again. With ferocity Beck had seen only once before, Rachel forearmed Leah across the throat, knocking her back several steps, turning her. Leah leaned into a step, about to lunge, when her eyes followed Beck's scream and Beck caught her gaze. Leah hesitated. She stretched her neck for a better view, concern clouding her face.

Beck screamed again, her hand extended.

Time stood still.

Leah was wide open. Rachel hammered her with a right to the chest, then a left, pushing, pummeling. Leah covered her head, struck back once, then backpedaled, still staring at Beck.

Beck cried out again, hand extended. Leah moaned, pain filling her eyes.

Rachel pressed her attack, snarling, hurling another double-blow.

Leah ducked, arms over her head, as Rachel delivered a steady and violent drumming. Then, at long last, her will broken, Leah turned tail and ran into the shelter of some trees.

Reuben's bravado drained in an instant. He whimpered, looking at Beck, then up the hill toward his mother.

Finish it!

Beck noticed she was on her feet. It hurt like crazy, but she was standing. A good-sized stick lay only two steps away. She took those steps, grabbed up the stick, raised it high, and climbed the hill, closing in on Reuben one last time. He was looking for his mother when Beck brought the stick down on his shoulders, raised it, brought it down again. Again! Again!

He flinched, ducked, put his arms over his head, then started up the hill, retreating, ducking, whimpering.

Again!

The GPS bounced onto the ground and came to rest in the shards of a rotting log.

Reuben ran, disappearing into the same trees that concealed his mother.

Beck teetered but remained standing, her fist still clenched around the stick, not sure it was over. Her upper lip and chin felt cold and she tasted blood in her mouth. She wiped her sleeve across her mouth and it came away red.

Rachel was coming to save her.

No, please, not yet. Where's that GPS?

It was close enough to grab just before Rachel enfolded her in those huge arms. Rachel settled to the ground right there, cradling her, licking the blood and mud from Beck's face with her big tongue, poking with grave concern at the weird stuffing inside Beck's shirt, yanking and tasting the grass that protruded from Beck's sleeves.

Beck held that GPS close, trying to find the on switch in between swipes from Rachel's tongue. *Lick!* She found it. *Lick!* She pressed it. *Lick! Lick!* Nothing happened.

She almost felt a wave of despair, but another thought held it off: *Check the batteries.*

The licking had stopped. Beck tried to open the back of the GPS, but her fingers were slick with mud and blood, and now the GPS was smeared with it. She pulled her handkerchief from around her head and wiped her hands, then the GPS.

Rachel was poking her, humming with concern. Beck nestled in close to let her know she was all right and, using her fingernail, wedged the battery compartment open.

The batteries were there, the ends blocked with a piece of paper. Clever! A safeguard, no doubt, to make sure only a human could turn it on. Beck pulled the paper out, closed the cover, and pressed the on button again.

A little light came on. The LCD screen came to life.

∎ ∎ ∎

Reed spoke into his handheld radio as he sat in his SUV just outside the Tall Pine. "Okay, 450 point 45. Hello?"

Sing came back from inside the motor home: "Gotcha loud and clear."

"All buttoned up?"

"Three Rivers, here we come. Oh. Sorry. Got one more thing." Sing set her radio in its rack on the dashboard and hurried back to secure the bedroom door. On her way, she remembered one more thing: the computer. Okay. It was time to turn it off.

She raised the lid and the screen came to life, the same old map of the surrounding forest with nothing showing but—

Something new caught her eye as her finger poised above the keyboard.

Was that . . . ?

No. It had to be dust on the screen, a bad pixel, the mouse pointer . . .

It was blinking.

She leaned in to make sure.

Yes, it was blinking.

She rolled out the computer chair and sat in it, digging her glasses from her shirt pocket.

The radio on the dash squawked, "Sing? Any problems?"

She put on her glasses and leaned close.

The blinking blip was labeled with a number 6.

"Reed . . ."

The radio squawked again. "Hello? Sing? You copy?"

"Reed . . . !"

Number 6. The GPS they'd left at the baiting site.

The Last-Ditch Attempt.

"Reed!" Sing bolted from her chair, ran to the dashboard, grabbed up the radio. "REEEEED!"

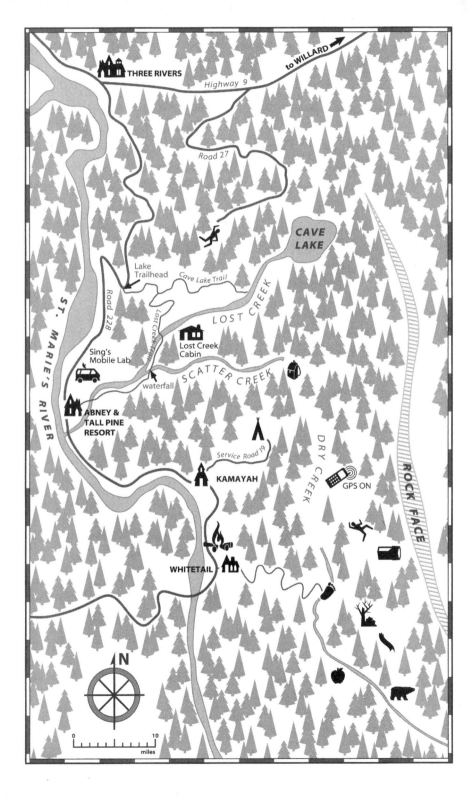

FIFTEEN

Cap drove up the Skeel Gulch Road, past quaint homesteads and run-down barns, freshly mowed hay fields, and a huge pond where a moose grazed on water cabbage. He found the bridge just as Mr. Dinsley had described it, a squatty rectangle of logs and rough-hewn planks with red reflectors tacked to each end. After the road took a left turn, Dinsley's directions ran out, and Cap was left to do the best he could with the man's broad-sweeping description, "It's up in there somewhere."

Cap drove two miles up the road, looking for anything that might be home to a scientist detached from reality. When he noticed recent tire tracks turning onto the road from a gravel driveway, he was desperate enough to check it out.

The driveway wound back through the trees for several hundred feet, then ended abruptly at a small, metal-roofed cabin. The parking lot was empty, so Cap felt safe pulling to a stop and climbing out for a look-see.

Just a few paces up from the parking lot, Cap could see past the cabin and into the trees beyond. The owner had added an outbuilding, a metal structure the size of an aircraft hangar.

Dinsley said Burkhardt had built a shop a few years ago. Cap may have come to the right place.

■ ■ ■

In an instant, Reed's entire universe had compressed to the size of a tiny blip on a computer screen. The blip was moving north, pulling the moving map downward across the screen pixel by pixel, blinking as it went, a little number 6 at its side. Reed didn't dare believe what it could mean; his nerves wouldn't be able to take it. "You double-checked?"

Sing, at the computer, was wiping tears from her eyes. "I cycled through all the GPS codes and every unit is accounted for, including this one: 1 through 5 are in their cases right here under the bench. Number 6 is out, and it's broadcasting—" Her voice tightened into a weeping squeak. She took a deep breath to clear it. "I tested it before you guys left it at the baiting site. This is it; this is the one!"

Pete, at Reed's side, couldn't have looked more intense if he'd been staring down a cougar. "You sure you wrapped those batteries?"

Reed was trying not to hope too soon. The whiplike reversal would snap his mind for sure. "I made double sure. Only an intelligent human being would have pulled that paper out of there and reset the batteries. This isn't an accident."

"What if it's a hiker who found it?" Sing ventured.

"The trails are closed," said Reed.

Pete pointed. "It's not on a trail. And look how fast it's moving. That's no hiker."

"ATV?" Reed suggested.

"Not in there. It's nothing but steep slopes, heavy forest, and no roads." He watched it a moment. "But something with eighteen-inch feet could move that fast."

Reed nodded, remembering that moment below the waterfall on the trail to Abney. "It's still carrying her."

Pete cautioned, "We don't know for sure."

"Right." Reed reined himself in. "What about radio contact?"

Sing replied, "I've tried to raise whoever it is, but the unit radio doesn't seem to be working. We've got GPS locating, but that's it."

There was a rap on the doorpost and Max Johnson stuck his head in. "Hey, we're all here!"

Reed went to the door. Max, Steve Thorne, Sam Marlowe, and Wiley Kane stood there, a firm set in their faces that almost overruled Reed's doubt. He still needed to be sure. "I need to know you guys are with me."

"I'm in," said Max. "Always have been. I want to finish this, Reed, and finish it right."

Reed wasn't satisfied yet. "Steve?"

"I don't care what's up there, and I'm not going to bicker about it," Thorne replied. "Whatever it is, if it comes between us and your wife, I'm prepared to take it out."

"Sam?"

Sam seemed so young, but the grim look in his eyes came from the heart of a man. "I know I'm the rookie here, but I'll give you my best and that's a promise."

Reed still couldn't address Kane by his first name. "Kane? Do you think I killed my wife and made up a story to cover it up?"

Kane sniffed a chuckle and wagged his head shamefully. "I'll wash my mouth out if that's what you want."

"I might."

"Fair enough." Kane grinned. "I just got me a record-breaking bear. Getting a big old Sasquatch, now, wouldn't that be something?"

Reed asked Thorne, "Think you can keep him in line?"

Thorne nodded.

"All right, then."

"What about Jimmy and the others?" Kane asked.

Max piped up, "We don't need the others. We know where your wife is."

"There isn't time," said Reed. He stepped back from the door to make room. "Come on in. Let's get organized."

The hunters climbed in and squeezed around the computer station, marveling at the sight of one little blip.

"So where is it now?" Kane asked.

"Four miles southeast," Sing replied. She zoomed in for a closer view of the terrain. "And it's coming our way."

■ ■ ■

The Sasquatch train was moving again, rushing through dense forest, brushing aside limbs, leaping over logs as they looked anxiously over their shoulders and gave off fear scent, pushing, pushing, pushing themselves to the point of exhaustion, an endless cycle. Only one thing had changed: Rachel and Beck were now second in line behind Jacob; Leah and Reuben brought up the rear.

The change was costly. Beck was sure she needed a doctor. The bleeding from her nose and mouth had gone from steady to sporadic, but it hadn't stopped. Her face felt puffy and her whole body ached, not just her ankle. With barely enough strength to hold on, she feared she had none left to survive.

She'd found a way to bind the GPS in the roll of her sleeve, leaving its antenna exposed to the heavens. Beyond that, she was living by faith. The case was bitten and bent in the middle, and she couldn't get the slightest hiss out of the radio. She could only hope the GPS part was actually working and that someone was watching.

Perhaps it was that person the Sasquatches were running from this very moment; hunters had encircled them before, and Reed was one of them. Beck cradled her head on Rachel's soft, furry shoulder, so tired, dizzy, wishing whoever it was would catch up and put an end to this.

Rachel's head turned, her leathery cheek bumping Beck's bruised face. It hurt.

"What?"

Rachel huffed and kept running, a new wave of fear quickening her step.

Beck raised her head, and through the rush of the wind and the snapping of passing limbs, she recognized a familiar, chilling sound: the cry of the banshee. The woman from Lost Creek was wailing again, her voice carrying like a faraway siren, following them like a distant shadow.

Wait. Following them?

Beck fought off her stupor and forced herself to think. All the Sasquatches were *here*, running together. She could see all four of them. Jacob wasn't making the noise; he was running from the noise.

She tightly clutched Rachel's fur as a chill went through her.

It was no hunter either.

She looked over her shoulder. There were so many trees, limbs, thickets, dark spaces. Anything could hide in there.

■ ■ ■

Max and Reed came to a wide-eyed, open-eared halt.

"Yeah, you heard it, and so did I," Reed said, answering the question in Max's eyes.

Reed faced south while Max faced north, both on high alert, watching each other's backs. They were working their way up the mountain slope above Abney, in a hurry and breathing hard, hoping they and the others could weave a net tight enough to catch a north-moving GPS and whatever or whoever might be carrying it.

Reed radioed, "Pete, we heard it to the south, down your way."

There was a pause before Pete replied, "It's north of me. It's in the circle, gentlemen—as soon as we get one."

Reed checked the screen on his GPS. He could see Blips 3 and 4, Pete and Sam, moving up the mountain to the south, but Thorne and Kane, sharing GPS unit 5, weren't on the screen. "Sing, you there yet?"

■   ■   ■

"We're at the drop-off point," she answered, just pulling the motor home to a stop at the end of Service Road 221, a road so old and unused that nature was taking it back. According to her Forest Service map, this would place Steve Thorne and Wiley Kane far enough to the north to intercept the blip *if* it continued on its present course and *if* they could get up the mountain in time to close up the circle.

Thorne and Kane were geared up, armed and ready, in the back of the motor home. Thorne had GPS 5 on his sleeve.

Sing killed the engine and set the brake. "Good hunting."

They jumped out the door like paratroopers and started up the hill.

Sing took her place at the computer station and scrolled the map to her present location. Zooming out, she found all the blips: Reed and Max, units 1 and 2, widening their position above Abney; Pete and Sam, units 3 and 4, farther up the mountainside a mile south, but swinging north to close in. And Thorne and Kane, unit 5, heading up the hill with a good climb ahead of them before they would cross the projected path of Blip Number 6. Because the radio on unit 6 wasn't working, only Sing could see the blip, via satellite. It would be up to her to guide the hunters to its location.

"Target is still moving north," she reported, "on a course roughly 355. Pete, bearing to target is 345, about half a mile; Reed, bearing to target is 110, three quarters of a mile. Steve, maintain your heading; at your present rate of climb you should intercept it."

It was like watching a fast-pitched baseball heading for home plate and hoping the catcher could put on his mitt in time to catch it blindfolded.

"I've found a sign," Pete reported. "It's more than one, maybe the whole family."

"So maybe they're going back home," Reed offered. "Back where this whole thing started."

Sing could see Lost Creek on the map just a few miles north. She wagged her head in absolute wonder and started trembling. She'd always believed the footprints at the first baiting station were real, and now being right terrified her. What had Beck gone through? If they found her, given she was still alive, would she even be the same person?

Cap had to know. Sing grabbed her cell phone.

■ ■ ■

Cap said good-bye and folded his cell phone, stunned, not knowing what to feel or think, except for one thing: he had to get inside this cabin.

He'd knocked on the cabin door several times and concluded

there was no one at home. Now he looked up and down the porch. Did Burkhardt have a particular habit when it came to hiding keys? From his two years as the man's unwilling protégé, Cap recalled Burkhardt liking overhead places: rafters, ledges, windowsills, light fixtures. He felt along the molding across the top of the door. Nothing. There was a hanging flowerpot next to the stairs. He reached and fumbled among the leaves.

A house key.

He stopped for one more cautious look around and then let himself in.

It was warm and homey inside, with pleasant, soft furniture, a bearskin rug, a stuffed deer head, a mounted trout with its weight and length proudly displayed on a brass placard beneath it. Fishing poles were mounted in a rack near the front door, and in a cabinet with glass doors next to the brick fireplace . . .

Rows and rows of glass jars containing Burkhardt's icons of evolution: the Galapagos finches with different-sized beaks, the white and gray peppered moths, the coelacanths and bats, the lizards and snakes, and on the top row, in a place of honor, four new additions—unborn chimpanzees, floating in a fetal position in the amber liquid, eyes half open, toothless mouths in a half yawn.

Baumgartner had listed three possible results of tampering with a chimp's DNA—a normal, unchanged chimp; a deformed, retarded chimp; or a dead chimp. Apparently, these were the dead ones.

■ ■ ■

Pete and Sam were moving north, following Sing's vectors while Pete spotted snapped limbs, bruised leaves, and soil depressions to cross-check their progress. From the sign Pete found, the targets were not moving in any lazy, meandering pattern that would indicate foraging but were heading in a fairly straight line north-ward, definitely on the run.

"How close are we?" Pete whispered in his radio.

Sing came back, "Still half a mile. They're moving just as fast as you are."

Pete halted at the edge of some soft ground, scanned it for prints, but found none. "Mm. We've veered off the trail somehow."

Sam stepped through and pushed ahead, peering intently in all directions. "Why don't we bag this tracking stuff and just fol-low Sing's vectors?"

"I want to know what those critters are doing," Pete said, his eyes searching the ground.

"Pete, come on, that thing's gonna pull farther away the longer we stand here!"

Then Pete found a footprint in a bare patch of soft earth.

Sam's.

He dropped to one knee and produced a blue diagram card from his pocket, quickly comparing.

When he looked up, Sam was watching him.

■ ■ ■

Thorne and Kane were pushing uphill, groping and climbing as silently as possible through tightly spaced trees and limbs, follow-ing Sing's vectors, primed for a deadly collision.

"Veer to the right," came Sing's voice through Thorne's ear-piece, "090."

Thorne whispered to Kane, about thirty feet ahead of him, "Kane, move right. Kane!"

Suddenly Kane jerked to attention, whispered a curse, and aimed his rifle uphill.

Before Thorne could caution him, the rifle went off.

■ ■ ■

Beck knew that sound and understood when Jacob turned on his heels and ran past, leading the group the opposite direction. Hunters. It was all happening again.

■ ■ ■

Thorne hissed at Kane, "What are you doing?"

Kane was nearly beside himself and had a tough time keeping his voice down. "I saw it! It was a Sasquatch—I am not foolin' you!"

Thorne caught up and put a hand on his shoulder to keep him calm—and corralled. "You weren't even supposed to be ahead of me. We were tracking with the GPS, remember?"

"I saw it! It was walking, standing upright. Man, it was huge!"

Thorne stared at him. "You're sure?"

■ ■ ■

Reed pressed his talk button and only half whispered, "Who fired a shot? What's going on?"

■ ■ ■

Blip Number 6 was heading south again, with Thorne's blip less than 500 yards northwest. "Heads up, everybody!" Sing said. "Target is moving south. Pete, Sam, it'll be coming your way!"

Pete answered, "Okay, moving north to meet and greet."

Sam reported, "I'll move uphill, spread out a bit."

Sing's eyes were glued on every player. "Reed and Max, it's going to pass you on the uphill side."

Reed answered, "We're heading that way."

. . .

Jacob lumbered to a halt, then barely stood, stooped and swaying, his breathing labored, his eyes darting about, his nostrils sampling the air. Rachel came up behind him, every breath a painful wheeze. Beck slid to the ground, barely able to move her arms. Leah trudged from behind, legs like lead, and plopped to the ground with Reuben still on her back. The forest floor became a hairy heap, huffing and steaming.

Jacob's gaze darted to the south, then to the north, then down the hill. He moaned, a mournful sound Beck had never heard before.

From somewhere up the slope, invisible in the forest, the woman whimpered, then snickered. She was closer, watching, waiting.

They were hemmed in.

Rachel lay on her belly, her body heaving with every breath, the wind from her nostrils wiggling the undergrowth in front of her face. Beck crawled to her and touched her shoulder. Rachel looked up at her through watery eyes, and Beck saw more than fear; she saw defeat.

"No. Rachel, come on, don't . . ."

Jacob sank to his haunches, still sniffing, still looking, his hair bristling. Reuben cowered behind his mother's prone body, and his expression was much like Jacob's. He was afraid, listening, sniffing, sensing the surrounding danger.

And then a searing awareness worked its way through Beck's pain and stupor: *It's me. I'm the cause of this.*

She struggled with her shirtsleeve and got the GPS loose. It appeared to be working. The map on the screen was now indicating a steep mountainside, and that's where she was. This thing was locating her accurately, and somehow those hunters out there were getting the signal.

Which meant . . .

She didn't understand what she did. It was the last thing on earth she wanted to do, but at the same time, it was the only thing. She turned the GPS off.

■ ■ ■

The blip was gone.

Sing lurched forward. "No, no, don't do that!"

She radioed, "I've lost contact with the target. It just winked out. Does anybody see anything?"

■ ■ ■

Reed and Max had split up and spread out. Reed was alone now in timber so thick he couldn't see more than ten yards in any direction. "This is Reed. Negative contact."

"This is Max. Negative contact."

"Sam here. Still moving, still looking."

"Pete here. Sam, I'll wait for you to come up even with me."

"This is Steve. Sorry for the misfire. There's something wrong with Kane's rifle. We're checking it out."

Beck, what are you doing? Reed had heard of lost people getting so nutty in the woods that they actually hid from their rescuers. Was she afraid of being found? Either that, or . . .

Had she made friends with these creatures? Was she protecting them?

He radioed, "Everybody, keep closing on the last known position, steady and quiet, and be sure of your target before you shoot. Sing, let us know when you get the target again."

"Will do."

Reed wiped sweat from his hands and a drop of sweat from above his eye. He mentally reviewed the sight of the dead logger and the mangled body of Sheriff Mills. No more of that. Whatever Beck's mental state, the hunt would end differently this time.

■ ■ ■

Cap wasn't finding out much in the little cabin, other than Burkhardt was a fastidious person who always made his bed and put away his dishes. He searched and inspected his way to the back door and then gazed cautiously across the graveled alleyway to his next frontier: that huge metal outbuilding. It was time to get out there and take a look. He was pushing his luck beyond acceptable risk to take any longer in the—

The sound immobilized him. He was stunned, a statue in the small enclosed rear porch of the cabin. Yes, he'd heard Reed describe it, and Reed sounded like a nut case when he did. But Reed was right on the money!

From the big metal building, clear as day, Cap heard it for himself: the eerie wail of a woman in pain and despair, the cry of the banshee.

SIXTEEN

Kane's voice was getting loud. "*What* did you tell them? There's nothing wrong with my rifle!"

Thorne put out his hand. "That rifle's pulling to the left. Let me see it."

"You're nuts."

"Let me see it."

Kane handed it over.

Thorne peered through the sight. "Eh, it might be a little off. Did you drop it or something?"

Kane reached to grab it back. "We're wasting time!"

Thorne jerked it away, then raised a hand to calm him down. "Easy, Kane. You don't want them to know you saw that thing."

Kane worked on that a moment and finally caught Thorne's drift. "In case they get the kill first, is that what you're saying?" He got agitated again. "But if we stand around here, they're going to get it for sure."

"Take it easy. If the others see it, they won't be any better off. They'll be in the same mess you are."

That changed Kane's demeanor. "What are you talking about?"

■ ■ ■

The heavy metal door to the outbuilding was locked, but it had an electric locking mechanism with a numeric keypad. On a whim, Cap entered a number Burkhardt consistently used for locks, entry codes, and passwords: 1-8-5-9, the year Darwin's *Origin of the Species* was published. The mechanism whirred, then clicked. The door opened with a slight push.

At first, Cap was unsure if he'd entered a lab or a warehouse. The building was cavernous but well lit, with a vaulted roof supported by steel trusses and enough floor space to host a convention. A half-height wall divided the front section from the rear. From beyond that wall came the occasional stirring, banging, grunting, and hooting Cap had become familiar with at the York Center.

Chimpanzees.

Filling the front half of the building in geometrically arranged rows was a lab most scientists—and most major universities—could only dream of. Cap performed a careful walkthrough, eyes and ears open for any human presence, which, at least for now, was strangely missing.

Adam Burkhardt's original basement lab had grown tenfold, dropped all superfluous décor and warmth, and taken on the appearance of an assembly line, dedicated to specific procedures executed efficiently and repeatedly: DNA and protein synthesis and analysis, DNA sequencing, viral transfer, site-directed muta-genesis, and in a large, dedicated section toward the rear, high-volume, assembly-line in vitro fertilization and cloning. The woman cried again, her wail coming over that half wall with the nerve-jangling volume of a fire alarm.

Cap saw an archway leading to that side of the building. Moving quickly yet warily, he made a beeline for it.

■ ■ ■

Thorne spoke reassuringly, the voice of reason trying to corral Kane's impulsiveness. "People can't handle this sort of thing, you know what I mean? They see something like this and they get all the wrong ideas. Sometimes it's better when *we* decide what they're going to know and what they aren't."

"I don't follow you!"

Thorne struggled a moment. "You just told me you saw a Sasquatch."

"You bet I did! It was huge, it was all black like a gorilla, and it was walking on two legs just like a man!"

Thorne chuckled and wagged his head.

"You think I'm crazy?"

"No, no, you're not crazy." Quickly, easily, Thorne leveled Kane's rifle at Kane's chest. "You're absolutely right."

He fired.

■ ■ ■

Reed got on his radio. "Who's shooting? Fill us in."

Thorne's voice came back, "Hey, we're sorry, we've got a problem up here. Kane's rifle's misfired again and now he's hit himself in the foot."

Reed winced. Kane. He should have known. "How bad is it?"

Thorne came back on, yet sounded distant as if he were addressing someone else. "No, try to stay off it. Yeah, just wrap it with something." Then, "Reed, he's okay, but I need to help him out of here."

Reed feared the hunt was as good as over. "Okay. Pete, Sam, any southbound traffic?"

Sam called back, "They're still in there, Reed, but after those shots they've got to know we're here."

"Max, can you swing north and fill in?"

"Will do," Max replied.

"Sing, let's mark a waypoint at Steve and Kane's last position so we can guide Max up there," Reed instructed.

"You've got it," she answered.

Reed scrolled his GPS over to Thorne and Kane's last position and marked that spot with a waypoint. Hopefully, he or Sing would be able to guide Max to that spot before there was no point in doing so.

■ ■ ■

Cap found a central hallway with doors to individual rooms on either side, much like a hospital ward. The place was well scrubbed and smelled of disinfectant.

The first door on his right was half open; some stirring from within drew his attention. He approached slowly and eased the door open.

Chimpanzees. Six of them, in six floor-to-ceiling cages. The chimp in the first cage immediately went to the bars and stood up, one hand gripping a bar of the cage, the other reaching through the bars toward him, her amber eyes meeting his imploringly. He knew that mannerism and expression and went to her, gently taking her hand and stroking it. Her eyes went across the room to a bin of oranges. He grabbed a few and passed one to her. She settled into the clean bedding and began to eat it.

From her bulging abdomen he could see she was pregnant.

The female in the next cage cowered in a corner, her arms enfolding herself. Except for one frightened glance, she wouldn't look at him. She was pregnant too. He rolled an orange toward her, and she reached for it but would not come out of her hiding place.

In the third cage, a female lay on her back in what appeared to be a drug-induced stupor. Her belly was shaved, and a large stitched incision crossed her abdomen.

The chimp in the fourth cage was the kind who liked to be friends with everybody. She had bright, expressive eyes and didn't amble up to the bars—she pranced. She looked him right in the eye and reached for the orange he offered. Her belly too was shaved, with an incision, but not as recent; the hair was growing back.

The female in the fifth cage was also pregnant, grumpy, and not interested in oranges.

In the last cage, an older female bore an old incision across her bulging belly. The incision had apparently been reopened several times; it was ridged with pink scar tissue that displaced the skin and hair along its length. She didn't acknowledge Cap's presence but merely sat on her haunches, endlessly counting her fingers.

Cap knew this mannerism too. She'd given up.

At the end of the room was a pulled curtain. On the other side of the curtain was a clean room divided into two well-lit cubicles, each with a stainless steel operating table such as veterinarians used, but with one troubling addition: leather restraints. Cabinets on each side were stocked with surgical instruments, dressings, gowns, caps, masks, and gloves.

Cap was getting a picture of how the process worked. When he opened the door to the walk-in cooler just past the tables, he got his confirmation.

On the shelves, in Ziploc bags that were labeled and dated, lay tiny, unborn creatures that could have been—should have been—chimpanzees. Two had legs, toes, and fingers so elongated as to be useless. One on the second shelf had gone the other way, with three-fingered stumps for arms.

On the bottom shelf, thrown into a tub, were four little females whose legs nearly matched human proportions and whose arms were intact. These must have shown promise—they were cut open and the ovaries were removed.

■ ■ ■

Beck huddled against Rachel, listening, watching, her body aching, her soul in turmoil, her finger poised over the on button. She and Rachel were pressed against a crumbling snag, blending with the redness of the rotting wood until they had become part of it. A short distance downhill, Leah and Reuben had found a way to blend and disappear within a sizable clump of serviceberry.

Only the top of Jacob's head was visible as he crawled through the underbrush toward the north, watching and listening, his eyes floating above the leaves. Beck had no idea what he was hearing, seeing, smelling, or even *feeling*, but she knew something had to have changed out there. Jacob wasn't in a hide or flee mode; he was planning something.

He stopped and became a big rock in the middle of the brush. Silence. Stillness.

When he gave a quiet sniff over his shoulder, the old snag and the clump of bushes became crouching, sneaking Sasquatches again. With stealthy moves and low postures, the group pushed north.

Beck slipped the GPS into her shirt pocket and buttoned the flap. The right time would come. It *had* to come. But not yet.

■   ■   ■

Sing saw Max's blip moving steadily toward the north, but he was moving far too slowly for her comfort. With Thorne and Kane on their way down the mountainside, the north end was wide open for the quarry to escape; with no GPS signal, Sing and the hunters would never know it. "Max? How's it going?"

Max's struggle came through in his voice. "It's pretty rough terrain in here."

"Kane's waypoint is bearing 024."

"Zero-two-four, okay."

She quickly scanned the other hunters' positions: Reed was to the west, trying to keep the creatures from running downhill, if he could even do that. Pete held his position to the south, sup- posedly preventing any escape in that direction. Sam was—

Where was Sam?

"Sam, I don't have you on screen."

No answer. No blip.

"Sam?"

■   ■   ■

With his eyes still fixed in horror upon the eviscerated bodies of mutant unborn chimps, Cap's nerves nearly melted when the cry of the banshee rose like a goblin over the partition walls.

He closed the cooler door and fell back against the wall to gather himself, take some deep breaths, talk sense to his mind, and make sure his bowels didn't let loose right there on the floor.

It was bad enough knowing that *thing* was in the same building.

It was far worse knowing he would have to find and identify it, which meant coming face-to-jaws with a savage, neck-wringing killer. He could only hope and pray it was in a cage *and* that the cage could contain it.

He looked around for anything he might use as a weapon. No crowbars or baseball bats were readily available. He crossed the hallway to what seemed the most likely door.

Careful, now. His hand shook as he grabbed the knob. He would open the door just a crack, take a look, then evaluate his next step.

The knob turned.

The door cracked open.

The banshee screamed in terror, anger, maybe both, so loudly, so piercingly, that Cap jolted back, slamming the door shut. The screaming continued, the sound of violent death knifing into every fear instinct Cap had. It was all he could do to stand still, be reasonable, and not create another window in the building trying to get out of there.

The screaming subsided to gasps and whimpers, and Cap noted that, as near as he could tell from the sound, it wasn't moving from one spot. Whatever it was hadn't stormed the door or come after him. Chances were good that it was confined.

He slowly opened the door again—

The thing screamed again.

He opened the door enough to look inside.

He saw another row of cages, larger than the cells that held the surrogate mothers.

At the sight of the first creature, he had to double-check not only his bowels but his stomach. In the first cage was a quaking, nearly hairless blob with blue-veined, leathery skin. On one end were stumps that should have been legs. On the other end was a head without a neck that turned only slightly when he approached.

Feeding tubes ran into the broad, flat nose, pumping in temporary life. It seemed only vaguely aware of his presence.

The next cage held a chimpanzee giant, grotesquely overgrown and suffering for it. Straightened out, it could have measured eight feet from head to toe, but this poor beast was bent and crooked like an arthritic old man, sitting painfully in the corner, its joints knobby, its fingers bent and useless. It tried to reach out to him, but the arm was a gnarled limb on a dead tree; it barely moved.

A shockingly white albino occupied the next cage, its cold pink eyes studying him with suspicion and loathing. It too was oversized, and judging from the crookedness of the fingers and feet, only slightly mobile. It huffed at him, then creaked and straightened to its feet to growl and threaten. The twisted legs buckled and it fell to its haunches again, resigned to making threats it could never carry out.

After what he'd seen so far, Cap thought he was ready for the next cage.

He wasn't.

At the first sight of him, the *thing* leaped at the bars, wailing and frothing—its eyes the crazed yellow orbs of a demon, its black fur bristling like a sooty explosion. It filled Cap's vision and he slammed against the opposite wall even before he felt the terror that put him there.

This was a malformation of the highest order, a creature far removed from a chimpanzee, but not better. Though smaller than Cap in stature, it had to outweigh him three to one, with muscles so pronounced they impeded its movement. It was deranged, drooling, out of control, and the cry from that throat— the scream of a madwoman!

It was urinating as it clung to the bars, tried to climb them, tried to bend them, tried to grab on with its feet, which only slid to the floor; the big, opposing toes looked to have been surgically removed.

Cap inched along the wall, maintaining distance from the huge arm that groped at him through the bars. Hoping to make it to a nearby exit, he passed the last cage, this one much larger—

It was empty.

The bars were bent, the sidewalls battered. Plywood was ripped from the back wall, and the two-by-six framing members were snapped aside like dry twigs. Foam insulation lay everywhere in broken pieces. The metal sheathing that formed the building's exterior was mangled and ripped open like a tin can opened with a hatchet.

The cage door was ajar, as if someone had already gone in to inspect the damage. Cap took one step inside, recognizing a familiar pattern of bite marks on the splintered lumber and a peppering of all-too-familiar diarrhetic droppings on the concrete floor.

Looking through the gaping hole in the rear wall of the cage, he could see no barriers between this building and the forest and mountains beyond.

■ ■ ■

Sing rebooted her computer, tweaked all the wires on the back of the satellite system, and double-checked her radio receiver. "Reed, can you hear me?"

He radioed back, "Loud and clear."

"I still can't find Sam, and now I can't raise Pete either."

"I have Pete on my screen."

"So do I, but he isn't moving and he isn't answering."

Reed called for Pete but got no answer. "Well, I sure won't buy this brand of GPS anymore. I'd better get over there." Then he asked, "What about Thorne and Kane? Where are they?"

"You don't have them on-screen?"

"No."

Sing sighed in exasperation. "Now I don't have them either. But they were almost back here."

"No number 6?"

"No. It hasn't come back."

"Max? Anything?"

Max answered, "Not yet."

Sing heard footsteps outside the motor home. The door opened, and Steve Thorne stepped up into the driver's area, his rifle slung on his back.

Sing was relieved. "All right. There's one warm body accounted for. We're having trouble with the system."

He broke into a tired grin. "So I hear."

She waited a moment, then asked, "Where's Kane?"

Her cell phone on the counter rang, Cap's special ring. She reached for it—

"Don't answer that," said Thorne, snatching it away.

She saw him raise a pistol and almost understood before the muzzle flashed and her awareness shattered into a starburst of fragments fading to black. Her body came to rest facedown against the bedroom door, a pool of blood spreading beneath her head.

SEVENTEEN

Cap hurried, his cell phone against his ear, waiting through ring after ring until Sing's voice-message system answered and gave him a beep. "Sing. I've located Burkhardt's lab and confirmed the source of at least one of the creatures. I'm ready to call the police, but first I have to get out of here. Tell Reed that—"

He'd only gotten halfway to the front door when the electric lock hummed and the knob rattled. He tumbled down behind a workbench as the door swung open, casting diffused sunlight about the room. Judging from the footsteps, three, maybe four, people came in, and they weren't little. He thought of the cell phone in his hand and frantically shut it off before Sing called back.

Now he heard Philip Merrill's voice. "Secure the exits—this one, the one in the rear, and the side loading doors. Then search every inch of this place."

. . .

By now Reed was praying, *Dear Lord, don't let me lose Beck again.* "Sing?" he radioed. "Any progress?"

She didn't answer, but Sam did. "Hello? Anybody hear me?" Well, here was one source of relief. "Sam! You okay? We lost you, buddy."

"I'm fine. I was trying to swing around to cover the east flank, but now I'm worried about Pete. Have you talked to him at all?"

"Negative. I can't raise him. The whole system's breaking down. Have you talked to Max?"

Max came on: "I'm still scouting the north side. It doesn't look good. They may have gotten through."

"Sing?" Reed still couldn't get an answer. "Now *she's* cut off."

"We may have to call it a day, guys," Max suggested.

Reed wasn't ready to concede that. "Max, why don't you stay where you are. Sam, we'd better check on Pete."

"You got it," Sam replied.

. . .

Cap heard someone coming. He ducked around the end of a workbench just in time to avoid being seen. With a quick, one-eyed glance around the corner, he caught sight of Tim the campus cop, now in civilian clothing but brandishing a gun. It seemed out of character. Cap wondered what Merrill must have told him.

Slam! Clank! The rattle of a chain and a padlock. That had to be the loading doors on the side of the building. Cap wouldn't be escaping that way.

They were working their way through the lab, and it was only a matter of time before—

He wriggled around the corner to the backside of the bench and just missed being spotted by Kenny, the other campus cop. Now, that guy was not to be tangled with. He had an iron-jawed feistiness and the muscle to back it up.

Clunk! Rattle! There went the rear door.

Did these guys even know what was going on in this place? Did Merrill know? They were locking him in, but they were locking themselves in as well. Would they be all that happy with the idea once they encountered—

The thing screamed one of its best banshee screams yet, and just faintly audible under the screams and the rattling of the bars were the voices of men screaming in horror, running footsteps, more hollering, cursing—a frantic retreat.

Cap didn't smile outwardly, but some quirky part of him was enjoying this.

Now Merrill was in the mix, cursing, hollering orders nobody was hearing, trying to hold his band of thugs together. Cap caught the words, "Don't shoot it!"

Well. Imagine that. Merrill was surprised too.

Footsteps! Apparently they'd satisfied themselves—with a little help—that Cap wasn't in the rear half. The lab was going to get a thorough going-through.

There had to be a cupboard, a cabinet, a garbage can, anything he could hide in! He scurried on his hands and knees across an aisle, peeked around the end of a counter, scurried across another aisle, straightened to peek over a bench—

His shoulder upset a pair of forceps that hung over the edge. He tried to catch them but missed. They clattered to the floor.

The footsteps started galloping his direction.

There was only one place left to hide, and that was in a huge walk-in freezer built into the partition. He knew he was kidding himself, but then again, maybe he'd be able to hide in the cold just a little longer than they'd be able to search in it. He slinked across the floor, reached up, pulled the handle, slipped through the cracked door, and managed to click it shut just one nano-second before his pursuers rounded the corner.

It was dark inside, and yes, it was freezing. The cold was already working its way through his clothing. He rose carefully to his feet to look through the small window in the door and his breath fogged it. Nuts! He backed up, trying to get used to the dark—

He wasn't alone in here.

The first nudge of a hairy hand startled him like a jolt of high voltage. He jumped involuntarily; his arms flew outward and struck a hairy body on either side. Twisting, he saw two rows of four—no, six—no, *eight* glassy-eyed, deformed chimpanzees, some whole, some gutted, all staring back at him in the light from the window. Their eyes were vacant, jaws slack, faces and fur glistening with frost. They hung from two rails by steel hooks inserted in their ear holes, and now he'd set them swinging like bells in a bell tower, thumping against him and each other.

The first one rolled off the end of the rail and bounced off Cap's shoulder before thumping to the floor. The second followed, glancing off Cap and spinning as it went down.

The third bumped into the freezer door as the door swung open and flooded the room with light. The fourth dropped, teetered, and fell right in front of Kenny the cop, now silhouetted in the doorway.

Kenny hollered and jumped back but recovered when he spotted Cap.

Cap was on the floor, tripped up by the first two corpses and trying to wrestle himself out from under the third and fourth. Kenny reached down, not to give him a hand up but to yank him off the floor, nearly dislocating his arm.

Before Cap knew it, he was out in the warm, habitable lab, held fast between Kenny and a Kenny wannabe. A third guy in an expensive suit slammed the freezer door shut behind him. Tim stood before him holding a gun, and next to Tim was Dr. Philip Merrill, looking pale, his hair out of place, his tie crooked, and sweat glistening on his brow.

"Dr. Capella!" he said, winded and shaking. "You never should have come back!"

■   ■   ■

One more hour, Deputy Saunders thought, *and we'll call it a day.* His volunteers were getting tired, cold, and hungry, and they had to get back down before the light was gone. The last discovery, a rusty pocketknife, was over an hour ago, and expanding the search area to include the entire Inland Northwest didn't seem like a wise use of time and manpower.

"Okay, everybody," he spoke into his handheld radio, "one more hour."

They came back with muttered acknowledgments.

A metal detector somewhere in the woods replied with a loud chirp.

"Officer Saunders! I found it!"

"What is it this time?"

"It's the shovel! I found the shovel!"

■   ■   ■

Merrill and his men took Cap to an office in a corner of the lab, a simple cubicle made from sound-baffling dividers, and sat him down in one of two available chairs. Kenny stood in the entry, big arms across his chest, expression not firm but troubled. Tim leaned in the corner as if he didn't want to come out of it, the gun lowered but visible. Merrill took the chair behind the desk and smoothed his hair back repeatedly as if trying to compose himself.

The other two guys stood behind Cap's chair to make sure he stayed in it. Cap offered his hand to the one behind his right shoulder. "Uh, Mike Capella. Dr. Merrill and I know each other, did he tell you that?" The man gave him a cold stare. He and his partner were definitely on edge.

Cap checked around the room. Only one entrance. The walls were too heavy to knock over, too tall to jump over. The room was too small to avoid being grabbed if he made a move.

A snapshot push-pinned to the wall above the desk hinted that this was Burkhardt's office. It was a photo of Burkhardt, bearded and ponytailed, decked out in a billed cap and fishing vest and posing with a good-sized cutthroat trout. Burkhardt always had been an avid hunter and outdoorsman, which was ironic, Cap thought. Merrill loosened his tie, unbuttoned his collar, and finally reached a level of composure acceptable for conversation. "I suppose you've seen everything?"

Cap studied him—and his men. "Looks like you have too. Didn't you know what Burkhardt was doing?"

"We had an understanding." Merrill leaned closer. "Sometimes the greatest scientific breakthroughs have to be made in secret, away from prying eyes, politics, and boards of ethics."

"So how do you like his results?"

Merrill rubbed his face.

"I don't suppose your so-called scientific community will be too wild about them," Cap went on. "*American Geographic* isn't about to publish them, and forget about Public Broadcasting and the Evolution Channel."

Merrill's temper brought some of his color back. "Such steps are necessary—"

"To prove what? That random mutations work? Look around you, Merrill! Does all this look random? It's planned; it's monitored; it's carefully recorded, and it *still* doesn't work." He spoke to the men behind him. "Burkhardt's planting mutated embryos in surrogate mothers and harvesting the eggs from the offspring before they're even born—"

Merrill interjected, "To compress the amount of time between generations."

Cap spoke to Kenny and Tim, "—so he can further mutate the mutants, implant the mothers, and start all over again."

"And thereby replicate the natural process—"

Cap was so steamed up he had to stand. "Nature doesn't load the dice! You're using a lab here, Merrill! You're interposing intelligence into the process! You're—" The two guards sat him down again. "You're not only proving that random mutations don't work; you're proving that *purposeful* mutations don't work!" He spoke to Kenny and Tim again. "Did you get a load of those monsters in there? Nice improvements on the original, don't you think?"

Merrill tried to argue to his men, "Mutations are the mechanism by which—"

"So where is everybody?" Cap said.

Merrill wasn't in control, and it showed despite his effort to hide it. "I suppose it's their day off."

Cap felt sorry for this man. "Philip, come on. You've figured it out just as easily as I have! You know Burkhardt! He's not about to let somebody accomplish something when he's not around to take credit for it! The staff isn't here because he isn't here, and he isn't here because . . . ?"

Merrill sat there, cornered and seething.

Cap answered his own question. "Because his monster isn't here. You saw that hole in the wall, right?" He asked the guards,

"Right?" He pointed that direction. "There went the whole experiment, along with your funding, Merrill, into the great outdoors for the whole world to see. You think Burkhardt can live with that? You think he'd want you to find out?"

Cap could tell Merrill knew, but the esteemed college dean didn't offer to discuss it.

Cap spoke to the guards, "Burkhardt's gone after it."

■ ■ ■

Deputy Dave Saunders, the housewife, the fireman, the heavy equipment operator, and the machinist found the shallow grave only a few feet from where the shovel had been dropped. It was the equipment operator who first hit something with his shovel—a boot.

The housewife turned away.

The others dug carefully as the stench of a dead corpse rose into the air.

The fireman dropped his shovel and ran, bent over, and vomited.

Dave could hardly bear it himself, but he kept going, carefully moving peat and soil with his gloved hands until he found out what Sing and the others needed to know. Gasping for fresh air, he waved for a halt. "It's Thompson."

■ ■ ■

Merrill was desperate to make Cap the liar. "You can't possibly know where Dr. Burkhardt is or what he's doing! Of all the arrogant, outlandish—"

"Can I stand up?" Cap rose, testing the disposition of the two guys behind him. They didn't slap him into the chair again, so he knew he was making progress. Slowly, making sure they could see his every move, he reached into his shirt pocket and pulled out some folded sheets of paper, digital photos Sing had e-mailed him. He unfolded one and showed it to them. "Recognize this guy?"

They stared at it blankly.

Cap went to the desk, reached for one of Burkhardt's pencils from a desk caddy, and scribbled a beard and ponytail on the man in the photo. He held it up. "Now do you recognize him?" He directed their attention to Burkhardt's fishing photo on the wall. Cap saw the light of recognition in their eyes. "He's out there right now, lying to my friends and pretending he's helping them hunt down a Bigfoot! But we know what that monster really is, don't we? And so does he."

"You are a trespasser, Cap!" Merrill lifted his voice. "I could have you arrested!"

"Trespassing where? Care to show this place to the police?"

Merrill fell silent again.

"I'm guessing Burkhardt cut the big toes off his monster so it couldn't be arboreal and would have to evolve into a ground-dwelling, bipedal something-or-other. I'm going to guess that Burkhardt engineered that thing to compete with any other primates it encountered—that's the natural selection thing, you know, competing with other species and prevailing—and that includes human beings. Well, it's not evolving, but it *is* competing. It's responsible for the deaths of four people, one of them a dear friend and one of them the Whitcomb County sheriff!"

Merrill leaped to his feet, the veins showing in his neck. "You can't prove that!"

"Ah-ah-ah! The hair, stool, and saliva samples, remember? Now, the hairs don't reveal much, but that's okay. All the police have to do is match the stool and saliva samples with the saliva and droppings in that broken cage, and bingo!"

Merrill looked as though he'd swallowed a bitter pill. "I knew nothing about all this! I had nothing to do with it!"

"Ah!" Cap pointed at him. "You believe me!" He walked over to Kenny and looked up at him. "I'd like to go now. I need to warn my friends before Burkhardt gets a chance to do something really stupid."

Kenny locked eyes with him a moment, then exchanged a quick look with the others. Tim slipped his gun back into its holster. Kenny stepped aside.

"Thanks." Cap wasted no time getting out of there and called over his shoulder, "You might want to wait here for the cops—and show them that photo!"

Merrill bolted for the entryway, but Kenny blocked him. "Where do you think you're going?"

Merrill was dumbfounded. "You work for *me*!"

"Sit down."

Merrill backed away, rubbed his hand over his hair, approached Tim to try to reason with him—

He grabbed Tim's pistol from its holster and swept it around the cubicle.

The men shied back, hands raised.

Merrill dashed out of the office and across the lab and caught sight of Cap racing for the rear of the building. He aimed wildly and fired as he ran. The first bullet put a hole in a wall about twelve feet from the floor. The second shattered glassware on a workbench.

Kenny and Tim raced after him, hollering to stop, to simmer down, but Merrill was beyond that.

Cap ran down the hallway and ducked around the partition.

Merrill shouted, "Cap! The doors are padlocked! Give it up! There's no reason to call the police! We can reach an agreement!"

The banshee started screaming then—a perfect giveaway of Cap's location! Merrill hooked a sharp left and ducked through the doorway into the hall of monsters.

The beast in the far cage had already gone berserk, leaping and pounding the bars, spitting, screaming, groping, drilling into Merrill with murderous eyes. Merrill recalled how Burkhardt's creations felt about competing primates, and ran sideways with his back sliding along the opposite wall.

The last cage brought no comfort. Even before Merrill got there, he knew what the open cage door meant. Directly opposite the cage, he quit running and fell back against the wall in dismay.

Yes, all the doors were padlocked, but there was nothing beyond that hole in the rear wall but the wide outdoors.

■ ■ ■

"Sam? Sam, you there?"

Reed and Sam had been converging on Pete's GPS blip and getting close, but now Sam's blip had vanished again, and Reed couldn't raise him on the radio. Reed rested against a tree and called again, "Sam? Come in, Sam. Sing? Can you read me? Can *anybody* hear me?"

He took the GPS from his arm, checked the batteries, then recycled it. Pete's blip appeared again, but Pete still didn't answer his radio. As for Max, Sam, and Sing, he wasn't getting a blip or a radio response.

Guess I should have known. This gremlin-plagued GPS system had been playing a cruel game with his hope all along. He tried not to let it distract him as he pressed ahead through heavy forest, following a game trail, closing on Pete's blip, the one thing he could call a "known"—maybe.

Like an airplane popping out of the clouds, he broke into an open area where rocks and shallow soil stunted the trees and undergrowth. Grass found root and sunlight here, providing pasture for elk and deer. Hoofprints and droppings were plentiful, and there were obvious patches of flattened grass where elk had rested.

Ah! He got a visual. Pete sat against a tree in the middle of the clearing, his back to Reed. Reed blew a sigh of relief and gladness. After all the gadget failure, it was great to have direct human contact again.

"Pete," he said quietly as he approached, "I'm coming up behind you."

Pete nodded slightly.

"I guess you know your radio's out. The whole system's on the fritz. Maybe it's sunspots, I don't know—"

"Reed . . ." Pete's voice was weak, barely audible.

Reed double-timed and knelt beside him. "Pete . . ."

Pete's rifle was gone. His face was pale, drained of blood, and he was holding his side. Blood oozed between his fingers. It looked like a knife wound.

Reed didn't ask how it had happened. That wasn't important now. "Easy, bud. We're going to get you out of here."

"S-sam!"

"What?"

"Get down."

Reed saw the terror in Pete's eyes as they focused across the clearing. Not thinking, just trusting, Reed ducked.

A bullet zinged over his head and thudded into Pete's chest.

Then came the *Pow!* of a rifle.

Reed hugged the ground, looked up at Pete—

Pete's lifeless body slumped over, revealing a bullet puncture and a red smear on the tree behind him.

Reed held his rifle in a death grip. He had a general idea

where the shot had come from, but he dared not raise his head to make sure.

Sam. Pete said "Sam."

Why began to enter his head, but the why didn't matter, not now. *Not being killed* mattered.

Reed rolled behind a clump of rocks, disturbing some brush, a telltale sign of his location.

There was a puff of dust and the whine of a ricochet.

Pow!

The slope fell away just below Reed's position, providing a protective dome of earth between him and the shooter. He grabbed his chance and ran, crouching, down the slope and into the trees. Dropping behind a protective log, he peered back toward the clearing as he cycled the bolt on his rifle, chambering a round—

It didn't feel right. He opened the bolt.

The firing pin was broken as if someone had punched it in with a nail.

Max had offered to load Reed's rifle and Reed had said okay.

Max and Sam. The cover-up! Them? Why?

The questions would have to come later. For now, there was absolutely no sense in sticking around. Reed barreled down the hill, not navigating, just moving, ducking behind trees, zig-zagging, always looking for cover.

The GPS! He glanced at it. He could see his own blip, and now he could see Sam's, coming down the hill after him, homing in on his satellite signal!

Reed clicked off his unit. The LCD screen went black. No Reed. No Sam. No signals. He was alone in the woods except for the men trying to kill him, out of contact.

Hunted.

EIGHTEEN

It was like awakening slowly from an anesthetic, coming out of the dark, reentering the world from somewhere far away. She heard a voice but understood no words. The floor felt wet and sticky against her face, and it was reeling as if the entire motor home were floating on stormy water. A sharp pain hammered her skull with every beat of her pulse, and she smelled blood. She became aware of her body in stages, first her hands, then her arms, and then her legs, but somehow, through the morass of tangled, swirling thoughts that were half dream, half coherent, she knew that she must not move, she must not appear alive.

She heard a voice from somewhere, and in a few more moments and a few more painful pulse beats, she remembered whose voice it was.

Thorne. She recalled the last image she saw before her awareness came to a shattering halt: Steve Thorne, eyes as cold as a shark's, aiming his pistol at her. As near as she could determine from the pattern of the pain and the state of her body, the bullet had struck her in the head. Where the bullet was now she cringed to imagine, but she was still alive and beginning to think again, which astounded her.

"No, he's got it switched off," came Thorne's voice. He paused as if listening to someone and then answered, "I know, but just keep moving, keep the pressure on.

She sensed from the direction of his voice that he was behind her. Carefully, she worked one eye open. The floor of the motor home wavered and then came into focus.

The first thing she saw was a pool of blood. How she'd managed to regain consciousness she had no idea, but one thing was certain: whatever consciousness she had would be temporary at best.

Just a few more moments, she thought. *If I can gather my strength for just a few more moments . . .*

■ ■ ■

Reed rolled over a log, sank into the cover of some willows, and lay still, listening, thinking.

Encouraging thoughts were in short supply. For all he knew, there hadn't been anything wrong with Wiley Kane's rifle, which would mean Kane was dead and maybe Sing as well, both at the hand of Steve Thorne. That left him no friends and three hunters trying to track him down. If he could turn on his GPS and pick up their locations—

That was the problem. If he turned his unit on, the others would be able to see him just as he would be able to see them. He could guess that he was in the middle of a triangle with Max to the north, Sam to the south, and Thorne downhill to the west. They were no doubt closing in on him right now.

He wriggled through the willows and ran for a stand of firs—
A chip of bark flew from a trunk and nearly hit him in the cheek.
Pow!

Well, at least he was maintaining some distance.

■ ■ ■

Jacob halted again, turned in place, sniffed, and searched as he
grunted at his females, yanking them to keep them close together.
They were still working their way north, but in zigzags, quick
sprints, silent hidings. The woman was silent, unseen, but Beck
trusted Jacob's senses and understood why he was keeping the
group together: predators went for the stragglers, the strays,
those left alone. If they stayed together, maybe, just maybe . . .

Beck had heard more gunshots behind them. She couldn't
make any sense of it except to guess the hunters were trying to
signal her.

She felt the GPS in her shirt pocket. For now, surrounded by
the frightened, fleeing family, she left it off.

■ ■ ■

"Okay," Thorne was saying, "try to keep pace with him and
don't let him flank you. I'm all set to torch this place as soon as
you're done."

Torch. Fire. Now Sing recognized a particular smell that didn't
belong: gasoline.

She concentrated, then raised her head a hair's breadth, gritting
her teeth against the pain. *I must be a stone. Lord, help me not to feel;
help me not to hurt.* She raised her head higher. She tested the fingers on her right hand. From somewhere, she found strength.

She couldn't see Thorne but could paint a picture in her mind from what she could hear: four feet away . . . sitting at the computer . . . facing maybe a quarter turn away from her . . . looking down at the screen, and—*Dear Lord, please*—his weight on the forward half of the chair.

She wouldn't be able to test her strength or her ability to move. She would have only one chance to move at all.

She envisioned where the knife rack must be: very close, above the cutting board, near the bedroom door. One quick leap would get her there—if she was able. She envisioned the carving knife in her right hand, the one with the sharpest point. She reviewed her memory of the various knifing victims she had examined, which wounds had killed in the shortest amount of time.

"Is she dead?" Thorne was saying. "Are you kidding? I blew her brains out. You want me to do it again?"

I am a stone.

She pulled in a long, steady breath, then let it out slowly, silently. She pulled in a second breath, then let it out. Without motion, she tested her muscles.

Thorne was listening again, drumming his fingers on the counter. Hopefully, he would talk again; his ears would be filled with the sound of his own voice.

"Adam, come on, now. You're in this neck deep with the rest of us. Let's get it done—"

With every reserve of strength, of body, and of spirit, Sing flipped from her belly to her back and then to her side, closing the distance to the computer chair. Thorne's head was turning toward the sound and he was saying, ". . . and go home," just as her hands gripped the wheeled base of the chair, yanked, and upset it from under him. He fell away from her, grabbing the counter, trying to recover as the chair clattered on its side to the floor.

She pushed to her feet, reached with her right hand, grasped the knife from the rack—

Her head emptied of blood and she sank to her knees, head down, vision clouded, pain raging through her skull. Her hair and scalp were sodden and dripping. She held the knife in both hands.

Thorne was on his feet immediately. He came at her.

She raised her head and saw her target: the femoral artery near the top of his thigh. Her head was swimming, her strength departing.

He put his hands on her, tried to grab her arms.

With both hands, she plunged the knife into his thigh near the groin.

He screamed in pain and horror, releasing his grip, backing off. The knife slipped from the wound with a spurt of blood. His leg collapsed under him and he staggered backwards, tumbling over the fallen chair.

He was distracted, disoriented, on his back.

Her chance would never come again. Unable to rise to her feet, she lunged forward on her knees, screaming like a cougar, pouncing like a bear.

Just above the belly, just below the breastbone, at just the right angle—

With both hands and all her weight, she put the knife through his heart. He stared at her in disbelief, gasping, trembling, until his eyes went blank, his pupils dilated, and his head clunked against the floor. His arms, then his whole body, went limp. Near his head were the mobile lab's auxilary gasoline cans. He wouldn't be using them.

Sing rolled to the floor beside the man she had just killed, her scream becoming a loud sobbing from pain, fear, and horror.

■ ■ ■

Jacob and the females were moving swiftly, their articulated feet padding silently over deep humus and soft green moss, weaving up and down, under and around immense, ancient pillars of old-growth forest with seeming indifference.

But Beck was sure she knew this place. Hadn't she once compared it to a Tolkien or Lewis fantasy, a wondrous, otherworldly place where hobbits and elves, fairies and princesses, knights and ogres had their adventures and intrigues?

She'd been here with Reed only a week ago!

Hadn't she?

Painfully clinging to Rachel's shoulders, she looked for a trail, a ravine, a creek with a log bridge, an old cabin torn apart by a savage beast—frightening memories to be sure, but it was the nearest boundary of her world, the last place she'd ever been as a human being.

Rachel slowed, faltered, then turned downhill.

"Wha—?" Beck started to say.

Rachel kept going, loping down the slope even after Jacob stopped, turned around, and grunted a question at her; even after Leah barked in alarm and Reuben whimpered.

Beck pushed herself higher up on Rachel's back and scanned the forest on every side, wondering where Rachel was going, and why, and feeling anxious about being separated from the group. "Rachel! Hello? W-what are you doing?"

Beck looked over her shoulder. Jacob, Leah, and Reuben were huddling together, fidgeting and grunting. Rachel's side trip was not in their plans.

Rachel was sniffing, on the trail of something. Beck had never seen this behavior before, a Sasquatch sniffing *after* something rather than running *from* something it happened to smell. "What is it, girl?"

They came to an immense log that had once been a majestic cedar unnumbered years before. A web of tangled roots clawed the air at one end; the other end disappeared in the forest, covered over with young firs and cedars that had taken root along its surface.

Rachel sniffed the air again as if trying to be sure of something, then circled around the roots to the other side.

A loud fluttering startled Beck; she ducked behind Rachel's head as a gathering of birds scattered into the air: ravens, an osprey, two bald eagles. Recovering, and peering over Rachel's shoulder, Beck saw that the birds had been here awhile—the surrounding thickets, branches, and windfall were spattered with white droppings.

Rachel straightened in that certain way that let Beck know she could slide to the ground. Beck released her grip around Rachel's shoulders and slid clumsily onto a mound of red crumbles, the remains of a fallen tree. Her legs were weak; she collapsed to the ground.

Rachel took a furtive step, then another, looking at something amid the broken, dropping-spattered branches of serviceberry, until, with a mournful sigh, she sank to her haunches, her head hanging.

Beck struggled to her feet, eased closer, and caught a scent she'd come to know: raw meat and peeled animal hide, this time with a reek of decay. From behind Rachel's slumped back, she peered into the broken bushes and saw a rib cage almost picked clean by the birds, the blackening meat showing red where it had been freshly torn by their beaks. Eyes widening with horror, Beck saw an arm, half eaten, half covered with reddish-brown fur, with an ape's hand—five fingers and a thumb.

Beck moved from Rachel's right shoulder to her left for a better look.

The innards were almost completely gone. The spine was visible through the empty chest cavity, and Beck saw that the neck had been violently twisted and broken. Lying crookedly, almost separate from the body, was the rotting head of a Sasquatch child, one eye closed, one eye gone, the face pecked and gouged.

The little female was Beck's size. The mouth was smeared with huckleberries, and the hair—the long, magnificent hair—was reddish brown, the same color as Rachel's.

"Sh-she was yours, wasn't she?"

Rachel's body began to quake as air rushed in and out of her nostrils like . . . sobs? Beck, already in a state of shock, was further astonished. Was Rachel . . . *crying*? Was it possible?

Tears flooded Rachel's eyes, overflowed, and ran down her face, something Beck had never seen or imagined in the great ape.

"Rachel . . . sweetheart . . ."

Beck touched her, patted her.

Rachel threw back her head and howled, a loud sound that rippled through the forest and carried for miles.

From above, Leah began howling and Jacob barked a warning. The forest was filled with the noise.

Beck covered an ear with one hand, stroked Rachel's shoulder with the other—

She recalled the bite marks on that shoulder, the patch of blood that had soiled Beck's leather coat, the howls she and Reed heard that night—not vicious howls of predation and threat as they'd thought, but howls of struggle and loss, pain and remorse, the same as she was hearing now.

Then, like a loathsome reminder, a third voice joined Leah and Rachel's from *out there*. The wailing woman, the demon of Lost Creek, began to answer the howls with her own eerie cry, matching them volume for volume.

The ghostly chorus from that night on Lost Creek was complete.

Beck *had* been in this place before.

■ ■ ■

Reed was not terrified when the howling voices floated his way through the forest, layer upon echoed layer. For him, it was an awakening of hope. He knew those voices well, and judging from the sound, the beasts were still within reach—if he could only live that long. He took a measured risk and raised his head from his hiding place between two moss-covered logs, scanning the forest all around. He saw no telltale movement behind the trunks of trees and the tangled stalks of bushes; he heard no snapping of twigs or crunching of leaves to indicate his enemies had found him.

Not that it mattered. They were hunters. They would be doing all they could to remain unseen and unheard. The last two bullets had whizzed by his head before he'd seen or heard anything else.

But he'd heard the beasts, and if they were nearby, Beck could be nearby, and if, on the outside chance that she'd decided to send a signal . . .

He turned on his GPS and the screen lit up. He could see Sam almost straight uphill from him—and knew Sam could see him. Max was still to the north and moving farther that way, not interested in Reed at all but going after the beasts—and maybe Beck. He last saw Steve Thorne's blip approaching Sing's motor home near the end of Service Road 221, but it was off the screen now, which could be the worst of news. Only Sing could update him on Blip Number 6, *if* Beck's unit was turned on and *if* he could raise Sing on the radio, and *only if* Sing were still alive—

A weak and faltering voice came through his earpiece, "Reed, I see you on my screen. Can you hear me?"

Reed felt as though he'd reconnected a lifeline! "Sing! I was afraid you were dead!"

"Almost. Steve Thorne shot me in the head."

He couldn't have heard that correctly. "Say again?"

■ ■ ■

Sing was slumped over in her computer chair, pressing a bloodied towel to her head, trying to view the screen sideways and work the keyboard with one free hand. Sometimes she could think clearly, and sometimes she felt she was dreaming. "It was a glancing blow." She touched the wound and winced. "It feels like a shallow depressed fracture, nonpenetrating." She looked at the bloodied towel. "The bullet missed the temporal artery, but there's still a mess."

"Have you called the medics?"

"Thorne smashed my cell phone and I can't find the police radio."

"Where is Thorne now?"

"Steve Thorne is dead."

"Did you say Thorne is dead?"

She looked at the corpse on the floor for a moment, her focus wavering. "I'm pretty sure. I severed his femoral artery and stabbed him through the heart. He isn't moving."

"Sing, Pete's dead too. Sam killed him. Do you copy?" She heard the anguish in Reed's voice, as if he were hearing the news himself for the first time.

Her wound pulsed out fresh pain in a faster rhythm. "Did you say Pete is dead?"

"Yes. Sam shot him, and now Sam's trying to kill me."

She rested her head on the counter, weak with shock and grief. Maybe she *was* dreaming, and this was a bad dream. It felt like one.

"Sing? Are you there?"

"The cover-up," came to her mind and out her mouth.

"We need to find Beck. Can you see her on your screen?"

Sing blinked and forced her eyes to focus on the screen. "Reed . . . Sam is coming down the hill, coming close to you." Sam's blip winked out. "Oh no, he's not—"

■ ■ ■

Ping!

Reed had just turned to scramble out of the logs when the bullet hit and chips flew only inches away. He ducked, rolled, plowed into some bushes, found a tree to protect him.

"Sam?" Reed called into his GPS radio. "Sam, you don't want to do this."

No answer. Reed looked at his screen. That's what Sing meant: Sam had turned off his unit. He'd gone invisible.

Well, it could work both ways. Reed switched off his unit. He knew Sam was heading down the hill from the south. Hoping to flank him, Reed started up the hill toward the north.

■ ■ ■

Beck heard the shot and searched that direction but saw no movement, no camouflage jackets or caps. She thought of shouting, but no, not here, not where they would find Rachel.

As if Rachel were not giving them plenty of noise already. She was still howling inconsolably, her head thrown back, her right hand beating her chest.

Beck tried to calm her, quiet her down. "Shhh, now! Shhh! Rachel, don't do this! The hunters will find you!"

Rachel shrugged her hand away, and Beck shied back a step, stricken by the tableau of a grieving mother and her dead, mangled child, incredulous at the revelation in the child's reddish-brown hair: "I was *her*! You thought I was *her*! No wonder you wanted my hair the way it was."

Ka-wump! As if he'd dropped from the sky, Jacob came leaping over the log and thudded like a falling timber right next to them. Beck jumped with a yelp, but Jacob paid her no mind. Growling and scolding, he yanked Rachel to her feet and shoved her against the log, trying to knock some sense into her. She quit howling but kept crying. He pushed her from behind, herded her, swatted her, got her moving around the log.

Rachel did not look back to find Beck. She just went around the log, still whimpering, with Jacob huffing at her to be quiet.

Beck stood there. Alone. Amazed. Nonplussed.

Rachel didn't look back.

When they reappeared on the hill above the log, Jacob was hurrying her along, pushing and grunting. She obeyed and climbed the slope in front of him, her soft feet taking hold of the ground with sure steps, her head hanging as she wiped her tear-stained face. They disappeared behind a tree, reemerged, passed behind another tree, then two, and then the forest shrouded them like a closing curtain and Beck saw them no more.

Somewhere in the deep forest, out of sight, Rachel quit whimpering and Jacob fell silent.

Beck backed up a step, and noticed that she could. She looked over her shoulder, down the hill, and realized she could go there. She looked up the hill. No Jacob. No Rachel. No group.

What about the woman? Beck listened carefully, rotating a full circle. The woman was silent, which could mean she was gone, or lurking, or stalking, or trailing the Sasquatches . . .

There was no time to fret about it. There was no option but

to get moving, to find a landmark or trail, to get that GPS turned on and make sure the hunters found only her.

She ventured One Small Step downhill, slowed by the pain in her body, her ankle complaining but carrying her. Other steps came after the first, from tree to tree to ledge to stump to tree to fallen log, farther down and still farther down, always peering ahead, always hoping to sight something familiar emerging through the ever-changing curtain of trees.

Just one more time, she looked back. The Sasquatches were gone. She was no danger to them.

She pulled the GPS from her shirt pocket and pressed the on button. The LCD screen lit up.

■ ■ ■

Sing just had to accept it. She couldn't explain it; she wasn't expecting it; she could hardly comprehend it, but there it was: Blip Number 6.

"Reed . . . I have Beck on my screen."

The screen faded to black; her thoughts disintegrated into nonsense and she began to dream.

She didn't know how much time had passed before she jerked awake, forced her eyes open, and brought the screen back into focus.

"Reed, Max is heading for Blip Number 6. He can see where Beck is. Reed? Reed, do you copy?"

No answer.

■ ■ ■

Beck studied the screen on her GPS as she hiked a meandering, limping course down the mountain slope, heading for what looked like a stream on the moving map, hoping to find another human being.

"Hello! Is anybody there?"

She was alone, and she knew it. She was a stray, a straggler, and a perfect target for a predator. No wonder Rachel never let her wander off.

"Hello! I'm Beck Shelton! Is anyone there?"

Keep moving, girl; keep moving. Find those hunters.

Was *she* making that noise? She stopped. The rustling she heard continued. It came from up the slope, back among the trees where anything could hide.

"Hello!"

No answer—just the snap of twigs, the rustling of some brush.

■ ■ ■

Reed crouched in a thick cluster of young growth, not sure enough of where he was to keep moving. He may have slipped by Sam on his way uphill, but there was only one way to be sure.

He pressed the on button.

The screen told him he was a little upslope and a little south of where he wanted to be. "Sing? Do you read?"

Her voice was weak but tense with excitement. "Reed, I have Blip Number 6, bearing 342, close to Lost Creek. Max is closing on it!"

Something in Reed came alive again. He zoomed out on his screen to find the creek, to orient himself to the bearing.

Sam's blip appeared like a ship out of the fog, closer than ever.

The bullet hit with a loud *whack!* Reed spun and went down with a cry, grasping his shoulder.

"Reed, Sam is coming uphill toward you!"

Reed had to grab a breath before he could answer, gasping with pain. "Sing. I've been hit."

■ ■ ■

Beck quickened her step. A human would have answered when she called. She moved downhill, ducked behind some trees, froze, and listened.

The sounds were following her, moving down the hill: a thump, a dragging, another stick breaking.

She leaped and limped to the next tree and listened again. She may have heard more noises, but now the gurgle of a creek was making it difficult to tell.

A creek?

She limped to the next tree and peered around it.

A ravine. A creek. It had to be Lost Creek!

Thump! Drag. Thump! Drag.

She ducked behind the tree and peeked uphill.

Through the spaces in the trees she caught a flash of black hair, a patch of yellowing flesh.

Whatever it was, it was walking.

Beck only whispered, "Jacob?"

The woman screamed in reply, so close Beck could hear the rattle of phlegm in her windpipe.

Beck spun, tried to run, but her legs were weak and she fell headlong.

The cry of the banshee blasted over her, around her, so close and so loud it hurt.

Thump! Drag. Thump! Drag.

NINETEEN

Reed disappeared from Sing's screen. "Reed, don't do this to me! Be alive, please!"

With a few fumbling tries, she zoomed in on Sam's blip. He was shifting back and forth as if searching.

■ ■ ■

Reed ducked and wove around trunks and undergrowth as quickly and silently as he could, mimicking the stalking techniques he'd seen Pete use, half-guessing his bearing, hoping, praying for enough time to live, to stay ahead of Sam, to get to Beck and end this. His GPS was off. For now, he would have to be invisible.

■ ■ ■

Beck rolled to a stop, righted herself, looked up the slope—
Thump! Drag.

It emerged from behind an ancient fir, thumping on one crooked leg and dragging the other, still raw and bleeding from a bullet wound. It wavered, grabbed at one tree and then the next with long ape arms to steady itself, wheezing hoarsely, teeth bared and canines glistening. It was every bit as large and powerful as Jacob, but bent, twisted, deformed. Its black hair was sparse and patchy, bristling like quills from its jaundiced skin. The wrinkled head was nearly bald, and one half of the face was peeling, blistered and scabbed from a recent burn. When it saw her, it glared with bulbous yellow eyes and screamed a scream Beck could *feel.*

It came after her, hobbling on uneven legs, careening, its long arms guiding it from tree to tree as it descended the slope.

Beck leaped aside as it rumbled past. It planted a hand on a tree and spun around, fell, rose again, and crawled up the hill on all fours, thumping and dragging, grabbing and pulling, a crooked, arthritic hand clawing to reach her.

Beck screamed as she turned to escape up the bank, her strength ebbing, the humus crumbling and giving beneath her feet. She screamed again with all that was in her as a huge hand swung close enough to strike her foot but not grab it.

Thinking like an animal, Beck wailed a Sasquatch wail of alarm, loud and throaty, again and again, grabbing roots and small bushes to pull herself away from those hands, those teeth, those glaring eyes.

■ ■ ■

Reed heard the screams—Beck's screams; he'd know her voice anywhere—and it was all he could do to keep his cool, stay smart, and not break into a blind run. Sam was still a factor, and Reed would never be able to outrun him.

He found a hiding spot behind some rocks and collapsed there, taking off his hat, struggling out of his jacket. *Hang on, Beck!*

．．．

The thing fell on its face as its legs buckled; it writhed and flailed until it was moving again, hobbling on twos, walking on fours, stumbling on threes, shoulders uneven, knuckles skinned and bleeding. It lagged behind long enough for Beck to break into a clearing where patches of maple and elderberry grew through a crisscross of wind-fallen trunks. She came up against a wall of brush and fallen trees with no way over or around.

The creature broke into the clearing, huffing and wheezing, froth on its chin, eyes crazed. *Thump! Draaaagg. Thump! Draaaggg.*

Beck turned, her back against the brush pile, her arms and legs tangled in an explosion of shoots, leaves, and branches. She cried out again, looking for a way out, over, under, *anywhere.*

The thing bared its teeth, reached out—

Boom! The left shoulder jerked violently as blood and flesh exploded out the creature's back. It cried out in pain and horror, afraid, wondering.

Boom! The right arm jerked and twisted, the bicep punctured and spurting red, the bone beneath snapping.

Boom! The creature reeled backward, a puncture in its chest.

It stood, glaring at Beck, teeth bared, reddening saliva seeping through its teeth.

Boom! With another blast through its chest, its breath became a gargle. It teetered and swayed, choking, its eyes locked on Beck with murderous intent until they slowly closed in sleep and the creature fell with a *wump!* that shook the ground.

It lay still. There was a momentary, unnatural silence.

Beck could not comprehend that the danger was over. She pushed farther into the thicket, tried to get a foothold on the log, slipped and fell into the elderberry branches.

Then she saw someone. A hunter in camouflage came into the clearing, stepping cautiously, rifle leveled at the creature.

Beck couldn't move. She couldn't speak. She could only stare through the leaves.

He went to the creature, now spread flat on its back on the rough ground. He poked it with his rifle, then pointed the rifle directly at the thing's head.

Beck turned her head away.

Boom! One last shot.

The hunter glanced around the clearing. "Hello? Beck Shelton?"

He spotted her through all the helter-skelter limbs, and he appeared a little puzzled. "Beck? Beck Shelton?" Why was he staring at her? "It's all right. The creature's dead."

Language had left her. "Whoo . . . hoo . . . hoooo . . ."

"Who am I?"

She nodded.

"I'm a friend. My name is Adam Burkhardt."

■ ■ ■

Reed lay among the rocks, unable to move. He switched on the GPS and spoke in a weak, trembling voice. "S-sam. Sam, why are you doing this? Why are you trying to kill me?"

For the very first time, Sam replied. "It's nothing personal, Reed. It's something I was hired to do."

"I don't understand."

"It's not that complicated. Just call it survival."

■ ■ ■

Sing saw Reed's blip on her screen, but it wasn't moving. Sam's was, changing course and heading directly for him.

She mumbled into her headphone, "Sam . . . Sam, I can see you on my screen. I'm a witness."

There was an ominous silence as the blip kept moving closer to Reed's position.

Abruptly, Sam radioed, "You've got a hole in your head, so I figure I've still got a pretty good chance of catching up with you later. Reed? You still with us, buddy?"

Reed's voice was barely audible. "Please don't kill me."

■ ■ ■

Beck pushed a few limbs aside. She studied the man, unsure about him. He was suddenly preoccupied, listening intently to the device in his ear. She could see a GPS on his sleeve.

■ ■ ■

Sam Marlowe got a visual: Reed Shelton down, propped against a log, hand against his chest as if he were having trouble breathing. Sam steadied himself against a tree, sighted Reed's back through his scope—"Sorry, pal"—and pulled the trigger. The body lurched with the impact, then remained still, flopped over the log.

He sighed with relief. "About time."

Keeping his rifle ready, he stepped carefully into the open, approaching his target. He could see a good-sized hole through Reed's jacket. He spoke into his radio, "Boss? You there?"

"Go ahead," Burkhardt answered.

Sam reached the body. "Heard you doing a lot of shooting. Did you get what you were after?"

"Uh, yeah, so far."

"Well, I just got Reed, so let's close this up and get out of here. We've still got Thorne's job to finish."

"Uh, roger. I'll get back to you." Burkhardt's voice didn't sound too sure.

■ ■ ■

Adam Burkhardt set his rifle down, removed the earpiece from his ear, and turned off his GPS. "I guess that's that." He looked at Beck, who was still hiding in the bushes. "Don't be afraid. It's all over now. I, uh, I spent quite a few years studying these creatures."

For some reason, she couldn't move.

■ ■ ■

Sam shook his head. Burkhardt sounded as though he was having doubts again, which wasn't good. Burkhardt set this whole thing up, and now he was becoming the weak link! Never send a boy . . .

Sam grabbed Reed's body by the shoulder and flipped it over.

It was Wiley Kane, dressed in Reed's jacket, his white mane stuffed inside Reed's cap.

■ ■ ■

Reed could move now. He aimed his rifle from his hiding place in the rocks, only fifteen yards away. "Sam, drop that rifle!"

Sam's face flushed with surprise. He raised his weapon—

Reed shot him through the heart, knocking him backwards. He dropped like a limp puppet.

Reed rose only enough to make sure Sam and his rifle landed separately, then got on the radio. "Sing? It's Reed. Can you hear me?"

■ ■ ■

Maybe being shot in the head had something to do with it: Sing was still hearing Reed's voice. "Reed, are you *alive*?"

"I had to do some playacting. Sorry to scare you."

"Sam . . . Sam's close!"

■ ■ ■

Reed stood over Sam's body and double-checked. "Sam is dead. I shot him with Wiley Kane's rifle." He looked about cautiously. "Do you have Max on your screen?"

"No. He's gone now. But I still have Beck."

"Get me there, Sing."

Sing was fading. Her answer came in disjointed pieces. "Head for . . . um, Lost Creek. The bearing is . . . 340. Less than a quarter . . . mile."

■ ■ ■

Adam Burkhardt sat on a log, wiping his close-shaven brow and staring at the grotesque, bleeding beast at his feet. "This creature was an experiment that went terribly awry." He laughed. "Makes me sound like a mad scientist, doesn't it?" He quit laughing abruptly. "Maybe I qualify. This is a terrible thing, just terrible."

Beck ventured to the edge of the bushes, eyes probing this man and the hairy, misshapen creature that had almost killed her. "Did it kill . . ." She could not recall the man's name.

"Randy Thompson?"

She nodded.

"Oh yes. It's killed several people. We thought it had killed *you*." His face was sad, and yet he seemed to marvel. "It was bred that way, bred to prevail—even though it can't reproduce." He pointed, almost proudly. "But did you notice it was trying to walk upright? We removed the big toes so it couldn't live in the trees and would have to navigate mostly on the ground. We may have confirmed our theory, but then again, the knee and hip joints are unsuitable for bipedalism, so it's hard to draw any conclusions."

She stared at him blankly.

He shook his head. "I'm sorry. This does take a bit of explaining, doesn't it? Well, have you ever heard how we're all 98 percent chimpanzee?"

■ ■ ■

Reed ran, ducked, swerved, jumped, ran some more, jamming more cartridges into Kane's rifle as he went. He still didn't have Blip Number 6 on his screen, but he had to be getting close. He'd entered a familiar stretch of old-growth forest; the terrain descended toward Lost Creek.

■ ■ ■

Sing's eyes were so heavy she could hardly keep them open. "Too far downhill. You want . . . 355."

Reed's blip changed course, but its progress seemed agonizingly slow.

"Sing, is Beck moving at all?"

Sing closed her eyes. The motor home was rocking again, heaving like the ocean. She was getting nauseous.

"Sing!"

She opened her eyes. "Uh, now it's, uh, 350."

■　■　■

"Anyway," said Burkhardt, replacing his hat and eyeing Beck with a strange look of pity, "what we've taught people to believe, we have yet to prove, and now . . ." He indicated the beast at his feet. "Some could even say we've proven the *opposite*, which would be very difficult for us, to say the least. We wouldn't want that fact to become too, uh, noticeable. Am I making any sense?"

Beck could only shake her head.

He stood, wringing his hands, obviously agitated, nervous. It made *her* nervous. "Well, here's the situation: many, oh, at least half of the search party, thought it was a bear, and when they shot a large bear, they thought they had the villain, and they all went home. That was excellent! That took care of half the problem!"

He stepped closer to her, his hands out in front of him as if gesturing. "And then there was a really wonderful hoax by some Bigfoot fanatics—oh, you should have seen it, footprints and everything! It provided an excellent dismissal of that contingent as crackpots that no one would take seriously!"

He came so close that Beck took a step backward.

"But then there were the people who actually saw our *creature* but were not killed—people like your husband, Reed . . . and you." He grimaced. "If you just hadn't been in the woods, things could have been different! As it is, you and your husband became a liability, and now, with your husband no longer a factor, that leaves you."

Beck pressed backward into the tangle, dismay becoming

dread, and dread becoming terror. *Reed no longer a factor?* What did that mean? Then it occurred to her—she was not back in her own world. This was not a human being come to save her, but an articulate, educated beast. She could see in his eyes what she'd seen only moments before in the eyes of his creature.

He was there to kill her.

She turned and bolted into the bushes.

He dove, grabbed her by her collar, and jerked her backward, off her feet. She fought, striking and flailing, as he dragged her out of the thicket by her collar, by her hair. "I'm sorry, I'm sorry," he kept saying.

■　■　■

Reed heard a scream, very close. He checked his GPS.

He was picking up Blip Number 6, uphill, bearing 005, not more than 200 yards through dense, young growth. "Sing! I've got her! 005! Can you confirm?"

■　■　■

Sing saw both blips on her screen, with Reed converging. The image was fuzzy, fading in and out of her awareness, becoming meaningless to her. "Go to her, Reed."

She backed her chair away from the computer and put her head between her knees. The pain made her whimper. She checked the towel she'd been using, and fresh blood dripped on it the moment she lifted it from her head.

She didn't remember toppling to the floor. She only remembered seeing the ceiling as high as the sky above her and hearing the faint sound of a helicopter before she fell asleep.

■ ■ ■

Beck was facedown in rocks, needles, and grass, trying to squirm free, flailing her arms at nothing, struggling for breath as Burkhardt's knee pinned her to the ground. He clamped his hands on either side of her head; she peeled them loose. He gripped her forehead and the back of her head and began twisting. "I'm sorry," he said. "I don't want to do this."

She grabbed, clawed, kicked, but couldn't resist his strength. Her neck twisted, twisted some more. Her scream became a gargle. He was going to snap her neck, kill her like all the others, carry out what his beast couldn't. Abruptly, his grip forced her head backward, and then—

He was gone. His weight lifted from her body as if a huge eagle had plucked him up. She got her arms and legs under her, ready to dig in and get away—

The sky was blotted out by blackness that moved, roared with anger, and held Burkhardt aloft as if he weighed nothing. With long, tree-trunk arms, the monstrous shape hurled Burkhardt across the clearing.

Burkhardt hit the ground, tumbled, struggled to right himself—

He looked up—*way* up—and the sight paralyzed him.

Beck was amazed, relieved, and terrified.

It was Jacob, vicious and defensive, taking position between Beck and Burkhardt with black hair bristling, fangs bared, and arms ready to dismember.

Burkhardt's rifle was only a few feet beyond his reach. He noticed it, tried to ease toward it.

■ ■ ■

Deputy Dave Saunders had an iron grip on the wheel and a determined set in his jaw as he drove his squad car through Abney, lights flashing, and veered onto Service Road 221. Behind him came another squad car carrying two more deputies, a squad car carrying two Idaho State patrolmen, an ambulance with four paramedics, and behind that, a light-green rig carrying three shotgun-toting forest rangers.

Cap rode in the squad car beside him, hand on the dash, eyes intent on the road. "How far?"

Dave got on the radio. "Chopper Oh-9, we are entering road 221 at Abney. Any fix on the motor home?"

■ ■ ■

High above, piloting a National Guard helicopter on loan to Idaho Fish and Game, Jimmy Clark eyed the old road that snaked through the rolling, forested terrain. Two sheriff's officers rode with him. Where the road began to fade from brown dirt to green weeds, Jimmy spotted the silver rectangle he was looking for. "Car 12, I have the motor home, about four miles up the road. No activity, but we'll stick around. Drive safe, everybody."

■ ■ ■

Dave drove as fast as "safe" would allow, the wheels pounding over ruts and potholes, the car nearly bottoming its springs. The other vehicles stayed right behind him.

■ ■ ■

Burkhardt had just grabbed his rifle when Jacob plucked him off the ground by a wad of his jacket. The scientist dangled in the air, legs kicking, face stretched with horror, trying to chamber a round, trying to aim his rifle. Jacob didn't wait for Burkhardt to resolve such issues but threw him into the brush, where he tumbled and thrashed out of sight in the tangle.

Beck was suddenly surrounded by reddish-brown hair as huge arms enfolded her and pulled her in. She fell against a familiar bosom, felt a sweaty heat, inhaled a disgusting stench, and for the first time in a week, felt perfectly, wondrously safe.

"Mmm!" Rachel grunted, looking down at her. Beck had seen that expression before, when she awoke in Rachel's arms in a patch of huckleberries.

Jacob tromped halfway into the brush, watched Burkhardt's still body for a short time, growled a last word, and then he was satisfied. He stomped out of the bushes and started to leave, but not without an obligatory glance in Beck's direction.

She wanted to smile, to thank him, to give him a hug, but of course, he would not understand such things. She only hummed her thanks, looking just below his eye line.

He huffed back at her as if to say, *This doesn't mean I like you*, and vanished into the trees.

Beck tried to relax. She had to deal with Rachel somehow, had to—

Rachel tensed, her arms closing tightly against Beck. *Danger*. Beck could read it clearly in Rachel's manner. Was Burkhardt still—

The brush across the clearing opened, and Beck gasped audibly. Her legs weakened and her hands began to shake.

It was Reed, hard-run and sweating, holding a rifle, suddenly motionless at what he saw.

She couldn't express what she felt in words, only a Sasquatch sound, a long, mournful cry as she hung in Rachel's arms, trying to believe.

TWENTY

Reed was prepared to confront anything, but the scene before him was impossible to fathom. It was as if time had folded back on itself and he was below the waterfall again. The creature he never quite saw that night stood across the clearing plainly visible, a reddish version of Arlen's photograph, but so much bigger in real life. Just as before, it held Beck—but what had happened to her? The pitiful woman in that creature's arms was dirty all over, smeared with mud and . . . it looked like manure! Her face was bruised, and one eye was puffy. Grass and weeds hung from every chink in her clothing, the front of her shirt was stained with blood, and now she was making sounds like an animal.

In the center of the clearing lay a grotesque, fly-infested corpse that shattered all of his previous assumptions.

■ ■ ■

Rachel growled low in her throat and began to back away.

Beck shot a hand toward Reed and cried out like a Sasquatch, pleading, "Ohh, oh-oh-oh, Reeeeed!"

Rachel hesitated, huffing air through her nostrils, her arms like steel, on the verge of fleeing. But something held her here; maybe, just maybe, she recognized this stranger.

Beck detected Jacob's stench. He hadn't left.

■ ■ ■

Reed didn't move, but he had a round in the chamber and his finger on the trigger.

Beck had cried out his name. He said hers, very quietly. "Beck."

"Look at me," she said, her hand extended toward him. "Don't look at her; look at me." Beck was *talking*!

"Are you all right?"

The big red beast was huffing, nervous, spooked, ready to attack, or ready to run—Reed couldn't tell which it would be, but he would shoot either way.

He heard a low growl coming from the trees behind the beast and recalled the multiple footprints, especially those of the alpha male. He forbade himself to be afraid, but his hands were getting icy.

"Reed," Beck called quietly, "you have to bow. You have to show them you're not a threat."

Reed had to be sure he'd heard her right. "Bow?"

■ ■ ■

Beck sensed that Rachel was warily checking out this intruder, which was a good sign. In a different situation, Rachel never would have stuck around at all. Beck kept her hand stretched out to show friendship and connection, hoping Rachel would read it that way.

"Bow, Reed." She pantomimed a slight bow. "Bow down."

Reed bowed only a few inches, his eyes taking in his target, his rifle pointing only slightly away.

"Yes, yes, that's right." He looked up. *"Don't look at them; look at me!"* He dropped his eyes and met hers. "We have to show them we know each other. Just look at me—and don't smile!"

He wasn't smiling anyway, but he relaxed his expression as best he could. "Good, good, good. Don't show your teeth; that's a threat. Now maybe you'd better put the rifle down."

■ ■ ■

No way. "Can't do it, Beck."

There came that growl from the trees again. Reed saw something moving back there—if that was the top of the thing's head, it was a lot taller than Reed would have expected.

Beck made that weird guttural sound again, reaching out with both hands, "Ohhhhh, oh-oh-oh!" Then she clicked her tongue. *"Tok! Tok!"*

Now what was he supposed to do?

"Reach out to me, like I'm doing."

Reed cradled the rifle in his left hand and slowly reached with his right, an eye on those trees.

"Look at me, Reed!"

How far do I trust her?

The big red creature huffed, eyeing him with obvious suspicion as the trees behind her quaked.

Come on, Big Red, he thought. *You know me. We've met before.*

■ ■ ■

Beck pushed to get free of Rachel's arms but was held tight. As for Jacob, Beck recognized his breathing from the last time Reed came too close. "Reed? Reed, listen to me. I don't think they're buying it."

He tightened his grip on the rifle.

"No! No, just put it down."

"Can't do it!"

"They've seen hunters before. It scares them."

■ ■ ■

Reed had to trust Beck or shoot. He looked into Beck's eyes one very long, final time.

■ ■ ■

"Reed . . ."

■ ■ ■

He found her. He finally saw, under all that filth, the Beck he'd known was there all along—the confident, competent woman he'd grown to love. He slowly stooped over and set the rifle down.

"Stay there now," she said. "Stay bent over. Don't look up."

He bent low, eyes to the ground, every bit of common sense telling him this was death for sure.

The growling behind the trees stopped.

■ ■ ■

Beck forced herself to relax. She looked up at Rachel and hummed in as calm and happy a tone as she could. Rachel gazed down at her, then cocked her head, eyes troubled.

Beck reached for Reed again, not pleading this time, but expressing happiness. "Hmmm . . . hmmmph."

Across the clearing, Reed sank to all fours.

Rachel's arms relaxed. "Hmm."

Beck told her, "Friend. My friend. Hmm. *Tok! Tok!*"

Rachel eyed Reed for a long, careful moment, as if she was finally sorting out where she'd seen that strange creature before.

"See?" said Beck, patting Rachel's arm. "You know him. You've seen him before."

Rachel quit huffing and just stared.

■ ■ ■

Reed stayed on the ground but was poised to grab his rifle if anything went wrong.

■ ■ ■

Rachel drew a deep breath, sighed it out, and slowly relaxed her arms. Beck stepped down, limping slightly, one hand holding Rachel's, one hand toward Reed. "Look at me, Reed." He lifted his face to hers, and she could see hope flooding his eyes. "Don't get up. Let me come to you. I have to come to you."

She gazed back at Rachel one last time. Rachel seemed perplexed and troubled, but when Beck let go of her hand, she withdrew it, letting it fall to her side.

Beck turned toward Reed and limped across the clearing, passing by the fallen monster. She could muster only a quick, fearful glance in its direction.

■ ■ ■

It was the longest wait of Reed's life, but he kept to the rules, watching Beck come closer, stepping and limping over rocks, easing through grass and low brush. When she was only ten feet away, she said quietly, "I think you can get up now."

He rose slowly, meeting her eyes, careful not to look at the—

She fell into his arms.

He embraced her as she held him, kissed him, clung to him, stinking like a sewer but totally, wonderfully Beck. He was still cautious, checking the area over her shoulder, almost dancing with her as he scanned a full circle, wondering what became of Max Johnson, checking the location of his rifle, wondering what the Bigfoot might do—

The Bigfoot. He stopped and stared.

Beck turned. "See, Rachel? He's—"

It was as if a dream had ended. The creature was gone. The brush and trees were motionless as if they'd never been disturbed.

■ ■ ■

Cap pressed his fingers against Sing's carotid artery. The pulse was weak but steady. "Sing! *Sing!*"

She opened her eyes. It took her a moment before recognition settled, but finally she smiled. "Cap, you're all right."

"So are you," he lied. He kissed her gently, almost imperceptibly on the cheek, afraid he might snuff out whatever spark of life remained.

"Hello," Sing said to all the wonderful people in uniform who were stepping around Steve Thorne's dead body to get to her.

The medics went right to work, assessing her vitals. One shined a light in her eyes. The pupils responded.

She pointed to the wall beside the computer station.

The medics were too busy saving her life to look. Cap and Dave followed her direction and found a thin spattering of her blood and some of her hairs on the wall. In the center of the pattern was a bullet hole.

Dave took a penlight from his pocket and shined it into the hole. He smiled. "The slug's in there."

The medic tending her wound smiled. "Pretty good scalp wound, but no penetration of the skull. She'll make it."

"Sing," Dave asked, "what about Reed and Pete?"

"Reed's looking for Beck." She gasped. "And Max is still up there!"

Cap told Dave, "Adam Burkhardt."

Dave eyed the computer. "Can you show us where?"

"Lost Creek." Sing tried to rise but couldn't. She gestured toward her computer. "Help me up there."

■ ■ ■

Reed gave Beck a kiss, giving no thought to the mud, blood, and filth, then immediately turned his attention to her battered face and bloodstained shirt. Her nose and mouth had been bleeding, then apparently wiped and smeared with a dirty rag. "Are you . . . what happened?"

"I got in a fight."

"Somebody *hit* you?"

"My snotty little cousin."

"But you're, you're all right? Nothing broken, nothing . . ."

"I've been worse. But I'm with you now, and—"

She gasped, her eyes looking in horror over his shoulder.

Reed spun, then froze.

Max Johnson emerged from the brush, limping, in pain, his shaved head scratched by branches and bleeding. He sighted down his rifle at them.

Reed spoke quietly, without moving a muscle. "Max, it's over."

He wagged his head, his eyes burning. "I'm sorry, Reed. I have to survive."

Beck whispered, hiding behind Reed. "He made the monster."

The pieces flew together in Reed's mind. "Survive as what? You want to end up like your creation? A killer?"

The man was trembling. The barrel of the rifle oscillated in erratic circles. "It's a natural process. It's been going on for billions of years."

"Max—"

"Burkhardt!" he spat. "Professor Adam Burkhardt!"

"Okay," Reed lowered his voice. "Professor Burkhardt. You see? You have a name. You're a person, a *man*; you're more than that thing you made."

The faint sound of a helicopter grew louder, coming closer.

Reed never broke eye contact. "And now, just look at yourself. Is this Professor Adam Burkhardt standing here? Is this something he would do?"

Burkhardt was shaking. "I don't *want* to do this! But I have to survive!"

Reed insisted, "As what?"

Burkhardt glanced at his creation.

The sound of the helicopter grew louder and then appeared from the southwest, heading directly toward them.

"Professor. When that chopper lands, what are they going to find standing here? A man, or a monster?"

Burkhardt could no longer sight down the rifle. His eyes

strayed, looking far away, filling with tears. The rifle drifted to one side and then sank as his resolve melted.

At last, his gaze fell and he began to quake, weeping.

The chopper rose overhead, circled, and began to settle toward a landing site beyond the trees.

"Professor. It's over."

Burkhardt sank to his knees, sobbing in shame and remorse.

Reed reached into his shirt pocket. The handcuffs were there, for this moment. He pulled them out. "Professor Burkhardt, you're under arrest." He took the rifle from Burkhardt's weak and trembling hands and handed it to Beck. "It's my duty to advise you of your rights. You have the right to remain silent . . ."

He cuffed Burkhardt's hands behind his back.

■ ■ ■

Jimmy Clark and the two sheriff's officers were aghast when they first arrived, and Jimmy had not yet recovered even as he snapped photos of the scene and of Adam Burkhardt's monster.

Click! Click! Click! The clearing from several compass directions.

Click! The location of the monster in the clearing.

Click! The monster, wide shot.

Click! The apelike feet, missing the opposing toes.

Click! A close-up of the burn injury on the side of the head, compliments of Melanie Brooks and her pan of hot hamburger grease.

Click! A close-up of the bullet wound in the leg, compliments of Sheriff Mills.

Click, click, click! Jimmy lowered the camera and shook his head—something he'd been doing incessantly since he and the officers arrived.

Reed had just finished using the chopper's first aid kit to

clean Beck's wounds and prepare a cold compress for her face. Now he came over to take one last look before they left for the chopper.

Jimmy gazed at him, struggled for words, and finally came up with, "I guess you've made your point."

"Well, next time—" Reed smiled and waved that one off. "No, we don't want a next time."

"No, we sure don't."

They shared a laugh and then a handshake.

The two officers had Burkhardt between them. Burkhardt wouldn't look at his monster; he wouldn't look up at all.

Jimmy hollered, "Okay, let's get these people out of here."

Beck sat in the coarse grass, holding the cold compress against her face with one hand while pulling itchy, prickly grass, twigs, and moss from inside her shirt with the other.

When Reed and Jimmy came over to help her up, Jimmy shied back from the filth. "*Eeesh!* What did you do to yourself?"

"Hey!" She got to her feet without any help and looked him squarely in the eye. "Just for your information, this is my family scent. It tells everybody who I am and what I've been eating and how I'm feeling about things."

Reed and Jimmy stared at her.

"It even tells you whether I like you or not, so read it and weep—"

"Beck," Reed began.

"—unless you can't read plain Sasquatch!"

"Beck?"

She turned toward him, her dignity reclaimed. "What?"

"What happened to your stutter?"

The question stopped her cold. Plainly, she hadn't noticed until this moment. "Uh . . ." She glanced toward the woods. "Maybe God took it."

He gave her a special smile and then pulled her in close. She clung to him unabashedly. "Ready to come home?" he asked.

"Anywhere with you."

He gave her his arm to lean on. "Come on. Let's get you to a hospital."

The chopper was parked on a rocky knoll a short hike up the hill. As it rose above the trees, Beck watched out the window and marveled: the mountains really were as vast and mysterious as they seemed.

Almost immediately, Jimmy started circling as Reed tapped her shoulder and pointed.

They passed over a deep, meandering ravine with a creek running down its center. Because of the thick forest, Beck could only catch a few quick glimpses, but it was enough for her to recognize a natural log bridge across the creek and the square, split-shake roof of a forlorn little cabin.

EPILOGUE

What in the world were they thinking?" A week later, Reed still couldn't get over it. "I mean, how were they going to explain all the dead people lying around? Didn't they think somebody would start to wonder?"

He sat at one of Arlen Peak's best tables at the Tall Pine Resort, debriefing and remembering with Cap, Sing, Dave, and Jimmy while they waited for the best barbecued steak dinner Arlen could whip up.

"The problem got away from them, literally," said Cap. "Even if Burkhardt and his crew had a containment plan, it had to be trashed the moment Beck got grabbed. These guys were desperate."

"Nice pictures, Jimmy." Sing, wearing a head bandage and a modified hair arrangement, was once again glued to her computer. "But Thorne cut us a nice break, right, Reed?" She was hinting. She still hadn't heard the full explanation.

None of them had. Reed had a rapt audience. "I figured Thorne had to leave Kane's gun with him so people would think Kane died from a self-inflicted gunshot wound. I had a waypoint in my GPS marking where Kane and Thorne left off, so I used that to find Kane's body—that and some lucky guessing."

"A mighty long shot, Reed," said Jimmy.

Reed shrugged. "That's all I had left."

Jimmy patted his shoulder. "It was brilliant. Pete would've liked it."

Reed, along with the others, fell into a somber moment at the mention of their old friend. "It does sound like something he'd do, doesn't it?"

Dave had plucked a cracker from the basket in the middle of the table and said with his mouth full, "So what were they going to do with that monster's carcass, let the birds eat it?"

"Bury it, I suppose," said Sing.

"Well, it's in a cooler now," said Jimmy.

"Just like Burkhardt," Reed quipped, and got a laugh.

"He and Merrill could end up being bunkmates," Cap ventured.

"Tell them about your job," Sing prompted her husband.

Now Cap had their undivided attention. "Well, it looks favorable. I don't know whether the university's had a change of heart or whether they're just trying to save face, but . . ."

"But you can't argue with Right," said Sing with an overacted pat on his hand, "and that's what you are!"

Arlen swept through to take drink orders. "And by the way, it's not such a bad idea to let the birds and the bears and the coyotes eradicate a carcass. They can make quick work of it, let me tell you." He directed his next sentence at Jimmy. "Which is why nobody's ever found a Sasquatch skeleton. Nature has a way of erasing things."

Jimmy smirked good-naturedly, hands lifted in surrender. "Whatever you say, Arlen."

"Didn't Beck find a skeleton up there?" Dave asked.

Reed put up a hand of caution. "That's a sensitive area."

Cap interjected, "But remember, Jimmy: Those hairs from Beck's backpack turned out to have clean DNA from a creature not yet catalogued. Nobody mutated that animal; it was the real thing."

Sing peered closely at her computer screen. "And you might take a look at this, Jimmy, especially since you took these pictures."

They all rose and gathered around Sing's computer. She scrolled through the photos as they murmured, reacted, and pointed. They'd seen these before but were more than eager to see them again. Sing clicked and enlarged one of Jimmy's wide shots of the clearing. "See those two fir trees and that bush between them?"

They did.

She scrolled to a medium shot of the monster's corpse on the ground. The two fir trees were visible in the background. She clicked and dragged over the fir trees and zoomed in on that area.

"Take a look, gentlemen. Take your time."

At first there was silence as they studied the blown-up image of two fir trunks with a splashing of green, yellow, and red leaves between them.

Green, yellow, and red.

But red only in one area.

"I think I see it," said Reed, as he traced it with his finger.

Sing clicked and dragged, enlarging the image until the saw-edge of the individual pixels began to appear.

Jimmy's eyes narrowed, glued to the screen. "I took this picture?"

They could all see it now: a domed head, a red brow, two

amber eyes, and a flat nose—a face peering through the leaves, keeping an eye on all that was happening in the clearing.

"That's her," said Reed. "That's Rachel."

"Beck needs to see this," said Cap.

"Where is she, anyway?" Jimmy asked.

Reed put out a hand to calm them down. "Outside."

"She okay?" they all wondered at once.

Reed nodded. "She'll be right back. She just needed to say good-bye."

■ ■ ■

Beck had not gone far, just enough of a walk up the Lost Creek Trail to stand still and silent among the trees, out of sight of her world, just barely within the boundary of *theirs*.

The swelling in her face was nearly gone, reduced to bruised patches of yellow, purple, and blue. Her cuts were healing. Her ankle was back to business as usual.

Her stutter had not returned. She could still lapse into shyness, but for the first time in her and Reed's marriage, she was answering the phone.

She'd gotten that shower and shampoo she used to dream about the first several nights in the woods—plenty of showers, as a matter of fact. Her skin was bathed, moisturized, and perfumed.

Nevertheless, the Sasquatch stench still lingered—in her memory.

She'd come to this place to wonder, she supposed, just wonder, and for how long, she couldn't guess. One moment, one night, one lifetime might never be enough to finish what felt so unfinished.

If only . . .

She listened for the voice of the forest. The birds were

singing their closing number, but there weren't too many. A light breeze moved through the treetops, but so gently that other sounds could still be heard.

She didn't feel foolish when she whistled; she only thought about how to achieve that particular, teakettle-like wavering in the main part and that curious warble at the end. The first attempt was only fair. The second was better. The third was delightful, almost exactly the way Rachel did it.

Then she stood quietly, listening, knowing how unlikely it would be, thinking she would never tell anyone, wondering if her whistle would carry far enough.

The voice of the forest continued to speak, but it had nothing to say to her.

Yes, it was a bit foolish. The mountains were so vast, the forests so deep. The wind could be wrong.

She turned to start back—

Somewhere out there, so far away, a teakettle whistled.

She held so very still, not breathing, straining to hear it again.

The teakettle whistled, wavering in the main part, warbling at the end—and so much better than Beck could do it.

There was nothing after that—only the breeze and the last verse of one bird's evening song. Beck cried a little, deeply happy and not having to wonder quite so much. She started back down the trail while she still had light to see her way.

It could have been a bird. It could have been the bugle of an elk or the squeaking of one tree swaying against another. She couldn't be sure.

But it was enough for now, and maybe forever.

READING GROUP GUIDE

1. Before you began the novel, what did you think the title referred to? What is the real monster Peretti is referring to?

2. *Monster* looks at the question of beneficial mutations and if there really is such a thing as a beneficial mutation. What did you think about mutations before you read this novel? Have your thoughts changed at all? What new questions do you have?

3. Many of us were taught certain things about evolution in high school and college. What are some of the facts about evolution that you assume are true because you've heard them all your life? What proof have you actually seen for these "facts"?

4. At the beginning of the novel, Beck, is worried about checking her makeup and ensuring that she has her hairbrush and compact. By the end, she has covered herself in mud, brush, and dung in order to survive in the animal world. Why are the proprieties of human society not the norm in the animal world? What do you think is indicated by the fact that Rachel and Leah are so fascinated by Beck's hairbrush?

5. In order to protect his theory, Burkhardt must eliminate all witnesses. He justifies this by saying it is part of the natural process, but in reality he has reverted to a savage animal himself with no rules, no propriety, and no morality. Is this the logical outcome of evolution?

6. Throughout the novel, Jimmy is convinced that they are searching for a bear—even when the footprints are much too large to belong to a bear and prove that the creature moves on

two feet instead of four. What things do you believe in spite of strong evidence to the contrary? Are there times when you should reconsider your position based on the evidence?

7. For a moment, try to put aside all of your feelings about the existence of sasquatches or Big Foot. What facts do you know about them? What information is presented in the novel? If our culture did not present them as a myth, what might you believe about them? Are there any other things you might believe if society did not call them myths?

8. What is it about myths—sasquatches, the Loch Ness monster, UFOs—that is so intriguing?

9. In *Monster*, sasquatches are treated as real animals and not as cartoons or King Kong prototypes. Do you agree with this treatment? What effect does it have on the story?

10. The sasquatches appear to be monsters at first because they are unknown, but the more time Beck spends with them and gets to know them, the less monstrous they become. How does knowledge empower her? How does this principle apply to everyday situations?

11. *Monster* is written from a cinematic approach. We learn about the characters by watching how they react in different situations. Why do you think Peretti chose this approach, rather than a more literary writing style?

12. Through the trials she experiences, Beck learns that she must take responsibility and rise above her situation in order to survive. What might you learn about yourself if you had Beck's experience with the sasquatches? What might you learn if you experienced Reed's role in the story? Cap's?

13. Has this novel raised any questions about sasquatches and myths that you had not previously considered? What advantage(s) do you see to thinking about an issue from a new perspective?

14. Are you afraid to be out in the woods at night?

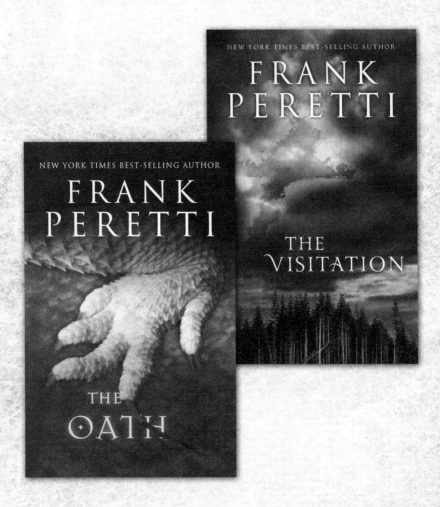

Also available from Frank Peretti

THE VERITAS SERIES
FOR TEEN READERS!

Nate Springfield, his wife Sarah, and their twin children Elijah and Elisha, are part of the Veritas Project team. Follow this group as they travel the country aiding the FBI and other organizations in breaking drug rings and solving mysteries.

These stories could have come straight from the headlines and will lead kids and young adults to an understanding of peer pressure and the pain that comes from being different. A riveting message on the wounded spirit that teens will never forget!

THOMAS NELSON
Since 1798

ABOUT THE AUTHOR

FRANK PERETTI, referred to by *Time* magazine as "the king of the [Christian fiction] genre," has more than 15 million books in print. He is the *New York Times* best-selling author of more than 21 books, including *This Present Darkness*, *Piercing the Darkness*, *The Oath*, *Monster*, and *The Visitation*.